Red Fortunes

Hugh Fraser

Copyright © 2013 Hugh Fraser

26 Star Street

London W2 1QB

hugh@storynory.com

All rights reserved.

ISBN:
978-1484040928
1484040929

Originally published for Kindle by Endeavour Press

Contents

Foreword 6

Prologue 7

Chapter One 13

Chapter Two 30

Chapter Three 36

Chapter Four 53

Chapter Five 66

Chapter Six 77

Chapter Seven 85

Chapter Eight 97

Chapter Nine 109

Chapter Ten 117

Chapter Eleven 133

Chapter Twelve 139

Chapter Thirteen 143

Chapter Fourteen...151

Chapter Fifteen 156

Chapter Sixteen..161

Chapter Seventeen...171

Chapter Eighteen...178

Chapter Nineteen 197

Chapter Twenty...205

Chapter Twenty One 210

Chapter Twenty Two 219

Chapter Twenty Three..229

Chapter Twenty Four..244

Afterword by Misha Munnings 282

From Hugh Fraser...289

Select Bibliography..290

Foreword

What follows is the Russian memoir of my great-grandfather, George Munnings (1893-1973), written in the late 1920s, and for the most part dealing with the years 1914 and 1920. It appears that he worked up the manuscript from journals that have since been lost. The Munnings family has a somewhat chequered history, and the author made no attempt to suppress embarrassing episodes and details. The covering page carries an inscription, 'The truth – for posterity', written in what I believe is the handwriting of my great-grandmother, Vera Munnings.

A number of interesting items from George Munnings's library, including his Russian guidebooks, phrasebooks, business manuals, and theatre programmes, have also come down to me. Of particular interest is his 1914 Baedeker given to him by his friend, Lady Lydia Hawthorne. I have drawn on his books to add footnotes and chapter quotations where I feel they are useful.

It was after I myself visited Moscow two years ago and noticed how, in many ways, so little has changed since 1914 that I decided to prepare George Munnings's manuscript for publication.

Misha Munnings, London 2005

Prologue

"It is not too much to say that the Coronation Season at Covent Garden has in preparation for the spoilt and blasé theatregoer a spectacle that should arouse even that pampered individual from his customary apathy."

The Programme for the Royal Opera and the Imperial Russian Ballet
Coronation Season, Covent Garden, 1911.

It was my eighteenth birthday and my father and a certain woman had brought me to Covent Garden to see the Russian dancers. The stage lay in wait behind a blue curtain decorated with silhouettes of Arabian horses, soldiers and scimitars. Papa looked around the theatre to see who in Society or the City or even among Royalty was in the audience. The crowned heads of Europe and the bejeweled princes of the Empire were in London for the Coronation of George V. All wanted to see the Russian ballet.

The orchestra struck up Rimsky-Korsakov's One Thousand and One Nights. The ominous opening bars soon gave way to a lone violin. Its voice was feminine, enigmatic, seductive. It seemed to speak to me and to me alone as it posed the unanswered question – why must we all submit to fate? Even now, after all these years, the melody plays in my head when I think of my Russian days and nights.

The curtain rose to reveal an oriental harem. Applause rippled across the auditorium. My father's lady friend whispered in my ear, 'What décor!' She meant the drapes, the carpets, the cushions and the passionately deep colours. The upper reaches of the harem were cooled by a virulent green canopy flaked with gold. Down below, a crimson carpet smoldered with desire. And desire was what I felt as three harem girls, clad in blue trousers and little tunics, began to weave a slow, sinuous dance, at first with their arms, and then with their bodies, tilting their turbaned heads backwards to the floor, and forming their spines into half-moons.

In the midst of the harem, the sultan and his brother reclined on ottomans, fashionably bored. Evidently, they had seen it all before. They upped and left.

As the saying goes, when the cat's away.... Tamara Karsavina, the Sultan's prima concubine, was asleep among the silken cushions. She began to stretch her exquisite arms. The music had an undercurrent of suspense, and the numerous slave girls were gathering around the Chief Eunuch, a huge man in very baggy trousers. They brought him jewels and caresses and implored him to open the metallic blue doors at the back of the harem. He did so reluctantly – the tassels on his tall wobbly hat shook with fear – for the slave girls' wish was a forbidden one.

In an instant, a black and gold streak shot out from one of the doors. This was Vaslav Nijinsky, whose sensational flights across the stage of Covent Garden were the talk of the town. At times he was little more than a glittering vortex. He seemed more than a little in love with himself, carrying off each implausible leap and pirouette with a flourish of triumph.

He danced for Karsavina – and then she for him – their two bodies never quite meeting. At first, her movements expressed haughty pride toward this slave who dared to be her suitor, then languorous sensuality, and finally submission to her rising passion. How I wished that one day I would conjure up such feelings in such a woman.

It was at the moment when numerous harem girls and black slaves were undulating on the floor that the Sultan returned. His hand gripped the hilt of his sword. His beard was thrust imperiously upwards. When he gave the command with a wheel of his arm, his guards surged into action. Now panic and a frenzied slaughter followed hard on the heels of the orgy. Slaves and soldiers flew this way and that. Nijinsky sprang and pirouetted just inches ahead of the scimitars. At last, he was clipped by a blade, and passed away in a series of spasms. Karsavina, unaware of her lover's death, pleaded with the Sultan for her life. Ah, that solo violin again! It was tinged with fate. Her lyrical gestures conveyed her whole soul to me. What man can resist the pleas of a woman in her moment of need? I wanted to jump down onto the stage and to rescue her; even the cruel Sultan hesitated. Must he give in to her pleas or slice his blade across her slender neck? She herself resolved the matter when she caught sight of her dead Nijinsky. Her body convulsed with despair. She pulled out a dagger and plunged it into her breast. Her back and the soles of her feet arched and then relaxed. It was a gorgeous suicide.

The audience was stunned, shocked, thrilled, and delighted by the spectacle. When the thunderous applause and cheering finally began to die down, we started to pull ourselves away, and a man emerging from the next-door box claimed, 'Honestly, my dear, the sex-element is quite negligible in the enjoyment of the dance. Speaking as a man, I would just as soon watch Nijinsky as La Karsavina.'

As we left the Opera House, my father's lady friend asked me: 'Did you enjoy the Russian dancers, George?' I was still in a daze, trying to take in all that the ballet meant to me. I was overcome by the intensity of the passion and the feeling that it is only the senses that make one come alive, albeit briefly.

'It was very east,' was all I could say, before adding, 'I should like to visit Russia one day.'

'And what is your view of the lovely Karsavina? I should think a young man could be quite enamoured of her.' As it happened, I was still in a kind of mourning for her.

'Her art is certainly remarkable,' I said, feeling somewhat shy.

'There's a moral in that story, young man,' said the lady wagging her finger at me. 'Too much of a good thing is bad for you.'

The woman herself was rather east that night, wearing a turban with a jewel that could easily have sat on the head of the Maharaja Holkar of Indore. She was on the receiving end of not a few glances and one or two downright stares. Her interest in the evening's spectacle had been aroused, first and foremost, by the stage decor and the oriental costumes. She tapped my father on the arm.

'What did you think of those lampshades, Gabby?'

'Shades?' I could tell that he was getting into a grump. We were standing on the crowded pavement of Floral Street, and he was looking out for Johnson and the Rolls. As far as matters such as lampshades were concerned, my father wanted only the most tasteful and the best, but he did not want to waste his precious time thinking about them. He had hired the lady to do that for him: she was his 'adviser on matters of artistic taste,' responsible for overseeing the design and furnishing of his future country villa, or at least that was the public pretence they both kept up. She gently chided him:

'You could hardly miss the vast lampshades: those celestial objects hanging from the ceiling. And as for those drapes; a woman could die for curtains like those, colours so primary they could have come straight from the Garden of Eden. And what about that mountain of oriental silk cushions?'

'All very well for a harem, I suppose.'

'Oh Gabby, you're so impossible! Russia is all the rage among people of fashion.'

We were jostled by theatre-leavers. The lady held onto my father's arm and continued trying to interest him in the decorative arts.

'Well what did you think of those trousers on the harem-girls? They say that women in Paris are wearing them this year. What would you say if they caught on over here? Would you write an outraged letter to The Times?'

'That'll be the day. I say, do you think that pretty little Russian ballerina does private engagements? We could invite her down to shake a leg one weekend. That would create an impression.'

'Karsavina is an artist,' said the lady firmly, 'She is not anybody's thrill-for-hire like Maud Allen and she is not about to dance the Seven Veils however many ready tenners you offer her.'

'Pity.'

'I do believe,' I said, 'that the Russian dancers have performed for Lady Ripon at Coombe Court.'

'Well there you have it. My son knows all about these things. They do dance at private engagements. My money doesn't smell any worse than Lady Ripper's, or whatever her name is.'

She finally shut up. That was the only sensible thing to do when the great financier was in one of his moods.

Three years were to pass before I was to visit Moscow. My father dispatched me there in January 1914 on a business trip. He had received a tip about a valuable mine that was in need of capital for its development — and when a hole in the ground of some far-flung territory required backing, my father was your man. My task was to fill out the very sketchy particulars that he had already received. The property contained a rich deposit of a rare and precious gemstone called alexandrite. The owners were the Mizinskies who lived in Moscow, and the property itself was situated in the Ural Mountains. Language would not be a problem as the youthful head of the Mizinsky family spoke excellent English. But it was certainly not the business venture that excited me as my train pulled out of Liverpool Street Station. I had not forgotten my lovely Tamara Karsavina.

Throughout the long journey across central Europe, I was dreaming of my very own ballerina. I might meet her, I thought, through our connections in Moscow. I would call daily on her home and pay my compliments to her, and one day we would find ourselves alone and she would dance for me before falling into my arms. I would know exactly how to handle the situation because I was no longer a scrawny undergraduate, a condition that had seriously undermined my earlier attempts at romance. At each major stage of the way, The Hook of Holland, Bentheim, Berlin, Alexandrovo, Warsaw, Smolensk, and finally Moscow, I felt that I had shed a little more of my youth.

I had been expecting to be met at Brest Station[1] in Moscow, but I could not see my name held up on a card as per our arrangements. Eventually I was rescued by a rascally looking but efficient porter who carried my bags through the crowd and negotiated a fare for me with a cab driver. The only words I was able to use were 'Hotel Metropole' and fortunately they proved sufficient.

The unaccustomed stillness of my bed in Moscow's finest hotel soothed my bones after their seventy odd hours of rattling on board the train. Even so, my excited mind would not let me lie for long, still dressed, on top of the covers, with my nose buried in the soft pillow. I arose to look out of the window at the snowflakes falling onto the spacious square. Across the way, I could see carriages mounted on blades as they pulled up outside a great white theatre.

I had been in my room for about ten or fifteen minutes when the telephone rang by the side of the bed. As I picked up the receiver, I expected to hear my prospective business partner. Instead, I heard the rasping voice of a woman who spoke in the language of international diplomacy:

'Est ce que Monsieur désire une femme pour ce soir?'

---

[1] The first station inside the Tsarist Russian Empire, and part of the Polish territory that was under Russian sway from the end of the Napoleonic Wars until it was occupied by Germany and the Central Powers in 1915. Baedeker states: "Alexandrovo – a halt of 1 ¼ hours is made. Passports and luggage are examined here. Between Alexandrovo and Warsaw the train traverses the plains of the present Government of Warsaw, the ancient Kujavia and Masovia. The country is dotted with miserable looking villages and is largely populated by Jews" - Russia with Tehran, Port Arthur and Peking – a handbook for travelers", Baedeker, Leipzig, 1914.

Chapter One

"The quaint custom of 'paying for conversations' prevails with the Russian man-about-town. His inamoratas of the moment sits with him at tea or over the supper table, and entertains with trifling chatter, or, perhaps, a song. As compensation for an hour of glitter and banter these birds of passage sometimes receive a palmful of gems to deck their plumage, or a cheque of staggering proportions. She who pleases a Russian pleases a generous child. The interview at an end, he rises from the table and bids his entertainer a polite adieu."
  Ruth Kedzie Wood, The Tourist's Russia, Andrew Melrose, 1912

The girl knocked on my door right on time. She belonged to just about the only class of person in her country who could be relied on for punctuality. Good time keeping is the whole secret of profitable prostitution.

She closed the door behind her and leant against it, looking up at me with her green eyes. A more experienced man would have known what to do with her right away. I was too afraid to move. Her dress was white, low cut, very simple. She had wrapped a red woollen scarf behind her shoulders and around her upper arms, and she twisted the tassels just below her ripe breast. Despite my orders, she had painted over her lovely pale complexion that contrasted so nicely with her dark hair.

About an hour beforehand, I had picked her out myself, refusing to accept blindly whatever goods the strange female voice on the telephone might send me. In the upper reaches of the hotel, I had found a room containing a gaggle of girls. An expanse of female flesh - arms, necks, lower legs, and half revealed breasts - shimmered before my eyes, and I felt a certain revulsion. I was pulled further into the room by the French speaking 'Madame', and introduced to two or three of the women, none of whom appealed to me with their fleshpot figures, false eyelashes, and bright red lips. This was the coarsest, most cynical sensuality: it had been quite unreasonable of me to have dreamed of finding anything else on sale. I felt an urge to leave, but Madame was very insistent on the quality of her wares and it was difficult to extricate myself. And then I noticed a dark hared girl perched on the windowsill. She had ignored my presence in the room completely, and was carrying on her discussion with a redheaded colleague. The girl of my fancy had an animated face that expressed a lively interest in the world. Besides which, she was nicely proportioned in the right places. As for her face, I did not think that she had worn it for more than seventeen or eighteen years, and at that moment, in sharp contrast to all the others, it did not show any trace of rouge. I paid the price demanded by Madame without any attempt to strike a bargain, arranged a postponement to give me time to wash and change, and told her to dispatch the girl as she was, without the addition of paint.

The hour-long wait had passed slowly for me, as anticipation mingled with trepidation. Now, as I stood by the bed, the girl was ambling slowly toward me, still playing with the tassels of her shawl. I felt the need of some preliminaries, but I did not even know how to ask her name in her language. The situation lacked any of the charm or playfulness for which I had hoped, and called for a more direct approach. I tried to swallow, but a confusion of desire and tension had dried my mouth.

Just then there was another knock on the door. The girl smiled and twitched her nose. We should have just stood still in complicit silence until whoever it was went away, but nerves or some devil inside me made me call out 'Who's there?' The door opened and a big, broad man with dark moustaches swaggered in. He was quite a swell with his embroidered waistcoat and fancy cravat.

'Mr George Munnings?' asked the man, looking first at me, and then at the girl.

I was about to deny it, but thankfully thought better of it. It would have reduced my stock of decorum even lower to have pretended to have been somebody else.

'I am Anatoly Alexandrovitch Mizinksy,' he went on. 'Welcome to Moscow.'

The last person I wanted to see just then was Anatoly Alexandrovitch Mizinsky. He was our prospective business partner in Moscow. Up until that moment, I had felt comfortably far away from home, almost as if on the moon like a character in a fiction by Mr Wells. Now I could envisage news of my debauchery travelling back as fast as a telegram. 'Think, George, think of something,' a voice in my head was urging me. There had to be a perfectly good professional reason to be talking to the girl. But no excuse came to mind. I did not have the knack of my father, who could look you in the eye and tell you a fib without batting a lid. I must have looked pretty stupid just standing there with my mouth open and no words coming out.

The girl said something to Anatoly Mizinsky in Russian. I prayed that it was not indecent. Apparently it wasn't. He explained:

'She says you are just about to go downstairs to dine. It is an excellent idea.'

I was amazed at her tact. Dinner had been the last thing on my mind.

'Yes, that's right. I was just going down. Would you join me?'
'Of course.'

As we headed down the corridor, Mr Mizinsky apologised for having missed me earlier at the railway station. He had arrived just forty minutes late and was staggered to discover that the London train had been on time. I felt my cheeks burning. I had been hoping to lose the girl when Anatoly had stood aside to let her through the door, but she walked a few steps in front of us in the direction of the lift.

When we set foot in the vast dining room of the Hotel Metropole, I realised that my concern about the girl had been quite out of place.

At least one gaudy lady sat at every table. It seemed like their natural habitat. It would have looked odd had I not brought along a scarlet woman.

Mr Mizinsky suggested that we take a private room, a 'kabinet' up on the balcony. A waiter in a white frock coat bowed deeply, but there were no rooms available. My host slipped one of the Tsar's notes into his top pocket and suddenly a private room became free.

On the way up to the private room, my new Russian friend suggested that we use first names, and I readily agreed. As for the girl, I did not like to admit that I did not yet know what she was called. I wondered if, perhaps, she worked under a false name anyway.

Our room was almost like a box in the theatre, though the scene below would have been better suited to a music hall. Up on the stage, the orchestra thumped out The Blue Danube and half a dozen couples waltzed drunkenly around the tables. One of the pairs was formed by two ladies. Even between waltzes it was far from tranquil. Knives and forks clattered, champagne corks popped and a woman shrieked with laughter. Above all this pandemonium, a glass canopy stretched serenely across the hall like a night sky. Every table was cluttered with bottles of all colours and heights. Goblets and crystal dishes were crammed in between them. Figs, pomegranates and caviar were piled high. A drowsy woman rested her head on a gentleman's shoulder. A man stood up and paced around the table and his fellow diners while he smoked a cigarette. In the centre of it all, a fat golden cherub poured water from his mouth into a pond. At first the general lack of decorum made me think of Genghis Kahn and his Mongol horde debauching themselves in their camp on the steppe. After a while, I ceased to feel that there was any bestiality in the Russian mode of extravagance. On the contrary, there was something reassuring about the disorderly abundance. There was a sense of freedom in the carelessness of it all – a devotion to enjoying the moment rather than observing the strict formalities. Looking down on this scene, I felt that I had arrived in a place where I could be myself.

The girls entwined an arm around my neck. I shivered. I'm not quite sure whether it was with fright or embarrassment or the thrill of a female touch. She pulled me back from the balustrade to the table.

'The girl wants us to choose the food,' said Anatoly.

Her large green eyes as intense as a cat's. There was a wild, desperate desire in those eyes: hunger, perhaps.

'I suggest we begin with an aperitif and caviar. For the next course, the sterlet.' Anatoly spoke with the air of a gastronome. The sterlet, as it turned out, was a small sturgeon from the River Volga. The freshness of the fish was not in doubt – they were skulking in the pond beneath the golden cherub, hoping to avoid the waiters' nets. Our waiter bowed so deeply he almost banged his nose on our table. He was an oriental, a direct descendent of the Khans, with shiny black hair lacquered back behind his ears.

Anatoly looked like a man who knew a thing or two about the gifts life had to offer to the senses. His hair was heroically thick, almost as if it was sculptured out of some grainy wood, and was swept back into a roll-top coiffure at the top of his high forehead. He was white and puffy around the gills, but apart from that he was good looking - perhaps too good looking for his own good - with a round, boyish face. It was the sort of face that was half-angelic, half-impish - you could not really say which, but there was no doubt that his manner was engaging. When the waiter placed a crystal jug of vodka on the table, he rubbed his hands together with eager expectation. He was going to enjoy this shot of spirit.

That night in Moscow I was a complete novice at drinking vodka, but nowadays I consider myself something of an expert. It is the one thing in Russia that has to be done just so. First a toast has to be proposed. Often these can go on for a while, but if in a hurry, something like, 'to our meeting' will suffice. Then you hold the silver tumbler to your lips for about half a minute and inhale the alcohol fumes with a far away look in your eyes. It is important to inhale deeply just before you throw your head back to tilt the glassful into your throat. You do not let the spirit touch your tongue, if at all possible, as the taste is too vile. The vodka shoots downward, leaving a trail of fire along your chest. Next you exhale like a dragon. A few seconds later, your senses are remarkably sharpened, and here lies the whole pleasure in the thing: you feel like you are looking at the world with the wonder of a new born baby. After a short pause, the flames at the bottom of your stomach are suffocated with a bite to eat. When we drank that night at the Metropole, caviar and warm bread were to hand. After one shot my head was zinging and I was set up for the evening. Let there be no doubt, vodka does have a fiery magic. As a beginner, you approach your first couple of shots with apprehension. After that, it is all plain sailing.

Anatoly told me about the three months he had spent in England in 1906. His late father, who had always been an admirer of the British 'system', had sent him there to 'study free enterprise in the land of Adam Smith' (apparently he did not know that the great economist was a Scot). I smiled when he told me that he had lived in Surbiton. He had boarded with a very respectable family who were 'rather particular about small things,' such as not being seen to walk back to the house on a Sunday carrying a shopping parcel. Almost every weekday he had taken the train up to London with the commuters and had seen how each the great mass of British humanity moved through the stations and underground passages, and along the pavements, without any jostling .

'It was almost as if they had woken up out of their graves on the last day of Judgement and were pulled along by the command of God. Such order! Such sense of duty! This will never be possible in Russia.'

He had made some valuable connections in England, and, more recently, his old acquaintances had helped to bring him into contact with my father concerning the business of the mine.

Soon we were chasing the vodka with sugary Crimean champagne. The girl's eyes seemed less intense after she had swallowed a pork cutlet. I could only speak to her through the auspices of Anatoly's translation, and he told me that she spoke with a heavy provincial accent that was hard for even him to catch. I asked where she was from, and she said a town about 1,200 versts[2] south of Moscow. To my surprise, she asked what sort of dogs we had in England. I said my favourites were Dalmatians, explaining that they were elegant coach dogs, with black and white colouring rather like her own. Her mouth formed a pretty 'o' which needed no translating. I thought that her thoughtful expression, as she considered what to say next, was very fetching. Then she asked, 'will he give me one from England?' Quite how and when she thought I was going to send to England for a dog, I could not fathom. I said I would think about it, which is what my father used to say when I asked him for something unreasonable.

I did not find out more about her just then, because Anatoly proposed a toast to our parents, swiftly followed by another to our long and profitable relationship in business.

We had cream chocolate cake and sorbets for desert. A violinist played the sobbing strains of a gypsy song. I could not say that it was quite as exquisite as the solo violin refrain that had moved me so much at the Russian ballet, but it was certainly played with passion. A glisten appeared in Anatoly's dark eyes. It was hard to say which sensual pleasure touched him most.

'I do believe that the whole secret of life,' he said, 'is to taste the purest vodka, the juiciest caviar, and the softest skinned women.'

The girl relished the deserts even more than the previous courses. Food and vodka transformed her face, lending it a glow as if she had been sitting in front of the fire. She gave me an appreciative squeeze under the table. I just want to mention that this was my first close encounter with a representative of her ancient profession. I had seen twilight streetwalkers on Sussex Gardens, and I had read law reports, recorded almost in code in the newspapers, about police raids on establishments around Piccadilly and Haymarket. A Russian hire seemed less furtive and hypocritical. There was no hiding behind net curtains.

---

[2] 10 versts = 6.63 miles - Baedeker

The bill came and Anatoly almost got away with accepting it for payment. I kicked up a fuss and signed a chit for a stupendous sum. Had I been sober I would have choked to see how much they dared to charge.

As we stood up from our places, the orchestra stopped and there was a general uproar. We stood at the balcony and watched as one of the revellers clambered first onto the shoulders of his friend, and then pulled himself up on to a branch of one the four golden trees which supported the candelabra illuminations in the hall. His comrades were throwing buns up to him, and he was hurling them from his vantage point at other diners and members of the orchestra. The musicians struck up a dance that began slowly, and built up to a crescendo. The audience clapped and sang along: Kalinka, malinka, kalkina maya until the bun-thrower flew from his perch and landed among the tables, sending plates, knives, forks and chocolate mousse flying in all directions, but mostly over the evening clothes and uniforms of his fellow diners. He ended up by dancing in the pond with the fish. There was thunderous applause and the orchestra picked up with yet another Viennese waltz.

I was ready for bed (the vodka had whetted my appetite for it) but Anatoly paused in the lobby: 'The atmosphere here is a little false. The people are putting on a show of wealth. The night is young still. We too are still young. Let's go to another place I know. It is quite authentic.'

'And what about her?'

'If it pleases you to bring her, feel free - but if you are tired of her, there will be other ladies.'

She was standing looking towards the lift, holding herself languidly but gracefully - a look fashionable just then in London where it was dubbed 'the slinker-slouch' - but no doubt it came naturally to her. It seemed such a shame to lose her now. If only she had been a little more subtle with the make-up, and had sent her dress for a bit of a press, she might have got away with looking like a decent woman. It even crossed my mind that were one to ship her to London, and escort her on one's arm to the right sort of party, she might be taken for a Russian ballerina. She might not have convinced as Karsavina, but surely she could have passed muster as a member of the Corps de Ballets.

'Well, if there are going to be ladies present, we absolutely can't take her along,' I said not without regret in my voice.

'These ladies are no better than her. Not much, anyway. No need to worry on account of decorum. Bring her, if that is what you wish.'

Soon I was floating up in the lift to get my coat and hat from my room. I lingered for a minute to take a look at my face in the mirror. I do not suppose I would have noticed back then, but there would not have been many lines of care or experience or much sin in particular. It would still have been a smooth, boyish face, full of innocence, able to take alcohol and late nights without too much toll. It had the charm of youth without any of the interest of manhood. Those lines of experience, rather than dissipation, are an elusive quality, even later in life, particularly among those who never truly grow up. I lifted up my chin, trying to convince myself that I was already a man who knew a thing or two.

'Listen', I said pointing to my reflection, 'Don't let her get away without delivering the goods.'

A thin layer of snow covered the passenger bench of our hired-sleigh, on which there was barely enough room for two to sit. The cabbie turned his hairy face around to protest about the three of us squeezing in together. He was a giant of a man insulated against the cold by a bulky blue caftan. Anatoly promised him a generous tip and he seemed satisfied. Our sleigh-taxi slid through the dark streets, bell tinkling. I caught shadowy impressions of wooden shop fronts with signboards in eerie letters – the Cyrillic had a supernatural feel, like a wizard's spell book. Occasionally I would see a word of English or French, such as 'Restaurant' or 'Hommes et Dames.' Vera's scraggy furs helped to warm my right flank, but the icy air bit my ear lobes and crept into the crevices of the Crombie overcoat that had seen off three cold winters at Cambridge. Now I understood why all those young idealists in Chekhov were always dying of nasty coughs.[3]

We dismounted in an unlit street, silent but for the crunch of the snow beneath our boots. The staircase up to the flat where Anatoly's friends lived was in pitch blackness. We followed the creaks of Anatoly's footsteps. On the first landing, I put my hand on the rail and Vera placed hers on top of mine. The secret communication in the dark stopped my breath until Anatoly banged on a door as if he meant to wake up the whole neighbourhood. The door opened to emit warmth, yellow light, and the scratchy singing of a gramophone. A slender arm entwined itself around Anatoly's neck and he was kissed on the lips. I thought that every man should have a girl like that stored away in a place like this. Nina – as Anatoly introduced her - had a silk kimono wrapped around her. Her hair was undone and loose and her eyes were sleepy, but she seemed ready to receive us. We stepped into a welcoming fug given off by a white stove. Silk stockings were drying on the back of a chair. She tossed them into a corner so that I could take a seat.

'Make yourself absolutely at home,' said Anatoly. 'Another girl, Katya, lives here normally, but she is away hunting.'

'Hunting for what?'

'An officer. He left for St. Petersburg. She is chasing him there.'

Perhaps the dishes on the floor, the orange peel on the table, and the heap of clothes, expressed a free, artistic talent, for our hostess was an actress. Nina swiftly whisked up a midnight snack – sausage, salted fish, cucumber, tea, vodka – all just seemed to arrange themselves on the hastily wiped table. She was a strong featured woman, with thick, slightly unruly hair: handsome rather than pretty like my own girl whose name I was still did not know. Even then Nina struck me as proud and independent, and no plumed bird kept in a

---

[3] 'Travellers in Russia are especially warned that, in the matter of wearing furs and keeping their coats buttoned up, "Discretion is the better part of valour." Britishers especially are apt to imagine that they can play with the climate.' The Russian Year Book for 1911 compiled and Edited by Howard P Kennard MD.

gilded cage. Anatoly pulled his chair up close to her and held her without any sense of restraint. On his thick finger I noticed a wedding ring. I sat in the largest chair, an incongruously grand throne given the humble surroundings, with lion's paws for arm rests and two Venetian lions guarding my shoulders.

My companion fed a piece of sliced sausage into my mouth.

Before long, the women were having an animated chat with each other. I sensed that they were perhaps talking about me, and I was correct.

'They are wondering what your English nickname would be,' said Anatoly.

'I don't have one.'

Anatoly relayed this to the women.

'What does your mother call you?'

I hesitated a moment. I rarely saw Mama, who had lived for some years in Biarritz for reasons of her health (seeing my father made her ill). I said simply,

'George.'

'Just George?'

'George and nothing else.'

This declaration shocked them. Were all English mothers so cold? Russian parents were not so stingy in this regard. One child could be called Vera, Verotchka, Verushka, Veronka, Veroonya. Now I learned that my girl went by all those names as she sat on my knee and stroked my face. She uttered lots of dark Russian 'l's and a string of words ending in 'inky' and 'ubchik'. I felt that she was caressing me with suffixes in her mysterious language. From now on, she told Anatoly, she would call me 'Golubchik'

'What does that mean?'

'Little Pigeon' he said. I am thankful that she failed to keep that particular promise. 'And Vera also wants to say to you that her name means 'trust' and therefore you must always have faith in her.' She looked at me with mock sternness.

'But I've just met her,' I protested. She gave me a brief but warm kiss on the lips, and I hoped it was a sign of her good intentions to deliver one or two more before the night was out.

We drank a toast to our meeting.

No Russian evening is complete without a few anecdotal jokes. Nina had a huge stock of stories which she told in a variety of funny voices and faces, shifting the position in her chair as she switched personas. Anatoly was clearly proud of her skills. He called her, 'My Scheherazade.' Occasionally, she would place her hand across her chest to stop her kimono falling away. Her nails were painted blood red and her fingers wore enough rings to do a gypsy proud. Vera, of course, had no jewellery. Unfortunately, I have a terrible memory for the punch lines of jokes, besides which, quite a few of Nina's proved beyond Anatoly's powers of translation, although he made a valiant attempt to keep up with everything she said. However, I do remember Vera's one and only contribution. As she sat thinking very hard, trying to gather all the elements of the story in the right sequence behind her concentrated forehead, I wondered how she could hope to match Nina's expertise as a story teller – but in her own sweet way she did. Her joke went something like this:

The Russian Empress[4] was, as everyone knew, in love with Rasputin, the wild, hairy, smelly, priest, who through his influence at court and his many devious dealings, was sending the country to rack and ruin.

One day, The Empress gave her favourite a new pair of riding boots with golden spurs. Rasputin said, 'God tells me that I shall visit you tonight to demonstrate my gratitude.' The Empress agreed but warned him not to make any noise in case he woke up her wimp of a husband, 'Nicky', who slept in the next room. He must remove his new boots to avoid clanking with his golden spurs.

---

[4] "His Imperial Majesty the Emperor Nicholas II married Princess Alix of Hesse, granddaughter of Queen Victoria, 13/26 November 1894. Has issue, a son, Alexis Nicholaevitch, born 30 July/12 Aug 1904 and four daughters."- The Russian Year Book for 1911 compiled and Edited by Howard P Kennard MD.

Late at night, she heard steps coming down the corridor - clank, clank clank clank. Rasputin entered her bedroom and she softly rebuked him:

'Darling, I told you to take off your boots. What a racket you made!'

'I did remove them – even my socks.'

'So what was that noise?'

'Your Majesty, it must have been my toenails'

Even before Vera had finished telling the story, she had a rather fetching fit of giggles. Her green eyes glinted in the candle light and her nose twitched as she laughed. When her face became too scrunched up with laughter, perhaps for fear that it was not pretty like that, she put her hand in front of it. For me, it was her mirth at her own joke that was the most charming part of her story telling. You may well consider that she must have been an extremely crude sort of girl, but I thought she was marvellous. I just hoped that I could get her back to my room before I fainted from the effects of the vodka.

Nina clearly enjoyed the seditious character of Vera's story. She stood up to propose a toast: 'Liberté, Fraternité, Égalité.' For a moment, she looked like Delacroix's Mademoiselle Liberté herself leading the French people to revolt. She was certainly a well-formed woman, a little décolleté in her kimono, though not quite down to the waist as according to the French painter's notion revolutionary fashion. Anatoly clinked glasses with her, but Vera and I looked at each other slightly baffled. The trouble with an actress, is that it is hard to tell when she is being sincere. Nina translated the slogan into Russian for Vera who then banged her assent on the table and hiccupped. I did not feel quite comfortable.

'I'm sorry Anatoly, but no Englishman can drink to the slogan of the French Revolution. And besides, it's an inauspicious toast for a businessman who hopes to keep hold of his property.'

'You may drink to British fair-play.'

I could live with that, but it did not have the same ring.

We needed a pause to refresh ourselves. Anatoly and I stood by a small open window to take in some gulps of cold air. Singing voices drifted up from the street. I thought they must be fellow drunks, but Anatoly said they were pilgrims from the provinces, come to visit Moscow's holy churches: 'Though of course they are almost certainly drunk as well.'

The women seemed to be getting on fine together. They were examining the contents of Nina's wardrobe, and holding dresses up in front of one another. Anatoly offered me a cigarette from his fancy enamel case and said:

'Like you, I can't take the side of the socialists, but don't you think that this whole rigmarole about having to make money to get through life is a frightful bore?'

As he puffed his cigarette, his face suggested that the tobacco gave him indescribable relief from the cares of life. I thought I could see what he meant by his odd remark. Our evening had been so spontaneous and perfect that it would be a shame if its memory was blotted out by tedious negotiations or, worse still, a squalid quarrel over money. I truly hoped that we could conduct our business along civilised and cultivated lines.

'You know,' I said, 'I'm not sure that I agree with you about business having to be boring. The best business is creative.'

'You're absolutely right,' he said, 'as far as England is concerned, but things are different here. My fellow countrymen are very conservative. They like to do everything as they always did. Any new idea is repellent to their nature. You see the samovar' – he pointed to a bronze urn on the table that Nina was refilling with water - 'It is heated down the centre by hot coals or ash taken from the stove. The design is extremely convenient and economical. No Russian need ever be without boiling water for his tea! The factories of Tula, south of Moscow, lead the world in the production of samovars. They are never short of orders. All this is very fine, but unfortunately, its invention was the highpoint of the Russian Industrial Revolution. Since then our industry has achieved absolutely nothing without foreign equipment and managers. But in principle you are entirely correct. There's no reason why a businessman cannot leave his impression on the world any less than a poet or a philosopher.'

'Or even more so.'

'Yes, perhaps even more so,' he conceded, though I could see that he needed further persuasion.

'I even think trade has a certain romance,' I claimed. 'Just walk into a grocer's shop. There you will find tea from Assam, coffee from Brazil, figs from the Lamont, saffron from wherever it is that saffron comes from. In short, all the scents, tastes and colours of the wide world are brought to you by a man in an apron.'

'Yes, but your romantic grocer spends his life weighing out goods on scales, counting out pennies or kopecks, and writing figures in columns. He is short sighted and narrow minded, and the only excitement in his life is giving his wife or daughter a good thrashing with a birch once or twice a year.'

I decided not to mention that my own grandfather had been a grocer, and that Anatoly's description was not far off the mark. I myself was determined not to acquire the usual tastes and habits of a man who dedicates his life to making money. Much as I loved my dear Papa, I did not want to be like him, with his gleaming new mansion in the stockbroker belt of Surrey, and his forest of furniture from Maples. It had to be possible to do things differently.

'But I truly believe that one can be cultured and idealistic as well as successful in commerce,' I said.

'I do not disagree with you. I simply wish to express a desire that we should do business together in a way that is both progressive and creative. '

'Of course we can and must. Take this mine of yours. What would you say is its current stage of development?'

'As of now,' said Anatoly stroking his moustache, 'it is a filthy piece of land in the middle of nowhere. But below the surface, there is great potential.'

'And,' I said, 'if we raise some money to breathe life into it, soon there will be buildings, machines, engineers, managers, workers. It will grow up into a small community that functions almost like a living being and will continue to work long after we have sold it and moved on. In short, we businessmen are creators like gods.'

I was very satisfied with my explanation, although to tell you the truth, it was a variation on something my father had told me. Anatoly's response was remarkable. He looked like he had just seen the way, the truth, and the light. He was clearly delighted with my speech. It was his duty to develop the Mizinsky mine to show that Russia too could build great and humane enterprises. This, he believed, was the only way to make the country safe from disaster. He told me how miraculous it was that we both had such similar thoughts and feelings about the world, and that our souls were brothers. We would make perfect partners in business. He was becoming so carried away that I thought he was about to embrace me. Just then, Nina interrupted us. She explained that Vera had something to say. My girl looked very concentrated and uttered slowly but distinctly:

'I – LOVE – YOU.'

Then she disintegrated into a giggling fit. I could not have been more taken aback if the cat had spoken.

'Thank you,' I said, and felt awfully embarrassed.

Before we left, we had one more vodka, 'for the road', and we rose rather weakly, at least in my case, to our feet. Nina had given Vera a present to take home with her – a dress from her wardrobe that had been a prop in a play. The two women parted with hugs and kisses, and I was pleased that my girl had managed to win the heart of such an artistic and stylish woman as Nina. There was not a single cab on the streets and we ended up walking while linking arms. Our route took us past the silent Moscow circus and down the icy 'Boulevard of Flowers.' The spirit glowing deep inside us kept us warm and seemed to carry our legs forward, albeit not in the straightest of lines. Vera chatted gaily about how much she liked Nina and how we must go to see her act on stage. I must buy her a string of pearls because she would need them for visiting the theatre. She carried on talking, but Anatoly gave up translating.

It was not until we reached The Metropole that Anatoly was able to find a cab to take him to his family home. I would have shaken him by the hand had he not pre-empted me with a suffocating bear hug.

Vera and I went into the hotel together. The lift was not operated in the small hours of the morning, and I had to help her stagger up the marble stairway to the fourth floor and my room.

Chapter Two

"I don't say that the average duke or marquis knows very much about business. And doesn't a title go down well with the good old British public, which dearly loves anybody with a handle to their name!"
Hooley's Confessions by Ernest Terah Holley, Squire of Risley Simpkin, Marshall, Hamilton, Kent & co Ltd London 1924.

At school, I had been aware that my father, Gabriel Munnings (known to the readers of the financial tip-sheets as 'Angel' Munnings), was more than just 'someone boring in the City.' After a parental visit, my housemaster referred to Papa as, 'a colourful character'. This aspersion on my family's respectability encouraged me to develop a reputation that was as un-colourful as I could possibly manage. I have always tried to exhibit gentle manners. I dress with a distinct lack of ostentation, and certainly not with a carnation in my button hole or a silk scarf wrapped around my neck, as was my father's style. I have never put money on a horse let alone a dog (my father owned and raced both). I did not, and have never, chased shop girls.

I have only recently discovered some of the details of my father's early career (my source is my Uncle Frederick), and I will give you a flavour.

My paternal grandfather had built up a successful grocery business with a line of twenty five or so stores in the south east of England. On his death, the business passed to the elder of his two sons, Freddy, who had no inclination towards business, and sold up at the first opportunity to the Sainsbury brothers. The transaction left him a moderately wealthy man, and he began his career as an essayist and politician, dedicating himself to what my father used to call, 'Socialist pamphlets and piffle.' Freddy settled a few thousand on his brother, but Gabriel Munnings was ill-suited to moderation. He was determined to become a millionaire or go smash, and he wasted no time putting his reckless plan into action.

He took a whole floor of the Liverpool Street Hotel at £250 a week. He hired various clerks, chorus girls, newspaper journalists, and assorted hangers-on to populate the rooms and the corridors - and he let it be known that he had recently returned from the Transvaal where he had dug up a pile of gold and now intended to speculate in promising investments. An inventor would come to see him with a patented cure for varicose veins or a design for a better bicycle. Father would cast his eye over the patent and quite often buy it on the spot for £100. A week later would either have sold the same patent for £1000, or put it in a drawer and written it off. A spendthrift earl or a bishop would appear at my father's door with nothing more than his name and title to offer. My father did not miss the opportunity of signing up the dignitary to decorate the board of one of his newly formed limited companies. He called his hired directors his 'guinea pigs', because they were supposedly paid a fee of one guinea for attending a board meeting, the proceedings of which they little understood or cared about. In fact, the value of a directorship of one of my father's companies was much higher than the mere salary, for whenever one of his 'guinea pigs' was facing financial difficulties, which was often, my father would be their first resort for a 'loan'.

After a year or two of building his reputation for financial dealing, he progressed to promoting gold and diamond mines in far-flung places. It was around that time that he gained the sobriquet "Angel" Munnings, as people believed that his operations were blessed from on high. All his projects seemed to go well both for him and his investors. There were also those who suspected that he was aided by darker forces: it was rumoured that his telegraph ticker had been persuaded, by the performance of certain occult rights, to print out tomorrow's financial results today. Thus he joined the ranks of the City's pre-eminent plutocrats and financial necromancers.

The one thing that always eluded him was his acceptance into Society. It was not for want of effort or expenditure on his part. He dined with the top wire-pullers on both sides of the House of Commons. Nothing came of it. According to Frederick, he made a present of £25,000 to a certain baronet to save his noble line from financial embarrassment, in return for which he was supposed to receive a title of his own. He did not. Now his chief hopes for the Munnings name rested on me.

If I had enjoyed a worse relationship with my father, it would have been tolerably easy for me to rebel more openly against all the vulgarity and self-indulgence for which he stood. Unfortunately, even I was not immune to his bounciness and unctuous charm, and for his part, he was uncommonly tolerant of his only son and heir's whims and fancies, or, at least, he always gave the appearance of being completely relaxed about whatever path I chose in life.

In truth, it had not been my first choice of career to follow my father into stock promotion. In my final year at university, I had fancied myself as a theatrical impresario. I had produced some college plays and imagined that in a few short steps I would become a worthy rival to Sergei Diagelev. The curse of being the only son of a wealthy and free-spending father, was that my ambition was all too easy to realise without the usual prerequisite of learning the ropes. Nine weeks of trying to explain to our company that the money at our disposal was not unlimited despite the backing of my father; of doing my best to smooth over the bitter artistic differences between the writer, the director, the musical director and the principal performers; of taking the blame from the cast for everything from the quality of the kippers at breakfast to the empty rows of seats in dreary provincial theatres; of turning up at hotels and finding that our booking for eighteen rooms had been lost and that we had nowhere to stay for the night; of apologising to theatre managers for the absence of our star female attraction who had stormed out after the second performance after calling me an 'amateur', a 'schoolboy' and more colourful names; and of general despair and humiliation, had convinced me that my talents lay elsewhere. Despite this bitter experience, I still believed that an artist and an entrepreneur happily co-existed within the personality of yours truly. I wanted to combine business acumen with my creative leanings in some way. This was my 'idea' for life at that stage.

I dreamt of establishing a hedonistic nightclub in the West End of London to rival the Golden Calf, and I had even found a vacant draper's basement off Regent Street that I thought would be the perfect venue; but it was too soon to tap my father to underwrite another of my fancies. I had become easy prey for his suggestion that I join the 'family firm' in the City.

After two months of coming into father's office to learn from his chief accountant about how to read balance sheets, capital accounts, engineering surveys, and company reports, I was beginning to wonder how much more of the share-promoting business I could take. My father must have noticed my unenthusiastic face in the morning, and invited me to lunch at his favourite chophouse – a modest establishment down an alleyway off Cheapside in the City. He sat back in his 'usual place' - a booth in a dark corner - and looked completely at home. Then he asked me directly:

'There are those who call me a speculator. Do you know what a speculator is?'

'Something like a gambler,' I ventured, but he did not seem particularly interested in my opinion. He wiped the claret off his lips with his napkin before continuing:

'A speculator is like a child who believes in fairytales. He hears of an idea that grabs his fancy and takes it into his heart. He writes out a cheque, but does not feel that he has parted with any money. On the contrary, he already feels richer. He dreams of the fat profits that his speculation will yield up to him. Now, can I ask you this: does your old Papa seem to you like a naïve child who believes in fairytales?'

'You never struck me that way.'

'Well I was like that once, but that was a long time ago. In my youth, I had a limitless capacity for belief. I would throw my money at any old whim and expect it to make me a millionaire within the month. Despite my ignorance and the long odds against me, I was hugely successful at it. And do you know what the secret of my success was?' I was forced to admit that I did not know his secret. His grey eyes squinted at me shrewdly: 'Luck,' he said. 'My successes were entirely down to Lady Fortune, but she's a capricious female. Just as an investor is starting to believe he's a genius, she sticks out her little foot and trips him up. I had just enough brains to understand this. That was why, as soon as I could, I switched to the other side and became a company-promoter. Now it's my business to supply the investing public with interesting speculations.'

He held his steak knife in his fist and sawed away at his steak. He had paid for me to learn expensive table manners at my public school, but he never saw the need to take them up himself. After about his fourth glass of claret, his cheeks started to go ruddy and there was a watery look in his eyes.

'A company-promoter is a master storyteller. He uses words to build a castle in the air. It's a beautiful edifice with turrets and ramparts and extensive gardens. At first, the investors cannot see it with their own eyes. But the promoter spins his tale with such force and conviction, that the day comes when they are falling over each other to entrust their money to him. Of course, only one enterprise in ten develops into a pillar of the economy. Such is the nature of risk taking, but the investing public needs great storytellers to persuade it to invest in the future. Without them, there would no great industries, no minerals except those still lying in the ground, no railways, no steam ships; mankind would still be picking berries in the woods.'

It became clear, as we walked down Cheapside back to the office and my dreary pile of reading matter, that his talk had been leading up to a proposition. When we reached the steps of the Stock Exchange, he patted me on the back and asked me if I might be interested in a visit to Russia. He remembered how taken I had been by the dancers, and his 'artistic adviser' was always telling him that Russia was terribly 'in'. He had found a project which instinct told him would go all the way through to a stock market flotation, and he thought it would all mean so much more to me if I could see the property with my own eyes and help to arrange its 'coming out party'.

Chapter Three

I awoke in my room at the Metropole feeling bad, but not that bad. No wonder Russians find temptation in the vodka bottle; it is a clean spirit, and without the retribution of a shattering hangover the next morning, what is there to hold you back? It was only when a light breathing sound permeated my senses that I realised Vera was still with me. I was soon absorbed in a pleasant recollection: the moulded ceiling spinning round and shafts of light stealing through the window pane as Vera made love to me. The violin from One Thousand and One Nights was playing in my mind as her hair fell in front of her face and swept lightly over my chest. Her nose brushed my nose. The tip of her tongue touched the tip of mine. Her touch was light and fleeting, teasing and tender. She seemed to float above me. I myself, did very little. Only at the end did I hold onto her, as if I wanted to keep her with me forever.

Vera was an honest girl. She could easily have had her fee and her night on the town without any extra service, because frankly I had drunk far too much vodka to even press my suit. Perhaps she was hoping for another night's patronage, or even for a Dalmatian dog. Anyway, Vera was my first experience of physical love in its fullest sense. If she had not provided that important service, I really cannot say who would have done so or how long I would have had to wait for it. It had cost me £1.[5]

In the semi-consciousness of morning, I studied Vera's sleeping head. Her crude make-up was smudged, and I resolved to somehow persuade her to wear less of it. Her fringe was scraggy and badly cut, but her hair was all the same fine and silky. I wondered if I could find

---

[5] For comparison, a night in George's room at the Metropole, one of Moscow's most expensive hotels, cost around a third of the price according to the tariffs in Baedeker.

a hairdresser to tidy it up, and then persuade her to let it grow a little longer. Her face, however, was a different matter. If I had a 'type', she was it. She had the same elfin chin and delicate cheekbones as Karsavina. The skin of Vera's neck was smooth and white. Potentially, she was as beautiful as my ideal ballerina. I would have to work on her, though. It would be nice to have a disinterested female friend to take her in hand and advise on mysteries like corsets, cold cream, face powder and so forth – but where to find such a woman?

Yes, I decided there and then that I was not going to let Vera slip away too soon. My only regret was that she was paid-for. Did that make her less valuable? We go to the theatre, we watch a beautiful dancer stand on her toes and make exquisite movements with her arms, our senses are pleasured, and it costs five shillings and sixpence for a seat in the stalls. Do we feel that money sullies the experience?

Vera stirred. I saw a green eye open and I came over to lie next to her and to hold her, filling my hand with her breast and snuggling up to her warmth. I felt a sense of unreality about the complete lack of any prohibition against touching what I desired to touch. For a few minutes, I was enormously content, but soon she stirred and sat up in bed holding the covers around her. I pecked her on the cheek and she smiled. I watched with fascination as she dressed and looked at herself in the mirror, before slipping out of the door; I presumed to the W.C. When she returned, she pointed to her mouth which was now minus the smudged rouge. I was pleased that she was not about to rush off anywhere. I picked up the telephone and used my limited ability in French to order quelque chose à manger. She sat in a chair and waited patiently. After about fifteen minutes, during which I pretended to read a book, but in actual fact thought only about her and how I might receive more of her for my money, sandwiches of smoked white fish and sliced German sausage arrived on a silver tray. The servant put the snack down on the table beside Vera's chair. When he had gone, I picked it up and placed it in the middle of the bed. She at first looked dismayed to see the food sail away from her, and then she giggled and came over to sit with me. I pretended to guard the tray and she playfully snatched sandwiches off it. My strategy proved a good one. A little food was a direct route to Vera's heart.

After a clumsy, but for me, at any rate, immensely necessary fulfilment of desire, I completely flopped on the bed.

Before she left, Vera ran her finger down my nose, and over my mouth. I doubted that all her clients warranted such a token of affection. When I heard the door click behind her, I found I was quite uncertain whether I was more happy or sad.

I sat by the window of my room, half in a dream, and gazed out at Moscow. I suppose that I had hoped to see Vera leave the hotel, but I did not catch sight of her. Instead, I took in the great white snowy space of Theatre Square, criss-crossed by traffic and people in chaotic fashion. There were many more uniforms than one is used to seeing in London: the thick blue coats of the cabbies; the red caps of the messenger boys waiting on street corners; a great variety of military greatcoats, most of them not fitting the wearer especially well; and the weather-proof jerkins of the numerous gendarmes, none of whom seemed very animated, despite the cold. This scene and my recollections of the previous night kept me happily occupied for perhaps an hour or more.

Anatoly knocked on my door in the early afternoon. He clapped his hands around my shoulders, and I think he would have kissed me had I not looked so startled.

'It is alright,' he said. 'I am not offended. Let us shake hands in the English fashion.'

I took his hand warmly with both of mine. I was struck by a familiar feeling which I could not quite place. When I had a moment to analyse it, I realised that seeing Anatoly that afternoon was oddly similar to waking up with Vera. We shared nocturnal memories. The night had brought us, previously complete strangers, together.

'How are you today?' I asked. His moustache looked spruce and shiny, but there were bags under his eyes.

'Not so good. My wife made me drink pickled cabbage juice. It is supposed to be useful for a hangover, but it is perfectly disgusting and made me feel quite sick. You look in full health though. Ah, to be young!'

'Come on Anatoly, you can't be that old yourself. May I ask your age?'

'Twenty-nine, but today I feel like ninety-nine. Now let me give you a word of Russian, 'poedyom': it means, 'let's go'. My wife and mother are expecting us. They want to see the Englishman who kept me away all night long.'

Once again, we caught a sleigh-cab in the middle of the grand Theatre Square, but the scene changed rapidly. Our route took us through a wide space filled with ramshackle, wooden fronted shops and market stalls spilling out onto the pavements. The street was busy with carts loaded with sacks. Boys carried crates and trays on their heads. Anatoly told me that this was the 'Hunters Row,' and was the best place to buy game. At the end of the market, Moscow again opened up grand and ornamental vistas. To the left we caught a glimpse of the curvy slope of Red Square through the twin arches of the Resurrection Gate. We continued alongside the Alexander Gardens; behind them loomed the ochre walls of the Kremlin that suggested a warmer influence than gentle flecks of snow that filled the air. The irregular towers, some round, some square, some squat, some slender, were clearly the product of an oriental imagination. I was already realizing that Moscow was in reality two cities - Baghdad and Rome combined into one. To the right, in a more classical vein, Anatoly pointed out the 'old' University where he had studied philology and ancient languages.

We turned up the hill away from the Kremlin and soon passed through a blizzard of musical notes and scales emanating from the Conservatoire. My eye caught a young woman carrying a violin case; she bore a passing resemblance to Vera although, of course, she was not quite so pretty. The side streets displayed the feminine side of Moscow's personality – not the one you normally hear about. The brooding legacy of Ivan the Terrible did not extend to these parts. Pink, yellow, sky blue – flirtatious, cheerful colours decorated the houses, each one a natural individualist, varying in size and shape from its neighbour.

Eventually we halted before a tall recent structure. The front was covered with green, shell-like tiles, and a couple of maidens held up the porch above the main door, smiling with virginal innocence and pointing their breasts at passers-by. This was Anatoly's home: a block of flats. I felt a slight disappointment. I suppose that I had imagined him to live in a palace with many superfluous rooms and ornaments, perhaps a little decaying and in need of some restoration, but resonant of decadent wealth and a noble lineage.

As we came into lobby of the building, the floor of which was in the process of being mopped by the concierge, Anatoly said to me in a low voice, 'The ladies might prefer to think that we spent the night listening to gypsy singers. The story is debauched enough to be credible without causing any special alarm.'

'Good idea,' I said, rather flattered to be invited to join him in a small domestic conspiracy. He thanked me and promised to take me to a gypsy nightclub before I left Moscow.[6] As things turned out, it was probably the only entertainment which he failed to show me on that trip.

The putting on and taking off of galoshes forms an essential part of the rigmarole of a Russian winter: we left ours on the rack by the concierge's cabin, and climbed the marble staircase to the fifth floor. Anatoly rang the bell as we entered the flat, and a maid came hurrying along the corridor to take our coats. There was pleasant aroma of cake baking. In the living room, we found the two ladies seated at a little table by a large bow-shaped window that was populated by a

---

[6] "Those who do not shrink from an expensive supper and somewhat bohemian society should make a point of hearing one of the Russian or Gipsy Choirs. The very characteristic performances of these choirs are generally given in the fashionable restaurants on the outskirts of the large towns, which on winter evenings are much frequented by the jeunesse dorée in their three-horse sleighs." - Baedeker

winter garden of green leaved pot plants. The elder Madame Mizinsky had a finely chiselled profile and her dark hair, streaked with grey, was clasped behind her long slender neck. The younger had a smaller and rounder figure, but her face was sweet and rosy. They were playing cards and drinking tea from little glasses.

Anatoly introduced me to the younger of the two women, his wife Julia, who said,

'So this is the Englishman who kept my husband away all night.'

'Please forgive me. We were detained by a band of gypsy singers.'

Julia spoke a few words of Russian to her mother-in-law, who responded by singing some lines of a ballad. Her hand circled in front of her. Her voice was low, her eyes glinting. It was a tease, but only just:

'Did the gypsies sing this song?' asked Julia

'Oh yes, I think I recognise it.' I said, 'What was it about again?'

'Black eyes, dark eyes, passionate eyes,' said Anatoly, rather flatly.

It struck me that the eyes of his mother could almost fit that description.

'They are more than just eyes in this song,' said Julia, 'This word means something like 'windows into the soul'.'

'Yes indeed, my dear,' said Anatoly. Then he turned to me and said, 'George, sit down next to Julia. I would like you to take a closer look at her ring.'

Julia proudly placed a white, slightly plump, hand on the table. A green stone was set in the ring on the first finger. Its hue was deep and verdant, and reminded me of the eyes of a certain girl. I expressed polite admiration for it.

What followed was something like a séance. A maid was summoned to bring matches to light the tapers of the candelabra and to draw the curtains. Only one electric lamp was lit in the corner of the room. We seemed to be sitting closer together than before, in an uncommonly intimate atmosphere, hardly separated by the table at all. I was aware that Madame Mizinsky was looking at my face, and I wondered if there was something different about me since my recent initiation into the rites of the Russian winter. Julia gave me her hand, as if for me to kiss, and I saw that the colour of the gem had turned to a gentle red.[7] In a low voice, almost a whisper, Anatoly said,

'You are looking at an alexandrite stone found by pure chance on our land. I think you will agree that the subject of our business possesses a rare and natural beauty. I doubt that a dealer in fine art could claim that his goods were more sublime.'

'It certainly is a remarkable stone,' I agreed. 'But is it truly valuable?'

'Extremely. A clear example with a strong colour change is rarer than the finest diamond. A true alexandrite can only be found in a small area of the Ural Mountains – although there are some inferior gems from Ceylon that are sometimes falsely passed off as alexandrite.'[8]

'And how did this land come into your possession?'

'Ah,' he said. 'Julia's dowry consisted of this ring and the land that goes with it.'

I smiled at Julia and she took back her hand. The maid opened the curtains and let in a cold sunlight, almost white in quality. The alexandrite was once again luxuriating in its greenness. Anatoly said to Julia:

'George and I have some business to attend to. We shall join you for tea in about half an hour.'

He led me into his study.

---

[7] "Alexandrite is especially remarkable for its strongly marked difference of colour, according as it is viewed by natural or artificial light. The finest stones present a bright green, or deep olive green colour, by daylight ; whereas, as night, artificial light, such as that of gas or candle, brings out a soft columbine red or raspberry tint, or purple. It has been said that the Alexandrite is an emerald by day and an amethyst at night." - *Precious Stones and Gems, Their History, Sources and Characteristics* by Edwin W. Streeter FRGS, MAI, 1898 edition.

[8] Streeter does not accord with Anatoly's dismissal of alexandrite from Ceylon: "The original Alexandrite came from the Emerald mine of Tokowoia in the Ural mountains, but was found only in small quantities. The principal supply is now obtained from Ceylon, where, however it is far from plentiful."

'Your wife seems very charming,' I remarked.

He gestured for me to take a seat. 'Yes, she is very charming indeed,' he said, almost yawning as he sat on edge of his desk. 'Unfortunately I suffer from a disease which did not know existed when I was your age. Its Latin name is Tedium Vitae. The best known cure for this condition is a love affair.'

I laughed at his frankness and looked around the room. There was something that aroused my curiosity:

'And may I ask one other question?'

'Ask anything you like.'

'Why do you keep that huge heap of rugs in your office? I've never seen so many outside a carpet shop.' I was unusually cocky that afternoon.

'Didn't you know?' he asked. 'My father dealt in oriental carpets. It is not a bad business. Unfortunately it refuses to run itself efficiently. My elder brother Fyodor is in charge now, but he is always being cheated by his accountant. It is impossible to say if we have more debits or credits to our name. If I go to the warehouse everyday, all is well with the roubles and kopecks, but my brother resents my interference. If I suggest even a superficial change, he tells me that it is all very well thinking up innovations, but our father always managed things in such and such a fashion, and besides the best way is always the one you know. It is better for our fraternal relations if I stay away. Besides, I am not attracted to that place: it is like a prison. There are metal doors and bars on the windows to protect the stock. My soul rebels against spending the hours of daylight in such an atmosphere. It's annoying to me, but perhaps it is God's will. There is no law that children must inherit all the characteristics of their parents. My late father loved carpets. It was his pleasure to travel to Bukhara in Asia to sit and drink tea and bargain over prices. He loved everything about rugs, and never ceased to wonder at the fine work and colours. But they are not my joy. I like carpets, but only so much. This is why I have decided to develop the mine. I find the idea of alexandrite far more appealing, and I need to be attracted to an idea before I undertake a project. The best thing about it is that I will be my own master and able to develop my own ideas without any interference from anybody. I think that this is the most important consideration for an entrepreneur.'

'Your father must have passed away at a young age.'

'He died of a broken heart. His mistress decided to be faithful to her husband.'

I really did not know what to say.

Anatoly laughed: 'Please don't look so shocked. It was just my little joke, in rather bad taste. I am sorry. He was much older than my mother and greatly in love with her. He died in her arms of purely natural causes and went to his grave a happy man. Now, let me show you something else.'

He opened a drawer with a key and took out a lump of rock, about the size of his fist. It was for the most part silvery and uneven in texture, but there were also some green planes. He handed it to me. It was surprisingly heavy for its size. It had both rough and smooth surfaces, and the sharp corners dug into my palm.

'You are holding a geological formation known as 'micha schist', and inside it are some crystals of alexandrite that would make some very fine pieces of jewellery. An alexandrite must be cut 'en cabochon' to display its remarkable qualities. We have left this sample in its natural state so as to be more useful for scientific examination. Do you mind taking that map from the shelf just by you?'

I unfurled the map on his desk and he placed a rock on it as a paperweight. He put his think index finger on a dark line of shading that ran from north to south through the vast emptiness that was the Russian Empire. These were the Urals that divide Europe from Asia.

'The mountains are not so very high, but they are rich in every type of mineral. Our property is here, on the river Tokovaya, near the City of Yekaterinburg. As you see, the Trans-Siberian railway runs through the area. There are many mining enterprises there. The best ones are managed by French and English managers.'

I explained that finance, not mining, was our business.

'I understand. With money one can find managers, and equipment. We need nothing else. When I spent three months in England, my father arranged for me to work in a merchant bank to observe how London feeds capital to the entire world. I would not wish to mortgage our property to one of our Russian banks – they are no better than thieves.'

'Like all banks,' I was tempted to say, but did not. It seemed best to leave him convinced that all things in England were superior. Instead, I asked when we could visit the property.

'Visit?' he said, as if I had asked something quite extraordinary. I thought he knew that the main object of my trip was to see the land. My father's instructions to me had been: 'Do some due diligence and all that rot. Check that the property exists. Talk to the neighbours about who owns it. You often find out more in an afternoon that way, than by paying an army of lawyers to spend weeks pouring over the documents at £1 per hour.' I knew that our office had cabled a more formal version of this plan to the Mizinskies, but Anatoly was set against any idea of travelling for the time being:

'Now is not the time of year. Our property is on the edge of Siberia. It is very cold.'

'Not possible?'

'Quite difficult. Much better in spring when the snow has cleared.'

Perhaps my geography was a little weak, but I had imagined Siberia to suffer from snow and winter all year round. It had not occurred to me that it might be better to wait a few months. Still I began to see the advantage of putting off the expedition. It would give me an excuse to visit Russia again.

'In that case,' I said, 'I hope you can help me gather us much paper work as possible and obtain official translations into English. I have a full list of what it is required back at the hotel. It includes mining permits, title deeds, a geological survey, an expert opinion from an engineer, and so forth…'

'I will do my best, but to obtain some of those papers we need to visit Yekaterinburg and the local mining office.

I could see that the circle was going to be hard to square. I just sighed. 'Well perhaps we can visit the area as you suggest,' Anatoly conceded. 'Let us consider this matter later.'

We joined the ladies for tea. I say 'tea' but it was an extraordinary spread. The table glittered with the whole spectrum of brightly coloured jams, and crystal jugs of kvas (a Russian rye drink) and fruit compote, not to mention various coloured vodkas, all lined up in full battle order. There were saucers of black and red caviar, plates piled with pancakes, and bowls of dates and cranberries. The maid tended to a silver-plated example of the famous Russian samovar that Anatoly had extolled the previous evening. I declined vodka, but I did not get away without a few toasts of red wine from the Crimea.

Julia spoke to me about Oscar Wilde. I had no idea that he was so popular in Russia, but she told me that some people she knew slept with The Picture of Dorian Gray under their pillows.

Anatoly's eyes looked like they might close at any moment. His mother stroked his head. I could see that women naturally adored him, but I wondered if his own wife numbered among his leading admirers. She and her husband took little notice of each other. They seemed to me, in this respect, not so very different from a great many English married couples, and I could not help wondering if she suspected that her husband's fidelity was not quite one hundred per cent.

Once again, I knocked tentatively at Temptation's door.

It was located in the upper reaches of the Metropole Hotel. On this floor, the columns of the stairwell were decorated with alabaster faces of young women. The waves of their hair and the outlines of their features were gilded. I wondered as to their significance. Were they nymphs or Vestal Virgins? Or perhaps honoured members of the hotel's harem? The door that I sought was denoted by a red heart painted in rouge. It was ajar. I knocked and it gently opened:

'Is Vera in?'

A girl looked blankly at me from behind her mask of white face powder. Further into the room I could see the semi-clad female form in all shapes, sizes, colourings and ages, draped over the couches and chairs like clothes thrown out of a suitcase. A great ginger beauty, the one I had seen speaking to Vera the previous evening, stretched out like a cat on the day bed, testing the seams of her corset. I must admit, I felt a tremendous pang of desire. But loyalty to Vera reasserted itself: 'Vera? Vera? Black hair?'

By now, several girls had gathered round at the open door. They hardly had enough clothes between them to cover one decent Englishwoman. I found it quite a struggle not to let my eyes wander too obviously. But why on earth shouldn't I? All their goods were for sale. Still, shyness, or shame, or good schooling, or some inner voice ordered me not to.

It was clear by now that Vera was not there. Perhaps she had taken the evening off. Now the Madame and her tawny beak was to the fore. Her bony face was covered in so much paint that she looked like a puppet. The skin on her hands glistened like wood varnish. She rasped:

'Monsieur aime la belle Vera, n'est pas? Mais nous avons beaucoup des autres belles femmes.'

If she really had been as French as she would have liked me to think, I probably would not have understood a word. It is much easier to follow someone on the same low level of a foreign language as oneself.

I pointed to the ginger-headed one and asked:
'Ca fait combien?'
'Roubles Dix'
'C'est chèr'
'Mais belle.'

I must admit, I was tempted to offer 10 roubles[9] there and then for the girl. She had flesh in all the right places and did not look at all hungry. The gentlemanly side of my character felt shy about haggling, but the financier in me told me to offer a lower price. The trouble was that it seemed insulting to go too low. I halved the sum when I should have at least quartered it. Even so, Madame shook her beak sternly at me and the oversized nostrils flared with reproof. 'Cinq roubles! Pour quelle une belle femme! Monsieur! Monsieur!'

I was humbled. It was like getting poor marks at school for a piece of ungrammatical French. At least no one bothered about grammar here. Ginger turned up her beautiful nose and went back to sit on the day bed. I felt really awkward about it; a real heel. I hardly recognised myself. Vera was my sort of girl; a well brought up and nicely mannered whore, considerate and not too bumptious. Now, I was revolted - not by Ginger but by my own greed for flesh. It would be like eating all the chocolates in the box and then feeling sick at the end of it. I was telling myself that I did not want Vera to be the start of a lifetime habit of debauchery, and that she was an exception. I had a soft spot for the girl. I wanted to get out of this room full of over-ripe women, so I said,

'Merci Madame. Je recherche seulement la belle Vera. Bon soir'

'Stop! stop! Pour vous, Monsieur, roubles cinq.'

Non. Merci!"

Now I knew her bottom price for the red head was 10 shillings. Vera – or my gullibility – had commanded an enormous price on my first night. My lust, my awkwardness, my mixed-up feelings had turned into annoyance. I am sure that a girl would not have cost more than two shillings back at Shepherd's Market. That was according to the gossip that I heard from boys who claimed to have discovered the

---

[9] Russian money before the Revolution: rough equivalents to British and American:
    1 rouble = 100 kopeks = 50c = 2s
    10 roubles = £1 = $550 kopecks = 1s = 25 cents
    4 kopecks = 1d = 2 cents
(see Baedeker and other reference books from the time).

prices for themselves. Somehow, the idea of a piece of English trollop did not tempt me. It did not strike me that English girls had a talent for prostitution, which is probably why they were so cheap.

The door to room sixty-six was still ajar as I turned to leave. Somebody knocked softly on it and started to enter - probably, I thought, another client. I would wish my fellow sensualist 'good hunting' and leave with as much dignity as I could muster. But it was not another man.

It might have been the pale and flat forehead; or it might have been the face which was out of bounds to any untidy expression; or it might have been the cut of her dress, fashionable but not chic, in the way that only Dickens & Jones or Liberty can manage; it might have been any or all of those things, but I knew right away that she was a fellow compatriot from a "good" family.

She nodded to me and addressed the room in general: 'Zdrastvutye.' Her greeting was met with stony silence. You could have heard a garter snap. She followed up with some other Russian words, but speaking slowly in what was clearly a foreign accent. If she was not blind or incredibly stupid she must have realised she had entered the wrong room. Why did not she apologise and leave? What the hell did she think she was playing at? I decided to tough her out.

'How do you do. My name's Munnings. May I be of assistance?' I was expecting her to be far more embarrassed than I was and to leave right away.

'How do you do,' she said, in a cucumber voice. 'My name is Lydia Hawthorne. I would like to talk to some of the women.'

'Well perhaps this lady can help you,' I said, indicating Madame. 'She likes to speak in French.'

Miss Hawthorne immediately started to communicate with Madame in far more fluent French than I could muster. A swot talking to a slut, I remember thinking as I walked back down the corridor. Suddenly I saw myself through the cold grey-blue eyes of Lydia Hawthorne; I felt exposed; I felt sullied; I was weak; I was an eroto-maniac; I was like my father. How too ..... too ..... sick-making.

I could not face the Hotel Metropole's European dining room that evening. There is only so much self-indulgence one can take on one trip. I had a light meal sent up to my room and I tried to read, but I could hold no concentration. My thoughts were on the rampage. I did not know what to do with myself, and so I went down to the bar. I found a table in the corner, and gazed at the strange foreign people; not all Russians, by any means: French, Germans, Greeks. And I found that I liked the unfamiliarity, the anonymity of the atmosphere. I could lose myself in it.

Over a large brandy, I imagined myself a few years hence – perhaps in around 1917. I would have made my million from Russian mining ventures and retired. I would marry some English beauty from an old family that was running short of ready cash. We would be on our honeymoon, probably staying in a French chateau, lying in a huge expanse of white linen with the scent of lilacs drifting in through the window, and my English rose of a wife, still warm from her initiation into married life, would ask in a whisper, 'Darling, have you ever been with, you know, a bad sort of woman, before we met? I won't hold it against you if you have. I just want to know everything there is to know about you.'

I would say: 'Whatever put such a silly thought into your pretty head? You know that I am repelled by all things sordid.'

The truth would surely be too cruel. There is an odd passage in Anna Karenina where Tolstoy's hero, Levin, makes his new wife read his journals in which he recounts his debaucheries. It is an extreme and insensitive form of honesty to inflict on the woman you love. Apparently Tolstoy pressed the very same 'honesty' on his own bride, and he was not short of confessions. I can imagine The Countess Tolstoy burning the midnight oil reading through pages and pages of filth, no doubt drawn-out in every sordid detail, since we all know that Tolstoy writes as if he is paid by the word.

On the way back up to my room, Lydia Hawthorne was standing by the lift. There was no escaping her up and down glance.

'I trust,' she said, 'that you found something to satisfy your appetite at dinner. I find there are so many dainty dishes to choose from.' Her ironic disapproval restored my confidence. The role of a young dissolute rake abroad was not so unbecoming after all.

We exchanged polite nonsense for a minute or so, as one does in a foreign country with a fellow compatriot, and it transpired that she was travelling on her own (with just one servant), writing articles for a woman's publication called Media. She obviously considered herself to be, oh so 'independent.' A man must have maturity and self-confidence to cope with such a woman – and in those days I wanted for both.

The lift in the Metropole was as elegant as a lady's boudoir with stained glass above the door embossed with motifs of African violets. It was quite small, and the fat attendant took up about a third of the space. I was standing next to my new acquaintance in an uneasy proximity, by English standards. As we were about to depart, two Russian gentlemen stepped in, talking loudly and laughing. They did not seem to mind the closeness. I was feeling a touch queasy and let my eyes close. We floated upward but my stomach stayed on the ground floor. I heard the lift operator announce the second 'étage', and my nostrils filled with a certain cheap rose-water smell. It was strangely familiar. After a few seconds I opened my eyes. I saw the back of a black head and ragged fur collar. We floated up to the third floor and the woman stepped out. She was arm in arm with a bulky bald man. She was holding the bastard steady as they zigzagged towards his room. Lydia Hawthorne said: 'Why must a man get drunk and make a fool of himself?' I replied that it was one of the eternal mysteries of the universe.

As I lay on my bed I knew exactly how a man got drunk and made a fool of himself with a tart like Vera. Fire was pumping round my veins. This time it was not shame - it was jealousy. Sleep was out of the question. I even thought of going back to the whores' staffroom to ask if Vera was back 'off duty'. I am glad to say that I held myself back from that final humiliation.

I can recollect few more uncomfortable nights than the one I spent lying in the Metropole being eaten up by my own Green Eyed Monster - and I speak as one who has signed on as a guest at a far more notorious hotel just up the hill from there. Fear or sexual jealousy - which burns you up most? I do not know, and I have experienced both in buckets.

Chapter Four

The next morning I telephoned down to reception and asked them to get me Anatoly's home on the line. It was five or ten minutes before the operator put me through. A woman's voice screeched 'Allo? Allo?' I just said Anatoly Mizinsky's name out loud and clear, hoping that he would be fetched. The telephone lady repeated 'Allo?' and hung-up. It jarred my nerves - not just sound of the hand piece slamming down - but the unseen woman's abrupt rudeness. I sat on my bed for a few minutes feeling slightly pathetic. I had not slept and I was still hung-over from two nights beforehand. My head and stomach felt much worse today. Finally, I came to the momentous conclusion that I would go downstairs and drink a cup of coffee.

Strong Turkish coffee on an emotionally upset stomach was probably not the best of ideas, but I needed something to clear away the debris of a bad night. As I was on my second cup, things went from bad to worse: Lydia Hawthorne came into the breakfast room. In order to avoid the rude entry of her clear, cold little eyes into my world, I attempted to contemplate the mysteries of my coffee cup, in the manner of a Russian émigré lady back in England who used to tell fortunes by interpreting the shapes formed by the coffee stains. She said,

'Anything of interest in the bottom of your cup this morning?'

In the thick residue of coffee a cruel smile was depicted. The foreseeable future consisted of Miss Lydia Hawthorne not only existing on the same Earth as myself but also sitting down and exchanging little jibes with me. I rose to my feet to invite her unwelcome presence to join me, bowing both to her and to fate. More coffee arrived and Lydia placed a cigarette into the end of a long silver holder, quite unabashed by smoking in public. I fumbled in my pocket for a match and lent over the table to offer her a light that went out as soon as she attempted to meet my flame. I struck another one. They were rotten Russian matches. The third time, as she sucked into her cigarette, I could appreciate that her eyes had an ironic glint, which was not unattractive.

'So how is your travelogue coming along?' I asked, trying to be polite. She had said the night before that she was writing something or other for a publication. I had assumed for some reason that she would be enthusing about the charms of Moscow.

'Travelogue? I would not write a travelogue for all the tea in China, Mr Munnings. My subject is social reality.'

Earlier that morning, she had been let down for an appointment with a high ranking official, the Privy Councillor in charge of the Ministry of the Interior for all Moscow. She had wanted his authority to visit the women's section of a prison and report on the conditions for her publication. She had waited two hours for him on a hard bench. 'Eventually I was informed that he was indisposed - which I translated as drunk,' she said, with evident disgust. 'Never mind. It's all gist for my article. And you - what brings you to Moscow, Mr Munnings?'

'Business.'

By the way she turned her cheek away and took a puff from her cigarette, I discerned that she disapproved of 'business' as much as she did of travelogues and, perhaps, men. At length she asked:

'So are you here as an advance party for the trade delegation of next week?'

She was surprised that I knew nothing of this event. A group of British parliamentarians, businessmen, financiers, and other Anglo-Russian business bigwigs were coming out to St. Petersburg and Moscow to promote commercial ties between our two countries. Lydia told me that she planned to attend one of the functions herself, an evening party thrown by a Moscow merchant in his palace which was decorated with paintings by the most outré and modern French artists. It was bound to be lavish beyond all imagining, and if I wanted to put my name down for it, she suggested that I apply to the

British Consul. I said that I was planning to drop in on the consulate in the nearest future.

'And what is the nature of your business?' she asked.

'I'd rather keep that under my hat for the time being, until it's signed on the dotted line.'

'But surely you would not wish to invest in so repressive and unstable a regime as the Tsar's?'

'It's a private project and it's none of the Tsar's business, as far as I can see.'

I did not want to give too much away. I hardly wanted my project to end up as 'gist' for one of her articles. I doubted that I would receive sympathetic treatment from her pen. To deflect her, I asked her what else she intended to write about.

'The principal objective of my trip is to interview Maria Spiridonova,' she told me.

'I'm afraid I've not heard of the lady.'

'Then you cannot have not been in Russia for long, for she is a cause célèbre here. She is a woman of principle who is undergoing the ordeal of imprisonment in a Tsarist gaol for what she believes.'

'She sounds like a Russian Mrs Pankhurst.'

'She is no less remarkable than the women-suffragist.'

Lydia then related to me the story Maria Spiridonova. I was not really in the mood for her version of Russia's 'social reality' but her story of cruelty, scandal and revenge impressed itself on my mind.

In 1906, the peasants of Tambov, in the South of Russia, were in revolt. The local satrap – a man called Luzhenovsky – decided to teach them a lesson. He rode with his Cossacks through the villages, whipping, burning, pillaging, and raping.

One bright winter's afternoon, he was about to board a train at a provincial railway station, when a young woman called his name. He turned to look at her. She was dressed as a schoolgirl. Her sweet face was the last thing he saw in this world. Concealed inside her muff was a Browning pistol which she fired five times into his belly. For a moment, a brittle silence stopped all motion on the platform. The stunned Cossacks who guarded Luzhenovsky could not pick out the assassin from among the crowd. Then Maria Spiridonova stepped forward and said: 'Kill me now! I lay down my life for truth and justice!'

The leader of the Cossacks dragged her by her pony-tale across the platform. Members of the public tried to object. Swords glinted and the crowd ran for it. A justice of the peace was obliged to hide from the Cossack blades inside the stationmaster's office.

They took Maria's unconscious body to a police cell. Then they stripped her. Then they whipped her. Then they burnt her nipples with cigarettes.

They took her to Tambov by train. On the way, she was violated by her guards.

A liberal newspaper in St. Petersburg got hold of the story. Her letters from her cell, which began, 'Dear Comrades,' were published. Her sufferings at the hands of the Cossacks elevated her status to that of a national heroine.

She wrote that she longed for her own execution. Her judge would have gladly granted her wish, but he was under orders not to provoke the people further. He sentenced her to lifelong penal servitude in the frozen East.

At every station through Siberia, her 'royal' train was met by cheering crowds singing revolutionary songs and strewing flowers onto the track. It was rumoured that the mob would set her free; at Omsk it was to be the workers; at Krasnoyarsk the soldiers; at Chita the Cossacks of Trans-Baikal. But all the people wanted was a glimpse of Maria Spiridonova and, if possible, her autograph. When the train ran out of track, she continued to the prison in Akatui in the back of a cart. The saintly murderess had remained in that desolate spot ever since.

Now Lydia wanted to visit Akatui to interview her.

'Not the most romantic of tales,' I said when she had finished telling me this.

'But it is a true story that touches the hearts of people from all walks of life, and has the power to inflict great damage on the autocracy. It is what brings me here. And you, Mr Munnings, no doubt, you are occupied today with your business?' Her eyes fell on my half-eaten roll and the little glass containing red jam.

'Not really. I thought I might do a spot of sight-seeing. Look at some of those golden domes and crosses you want to avoid.'

'Well actually, I'm not altogether against sight-seeing. I have nothing to do following my lack of success this morning. Perhaps I might accompany you?'

The Kremlin was close by, but the chill wind made it particularly unpleasant to walk outside that day. At least the cold air seemed to freeze the flow of Lydia's questions. A few yards down the pavement I slipped on an iced-over puddle, landed on my behind, and bit my tongue. Lydia helped me to my feet and insisted on brushing every last fleck of snow powder off my back. She even irritated me when she was helping me. My feet felt wet already and my shoes were skating every few steps. I was beginning to hate that morning. It was a hazardous place, this Moscow. Lydia told me a story she had heard from a Russian woman in St. Petersburg. It concerned an icicle falling from an over hanging roof, cutting straight through the canvass top of a baby's perambulator, and piercing the heart of the infant sleeping within. Damocles' sword was dangling from every roof-gutter.

As we walked through the Alexander Gardens under the great red walls of the Kremlin fortress, Lydia pointed out the Nikolsky Tower. Just there, in 1905, a bomb had ended the reactionary life of The Grand Duke Sergei Alexandrovich, a favourite uncle of Tsar Nicholas II, or so Lydia informed me.

'I hope you don't have a bomb under your furs,' I said.

'Good gracious no. My sword is my pen.'

We wandered over a stone bridge and into the heart of Holy Russia, quite unhindered. The shaggy, slouching guards at the Troitskaya Gate would not have passed muster as British Grenadiers.

I found their relaxed postures rather reassuring. They did not look eager to stick anybody with a bayonet, which was more than you could say about our boys when they are on motionless guard duty - but appearances can deceive.

The three cathedrals of the Kremlin are as beautiful as the Russian soul on a good day - and the Russian soul at its best is truly wonderful. Needless to say, on a bad day, when it has a hangover or is suffering from one of its periodic bouts of paranoia, the Russian soul is not a pretty sight - and when seen in a certain gloomy light, the shadowy Kremlin broods like a medieval head-splitter.

Lydia was equipped with Karl Baedeker's Guide to Russia with Tehran, Port Arthur, and Peking. Her nose was in Karl's pedantic print while mine was pointing up at the incredible interior walls of the Uspensky Cathedral, the holiest of holy Russian places where the Tsars had been crowned since the fifteen-century. The air was heavy with the scent of burning candles and the frescoed saints. Sinners and holy hosts watched us in a dusk-like serenity. Only in the centre of the Cathedral did a shaft of light fall from a skylight in the roof like a giant bar of gold. The shadow of priest passed through the shaft walking towards us, and it seemed to me that he had emerged out of a world beyond, at least several centuries old.

Lydia explained in a whisper that the Tsar threw the Italian architect of the Cathedral, Ridolfo Aristotele Fioravanti, into prison in 1485 for daring to request permission to return home to Bologna. 'That's a tyrant's gratitude for you,' she hissed. 'Make sure you get your passport back from the police.' The hotel had sent it to the police station, as a matter of routine, for checking, registering, and stamping.

A magnificent Iconostasis was studded with icons, pearls, and precious jewels. If you cranked your head up to look into one of the domes, your eyes met the almond shaped eyes of the Saviour, with his perfect aquiline nose, long black hair and pointed beard. Lydia was unimpressed.

'Don't you find the religion of the Russians is so very material? Their God is made of gold. Their idea of spiritual devotion is a display of wealth. It is so very oriental. Even as an unbeliever I find it distasteful.'

'I don't know,' I said, 'Perhaps we English are a bit too niggardly when it comes to worship.' Lydia gave me a look as if to say I was a hopeless vulgarian.

The thing I found most curious about the interiors of the Kremlin buildings was that, despite their thrones of gold and swinging incense holders, the medieval palaces with their arches and low ceilings covered in frescos, were rather cosy. The haunts of Tsar Ivan the Terrible were not half as chilly as our own Tower of London. Cosiness is a Russian talent. Given half a chance they can make a prison cell cosy, as even Lydia remarked in one of her articles. As ever in Russia, the rule always had an exception. At the top of a granite staircase, we turned into the celestial Hall of St. George. [10] This was the whitest room I have ever set foot in. Here it was possible to imagine the Lord Almighty and his host of angels sitting in judgement, but of course it was God's right hand-man on earth, the Tsar Emperor of all the Russias, who used to sit on the throne. Alcoves in the marble walls were inlaid with golden letters listing the Russian soldiers who had received the 'Order of St. George' for valour in the field. In this room, if anywhere, one could believe that the Romanov Tsars were divinely inspired, all-powerful, and would reign for all time.

---

[10] "To Anglo-Saxons the statement might be surprising that the Russians were the first to show the symbol of St. George and the Dragon on a coat-of-arms. "St. George the Triumphant" appeared first upon the arms of Moscow and was later, in 1472, incorporated with the two-headed eagle and the cross by Grand Duke Ivan II, as the arms of all Russia. The most treasured decoration for military heroism is named The Medal of St. George. It is given to the most courageous whether he be private or general" - Ruth Kedzie Wood *The Tourist's Russia.*" *Baedeker* records that room is the largest in the Kremlin (200 ft long, 70 ft wide, and 60 ft high) and that the six candelabra contain 3200 bulbs.

At the top of the bell tower of Ivan the Terrible, after Lydia had dragged me, puffing up all 250 steps, I lit a cigarette, before remembering to offer her one, and pulled up my collar to keep out the chill wind. Despite her desire not to write a travelogue, I wondered how Lydia's report could be complete without mention of Holy Moscow. Our eyes harvested a crop of golden domes and crosses glittering amongst the snow which lay in heaps upon the Moscow skyline. It was one of those travellers' moments when you feel like Marco Polo. You just want to gaze and wonder. The biggest onion of all was that of The Cathedral of Christ the Saviour, built by the people to celebrate the victory over Napoleon in 1812. It struck me as the most masculine and the least appealing of the structures before our eyes. For the most part, Moscow's skyline was curvy and buxom. In the opposite direction, we easily picked out the green roof of the huge 'Foundlings' Hospital'. Lydia sniffed when she read from her Baedeker that thousands of orphans were raised there at the Government's expense.[11] It was a fact which did not fit comfortably with her views on the nature of autocracy. The river itself was filled with lumpy ice; on its opposite embankment, elaborate villas vied with the Kremlin's palaces for splendour, and behind them stood hundreds of churches built by Moscow's merchants who were, as Lydia remarked, 'a pious bunch of speculators'. As we looked over it all, it seemed to me that no building was quite straight. I am not sure if the unsteady effect was created by the passing of centuries, or the lie of the seven hills, or by drink.

Lydia was thinking about England:

'You wouldn't, by any chance, be related to Frederick Munnings, the Socialist Candidate for Parliament and the advocate of women's rights?'

---

11   What Baedeker actually says is: "The Foundling Hospital (open to visitors on Thurs and Sun, 1-4) is a colossal white block founded by Catherine II in 1765… In 1812 it served as a hospital. The Institution receives a yearly subvention from the State amounting to upwards of 1,000,000 rb, chiefly derived from the sale of playing cards throughout Russia. The Foundling Hospital accommodates 25000 children, besides which 30,000 are boarded out in neighbouring villages."

'He's my father's brother.'

'Does that mean that you're the son of 'Angel' Munnings, the financier?'

'Indeed.'

'I think that you must take after your uncle. I've seen him speak at meetings several times. You've got the same voice and his nice, sensitive, eyes. I mean it as a sincere compliment.'

'I think I take after my mother, actually.'

'Better still.'

We came out of the Kremlin onto Red Square. I was beginning to freeze. The side of the square opposite to the Kremlin is formed by a vast emporium, the Upper Trading Rows. I felt the attraction of its cosy lights of commerce, but Lydia turned the page of her Baedeker and found just one more church for us to visit: The Chapel of The Iberian Virgin, a miniature place of worship built into the Resurrection Gate that forms the entrance into Red Square. She said, 'It's Moscow's most popular church and a perfect spot to study the superstition of the masses.' [12]

We stood for a moment in the vestibule. The warm glow of golden icons and the flickering candles drew me inside. Yes, the decor was showy from the Anglican point of view, but its magnificence warmed the heart on a cold day - as did the body warmth of so much human company gathered under one small roof. Some of the worshipers were kneeling, others standing before the icons lighting tapers and mouthing prayers. This was religion at its most disorganised. There was no particular service going on, just an ad hoc melee of devotion. The Virgin brought the high and the low born shoulder to shoulder. The smell of poverty intertwined with the perfumes of French scents, flowers, and incense; it was a truly democratic place. Some of the

---

[12] Chapel of the Iberian Virgin built in 1669, and one of the most highly revered in Russia. Each time that the Tsar comes to Moscow he visits this chapel before entering the Kremlin. The chapel is generally crowded, even at night, and the traveller should be on his guard against pickpockets." – Baedeker.

people there carried ragged bags. I thought that perhaps they were pilgrims who had trudged on foot with their bundles and teapots across the steppe. Later on I realised that ordinary Russians are never without a few bits of tattered luggage. Bag carrying is a national characteristic. The entrance to the small church was so packed with worshipers trying to reach the miracle-working icon of the Virgin that I succeeded in becoming parted from Lydia without seeming too ungallant.

A young woman in a fur coat made from patches of various shades of brown was waiting her turn to kiss the glass in front of the Iberian Virgin. She stood in the huddle of worshipers holding wax tapers in her hand. I worked my way, shoulder first, through the pilgrims, up to the girl. She did not say anything. She just touched my arm. We stood together in silence, occasionally shuffling forward, until we reached the foot of the icon. The face of the Iberian Virgin was dark, whether because of her southern origins or because of age, I was not sure. Her halo was a net of pearls. A chunky jewel clasped her raiment on the shoulder. Vera crossed herself, and her lips mouthed a prayer for about a minute, oblivious of the queue behind her. One by one she lit her tapers and planted them upright in the sand of the incense burner. She lifted up her head and planted her kiss, and then crossed herself again. It was all done with such grace and humility that I had no doubt that she would have willingly washed the icon with her hair. Now it was my turn. As I contemplated the smudged glass, wondering whether to follow the local custom, a clear English voice said behind me:

'Half of Moscow's germ population must be living there - but then, men are never ones to fuss about oral hygiene. When it comes to a kiss, they will adjoin their lips to almost any surface.' I turned around and met the eyes of Lydia Hawthorne. She added, 'If you have matrimony on your mind, the icon is particularly helpful at speeding along affairs of the heart.' I turned back and prayed silently to the Iberian Virgin that she help me to keep Vera with me throughout my stay in Russia, and that she help me to 'save' Vera – I meant from herself as much as anything - on a longer term basis; but I did not go so far as to kiss the glass. My lips just stopped short. Whatever you think about the efficacy of Russian icons, you might say that my heart's desire was silly, spontaneous and naïve - but that is how young hearts desire. Indeed, now that the icon had re-united us, I felt a sudden duty to rescue Vera from the drunken clutches of future visiting businessmen. It even crossed my mind that I should 'set her up,' especially if I was to be visiting Moscow on a regular basis.

Outside the Church, a group of old ladies were selling reproduction icons. They did not try to press anybody. They just waited by the door holding up their wares as the snowflakes collected on the shoulders of their threadbare coats. I pressed a coin into one of the old lady's hands. She wanted to give me her biggest reproduction icon, but I took a little papier-mâché oval bearing the face of the Iberian Virgin. It fitted easily into my pocketbook.

By now, Vera was holding onto my arm and things might have been getting a little awkward for Lydia were it not that, for her, embarrassment was an unknown quality. In us, she had some fascinating 'material.' She said, 'Well, are we going to stand here and freeze?' Vera seemed to understand as if by instinct, for she started to steer me back through the Resurrection Gate, and Lydia followed us with a bemused expression on her face – I think it was more her custom to take the lead. We did not have far to walk, for Vera turned sharply off Red Square and into a side street. I found that we were entering through the doors of a vast, echoing emporium that ran an entire length of Red Square, facing the red walls of the Kremlin. You could wander for a whole afternoon up and down the trading rows on three floors, each painted in its own gay colour: peppermint green, light blue, or peach. The nursery colours were very much those of old Moscow – you often saw a trading booth or a church or a merchant's house painted in them. Pretty iron bridges connected the rows on the upper floors. And it was all illuminated by natural light. The roof of glass welcomed in the winter sun. The arches, nooks, and crannies hid a thousand and one stalls and shops. Vera swiftly guided us to part of the store where there were piles of enamel, cheap mosaic, coloured crystals and amber. If we had let her, she would have tried on every single one. While she was engrossed in one particular pile of trinkets, Lydia said out of the corner of her mouth:

'Pretty little thing. Where did you find her?'

'I had dinner with her and my friend Anatoly Mizinsky on my first night,' I said. 'She's a student at the ballet school, you know, at that big theatre…'

'The Bolshoi.'

'Yes, that's it.'

Vera tilted her head slightly as if trying to catch our words. She knew instinctively that we were talking about her - like a dog 'who understands everything but can't say a thing,' as the Russian saying goes, and which I was to hear said of myself on several occasions while in Russia (it's not meant to be impolite). She tried on a necklace made of thin silver and bearing a largish green stone. Vera admired herself in the mirror from various angles and turned around smiling to seek my approval.

'Do you know what sort of stone it is?' I asked Lydia.

Lydia spoke to the storekeeper. Her Russian language was obviously quite serviceable. 'He says it's from Afghanistan. You can have it for one rouble and fifty kopeks. Are you sure you can afford to spend such a stupendous sum on a lady, Mr Munnings?'

'Well, of course.'

She spoke to him some more, and the storekeeper, who may well have come from one of the Asian 'stans' himself, laughed and shook his head, threw his arms up in the air, frowned darkly, and then at last shrugged his shoulders and placed the necklace in a little box.[13] Lydia informed me that she had beaten the man down to one rouble. He pressed us to join him for a glass of black tea. We politely refused and

---

[13] Lydia bargained well. Baedeker advises, 'In making purchases in Russia the traveller should not rely quite so implicitly on the bona fides of the shopkeeper as he does at home. It is quite customary, especially in the less fashionable shops, to accept 10-20 per cent less than the prices originally demanded.'

when I proffered a note, he shook my hand and a wide toothy grin stretched across his half shaved face. Vera rewarded me with delightful smile which, in contrast to the storekeeper's, contained a complete set of pearly white teeth. The whole transaction seemed to give satisfaction to all sides. The act of exchange – a rouble for a necklace – fulfils a deep human instinct, but it is even more rewarding when people come together from countries far apart and transact.

Lydia came all the way back to my room with us. There was nothing else to do but to call reception and ask for some tea and refreshments; I let her do the calling. I suggested gooseberries but she did not take the hint. A tray of sliced oranges, pancakes, and a silver bowl with black caviar duly arrived along with the tea.

Lydia was content with a glass of tea, and ignored the caviar and pancakes. She began to speak to Vera, and their conversation seemed to develop into an interview. Vera answered the questions quite freely and gaily - only pausing to look round for a napkin when orange juice dribbled down her cheek. Lydia began to take notes with a silver pencil. At length, she said, 'I must go back to my room and write out some impressions of the way ordinary Russians set about religion, what they pray for and so forth. Vera here has given me some valuable ideas.'

I couldn't help wondering what Vera had said and what impressions she had made. She had almost certainly blown up the story I had concocted about her being a ballet dancer because she herself did not know it. I had an idea that women like Lydia chiefly wrote earnest tracts on 'the sex question,' which was so very heated in those days. It did not take Vera and me long to get down to a more interesting approach to the topic. A mere forty-eight hours before, I had tasted neither black caviar nor a woman. Now Vera showed me how I could lick one off the other.

Chapter Five

I awoke the next day to the sound of quiet sobbing. Vera was sitting hunched on the end of the bed; her shoulder blades heaved and her skinny body quivered every now and then. What a man do with a woman in tears? Generally he feels helpless and panics. Well, I speak for myself here, at least. I suppose there are those who are masterly with women and manage to make the most of such tender moments. I fell back on a repartee of 'Cheer up old girl,' and 'Life can't be as bad as all that'. I'm sure she didn't understand a word of this foolishness but she sobbed even more. Only then did it dawn upon me that this was a cue to sit by her and put my arm around her, which I did, patting her shoulder and saying, 'There, there,' and generally feeling useless while thinking 'God, isn't she just gorgeous,' and 'What the hell should I do next?'

She changed her position and looked at me. She put her hand on my knee and uttered a word that sounded like foonds. 'Foonds, foonds,' she repeated. There was an expression of great perplexity in her glistening eyes. I wished that I could fathom what was going on behind that furrowed forehead. For the first time, I felt an intense regret at our lack of a common language. So far, it had not seemed to matter.

I do not know how many minutes passed before there came a masculine knock on the door, which gave me hope for deliverance. I called out, 'One moment', as I grabbed my dressing gown, but Anatoly strode in looking fully recovered from his hangover of the previous day. Vera gathered the bedcover around herself, in no particular hurry. She dabbed her eyes with the back of her hand, exposing a bare arm and shoulder, and tried to look brave. Anatoly wished me good morning and behaved just as if she was not there at all. All my upbringing told me that his manner was a discourtesy to the fairer sex. I cleared my throat loudly, and ushered Vera and the trailing quilt into the dressing room. When I had closed the door behind her, I said to Anatoly:

'The girl was just trying to tell me something. It seemed rather important. She's a bit upset. Perhaps you could assist with a spot of translation?'

'Of course!' he said with a friendly smile. He seemed to be in a good mood.

She returned wearing the dress that Nina had given her, barefooted, and her eyes cast modestly downward. Anatoly spoke to her in what even I could tell was rather haughty Russian. She listened attentively and then replied at great length accompanying her speech with plenty of gestures and expressions. After several minutes of this, he summed it up: 'She wants money.' I had been hoping for a more romantic cause to her troubles: one that called for the protective and sound common sense of an English head. I gave her an annoyed glance, and she shrugged her shoulders and went over to the window to look out of it with her back to us. Surely something must have gone missing in the translation? I explained that she had been trying to convey something specific to me: a word that had sounded like 'foonds.'

Anatoly thought for a moment: 'I expect she meant English "pounds". In Russian we sometimes say "Funds Sterling."'.

Vera turned around from the window. 'Yes, yes,' she said in English. 'Foonds Sterling.'

I felt winded, as if I had received a blow in the stomach. I tried to hide my disappointment. I had truly believed that the night we had just spent together had been courtesy of the Iberian Virgin.

'How much do I owe her?'

'She does not say that you owe her this money. She is asking you as a special favour for a small loan. About 200 roubles.'

'Twenty pounds!!!'

She says that she must pay this to her Madame. And Madame says she will throw her out onto the street naked if she does not provide this money by tomorrow night, and she will surely die of cold.' Anatoly gave a little ironic smile as he said the last part.

'And how did she come to owe this fortune to Madame?' We both looked over at her. She had sat down on the window seat and was examining her fingernails.

'Verotchka!' said Anatoly sharply, although he was using the diminutive that I had heard on the first night at Nina's place. For the first time I noticed how he pronounced the 'e' in her name as 'ye' where I said 'ee'.

V(y)era took my question as a commission for Act Two of her pantomime. She gesticulated. Anatoly nodded. I watched. To me, it seemed that she was truly distressed. I still wondered if she really did have some genuine and pressing difficulty. At length came Anatoly's single sentence summary:

'Now it seems that this money is for her sick mother in Smolensk.'

He could hardly be putting the most favourable slant on her words through his curt translation. No doubt he was trying to shield me from her appeal, but it was frustrating that I could not judge her story properly on my own accord. I studied her face: she was communicating to me through her eyes as if I were her last hope on earth. 'No' was not a word that came easily to me. I thought of her kneeling before the icon in the church and said to myself, 'Well she's obviously poor and some money might set her on the right path. And perhaps she does have an urgent need. She was praying pretty hard for something yesterday.' 200 roubles happened to be slightly more than I had in my pocketbook. I had already begun to wonder how I might get hold of some more cash so that I could stay a little longer than I had planned. I asked Anatoly which was the best bank to use. He did not give me a direct answer:

'My friend, do not trouble yourself about the girl. Everybody in Russia is asking everybody else to lend him money. It is natural for her to think up these stories. She is a harlot. She will surely find this money, even if she has to lie on her back from now until Mass on Sunday.'

'Of course I know that I could just give her ten roubles for her favours, but somehow I don't want that anymore'.

'For ten roubles you could have love with her for a fortnight! You could have every type of love you have ever dreamed of and some types that have not yet occurred to you.'

I could feel my cheeks burning. He sat on the edge of the desk, and I wondered if its narrow legs could support his weight. He asked me how much I had paid Vera and what presents I had bought her. I told him about the necklace, and I slightly understated the stupendous sum of ten roubles that I had paid to 'Madame' on the evening of my arrival (actually I halved it). My new friend looked at me fondly, but regretfully. He reminded me of my House Master at school – a man who obviously had a liking for me, but who seemed to think that I would never apply myself to anything in life. His next question confirmed the impression. He asked me if I had read Plato's The Symposium. I confessed that I had not.

'When I consider a social problem,' he said, 'I like to think of the ancient world. I see it at a distance and it gives a perspective on modern times.'

'And is this a social problem?'

'It is perhaps the oldest and most interesting question of all: what is the ideal relationship between a man and a woman? I believe that the ancients answered this better than we do today. They believed in the god of Eros, and they worshiped him without shame, and so should we. This is why I support the progressive element in politics. I despise all hypocrisy and wish to end it.'

'Well so do I.'

'The Symposium looks at each and every side of love, and, of course, Eros only represents one aspect. From time to time, we experience an intense yearning for one woman in particular. The Greeks had an explanation for this. They believed that at the beginning of the world, man and woman had been joined together. They lived in perfect happiness, but the great god Zeus was jealous and split them in two, creating separate men and women. Ever since that time, each man has been searching for his former partner. Only when he finds this singular woman – or in some cases, man - can he feel himself complete and perfectly accomplished.'

Vera sat down on a chair and looked over at him, and then at me, clearly wondering what we were discussing. I thought that she was prettier than ever when that mystified look came over her face.

'I know,' I said, 'that Vera is not my true love. Of course....'

My friend shook his head:

'Nor will any woman be. On this point, Anatoly Alexandrovitch Mizinsky must respectfully disagree with Plato, Socrates and Aristophanes, and all the other learned Greeks who took part in discussion described in The Symposium. Your other half does not exist, not in one woman. A man must complete himself in various women at various stages in his life. At first it might be his mother or his nurse. Freud has written about this. Later, when a man marries, he feels fulfilled for a while, but then he starts to feel that intense yearning to complete himself all over again. In short, he resumes the pursuit of woman, although he most probably does not understand why he does it. This is where Society and the Church are completely wrong about marriage... I see that you are shocked!'

'No, not at all,' I said. 'I'm fascinated.' I wondered at my friend's capacity to veer into philosophy and ancient history, but I could not help thinking he was an amazing character. He started to pace around the room as he spoke. Vera's eyes followed him for a while, and then gave up.

'The Athenians built their city on solid foundations: love of truth and hatred of hypocrisy. Their goddess was Athena; the divine wisdom. Under her guidance, they organised the relations between the sexes in a systematic and rational fashion. A man had different women to complement different sides of his character and its needs. We know, for instance, that an Athenian man had a lawful wife - his gynaike - who gave him children. She had to be a pure woman, satisfactory to one's parents, but most probably dull.'

'We make them in England too,' I said. 'But I wouldn't put your Julia in that category....'

'My wife, as you said yesterday, is most charming and clever and an excellent mother. But she wants to keep me prisoner and drive me mad. All wives are the same, or most anyway. It is in their nature.'

'Perhaps....' I remembered my own parents and the sounds of rows emanating from their rooms.

'For intellectual enjoyment, an Athenian man goes to a hetaera. She is an artistic woman: a ballerina or a singer, or perhaps an actress, like Aspasia, the mistress of Pericles of Athens, or like my own Nina. She is intelligent and can make a man laugh or cry as she wishes, but she is not suitable for marriage.'

'It seems a pity.'

'It is a pity. But it would be a tragedy to marry her. Such a woman is interesting precisely because she is free. Now, there is a third class of Athenian woman. She is the most relevant to the present case.'

'You mean her.' I did not turn to look at her.

'Indeed. A pallake is a good choice for a busy man. She is a low and simple girl. She performs her duties with her body. In ancient times she would be a slave. She does not bother a man with unnecessary thoughts, or moods, or reminders of anniversaries, or requests for gifts, or any of the other unfortunate symptoms of a love affair. This girl here' – I looked over to her and she tilted her head inquisitively - 'is your pallake. She has her role and she is suited to it. You pay a certain price, she gives. This is how it should be. Do not confuse one type of love for another. Do not imagine her to be what she is not. This mistake is always fatal.'

Vera reached down to pick up one of her shoes from the floor. The buckle had half fallen off it and the heel was almost worn down. She shrugged and looked up with her green eyes. This vision was too much for me, far more powerful than the even the tears had been, especially when a fragile, expectant little smile was added to it.

I said:

'Well, even a pallake needs new shoes sometimes.'

The cashier in Muir and Mirrielees (the owners of Moscow's first department store were Scottish), looked doubtfully at my cheque and then peered into my eyes apparently trying to find my true character there.

'Excuse me sir,' he said in English, 'You are a young man far away from home.'

There is nothing more insulting than to be called 'a young man' when you are standing on the threshold of adulthood. I wanted to say, 'damn your insolence,' but I knew that none of the clerks at Coutts in London would count out fifty pounds to any tourist who walked in with a foreign cheque book. I had decided to draw more than was necessary for my immediate purposes. I would sooner go overdrawn for a lot than a little. No doubt my bank-manager back in London would write me a sniffy letter, but he was hardly likely to bounce a cheque written out by the son of 'Angel' Munnings. Anatoly came to my rescue. He explained that if a cheque drawn on a solid and world famous English bank was not security enough, then he, Anatoly Alexandrovitch Mizinsky, would lend his own personal guarantee. The cashier accepted this assurance with no further quibbles. In the event, he did not actually have to sign any formal pledge.

I went to look for Vera behind the pillar where we had stationed her so that she could not observe me drawing money too closely, but she had moved off. I spotted her a few counters away admiring herself in a mirror with a black evening bag swinging from her shoulder. When we caught up with her, she whispered something in Anatoly's ear which he passed on to me: 'The lady says you have been so kind to her that she would like this handbag to remember you by. I suppose she means every time she takes your money out of the bag she will think of you.'

It was an elegant bag: jet-black with some sparkly stones along the clasp. I felt the material and it was terribly soft. The shop assistant informed us that it was reindeer skin with silk lining and decorated with semi-precious stones.

'And how much might it be?' The assistant frowned as if it was rather a low sort of question. It came to £12.

'No,' I said. It was a difficult word.

'Nyet,' said Anatoly, and started to move away. Vera did not look offended, just a little surprised, but I wished that I could explain to her that a reindeer bag was not her most pressing need. I looked at her shoes, and said, 'Well, perhaps you need another pair of those.' This did not need any translating.

Vera was radiant when I had bought her two pairs of respectable foot coverings – one for indoors and one for walking. To these, I added a pair of gloves, for she wrapped her hands in strips of cloth, and I thought that looked just too downright poor. The presents had been quite affordable, and she had forgotten about the urgent need for cash. I had got away with spending no more than about £6. She planted the warmest of kisses on my cheek. I loved that kiss because it seemed to be genuine. I felt that I had a bargain.

On the way out, she lingered to stroke the silky fur of one or two coats. I took her by the arm and led her to the door. Anatoly wanted to visit the cigar shop further up Petrovka Street. It was the first, but certainly not the last time that I was to walk with Vera along that way. Petrovka is far from being Moscow's widest or grandest thoroughfare, but it is in the heart of the best shopping district and is always thick with people and traffic. Strangers walked at our side in unembarrassed proximity. I found myself stepping sideways into order to slip through the oncoming bodies. All styles mingled here. European dress was predominant, but by no means exclusive. An Eastern gentleman in a high conical cap of black sheepskin was followed by a line of three veiled women. In those days, the elegant shop fronts used to run up the gentle hill until a bend in the street where the Orthodox Church interceded in the form of a monastery.

As we walked along together, I began to wonder if I had been mean not to buy Vera a coat. I felt a little embarrassed by the ragged woman at our side, even though she was now well shod and her hands decently covered. She wore a red flowery scarf around her head, which was rather fetching, but not exactly the mark of a lady. I think most people must have assumed (correctly) that my relationship with her was improper, but nobody stared. I noted that men and women of all classes and ages in Moscow walked arm in arm, as we did; it did not seem to be considered at all vulgar.

After we left the tobacconist, a policeman approached us. For a moment I felt nervous that he might enquire about the young foreigner and the woman of ill-repute – but all he wanted was tobacco. Anatoly provided him with one of the good cigars he had just bought and lit it for him. Where else in the world would you see a uniformed officer smoke on the street, let alone a cigar? It struck me that the subjects of the Tsar's autocracy enjoyed a great quantity of small freedoms, even if they came at the expense of the greater freedoms which an Englishman considers his birth right.

A minute or two later, we passed a coffee shop where they sold little French cakes. My arm received a sharp tug.

Inside the shop, Vera held her cake fork like a lady, and Anatoly pinched the little coffee cup handle with his big finger and thumb. We two were the only men in the refreshment room, which was filled with female shoppers. Vera was the prettiest - her nose and cheeks bright and glowing from the cold air and sporting a few tiny snowflakes glistening in her hair. Some of the other women glanced over at her. I think it was the pleasure she took in the cake, in the coffee shop, in her own attractive appearance that lit up her soul and made her stand out. Even her simple haircut was somehow fetching: it accented the natural attractiveness of her face. I had reason to be proud of myself. It had been my eye that had picked her out, in the rough so to speak, before she had a chance to show herself off to the best advantage. I said to Anatoly,

'You've got to admit, she's coming up nicely.' He shook his head and smiled. I continued, 'Well, I look at it this way; if you find a precious stone in the ground, first you have to clean the mud off it, then you have to polish it and cut it. Only then will any other person see that it's beautiful. I want to find her soul and polish it so that it shines. She's not too old and I'm sure there's still time. Perhaps she can learn to live another way.'

Vera was blissfully contemplating the cake on the end of her fork. Anatoly did not seem to notice her.

'You speak most fittingly,' he said, 'and it reminds me that I must take you to see an expert in precious stones at the University, but you make the wrong conclusions. If you find an amethyst, no matter how hard you polish it, it will never become a ruby. And if you cut a rock crystal, you cannot turn it into a diamond, not a real one. Of course, in a certain light, unprofessional people might mistake the stone – but it will never possess the fire that makes a genuine diamond special. An expert will always see the difference.'

Vera's ankle had gently hooking itself around mine.

'Well, I think a person can change,' I said defiantly. 'Especially if somebody applies a little kindness and of course, a little firmness sometimes.'

Anatoly laughed.

'Your case is hopeless. You are an incurable romantic, but I suppose there can be little harm in trying to prove your theory. You will escape back to London before she ruins you.'

As we left the shop, I was half-wondering if London really existed. My life there seemed remote and insubstantial. Out on the street, I said to Anatoly, 'Perhaps I needed to come to Russia to complete myself.'

Vera held onto my arm, and we edged our way through the crowds again.

When we reached Theatre Square, Vera pointed up the roof of the great creamy palace that housed The Hotel Metropole. Its upper echelons were decorated with freezes and murals, the largest of which was an arc-shaped panel made from a myriad of ceramic mosaics, predominantly purple and green, and depicting an extraordinary scene: a boat riding the waves, crewed by medieval mariners, and along by its side the soaring, horizontal figure of a woman with flowing blond hair. The overall effect was of a dream where you enjoy the faculty of flight and come across your heart's desire in mid-air. Vera tapped herself on the chest. The woman was her.

As we looked up, a street-vendor approached us offering pamphlets and books. Anatoly gave him a firm 'Nyet,' as he called out to us, but Vera took one of his volumes and looked at it. I would not have put her down as the reading sort. I asked Anatoly what it was called. He translated: 'A self-teacher of social etiquette and dance.' Vera wanted it, and so I made it the final purchase of the day. It cost fifty kopecks, proving that a present can sometimes be cheaper than the one that preceded it.

Back in the hotel room, Vera arranged her hair in the mirror and admired herself from different angles in her new clothes. I enjoyed watching her look so happy. The small fibs about her urgent need for money were easy for me to forget. They had been so simple; almost naïve (although effective enough on me). The more elaborate a fabrication, the harder it is to forgive.

Chapter Six

"The British Consul at Moscow, in his annual report, remarks that as the result of the strikes and troubled times in 1905-06, the men gained considerably; pay was increased and the working hours were at the same time shortened. Now, however, that order has again been firmly established, the reverse is taking place and the tendency is for wages to be cut down, while the working hours are being again made longer."

Howard P Kennard, "The Russian Year Book for 1911"

'Would you care for a spot of tea?'

When a British vice-consul said 'tea' he meant 'tea' with milk and sugar if one wished, but not with alcohol. It came in a rose patterned pot and Robert Campbell Fitzgerald, the young diplomatist, poured a smidgen of milk into two china cups. Then he lifted the lid of the pot, gave it a stir, and poured the tea through a silver strainer. It blended with the milk into a beautiful mahogany colour. The simple ceremony was immensely comforting.

'I know what you are thinking about the room,' he said, 'because I think it every time I walk in. It's more like a W.C. than an office.'

'Well, it's funny you should say that…' I liked the man already; he was not much older than myself. We immediately recognised a kindred spirit in each other – the spirit of a young man far enough away from home to discover his true self.

'The Foreign office sees Moscow as a glorified souk. All the prestige adheres to the Imperial Court in Moscow,' he said,

His general information on labour relations in Russia was less than comforting. The worst incident had taken place in Eastern Siberia at the Lena Goldfields where 230 miners had been shot dead. The shooting had been done by the Russian army, but that did not alter the fact of political significance that 70% of the shares in the Lena

Goldfields company belonged to British investors; the episode had done little to endear us as employers to the Russian worker. But none of this had stopped the brave and the foolhardy trying their luck in the 'Klondike of the East', as he called it, and about 100 or so British companies had obtained mining permits.

On a brighter note, he told me all about the British trade delegation that was arriving the following week and the various functions in the honour of Anglo-Russian friendship.

'Whatever you do, come to this one,' said Campbell-Fitzgerald. 'It's at the house of a merchant who likes to collect the latest paintings from Paris. Some of them are a bit naughty, between you and me; I don't think the Consul realises. It's going to be interesting. Perhaps we'll blame it all on the French.'

I said that I would most certainly come, and he put my name down on a list adding 'and guest.' Then he wrote out an invitation card. I still have it in my collection of papers. The form of the date written on it is a curiosity; an era in Anglo-Russian relations that is gone forever: The 14th / 1st of February 1914.[14]

There was a period of inaction while I waited for Anatoly to arrange our visit to Siberia.

In the evenings, he would often take me out, sometimes with, more often without Vera, to experience Moscow's colourful nightlife. As he had promised, we drank champagne around a roaring fire while a troop of gypsies stomped and sung. On another occasion we saw Nina play the part of a ruthless woman hooking a wealthy husband. The lines were, of course, unintelligible to me, but the audience laughed heartily at her vulgar manners and meretricious schemes. Vera would have liked to have come to the theatre with us, but

---

[14] "In all parts of Russia except Finland, the Julian calendar established by Julius Caesar in 46 BC and adopted by the Council of Nicaea in 325 AD still remains in force. This reckoning is 13 days behind the rest of Europe, which long ago adopted the Gregorian calendar." Baedeker, 1914.

Anatoly made it plain that he did not approve of the idea, or of her in general, for that matter.

During the day, my favourite occupation was to walk arm in arm with Vera. I say 'my' rather than 'our' because at first she seemed to regard the whole idea of going anywhere on foot as an English eccentricity, perhaps motivated by my being too mean to pay for a cab. We could not go very far before she would pull me in the direction of some warm pavilion, shop or café. And so I started to consult my guide book. We would take a sleigh to some interesting point in or near the city and promenade just a little. We might go to Petrovsky Park and walk beneath the trees laden with snow, or we would take a trip out to the Sparrow Hills from where you can see all Moscow entwined in the sensuous curves of the river. This was the vantage point from which, in 1812, Napoleon had looked down on Moscow and found it deserted by its population and left to burn. When we watched the sun set over the gilded city, the red rays set the golden domes ablaze. Once again, I was struck by the oriental side to Moscow's character. At other times, it seemed more like Paris than Constantinople.

If the weather was not too cold, we would stroll or drive along one or two of the elegant garden boulevards which form concentric circles around Moscow's centre. The street running in each direction is separated by a garden down the middle, which makes for pleasant walking. Our route would meander up and down hills, and we would encounter all manner of interesting obstacles on the way. I never knew what to expect on these walks: a shop selling the latest fashions could face onto an unmade street, so full of potholes that wheels and sleigh blades could not negotiate their way across the ruts. A heavy fall of snow actually improved the condition of some of the roads. You could find a rustic wooden house with curly gables and flowery patterns painted around its windows standing next to great palace guarded by stone lions. And some buildings were entirely original: one house, I recall, was covered with impressions of make-believe beasts, some with two heads.

One Sunday we came across the 'Thieves Market' held under the Sukharev Tower. Here we could have bought, had the inclination taken us, silver spoons, gold watches, or old boots. At 'The Clean Ponds' we stopped to look at the ice skaters. We watched a woman dressed in mink pull a small boy on a sleigh across the snow. Like all the wealthy children, he was quite spherical in his winter things. Vera gazed with a smile on her face. I wondered if she felt maternal - or if she was dreaming of a fur coat like the lady's.

During those days I felt a kind of light headed happiness and freedom from my own inner demons which I had not known since I had been a small child. I cannot say that it was 'first love', because I had experienced that already, and it was characterised by frustration, self-doubt, and pain. Nor was it mere animal gratification. I tried that later on in my life, and it does not bring much happiness. That feeling, I think, was that of an affection that was returned, and a knowledge that somebody else felt about me the way that I felt about her. Of course, there were moments, such as when I was buying Vera a present, that I wondered about her motives, but there were other times when I buried my nose in her hair and she nestled her head into my chest, that I could know that she had developed feelings for me too.

Of course the best thing about a walk in the snow is the need to warm up when you get back to your hotel room. Hot tea is only part of the formula.

I would sometimes bump into Lydia Hawthorne, usually in the lobby or the café. Often she seemed to be in a rush. I was impressed with the way she managed to be so purposeful in a city where purpose was always able to wait until the next day. On one of these occasions, I was coming down in the lift with Vera when Lydia joined us. She looked harassed. I asked her what the matter was.

'One step forward, two steps back,' she told me.

'I know how you feel.'

She said she was giving up her endeavours for the day, and instead she planned to visit the Tryetekov Gallery, asking if we would care to accompany her. I thought that a museum was the last place to interest Vera – but when Lydia explained the plan, her face lit up with excitement. I wondered what she expected.

The taste of the nineteenth century merchant Pavel Tretyakov, had been for ancient icons and for realistic depictions that held a mirror up to Russian life – a couple of titles will suffice to give you the idea – 'Prisoners Feeding Pigeons from the Window of a Train,' and 'Preparing the Ground for Flax Sowing in Vologda Province.' Vera lingered in front of each one. Lydia gave a brisk glance and moved on. Soon Lydia was a couple of rooms ahead of us on the tour of the museum.

The most interesting paintings had stories to tell. I recall one in particular depicting an aristocratic lady being dragged in a cart through Moscow on her way to exile in Siberia. The wealthy and poor alike lined the snowy street to see her off. Some bowed their heads, others laughed, some just stared. Vera spent a particularly long time studying each face.

By the end of our tour of the long halls of the Tryetekov I felt exhausted – but Vera looked radiant. She was talking excitedly to Lydia about her impressions. As we walked along the pavement to the two sleighs we had hired to bring us over the bridge to the gallery, Lydia said to me:

'Your Verotckha has a passion for paintings. You must try her on some modern art. Are you going to bring her to the reception next week organised by the British Embassy?'

I told her that vice-consul had let it slip that some of the paintings might be a little controversial.

'Then we must all go,' said Lydia. 'I'd love to see some official red faces.'

I did not think that Vera would fit in to such a high-society affair, but before I could express any doubts, Lydia asked her if she would like to go. Of course the answer was in the affirmative, and she added that it was her birthday that day.

I was about to take tea in the Metropole's cafeteria on my own, when I heard Lydia's crystal clear voice:

'Mr Munnings, won't you join us? The blini here are too divine.'

I resisted the temptation to adjust my collar, even though I wanted to be absolutely sure that a small imprint of Vera's teeth was not showing on the side of my neck. The young lady had gone off on some business of her own. One of the benefits of conducting a love affair in a foreign language is that it is not possible to question the object of one's affections about her movements or intentions. One just has to accept the other person as she comes and goes. It makes for constant surprises, which one hopes will, more often than not, be of a pleasant nature.

Lydia and a female companion were tucking into pancakes with honey and jam like naughty schoolgirls. I wondered what might be the cause of Lydia's unusually frivolous mood until I noticed a carafe of some sort of cherry colour drink that was sitting in front of her. The prospect of a tipsy Lydia amused me. I had put her down as strictly temperance.

'Don't mind if I do, but I'll have just tea,' I said. I was still bleary from my long night out with gypsies.

Lydia's companion was called Irena Victorovna. She was a journalist but of a different breed to Lydia: she wrote a column for a Moscow newspaper under the title, 'The Lady in the Mask.' Apparently it was very witty and a widely read by people who hoped to see their own names mentioned. I found her to be pleasantly flirtatious:

'Mr Munnings, would you like to finish my crêpe? It is very tasty, but I cannot eat it all. The waiter will bring a new fork,'

'Well it would seem a shame to waste such a nice crêpe. Thank you Irena.'

'It's an interesting ceiling, don't you think?' she said. We both looked up. It had been painted with pictures depicting naked men holding skipping ropes for women in long white dresses. It was hard to think what thought had inspired the artist, but it did seem to express Moscow's liberal atmosphere as regards the sexual life.

Lydia had a fit of giggles. I was astounded:

'Why are you in such a gay mood?' I asked.

'Oh, I just decided to give up. I spent three days in a row waiting at the Moscow branch of the Ministry of Interior for a permit to visit Maria Spridonova in her Siberian place of exile. An official hinted that in exchange for ten roubles, I might be granted an audience with the Minister himself in St. Petersburg. I told him that I would not want to corrupt his morals. Wasn't that silly of me? After that I realised that I had no hope. And now I have decided to be gay.'

'Jolly good show,' I said.

Irena asked me what I was doing in Moscow, and let it slip that I was planning a trip to the Urals.

'To see the gold mines?'

'Something like that,' I said. Now that I knew Lydia better, I did not feel so cagey about discussing business in front of her. Even so, I regretted my small indiscretion when I saw her grey eyes light up with almost fanatical interest:

'Take me with you,' she said abruptly. Then she dabbed her thin lips with a napkin. 'George ... I mean, Mr Munnings; I would be so grateful. I give a solemn vow that I will not mention your name or the name or your business associates in anything I write about the trip, but the conditions of the mines and the miners' families would interest me most terribly.'

I replied – with surprising social skill – that I would have to consult my business partner.

As I got up to leave, Irena offered me her hand to kiss, which I achieved with a reasonably elegant bow.

'You will be seeing Mr Munnings again shortly,' said Lydia. 'He will be at the soirée tomorrow evening'

'Well, 'till tomorrow evening.'

'And you will also have the pleasure of meeting his beautiful companion, Vera Borisovna,' added Lydia.

Irena smiled graciously.

Chapter Seven

We arrived in a spacious courtyard, crowded with parked sleighs, carriages and automobiles. The merchant's two-storey mansion was tucked away from the city by a garden and a fringe of snow covered trees, so that it felt as though we had been admitted through the gates into a secret hideaway. Strains of chamber music emanated from the upstairs windows as I helped Vera step down from our hired sleigh. Beneath her fox-fur, she wore the green dress that we had purchased that morning for her birthday. Underneath the green dress she wore the latest thing in half-corsets which had improved her posture no end. And around her neck hung a string of pearls on loan from Lydia.

Lydia and Irena Victorovna arrived shortly afterwards. Our path to the door of the house was illuminated by an oil lamp held aloft by a fur-coated servant. As soon as we entered the great, oak panelled entrance hall, our nostrils were filled with the scent of roses brought, according to Irena, all the way from Nice.

I watched Vera write her name in Cyrillic in the visitors' book, and was pleasantly surprised to note that she wielded the pen with apparent confidence. Lydia scrawled a sexless: "L. Hawthorne, England".

English and Russian voices intermingled on the staircase as we joined the upward cascade of satin, mink, and diamonds. At the top, we were welcomed by the vice-consul, Campbell-Fitzgerald, who was so pleased that I had come, and was most charmed indeed by my three companions to whom he bowed, each in turn.

The flow of guests was pulling us further into the house toward the sound of the string quartet, but Vera stopped and placed her hands on the balcony of the stairwell. Her green eyes opened wider than I had ever seen them do before, and I thought for a moment that she was giddy and might faint, but then I realised that the look on her face was of astonishment. On the wall directly in front of her, above the glittering tiaras of the guests mounting the stairs, hung a pagan work of art. It was a huge panel on which were depicted the crude, luminous red figures of five men and women dancing ring-a-ring a roses. The scenery behind them was flat, as a child would paint it: an emerald green hill and a sky of royal blue. I wondered what sort of man would hang such a picture in his home, and I discreetly asked Campbell-Fitzgerald for some information about our host. I tapped his name on the invitation card. It was spelt 'Sergei Ivanovitch Shchukin'.

'He's Moscow's wealthiest textile merchant,' said Campbell-Fitzgerald, 'and as you can see, he's an enthusiastic collector of modern works of art. And talking of objects of great beauty....' The Vice-Consul was taking a good look at Vera who was still absorbed in the picture.

'She's a friend of a friend,' I said. And then I thought, 'what the heck, he's a man like me, after all,' and I added. 'Actually, she's rather a good friend.'

Campbell-Fitzgerald gave me a sly smile, and returned to his duty of welcoming the guests.

Lydia looked a little impatient while we waited for Vera who was still staring at the picture. After a minute or so, she asked me:

'Did you catch the post-impressionists when they came to the Graffton Street Galleries?'

'I'm afraid I missed them,' I confessed, 'but I do recall there being some sort of hoo-hah in the newspapers a couple of years back.'

'There certainly was,' said Lydia. 'Some people couldn't wait to pack the pictures back to France soon enough. And looking at this effort by Monsieur Matisse, I'm not sure that they weren't right.'

I took another look at the five figures on the hillside. Yes they were primitive, but they seemed to be propelled around that grassy knoll by powerful witchcraft. You could feel the centrifugal force. Only the man leading the dance was proportioned along classical lines. He had a curved, muscular body and a proud scissor step. He drew the woman to his right through the air like a handkerchief, although on closer inspection her hand did not quite reach his. The three other dancers were doing a sort of Bacchantic knees up, one of them with bouncing breasts. But what fascinated me more than the picture itself, was the impression it made on Vera. She seemed to be flying in the same orbit as the figures.

Irena relayed a little gossip about our art-collecting host who had commissioned this strange work of art. He was a great eccentric, she said, and his idea of a holiday was to travel to Palestine and to fast in the desert on a diet of figs and water. His other favourite place was the Egyptian room in the Louvre. A few years ago, he returned from his annual pilgrimage to Paris bearing some peculiar modern paintings. Ever since then, he had become obsessed with the idea of transforming his mansion into a museum of Western European art. His plan was to leave it to the people of Moscow, but it was not entirely clear how much they appreciated the gesture. The general feeling was that the collection was an oddity and its owner was a dupe for unscrupulous Parisian art dealers.

On the wall at right angles to the vast panel of the dancers was an equally remarkable painting – its companion piece in the same colour scheme of red, blue and green. It was a scene of ancient tranquillity: a primitive figure stood on a hillside and blew on a panpipe as his companions sat and listened. Vera had turned her attention to this second picture and I had to prise her away and into the rooms containing the focus of the evening: the fabulous buffet that was piled up on the tables. Vera seemed only slightly interested in the food, which was not her usual way. She was still far-off. I hoped that she was not overawed by the throng of dignitaries.

The crowd was thickening and I could hear English voices exclaiming at the extraordinary place we had come to. I caught a loud whisper behind us: 'What a concoction! It's just like one of those American cocktails!' And it was true; we had arrived inside a room of interior contradictions. The décor and the furniture were in the grand

French fashion: Louis XIV, I believe. The tables and chairs stood on gilded feet. Moulded cupids fluttered and flirted over the doors. The wallpaper was pink, but you could not see too much of it, because the most modern, outré and brightly coloured works of art were hung in two decks all around the walls. I doubted that such a display existed even on Paris's left bank.

'It's hard to say,' said Lydia, 'where the wall paper stops and the pictures begin.'

I could see that many of the paintings betrayed the owner's interest in textiles. Some of them depicted highly pattered shawls and carpets. Overall, the combined effect of the pictures and the pink wallpaper was very light and colourful. I asked Irena to find out what Vera thought of it all. At first I did not quite understand her reply:

'These paintings smell of summer and apricots and the sea.'

'They do?' I said. And I asked if Vera had ever seen the sea. Irena listened to her story, which was punctuated by exclamations of pleasure such as 'oi!' which I had heard her make under rather different circumstances. As usual, Vera's words went on for rather longer than the translation:

'When she was a little girl, her mother sent her to stay with relatives in Batumi for the summer months. It is on the Black Sea near Turkey, and she went on a long dusty journey for several days. But when she arrived she found a heaven. She remembers the colours, the smells, the sand between her toes, the warm sea, and the spicy Caucasian food. This room and these paintings remind her of that summer.'

I was pleased by this, the longest piece of Vera's biography that had been revealed to me so far, but I could see that her gaze was beginning to focus on the other people in the room.

The British contingent could barely conceal their astonishment at the appearance of the Russian guests, at least those who exhibited some rather individual notions of evening dress. A variety of patterned ties, light trousers, and fancy waistcoats were on display. One man was dressed from head to toe in white: 'That's Andrei Bely, the famous novelist,' said Irena. The wives and daughters of the Russian merchants were no less extraordinary. They seemed to come in three sizes – large, extra-large, and giant. Purple taffeta, wafting feathers and sparkling diamonds were their order of the evening. Lydia's eyebrow made one of its question marks as a small flock of these women walked past us, but it was Vera who whispered a remark in her ear that made her chortle. Lydia passed it on to us in a low whisper:

'All that's missing are the rings for their noses.'

Vera was obviously pleased with her remark and was still smiling to herself as she picked a tall glass of Champagne from the tray of a passing waiter. We moved into a more comfortable space, and found ourselves in full view of one of those 'naughty' paintings that Campbell-Fitzgerald had promised: a hairy satyr loomed over a naked nymph as she slept unaware on a hillside. I was relieved that Vera did not stare at it with indecent interest. Instead, she gave it a modest glance and giggled. Now, she seemed to be enjoying herself, and her radiance shone brighter than all the diamonds on display. She was very much in a world of her own: poised and beautiful. Occasionally I would smile at her, and her eyes would sparkle back at mine. Once or twice she twitched her nose at me playfully.

Lydia spotted a British Member of Parliament: 'Quick, look the other way,' she said. When we had turned around, she explained, that the man was a friend of her father's and she had no particular wish to spend the rest of the evening exchanging family news.

While I had been distracted, a slightly built, immaculately attired gentleman had fallen into conversation with Vera. As soon as I noticed him, I cast a jealous eye over his face to try and read what dirty thoughts were going through his mind. I could see playful glint in his narrow, slightly slanting, eyes, and he was clearly enjoying his exchange with her. Irena nudged me. She said one word under her breath, hardly moving her lips.

'Shchukin.'

Our host understood, perhaps from my anxious interest in him, that I was accompanying Vera. He bowed and extended a delicate, almost feminine hand, for me to shake. There is an old saying: 'Only scratch a Russian and you will find a Tartar.' In this gentleman's case there was no need for scratching. The bones beneath his white skin were perfectly oriental. The whiskery, silvery tufts of his moustache and his pointed beard gave him the air of a slightly shy Persian cat. For a moment, I could picture him seated on a pile of cushions in some oriental souk, casting an expert eye over rich fabrics. It struck me that he might have run into Anatoly or his father or brother, seeing as they were both in the same line of business:

'Mizinsky,' repeated Mr Shchukin thoughtfully after I had mentioned the name. 'We have much in common.'

'Yes indeed,' I said, truly gratified that that such an eminent businessman should speak of my business partners on equal terms. And then he added: 'We have both been touched by similar tragedies, more than once.'

'May I ask,' I said, 'if it is not too delicate a question, what sort of tragedy?'

Mr Shchukin assured me that he did not mind: 'Both our families have been touched by the tragedy of one who takes his own life. Sometimes I wonder why it is that the merchant classes are so prone to this circumstance. Perhaps it proves that one must find other things in life besides business.'

I was most intrigued by this, but I thought I had pressed him enough as manners would allow. 'I am sorry to have asked you about such a personal matter,' I said, and changed the subject. I mentioned how taken Vera had been with his painting over the stairs. He replied in his excellent English, but it became apparent that he suffered from a slight stutter. It seemed amazing to me that a man of such varied talents should suffer from an impediment that gave the impression of shyness.

'She has already been kind enough to compliment my collection. I am honoured by Vera Borisovna's op-p-pinion. I wish that others shared her view. P-Prince Shcherbatov said to me the other day, "Tell me Sergei Ivanovich, why did you buy this – forgive me – bad Matisse? And at such a p-price!"'

'What a thing to say!'

'He is not the only one. But it gives me happiness when others take p-pleasure in my collection. I have already invited Vera Borisovna to return when the house is less crowded. It will be easier to view the pictures properly. I will be honoured if you will come too before your return to London.'

I thanked our host for his kind invitation. Before leaving us, he made his apologies with a gracious bow, and moved on to mingle with his other guests. When he had gone, I said,

'Nice old boy.'

Lydia raised that questioning eyebrow of hers:

'I'd watch out if I were you. The old boy seems to have an eye for more than just a pretty picture.'

But I felt pride. Vera had obviously made a favourable impression. For the time being, I forgotten the remark about suicide, but it came back to me later. Now Vera was chatting with Irena while they stood before a painting that depicted goldfish of such luminous colour that they seemed to illuminate Vera's face. Personally, I thought that she was the most elegant and beautiful woman at the whole gathering, and I doubt that many would have disagreed with me. Probably for the first time that evening, I began to wonder whether the words that came out of her mouth might be worth hearing. She had not been lost for words with a cultivated man like Shchukin. In the ten days I had known here I had found plenty to interest me about her other than conversation. In fact, it had struck me that our lack of common language had been a positive advantage. Few lovers can be so fortunate as to have no future and no past. The immediate present provides very little reason for care or disagreement. But I could not help wondering at the obvious success Vera had made with Shchukin. Anatoly had given me the impression that she had little more refinement than a village milk-maid.

'Lydia,' I said, 'would you notice if Vera had a provincial accent?'

'I expect so because I would find it hard to catch her words, but she speaks clearly enough.'

'And does she seem reasonably educated?'

'As far as I can tell. Why the sudden interest in the young lady's mind?'

'Oh, just wondering.'

I decided not to risk any more of Lydia's barbed remarks at my expense, and we spent the rest of the evening pleasantly mingling and listening to Irena's lively gossip. I remember one story about Madame Scriabina whom she pointed out sitting on the pink sofa. Shchukin had been in love with her after his first wife had died. He thought his moment had come when Scriabina's husband, a noted composer, left her with the words, 'It is time for me to seek inspiration from another woman. Make this sacrifice for art.' Shchukin had inundated Scraibina with letters and bouquets, but to no avail. Now he was marrying another woman, - just as soon as she divorced her present husband.

'See I told you,' said Lydia. 'It's always the quiet ones.'

Before we left, the servants gathered up the flowers from the bowls around the mansion and arranged them into bouquets to present to the ladies Even Lydia's steely eyes softened when she was given an armful of flowers. My trio of women smelt each other's bouquets with delight. Campbell-Fitgerald was standing nearby to see his guests off. He said to me,

'You must feel like Paris choosing between the three goddesses.'

I laughed: 'I think you can guess which one's Aphrodite.'

'I think I can,' he said.

I bid the Vice-Consul goodnight with a light hearted confidence in myself. The bells on our sleigh never sounded more delightful than that crisp, clear evening as we drove back to the Metropole. Vera snuggled her head against my shoulder as we went. We arrived back at the Metropole, and doorman gave us his usual respectful bow. The management never once even hinted at the proprietary or otherwise of my coming and going with this young lady, who, from her much improved appearance, had obviously been doing well out of her acquaintance with me. A slightly unpleasant thought passed through my mind: I wondered if the staff all benefited from her trade. It also struck me very forcibly, for the first time that night, that it was going to pain me very much to abandon her back to her old life once I departed for England – and in the meantime, I was heading for Siberia. Could I really leave her at the Metropole while I was away, and then come back to her, not troubled by what she had been doing, with whom, and for how much, in the meantime?

In the hotel room, as I helped her unlace her corset, I tried to put such thoughts far away from my mind.

Anatoly arranged our expedition to Siberia quite suddenly. He came to The Metropole the day after the Shchukin party and told me that everything was prepared for our journey, and that our train was to leave the following evening.

I mentioned the existence of Lydia Hawthorne and her wish to join us.

'They say a woman on board brings bad luck,' he said.

'But we won't be at sea.'

'I was only joking. Of course bring her along. The more the merrier.'

He would send a messenger to the station to book another compartment on the train.

A little later, I went to Lydia's suite on the third floor where the most expensive rooms were situated. Her door was answered by an English maid. When I broke the news to Lydia she said to her servant:

'So Lucy, we're off to Siberia. Make sure you pack all our warmest woollies.'

The look on Lucy's face was one of resignation, perhaps in the sense of handing in her notice.

I asked Lydia for a small favour: could she help explain my plans to Vera?

The three of us met for lunch at a table in the giant restaurant. I heard Lydia say the word 'Sibir' to Vera, which I took to mean Siberia. Vera's mouth formed that 'o' that it sometimes made, and she looked down at her soup plate to think it over. Then those green eyes looked up at me across the table and she said:

'Ah, ya ?'

'And what about her?' translated Lydia mechanically, though I detected a strong degree of interest in what I might reply.

'You, darling, will wait here for me to come back. I'll give you money to live on.'

When Lydia had translated this, Vera thought for a few moments before stating that she wanted to come with us. I was amazed. I had never dreamed that she would volunteer herself for such a trip. She insisted that it was a tradition: Russian women always followed their men to Siberia.

'I'm going on business, not into exile.'

She giggled: 'Giorgi Pasadili!'

'She says they've imprisoned you,' said Lydia, adding, 'It's a joke.'

'I guessed it was.'

Vera touched Lydia's arm and spoke some more words:

'She says that Siberia would be a change from The Metropole.... I should think it certainly would be!'

I thought that I understood what Vera meant to intimate by that odd remark. She did not want to be left as prey for 'Madame' and visiting businessmen, or perhaps for her own temptations. Or was it just wishful thinking on my part to believe that her feelings tallied so exactly with my own?

'Of course she can come if she wants to,' I said.

I would not say that Vera looked overjoyed at the prospect of the trip to Siberia but nor did she seem unhappy. Lydia asked what Vera might need to buy for the journey - not much, as it turned out, just a fur hat, underskirts and warm stockings - but the conversation took up most of the second course.

The following evening, Anatoly met us in the lobby of the Metropole. Nina had come with him to see him off at the station. She swept into the Metropole like a princess of Bohemia, and the doorman gave her a particularly low bow. Vera and Nina greeted each other with kisses and exclamations like old friends. As Anatoly had arrived three quarters of an hour later than agreed, there was a general kerfuffle to get the trunks and ourselves into the sleighs. Vera and I travelled together to the station, and it was only when we were all walking across the concourse towards the platform that I had a chance to say to Anatoly:

'By the way, I'm bringing some extra luggage along with me. Vera wants to come too.'

'She doesn't have a ticket!' he exclaimed. He was looking straight ahead as he spoke: our trunks had disappeared with two porters and Anatoly's man-servant, Ivan, or 'Vanya' as Anatoly called him. Vera and Nina were way behind us, ambling arm in arm.

'Surely we can come to an arrangement with the purser on the train,' I pleaded.

'She'll be a hare,' he said contemptuously.

'A hair?' (that was what I thought he had meant).

After some grappling for the correct English word he said:

'A stowaway.'

Anatoly had booked two first class compartments – one for Lydia and a second for him and me. Some money changed hands with the chief guard, and an extra compartment was made ready. There was plenty of space in ours for Vera. We had two upholstered couches which we could pull out into beds at night - or during the day if required. The designer of the carriage had thoughtfully included a bottle opener on the underside of the table by the window. In other words, we had everything one could possibly need for a long journey to Siberia.

A certain amount of discussion took place between Anatoly and Lydia about where their respective servants should sleep. Lydia tried to persuade Anatoly to keep his voice down so that he could not be heard by Lucy, but he boomed:

'Do as you find convenient. I'm sending Vanya to third class, but your girl can sleep in your compartment if you like. I expect she doesn't smell as badly as Ivan does.'

Lydia looked horrified:

'The point is that I don't think we should treat them differently from each other,' she said.

And so Lucy joined Ivan on the hard benches at the other end of the train. Nina went into Anatoly's compartment to wish him goodbye and spent rather a long time there.

Chapter Eight

"The Russian workman on the mines is not accustomed to consider time as a factor. It is his temperament to take life slowly, and a matter of indifference to him whether the mine makes a profit or not."

J.H. Curle, "The Gold Mines of the World", Third Edition, 1905

On board the train, Vera and I were like a perfect married couple, in that we could spend hours together, not exchanging more than half a dozen words if that many, (we had no more between us, after all), and be perfectly content with one another. You do not need words to say, 'Let's love,' and when Vera wanted something else, say a chocolate, she would point to the box and - even if she was sitting within arm's length - she would expect me to fetch one and pop it into her mouth.

I spent a good time on the journey reading and looking out of the window at the silver birch trees that lined the track. Russia must have many millions of those trees. Vera studied her primer on etiquette, only turning each page after a long while. Most of my journal covering those early days in Moscow was written at the table in our compartment in wobbly scrawl. It is not easy writing on a train, but I am glad that I made the effort, because those lines now form the main props for my memory. Cities, people, experiences, are all most vivid when you see them for the first time – and besides, the Russia of my early manhood is now gone for ever.

Although we were content in our fuggy warm carriage, I must say that pulling into a station for half an hour or so was a real treat. Walking on two legs never felt so pleasant as when we stepped onto the steady platform after many hours of sitting. The crisp winter air felt like the gift of life itself. The pink colour ran back into Vera's cheeks. It would not take long for the platform to fill up with all manner of passengers who would mill up and down and perhaps venture out into nearby streets. It was a motley crowd. Our fellow travellers included members of the 'intelligentsia' with trimmed beards and rimless glasses, as well as sleek and cheerful bourgeoisies. There were also those who were practically in rags, with coats that looked like they might disintegrate any moment. At the larger stations, the passengers could make use of the restaurant. Some would head for the bar where vodka was served in little cups called 'rumki.' Others would press around the buffet where you could pick up a plate with a chicken leg or a cutlet or a salad. Each dish would sit on a ticket with a price. You could eat a decent meal for between fifty kopecks and a rouble, but you needed to make good use of your elbows to force your way to the front of the diners and pick out the best dishes. Vera was to the fore, and after the first couple of stops, Lydia was not far behind. I never got the hang of it, and usually ended up making do with titbits off Vera's plate. Fortunately she liked sharing her food with me, and even forked salad into my mouth, sometimes teasing me by pulling the fork away just as I was about to bite. The cheaper and, in my view, more civilised, alternative was to purchase food from the local traders on the platform. I enjoyed giving them my custom, which rarely cost me more than a few kopeks. Once, I bought four bottles of beer from a long haired priest and received his benediction, and even the peasants gave me the sign of the cross when I bought their offerings.

The stationmaster rang a bell fifteen minutes before departure. This was universally ignored. When, with five minutes to go, he rang twice, a few of the passengers would start to gather their things. I would look anxiously around for Vera who was inevitably carrying out some small transaction with a local dealer. Most of the Russians would leave it until just before three bells before scrambling in a great crowd to clamber on board. Fortunately the train left the station very slowly, as some people were running and jumping up as it departed.

Hot tea was available around the clock from the guards who were easily recognisable, dressed smartly in black tunics and wide trousers. Lydia would call in to our compartment to see us and share her English ginger-nut biscuits. Sometimes she would sit in our carriage and swot up her Russian. Once she asked if there was anything that Vera and I would like to say to each other: 'I will translate and I promise to forget instantly your secrets.' I was pretty sure that she was just being a nosy-parker. I declined.

'It's not that I feel private. It's just that I don't really want to know anything more about Vera than what I know already.'

This was not strictly true – but I felt that Lydia did not make an ideal Cupid.

'What need would a man have for words of love?' she said, 'Except when it comes to false promises, of course.'

Gosh, I thought, Lydia harbours some bitter feelings within that white, starchy-fronted breast of hers. I said:

'Have you ever been in love?' I don't know why I asked such a silly question.

'Once,' she said. 'Have you?'

'Of course.'

I thought briefly of a passionate kiss with a girl from finishing school near Cambridge. She had shown no interest in seeing me again after that. There had been others, but most of them had been more in the desire than the realisation. As I have confessed already, Vera had been my first 'true love' in the physical sense. Some of my friends were expert at picking up waitresses and shop girls who would 'go', but I did not have the knack or the inclination. I suppose that, in an odd way, I was going against my father who had both qualities in buckets.

Vera, who had already picked up the word 'love', tried not to look interested, but I could tell by the way she turned her head that she was trying to pick up the odd word. I was curious to find out what sort of 'affair' Lydia might have had, and so I asked her to tell me more. I did not really expect an answer, but her brow knitted, and she looked at her most earnest. She told me,

'I was nineteen. My father did not approve of the young man. I did not agree with his reasons – money, family, prospects – those sorts of considerations - but naturally I respected my father and knew that he had my interests at heart, and so I broke it off. I cried every night for two months, and at the end of it, I swore that from henceforth I would make my own decisions. I owe my freedom to that incident.'

Lydia crying over a broken heart! I was amazed to hear such an admission. I wished that I could share it with Vera, whose eyes had looked up from the pages of her book and were focused on Lydia.

'You're a queer fish Lydia. I never know quite how to take you,' I said.

I immediately regretted embarking on such a risky line.

'How come?' she asked.

I had not intended to expand on what I found so peculiar about her, but she would not let me off the hook. I found myself being pressed to make myself clear. I was glad that the pitfalls of conversation where not a risk in my relations with Vera.

'I thought that you might find me and my behaviour with – you know, my young lady – (I did not want to say her name out loud) to be, perhaps, shocking.'

'I am not easily shocked. Besides I hold progressive views.' She looked at me with quizzing grey eyes and added. 'I do hope, of course that you will not leave your young lady in a worse-off condition than you discovered her.'

In actual fact, I did do my best to ensure that I did not leave Vera in a 'worse' condition, but a man can only do so much and damn it – I said to myself – a professional woman must take her own chances. I state this here for the record, but it was not something I wanted to discuss with Lydia. It was convenient for me to take her question another way:

'I give you my word,' I said, 'that I have already spent some considerable sum of money on improving her condition.'

'A businessman's answer,' said Lydia.

I looked over at Vera. She had obviously been listening to our conversation – or the sounds we made – but all she could contribute was a little smile. I smiled back. This was communication on a pleasant level, but could not help wondering if she ever thought of the future, and how she would fend for herself once I returned to London. At least I would be leaving her with some clothes and some money – and whatever Lydia might think – that would count for rather a lot to a woman who knew what it meant to have nothing. And then I said to Lydia,

'There is one thing you could communicate to her. After this trip to Siberia, I must return to London. I hope to come back to Russia, but I can't promise when. Is there anything I can do for her before I leave?'

Lydia nodded. I do not know if she believed that I was sincere in my desire to help, but she conferred with Vera.

'She must think about it before answering,' Lydia told me. And Vera looked out of the window for a moment, her index finger on her chin while she thought. Then she turned around and gave her answer with wide-eyed excitement, as if she had already opened some present. Lydia exclaimed at her reply, but Vera just said 'yes, yes,' in English.

'She says,' said Lydia, with an expression of rye amusement on her face, 'that she would like a painting by Monsieur Matisse.'

I tried not to look astonished. I did not want to hurt the girl's feelings. I spoke without thinking out a coherent reply:

'Tell her I will have to go to Paris for one... no, on second thoughts, better not, she might believe me. She needs four walls before she can think of paintings... I was thinking of something more practical.'

'And cheaper,' said Lydia.

'Well within the bounds of possibility.'

Lydia explained something to Vera, but I was not sure what it was they were talking about. Eventually Lydia left us, and Vera sank back into a daydream - a daydream, I supposed, about owning her own Matisse. I listened to the clackety-clack of the train. It was a sound that I found more soothing than conversation.

It was in the corridor, as we were stretching our legs, that Vera and I encountered Anatoly.

'Ah! Those rare birds of love!' he said.

At first, I thought it was the motion of the train that was distracting him from his usual poise. The way he greeted us, the way he offered me a cigarette from his case, and the way he leant back against the wall of the corridor, were a touch slower and a touch more deliberate than usual. I caught a whiff of spirit on his breath. I asked him if he would like to join us for tea in our compartment.

'Not now. I am going to see my man, Ivan.'

'Well I'm terribly sorry we haven't seen much of you.'

'No matter. Come with me. It will be merry.' He started to walk off, saying, 'Ivan will make us welcome. It is the proper way to travel, among the people. Songs, stories, vodichka.'

I was pretty sure that the third class would hold no novelty or interest for Vera, but she followed us tamely. It was an open carriage with wooden benches in rows. The air smelt of tobacco and sheepskin. People, coats, and bags were one big heap. There were pudding bowl haircuts on the men, and red headscarves on the women. I noticed one woman sleeping up in the luggage rack:

'She is a hare,' said Anatoly, looking up at the stowaway.

'A what?'

'She has no ticket. When the inspector comes, they will throw a coat over her. See that sign? It reads, "Hares absolutely not allowed," but most hares cannot read. If you look under the benches you will probably find others have made nests there.'

Ivan was playing cards with two other men. He was by far the smartest of the trio, dressed as he was, in a clean-ish collar. He stood up and greeted his employer like a comrade. He took Vera's hand, which she had not offered, and kissed it. I thought he was damned impudent, but I did not say anything. I supposed that he sensed that she belonged to his social class, or lower. Everyone moved along the bench; a woman got up and went to sit elsewhere; a child sat on a mother's knee, and somehow we managed to find room to sit down.

Vera said 'hello' in English to Lydia's maid. Lucy turned up her pug-like nose. She could not, I think, have looked more miserable and out of place if she had been sewing mail sacks in Holloway Gaol. I asked her how she was faring.

'Oh, Very well thank you sir, apart from the fleas and the want of a good wash and the lack of sleep. Not that I'm one to grumble, mind. Just seeing as you asked. I'm itching something frightful.'

'Why don't you take a wash in our carriage? We have a very adequate facility.'

'Why not indeed? A fine question, if you don't mind me saying so, sir. I would not presume.'

'Here's the key. Ask the purser for hot water. Just point to the washroom if he doesn't understand.'

After good deal more persuading and cajoling, Lucy took herself off. At least the removal of her sizeable behind gave us more room on the bench. I felt a powerful urge to scratch my leg.

Anatoly had produced a small bottle of vodka from inside his coat and handed it around, followed by cigarettes from his silver and blue enamel case. The men were eating a Ukrainian delicacy called sala. It was sliced lard. It was supposed to be good with vodka.

'Nyet, spasiba.' I said. I had learned how to say 'no thank you.' Vera, whom I knew to be hungry, also declined.

Ivan wanted to play a game of cards with me called fool. I was pretty sure that I knew which fool was being set up to lose his fifty kopeck stake. Anatoly explained the rules, and had me foxed. Perhaps they only make sense after a bottle of vodka. The deck is made up of 36 cards. Denominations lower than six do not exist in Russian packs, no doubt an economy measure by the Government monopoly that produced them before the Great War. Anatoly cut the deck to choose trumps - I understood thus far – and then Ivan and I took it in turns to pick up and put down cards in accordance with arcane rules. Ivan looked me in the eye trying to divine my thoughts, but all he could have seen there was confusion. Vera leant in close to me, looked at my cards, and played my hand. She selected a particular card, winked at Ivan, and slipped it next to her bosom, so that it stuck out just above the top of her dress. Ivan looked baffled. Was it a great card, or was she bluffing? After several rounds, he ended up holding all the pack. For a moment, I thought we had lost – but it was the other way round. The fool is the one left holding all the cards. Vera held out the hand which he had so impertinently kissed and he placed the coin in into her palm.

Everyone offered us a little something: sweets, boiled eggs, crusts of black bread rubbed with garlic and sprinkled with salt, foul cigarettes, and yet more lard. A man had a flower in his buttonhole which he gallantly presented to Vera. Anatoly was in his element. Nobody seemed to notice his fancy tailoring or careful grooming. His lips were pink with inebriation, but the dullness I had noticed earlier on seemed to pass. There was an impish look in his eyes which outshone even Ivan's.

A boy - well he was probably just younger than I - gave us a song while accompanying himself on a guitar. He breathed deeply in between the lines, strummed with passion, and reached a kind of climax where he punched the air with a deep baritone voice which overcame the rattling of the train. He seemed to find nostalgia for some long lost love in his young chest. At times that feeling was directed toward Vera whose face he gazed into for inspiration and romantic effect. We all applauded, Vera especially, and I felt a pang of jealousy. The boy chatted to everyone, but to her in particular.

After a while, we left Anatoly chatting to a pretty plump woman who bore a passing resemblance to Julia Mizinsky. The woman's husband, who was playing cards at the other end of the bench, gave the occasional anxious glance in his wife's direction.

Once we had passed Samara on wide iced-over River Volga, we were increasingly joined by Mohammedans - Bashkirs and Kirghiz - the descendants of Genghis Khan. The women wore long red scarves and baggy trousers. The men had a preference for narrow brimmed round hats which they tilted at rakish angles.

As we progressed, the soldiers guarding the great iron bridges looked colder and more miserable. Our journey was anything but speedy. We would sometimes stop in a side loop of track for hours on end at the behest of a signal-box, until an endless goods train laden with two or three hundred trucks heaved its way past us in the opposite direction. At night, halted on the edge of some godforsaken station, I would lie awake listening to clanking and heaving, railwaymen calling out to each other, and the hissing of a tired locomotive. Once, during the day, we halted for a couple of hours or more while men muffled up in thick coats loaded our train with logs for the engine.

The ascent became gradually steeper, though I never received the expected impression of a mountainous equivalent of the Kremlin. The Urals are a gentle range, and are rather more pretty than dramatic, at least at this more southerly point. We passed frozen lakes and isolated chapels. At some points the train ran along the top of a construction like a Roman aqueduct.

After we left the city of Ufa, both Lydia and Anatoly gave us the honour of their company in our compartment at the same time – the latter bringing vodka and preserved cucumbers. I was pleased, as I was growing concerned that my affair with Vera was keeping us all apart. Urged on by Anatoly, we all took a sharp shot of spirit followed by a taste of something pickled. I was slightly surprised when Lydia joined us in this tradition – but not as surprised as she was, judging by the expression on her face, when the vodka hit the bottom of her stomach. She coughed and Vera patted her on the back. I found a bottle of gaseous water and filled a tumbler for the patient.

It was the most interesting day from a scenic point of view. The railway ran alongside an immensely wide river, and for a long while we passed satanic factories billowing smoke, one of which was a government gun foundry. Souvenir salesmen on the platforms offered us swords and other metallic objects. The industry was, as industry generally is, ugly: but the giant of Russia's nature seemed amply able to take any of mankind's puny blows against it. The overwhelming impression of our journey was of a pristine, almost primeval landscape, only blemished here and there by human vandalism.

It was Vera who looked out for and spotted the grey stone column that marks the end of one continent, and the beginning of the next. All boundaries are artificial, but perhaps this one even more so, as it was not even a political border. Even so, it felt like we had passed the point of no return:

'Let us drink to Siberia!' said Anatoly, and he filled our glasses, including Lydia's – only this time to the brim. A full tumbler of vodka is a scary sight. It looks just like life-giving water, but you know that it is something quite different. Lydia stared at hers, and I thought for a moment that she was going to be sick, but she then she simply poured most of her vodka back into the bottle, leaving herself a neat little shot. Vera copied her, and when I did the same, Anatoly gave me a dark frown and growled, 'Et tu Brute?' I shrugged apologetically.

Anatoly held up his glass and looked into the mystical spirit. His face was so strong – almost carved out of wood – that he truly did seem equal to such a large quantity of vodka. His youth still had plenty of vigour to expend.

'Let us drink to the great white goddess of Siberia, and may she yield up some of her wealth to us!'

And all clinked glasses. Anatoly took the whole tumbler in two or three gulps.

In the late afternoon light, some of the distant peaks looked to me as if they were made of silver or gold. I thought of something I had heard my father once say - that every investor wanted to believe in the pot of gold at the end of the rainbow. I was starting to believe in it.

Lydia drank the toast with more success this time, but when she had downed her sensible portion of spirit, she said to Anatoly:

'How can you be sure that your goddess will yield anything up to you? Surely, if this wealth you speak of belongs to anybody, it is to all the people of your country?'

Anatoly looked at her with a deliberately steady gaze, which I knew by now to mean that he was pretty drunk (he never dribbled or slurred in his cups):

'You are right my dear lady,' he said, 'This wealth probably does indeed belong, not even to all the people, but to nature itself. But there is a phrase which my English governess taught us children when we were small, as a warning when we kept our toys in disorder: "finder's keepers."'

'Yes,' said Lydia, 'I suppose human justice has not yet progressed out of the nursery.'

'Then we are agreed, because I suppose the same thing.' Anatoly asked Lydia, for the first time what it was that had inspired a young woman to come all the way from comforts of England and to expose herself to the 'perils' a journey through this 'barbarous' terrain. She replied that Russia was a good place to study human nature because all its traits were blown up into extremes and could be seen all the more easily. I thought that she was quite tactless, but Anatoly seemed to agree with her.

Vera had been gazing out of the window. Now she turned into the compartment and tapped Anatoly's forearm. She had something important to say:

'She wants you to know that his is her land,' said Anatoly. 'Yes, she insists that all this belongs to her. You know, in the spiritual sense, she is quite right. Perhaps we can all agree on this, my dear Miss Lydia. I think every Russian has this vast space in his soul. It expresses our nature. We have a special word for it. We call it prostor. It is an area so big that it is beyond all measure.'

'Which is why,' said Lydia, 'Russians never know when to stop.'

'You are correct,' said Anatoly. 'And at least in my case, my shamelessness has no limits.' And then he added with a nod to Vera. 'And no doubt the same is true for her.'

Lydia and I glanced at each other, but we both let the remark pass. There was no point in making a fuss when Vera did not even know that she had been insulted.

Anatoly poured three glasses of vodka – this time giving himself a much more modest amount - and he hesitated over the fourth for Lydia. She told him to 'go on' and he poured for her. We drank a toast to prostor and the slight unpleasantness between us was healed in the fire of the spirit. It was not long before we all began to feel dozy. Anatoly rose to his feet rather slowly and returned to his carriage.

We reached Yekaterinburg the next day, around lunchtime, not more than five and half hours later than scheduled.

Chapter Nine

'The stones offered by the street-vendors , especially emeralds, are mostly spurious'

Baedeker, 1914.

'Psst, want to buy an emerald? Cheapest price.'

Gem touts loitered around Yekaterinburg like thieves. Those with good connections hovered in the warm lobby of our hotel; others drifted along the misty banks of the River Iset, and waited outside the portals of the Imperial Lapidary where precious stones from the Urals were cut. They intercepted us as we crossed a large empty square in the centre of which stood a lonely statue of the late Tsar, Alexander II. Some even ambushed us on the steps of the pale blue Vosnesensky Cathedral. They seemed particularly attracted to me and could not take my polite nyet for an answer. It occurred to me that Vera could do with a small ring as a symbol of our affair. They could smell my weakness.

'Go on! Bris!' said Anatoly. Bris is Russian for 'shoo': a word I learned to understand, but could not use with conviction like Anatoly. Lydia could, though. She would brush the touts away with her hand like mosquitoes. Vera walked straight on, ignoring them.

I needed to make sure that all the mining permits and licences were in order, but Anatoly went on his own to visit his 'friend', the local mining inspector. He thought that the inspector's tastes, expensive as they were already, would become yet more refined if he knew that foreigners were interested in the mine. When he went out he was dark and gloomy, but he returned much brighter and drunker. The result of his lunch with the inspector, which had taken an entire afternoon, was a renewed mining permit for another year. It was a miserable looking document, printed on thin yellow paper, with blank spaces filled in with Cyrillic scrawl and stamped with red sealing wax that looked like dried blood. Anatoly waved it triumphantly as we sat having tea in the hotel restaurant.

'Did it cost you much?' I asked

'We mine owners are generous fellows. We cannot bear to see a poor government official of the fifth rank struggling to feed his children on a salary of 75 roubles a month.'

He read out some of the conditions of the permit. The holder undertook to log every particle of mineral found at the mine for the purpose of paying royalties to the local administration. In any one-year, the mine owners would be liable to huge fines if there were more than two strikes, three major brawls, or five serious injuries among the employees.

'Surely that opens you to blackmail by the workers?' I said.

'Of course, these conditions are completely impractical. That is why we must keep the mining inspector acquainted with Monsieur Bolinger.'

Yekaterinburg was an elegant city, the more so thanks to the classical mansions built by the merchants who had grown rich out of the region's mines. One or two were boastfully immense, with columns and domes and extensive parkland. Anatoly told us that, in another part of the city, his wife's grandfather had built a medium sized house, having made a fortune out of gold prospecting, but that Julia's father had found life in the City insufferably boring, and had sold up and moved to Moscow. Fortunately he had

kept hold of some forest land in the region which was now the object of our trip.

I could understand why Alexander Mizinsky had wanted to leave. After the crowds and bustle of Vera's beloved Petrovka shopping street, the avenues of Yekaterinburg were tranquil but also a touch sad and lonely. I always felt that the people we encountered had a look in their eyes that was six days by train away from Moscow or St.

Petersburg. Even the horses seemed to pull their carts and coaches along with a note of tedium in their stride.

The local light gauge railway that took us out of the city the next day, seemed like a toy-train set compared to the Trans-Siberian. We enjoyed a pretty ride through woods and past little villages and ramshackle farms, about 40 miles to the settlement of Galino.

Galino was a prospecting town whose inhabitants exhibited all the decorum you might expect of those who hope to strike it so lucky in one day that they never have to work another day in their life. We hired a droshky to take us to the hotel. The sights on our short journey were far from edifying: men lay snoring outside the drink shops. A dog was licking a man's vomit. One could imagine that most of the buildings had been put up by drunks. A straight angle was a novelty, nails stuck out of timber, and the cement lay, not just between the bricks, but smeared around the edges like chocolate around a little boy's mouth. I thought of my father back home. He was forever bewailing the failings of his builders - but I doubted that he had to put up with work as shoddy as this. Further along, a gang of brickies, some carrying hobs, others mixing cement and spreading it with trowels, was putting up a new shop. Their work looked good. The brickies were women. Lydia drew a conclusion that was so predictable that I will not bother to record it here.

Inside the hotel, a different example of womankind leant against the reception counter watching Anatoly sign us in. I asked Lydia:

'Is her hair naturally that colour?' It fell in straight lines from beneath the woman's straw boater.

'Hydrogen peroxide,' said Lydia. 'Are you tempted by her?'

'Not in the least. Why should I be?' I thought it was an extraordinary thing for her so say.

'If that woman was fifteen, or perhaps ten, years younger, she might have stood a better chance.'

'I don't think so,' I said. It was unthinkable that I would ever have been attracted to woman who bleached her hair and stood on one leg, sticking out her hip.

'I don't speak of morality. I just mean that perhaps once she was attractive. Hers is the fate that awaits all women who live by their looks. It is a cruel fate, but it is inevitable. You should bear it in mind.'
I kept my eyes fixed on Anatoly at the desk and said: 'Lydia, I would rather you did not talk like that in front of her. It doesn't seem right.'
I quietly took Vera's hand, sliding my fingers between hers. I squeezed tight. It was unthinkable that she might end up in a place like this. Then I remembered, she had come from a place like this, only more exclusive.

Anatoly turned round and said, 'There's only one room for the servants.' Ivan and Lucy were waiting by the door with our bags, well within earshot.

'Well Lucy will have to sleep with Ivan,' called out Lydia, her eyebrow at a teasing angle. Before Lucy could protest - and I think it was going to be a mighty whirlwind of protestation, because she had already turned a bright shade of red - Anatoly said:

'Ivan is too shy. He will sleep with me.'

It was a noisy night with singing, shouting, sobbing, howling, screaming, and eventually shooting on the street. And women kept on knocking on the door and calling out, Nochnaya Sloujhba! - 'Night Service!' Vera got out of bed, opened the door, and gave them a piece of her mind. I expect it was a fairly filthy piece too, but in any case, it seemed to do the trick.

It was fortunate that we had brought our own sheets, because the hotel provided no more than a bare mattress and some blankets. As I lay in bed, I thought of my first night in Moscow, when a voice on the phone had summoned me to a room where I had picked out Vera. I was still not quite sure if my choice had been my good judgement or simply 'fate' as the Russians liked to believe. I wondered though, if I had gone for a woman like the unnatural blonde, would it have been better? I would not have had a growing sense of responsibility. I would be a freer man. Perhaps I should shake off my sentimental feelings about the woman whose leg was warm and next to mine. I was sure that was what Anatoly would have advised.

The renewed knocking on our door was particularly vociferous. A woman spoke in an accent honed at an English girl's school.

'George! Are you asleep?'

I put on my dressing gown and let Lydia in: 'This place is terrible. It's frightening.' Vera sat up with the sheet around her bosom and blinked at Lydia's candle. The Englishwoman sat on the end of our bed: 'I don't want to go back to my room. There are strange people outside my door the whole time.'

'Well you'd better get in with us,' I said. I meant it as a joke. I thought it would scare her off. But she got in. There was just about room. I wish, I wish, I knew what Vera thought of this strange Englishwoman. She did not seem to mind. I suppose she had shared a bed with less wholesome companions.

At first light, Lydia got up to return to her room. She saw the peroxide woman come out of Anatoly's door – from the room he was sharing with Ivan. She told me later that the woman had winked at her.

By midmorning, a convoy of sleighs was waiting for us in the street outside that frightful hotel. Our conveyances were not the usual one-horse affairs for use inside the town. I had almost got used to travelling around in one of those with Vera under my arm. Anatoly had rustled up a faster and more prestigious method of transport: the Russian troika.

The troika in motion is a noble sight. It is pulled by a trinity of horses. The central horse, harnessed under a large arch called a duga, trots forward. The two horses on either side point their heads outwards and gallop. Ideally, the duga is brightly painted, and the harnesses and reigns sport pretty patterns. The horses' necks are haughtily arched, like those on the Parthenon Freeze or a Staunton chess set. Icicles dangle from their flaring nostrils. Most probably, they would be silver and dapple coloured. The driver should be a tall fellow with a flowing red beard who stands on the box, with reigns in one hand and whip in the other, and shouts 'Yah!' as you fly across the snow fields in a cloud of white powder at the spanking pace of twelve miles an hour. It's not impossible to imagine a pack of wolves chasing behind, and one having to turn around in the seat to shoot a couple of them. At least, those are the sorts of ideas that come to mind when looking at the troikas depicted on the pretty lacquer boxes which tourists are always being asked to buy, or when reading Gogol who was a big fan of that way of getting around and who made it the symbol of Russia hurtling forward in his 'Dead Souls.'

Lydia, who knew a thing or two about horses, said that if the owners of the beasts dragging our sleighs employed a groom, he could have benefited from a good thrashing. We examined the equipment made out of horsehair rope and wood with rusty nails sticking out, and wondered how it would hold itself together. Before leaving, Anatoly gave each of the drivers a bottle of the cheapest vodka for the journey. Our man, a great hulking fellow, stuck the bottle between his teeth and bit the lid off.

We set off with an enormous jerk. I heard a shriek behind us. Lydia called out: 'Lucy, dear, just hold on tight to Ivan.' We travelled down the main street at a cracking pace, sleigh bells clanking like pots and pans, and sending drunks staggering and cursing for cover. Soon we were out of the town and slipping across virginal white snow. The silver birch trees stood on either side of our path like slender girls. We felt every bump and clump and rut. Vera's face was pink from the cold air, and her nostrils flared a little, but she seemed to be enjoying herself. I turned around to look at Lucy who was clinging on to Ivan as though he were the love of her life. We passed through copses and fields and from the brow of a hill we looked back at Galino and the bells and copulas of its two churches. From about a mile away it looked quite picturesque.

The final part of our journey had us holding on even tighter. The road, if you could call it that, was really just a way through the birch trees, and it took us skiing down a steep hill. The troika carrying Lydia and Anatoly went hurtling down the slope. Our driver sucked at his vodka bottle like a babe at the nipple and whipped up our horses. Soon we were on the tail of the troika in front. Behind us Lucy's voice was in full wail. I was fearful we might run into a tree or get knocked by a branch. We tore round a corner and briefly I had a fantastic view of the frozen River Tokovaya down below, and at the end of the valley a mountain in the shape of a blue triangle, the sort of mountain that a child would draw in a picture book, and above the mountain a scimitar of a moon suspended in the daylight sky, and I would not have been surprised to see a cow jumping over it, but the rungs of our sleigh were half way up a bank and silver birch trees were turning sideways, and, before I knew it, Vera and I were tipped out into the snow; for one second, blackness and for several more, whiteness. Somehow the driver and the horses kept hurtling on. My next fear was that we would be run-over by the troika bringing Lucy and Ivan. Vera was on her hands and knees, her fur coat dangling down, looking like a Scotty dog but, thank God, when the next sleigh came round the bend, the driver went up onto the bank and managed to avoid her toes by inches. I helped Vera stand and was pleased that we could both run to the trees before the fourth troika with the luggage came round the bend.

We were both shaken and covered with snow and Vera was cut above the eye. I was searching frantically for my handkerchief to dab the blood. It occurred to me that she was going to have a nasty shiner by evening. Our driver tramped back to meet us on foot, and seeing that we were all right he laughed and banged me on the back. 'Nichevo! Nichevo!' he roared, which I knew already to mean 'It's nothing at all.' The Russians use that word a lot. Bloody cheek, I could have done with an apology, but he proffered me his bottle of vodka - Russia's solution to every problem. I was about to swig it when I saw that Vera was looking at me crossly. She took the bottle, applied vodka to her own handkerchief, and gave it to me. I used the antiseptic alcohol to dab her cut. By now the sleigh out in front had returned to the scene of our accident. Anatoly jumped down onto the ground.

'Oh, Englishman! Where are you flying to?'

Now that I am better read in Russian literature, I know that he was misquoting a famous line of Gogol.

'Where the bloody hell indeed? Why don't you ask that blasted fool of a driver why he doesn't take more care of his passengers?'

Chapter Ten

A rickety log bridge spanned the River Tokovaya, but our drivers did not make use of it, cutting instead across the ice. Looking back at the bank that we had just left, we could see wooden cottages with smoking chimneys, piles of logs, and shadowy men working at machines. I realised that the whole complex must be a mine. I assumed, until corrected, that it was the same mine that we had come to see, but that it was in a rather more advanced stage of development than I had expected, and I was surprised and impressed by its business-like appearance. My delusion did not last long. Anatoly, whose sleigh had drawn up alongside us, waved his arm in its direction:

'Over there is a great mine owned by shareholders from England and France. The director is French and lives in that big white house. One hundred and fifty men wash the mud to search for precious stones. If there are riches on that bank of the river, they must exist on our side too.'

'It stands to reason,' I agreed.

Up on a slight hill, the Mizinsky dacha commanded a fine view of the bend in the river. Ten or even five years beforehand, it would have made an imposing sight, but now its wooden walls and verandas could do with more than just a lick of paint.

'All this from the top of the hill down to the river is our land,' said Anatoly.

The area we were now crossing, had also been cleared of the tall straight trees of the forest which surrounded us Tumbled down buildings looked as if they had been raided for firewood. Bits of rusting metal stuck out of the snow like burnt trees.

'Has an army camped here?' I asked.

'Maybe. It is possible.'

We had arrived.

Anatoly clanged the old bell on the veranda of the lodge and pushed the door open.

'Akulina! Privyet!'

An old woman emerged out of the shadows. The look on her face said, 'What the hell do you think you're doing turning up like this?' but Anatoly did not seem to notice: 'My dear Akulina! How delightful it is to see you!' Or at least that's what I interpreted him to be saying from his beaming face and wide-open arms. If the sentiment was reciprocated, not one wrinkle on Akulina's face moved to show it. We came further into the dark hall and she hobbled off to get our rooms ready. It did not seem that she had been expecting us.

One thing you could say about the house - it was very well heated. The Russians know how to keep warm. In the corner of the living room stood a tall stove with a chimney that retained the smoke for two or three days after the fire had died out. Lydia was already pulling off her green jersey. On the table, which could have done with a good dusting, Anatoly found two telegrams he had sent: one from Moscow and the other from Yekaterinburg, both warning of our visit. Obviously they had not made much of an impression on the Mizinsky's house keeper.

'Perhaps she can't read,' suggested Lydia.

'What do you mean?' said Anatoly. 'She taught me to read my first words in the nursery.' After he had married Julia, the family had too many servants in Moscow. They thought that Akulina would enjoy living in the countryside as the city was 'too hectic' for old people.

For dinner, Akulina boiled potatoes and served them with preserved tomatoes. Vera's eye had turned black and she looked like a woman who had taken a beating. Her expression was the glummest I had seen. I kept on looking at her, trying to elicit a smile, and eventually she twitched her nose at me.

'I'm so furious with those drivers for risking our lives like that. Vera might have broken her neck,' I said.

Anatoly shook his head. 'When the Devil wants to break her neck, he will find a way.'

The choice for the evening's entertainment amounted to homemade vodka or sleep. We retired early.

Vera and I were awoken in the middle of the night by a loud tapping on our door. Before I could rouse myself out of bed, Lydia came in. She placed her candle on the table and stood above us, her arms folded.

'I can't sleep. This place is intolerable. The whole house stinks. All manner of wild life is living in every crack and crevice. I turned the tap and it made an enormous heaving noise but all that came out was a dribble of red slime. The heating is screwed up like a Turkish bath. The windows are sealed so that the only way to get a breath of fresh air inside the room is to smash a pane - which I'm sorely tempted to do. The Russians don't seem to have heard of such a thing as fresh air. It's quite unfit for human habitation.'

'Well it is a bit fuggy.'

'Fuggy? I can't breathe.'

'Calm down Lydia. It's only for a couple of nights.'

'I won't calm down. Can't you see that your friend Mizinsky is good for nothing. It's obvious this place isn't worth a farthing. If you can't see that, you deserve to lose all your father's money.'

It was not the time to explain to her that the whole point of the project was to develop the property. It was what lay underneath the surface that mattered. She left and slammed the door behind her.

The heating had parched my mouth. I went downstairs in search of drinking water. The gaslight was still on in the living room. I discovered that Anatoly had not made it to bed but had fallen asleep on the divan. His servant was stretched out on the floor. The sound of the door creaking woke Anatoly while Ivan snored on. We had a little midnight chat and I told him about Lydia's intrusion into our bedroom. For tact's sake, I did not mention that it had happened before, and that the previous time she had stayed. He shook off his sleep and laughed:

'If she wants cold air we can make her a tent outside.'

I explained that the British are taught that fresh air and sleeping with an open window is the key to a healthy constitution. If they felt the cold they put on woolly underwear. Some even wore woolly hats in bed.

'Do English women wear woollen underwear?'

'In winter they do.'

'How can you make love to a woman who wears wool next to her skin?'

'Well that's why I have a Vera and not a Lydia.'

'I have often wondered why English people have such pink cheeks like you and Lydia.'

'And I always thought Russians had pale cheeks to look more interesting and intellectual.'

The next morning, Ivan stoked up the steam bath in the shed in the garden, and Anatoly said he was going to take a sauna and suggested that we do the same. The interior of the shed was as inviting as sheds generally are. Lydia was not tempted.

'I bet the French manager of the mine across the river has running hot and cold water in his bathroom. Let's go and pay him a visit,' she said.

'To cadge a bath?'

'Why not? I will write an article about his mine. It will be free publicity.'

Anatoly promised that Ivan would soon get the shed 'spotless.' Lydia frowned. I do not think that she trusted Ivan's sense of 'spotless' to coincide with her own. I was torn for a moment about whether to stay or go – but I decided to escort Lydia. The wilds of Siberia were no place to let a lady go wandering around on her own, and besides, I wanted to meet our neighbours. As they were in the same business as us, only far more advanced, I could hope to learn something. Lydia was against trying to rouse one of our drivers. She said that she wanted a bath while it was 'still daylight.' It was not so far, and so Vera, Lydia and I wrapped up warm and set out on foot down the hill and across the bridge.

Lydia would have shown off her French, but fortunately for me, Monsieur Cuny, the manager of the mine, was effusive in English: 'This is most unexpected; a great pleasure. We have so few guests from Europe here.'

I felt that we had turned up in the front room of his house like three children asking for a penny for the guy. Vera, with her black eye, looked like a young brat who had been in a scrap. I wondered how Lydia, the obvious leader of our band, would work the conversation round to the subject of baths. She did not. She simply asked him straight out:

'Monsieur Cuny, I hope you won't find this request too unusual, but would you mind if we each made use of a hot tub? You see, where we are staying, the facilities are somewhat non-existent.'

Only a shimmer of surprise travelled across his elegantly arranged face. I suppose, when it came down to it, we did look like we could all do with a good wash.

'But of course.'

A maid led Lydia off across the gleaming parquet floor to the bathroom, leaving Vera and me in the front room with M. Cuny. Bright winter sunlight poured through the French windows and filled the room with a sleepy haze. I was suddenly aware of how quiet it was. Vera and I sat with M. Cuny and I admired the fruit in a silver bowl on his mahogany table. The apples were as highly polished as our host's high bald crown. There were even oranges and figs. I asked him how they had arrived there and he said that he had them sent up from Samarqand:

'Little comforts make all the difference when one is so far away from civilisation.'

He was a big man, and he filled a large leather armchair. What hair he still owned was shiny and black and he compensated for his baldness with a saturnine beard.

I did not want to mention my interest in the land across the river, for fear that the Frenchman's company might make a rival bid. I said that we were here to see 'the real Russia'. I felt obliged to explain how Vera had come by her black eye, and when I had told the tale of how our sleigh had turned over, Monsieur Cuny looked at Vera sympathetically and said 'Nichevo?'

It was that universal word again which literally means 'nothing', but in practice sometimes means 'Ca va?' I believe that his Russian vocabulary was not much greater than mine.

'Nichevo,' she echoed, which in reply means, 'quite alright, thank you.'

He smiled at her gently. I realised now that the bruise around her eye lent a certain tomboy charm to her pretty face. I claimed that Vera was Anatoly's cousin. He might not have believed the explanation, but it sufficed for polite company, and I do not think that he found her hard to look at:

'You must stay for lunch. I insist. The food is not bad. My chef came with me from France, naturally.' I did not refuse. Since our arrival at the mine we had eaten nothing but potatoes and buckwheat porridge - and the cold air gives one an appetite.

Lydia returned with her hair shining, looking quite feminine, despite having changed into her tweed suit that would have been suitable for wear on a golf course, but was perhaps a little more modern than they were used to seeing Siberia. Our host complimented her, somewhat excessively I thought. I wondered if he had taken a fancy to her.

While Vera was in the bathroom - she took her time, as was her wont - Lydia and I engaged in small talk with Monsieur Cuny. He leaned over in her direction and seemed to be flirting with her, but perhaps it was just force of habit. Even so, her quizzical and ironic look was not entirely without allure, especially that morning when she had just been spruced up.

When it was my turn to bathe, the hot water and perfumed soap put me into a wonderful torpor. I smiled to myself as I thought of how Cuny's day had turned out – two unexpected female guests dropping in for lunch. I felt that I myself was a little bit extra - he had not seemed at all interested when I had brought up the subject of the Mizinskies and the mine. He had preferred even to listen to Lydia's complaints about Russian plumbing and heating.

When I re-joined the company, I found that he had brought his treasures in from the strong room. He had spread the contents of his 'museum' out on a piece of green felt laid on the table. I thought of a schoolboy with his prize conkers, but these half a dozen exhibits were worth keeping under lock and key: they were some of the most interesting gems found at the mine.

Vera was holding her hand over the table. Cuny placed a crimson stone in the crevice between her fingers. A speck of light played inside it, almost like a glint of human intelligence. Vera's black eye seemed to have opened up and any hint of grumpiness had fled her face.

Mr Cuny admired the stone and Vera's hand and said: 'Chudesna.'

She looked up at him, her face full of childish wonder. 'Da, chudesna' she repeated.

I asked what the word meant:

'It is a miracle,' said Cuny, which struck me as going a bit far.

'Now please take it over to the window,' he said to Vera pointing to the French doors.

'Aaah!' she said and looked up with a radiant smile. The stone had changed colour from crimson to green. I came over to have a closer look. I had already guessed that it was an alexandrite and would display its dichotic properties, but it had another trick which I had not been expecting. Vera tilted her hand slightly and the eye of light inside it shot out a tiny ray. This was no sparkle. It was a straight line of light, so sharp that you could almost prick your finger on it. The stone was quite a bit more fabulous than even the alexandrite stone worn by Julia Mizinsky. Its twin colours were richer and more contrasting. Its inner surfaces hinted at some secret meaning. Yes, this Gemini of a jewel was worth travelling all the way to see. One moment it possessed the tranquil green of youth and innocence, and the next, the smouldering red of desire and revolution. It had all the mystery and exoticism of the East about it. Indeed, it reminded me of my strong impressions that time I had seen the Russian ballet dancers perform, and I must say, it seemed made for the hand of Vera. I could see that she was thinking the same thing too. You could not fault her taste. An alexandrite mine truly was a business that gave aesthetic satisfaction. It could almost have been made for me.

'It's a nine carat alexandrite with a cat's eye,' said Monsieur Cuny, 'which makes it exceptionally rare. But be careful my dear. Legend holds that a woman who coverts an alexandrite stone will become a widow.'

Lydia translated this remark for Vera:

'I do not believe in fairy stories,' came the reply.

'Ah but it is true!' said Cuny. 'This stone was named for your Tsar, Alexander II, and he was blown to bits by a terrorist bomb.'

Lydia translated this too. And Vera replied,

'Then you would not wish to give this stone to your wife. So give it me. I'm not married. I can't become a widow.' She looked quite serious, but of course we understood it as a joke:

'My dear, it would give me the greatest satisfaction to find such a beautiful wearer for this stone. By daylight, it possesses the same shade of green as your eyes. But unfortunately, it is not mine to give. It belongs to the company.'

Lydia had joined us by the window and was examining the stone herself. She explained Mr Cuny's regrets, and Vera gave a little shrug:

'Nichevo,' she said, taking the alexandrite back from Lydia. She went over to the table and popped it into the little velvet bag where it was kept. Mr Cuny placed the bag with the others inside a metal box, and asked us to excuse him. He was obliged to leave us for a few moments: only he and his foreman knew the combination lock on the door to the strong room.

While he was away, I remarked that it would be an exciting day if we found a stone like that on our side of the river. Privately I was thinking that it might be possible to set one aside 'on loan' from the shareholders while it adorned Vera's hand. I had a feeling that a similar idea might already have occurred to Vera herself.

'Don't count on finding anything over there,' said Lydia. 'Mr Cuny was telling us while you were bathing that the Mizinsky side of the river is worthless.' She refused to elaborate, saying that I should ask for the story, 'straight from the horse's mouth.' I thought it was typical of Lydia to put a dampener on things, just as they were getting interesting. I tried hard to look unconcerned.

Over lunch, Lydia quizzed Cuny about the conditions of his workers. He admitted that they were paid five times less than British or French miners, but he insisted that they were five times less productive:

'Has that measurement been made scientifically?' she asked.

'It is a guess, but one which is perhaps too generous to the Russian worker.'

I was a little annoyed with Lydia for putting our host on the spot in this way: it did not seem quite right while were enjoying his hospitality, and I wanted to ask him about more capitalist concerns, but I found it hard to make an opening in the conversation.'

'Miss Lydia, please be assured,' he was saying, 'We have no deficit of men wishing to work for us. The conditions here are considered to be far superior to the Russian owned mines. Our equipment is the most modern. Our safety record is the highest. The men work ten hours per day - not twelve, as is usual. We grant them baths twice a week.'

I chuckled at the mention of baths, and for a moment I put Cuny out of his stride. He recovered himself, to add:

'I am very happy that you ask about such matters. It is important that the outside world receives the correct information. There are so many wrong ideas about the mining industry in Siberia. By the way, we have built a hospital and a school at the local town.'

While this conversation continued, Vera sat quietly. She was holding her fork more carefully than usual. We were eating wood pigeon, and I had been afraid that she might pick up the wings in her hand, as she had sometimes done with great relish and sexiness when had eaten in our room at the Metropole. The book on etiquette had been a good investment. And she had more natural grace than Lydia; you might have taken her for the lady.

When I eventually succeeded in mentioning the Mizinsky mine again, Cuny did not take up the subject with great enthusiasm.

'It is very strange,' he said.

'Why strange?'

'That land over there' – he briefly turned his bald head in the direction of the river – 'is dead land.'

'Dead, you say?'

'Yes, quite dead. It was mined for over twenty years. There is nothing of value left.'

'Do the Mizinskies know this?'

'Of course! Better than anyone. Anatoly Mizinsky came out two years ago and offered us the opportunity to buy this land. Our experts looked at it and we made enquiries. We discovered that it had been mined for about twenty years and not too much of value had ever been found. He told that he did not mind. He would keep the dacha for a hunting lodge. It is completely worthless from the point of view of a miner. Perhaps the trees have some value for timber.'

I was clutching at straws, but I suggested that perhaps the earlier attempt to exploit the land had been hampered by out of date methods and equipment but he was having none of it:

'You will excuse me if I speak too directly. It is perhaps not courteous for a host. But I wish to save you much bother and much money. Can't you find snow in Scotland? Do you not have rocks in England? That is all you will find on that land over there.'

If I was not much mistaken, Lydia found quiet satisfaction in his words. She certainly gave me one of her most quizzical of looks. Those eyebrows of hers were most expressive. I was not sure what I myself felt yet. Should I believe him? A stupid joke occurred to me;

'Well it's a good job I came to you today without our unusual request. It's better than taking a financial bath.'

He smiled politely: 'I hope that your trip has been interesting?'

'It certainly has.'

I found it rather hard to enjoy the tarte-tatin followed by smoked cheese as much as Vera evidently did.

After lunch, Lydia asked if we could take a look around the mine. A Scottish foreman was summoned to show us around. He was an engineer and his name was Mr Bruce. He was most obliging, and as we picked our way over some of the rougher ground, on several occasions he gently took Vera's arm and stopped her from slipping. Lydia, as ever, was as sure on her feet as a mountain goat. Vera asked a question, and Lydia said in English, 'That's just what I was wondering. Where are your men today?' Not a single worker was in view.

'Ach, it's St. Dimitry's Day' said Mr Bruce, who explained that there were over 100 holy holidays a year when the Russian workers spent time in religious contemplation. Most of the workforce had 'gone to church' in Galino and would not be allowed to return to work until they had sobered up. For some of them, that would take several days.

But when the miners did work, they clearly made progress. Mr Bruce showed us how they had cleared the area of trees and used the tall straight trunks to build cabins. They had dug evenly spaced trenches. They had laid rail tracks so that rocks and material could be moved around easily on carts.

He told us that men have washed river sediment through sieves in search of gold or gems since ancient times. This 'placer mine' worked on the same basic principles as the Cleopatra emerald mines in mountains of Egypt, but all the equipment for sifting and separating alluvial material was the very latest. A generator driven by the river (when it was not frozen) gave them electric light in the houses: they had hydraulic pumps, sluice boxes, separators (that looked like cement mixers), and a steam powered stamping machine to crush the larger rocks and to break the ground in winter. Mr Bruce told us that quite a few of the more traditional Russian mine owners did not trust the new equipment and methods, and preferred to use donkeys and carts instead of rail tracks, even though it was difficult to feed the animals in winter.

For the sake of a second opinion, I asked Mr Bruce about the Mizinskies' side of the river. He told us that when the snows melted, it was possible to see that the other bank had been thoroughly dug up over the years, and anything of any value had surely been found. In any case, he said, the lay of the land meant that most alluvial material had settled up on this bank.

'Which is why,' said Lydia to me, 'You were brought to see the property in winter.'

'Perhaps,' I said, remembering that Anatoly had at first been against travelling in winter, and then had changed his mind. I felt a certain confusion about what to believe, but Mr Bruce did not strike me, by any stretch of the imagination, as a man who made his living by telling tall stories or talking about what he did not understand: he was too straight, and too proud of the achievements of his workers. After the brief tour, he left us at the gate to Mr Cuny's house, but Lydia spotted a sign of human activity – a young girl of about nine or ten years of age was going through the door of one of the out-buildings. 'Let's see if we can talk to her!' she said. I could almost read the headline 'exploitation' passing through her mind.

We knocked on the door of the cabin and called out before entering. Inside we found a room with a bunk beds and whitewashed walls. A large pot was boiling on the top of a stove and a smell of cabbage pervaded the close air. Three women and the child we had seen were sitting around the stove, chatting and eating sunflower seeds. They turned around to look at us – and rose to their feet. Lydia spoke to them, and soon we too were sitting around the stove with glasses of tea. Vera sat next to the young girl and gave her a sweet from her pocket. As I could not join in the general conversation, I spent most of the time admiring Vera and the child as they conversed together, and wondering whether Vera seemed more like a mother or like a big sister.

An account of Lydia's conversation with the women appeared later in her article for Media, and I refer to it now:

'What do you do here?'

'Women's work. We wash and cook and keep an eye on our husbands.'

'Does this young girl go to school?'

'Yes, Anyushka goes to school in Galino. But today is a holiday.'

'Are you comfortable here?'

'The Lord be thanked, we are warm and we do not starve.' The woman crossed herself as she said this.

'How much do your men earn?'

'Seventy five.'

'Roubles?'

They laughed in merry voices and shook their heads.

'Kopecks.'

'English miners earn five times as much, and still they strike for more.'

'Molotsi!' The women chorused, 'Good Lads!'

'And what is your opinion of Monsieur Cuny?'

'Napoleon!'

'He is always walking so quickly!' said the mother of Anyushka, and she stood up and imitated his speedy march, much to everyone's amusement, especially the little girl's.

When we returned to Mr Cuny to give him our thanks and to take our leave, Lydia asked him casually if he knew that the workers called him 'Napoleon.' How I wished that she would employ a little more tact! But he took it in good humour and smiled graciously and said:

'Bonaparte lost everything in Russia. We do not intend to follow his example,'

As we left, Vera waved to two of the women whom we had met earlier on. They were standing outside their hostel. They waved back and called out 'Zabastovka!'

'What does that mean?'

'Strike,' said Lydia.

'Gosh! I hope they don't really mean it.'

'Well it would be difficult to go on strike while on holiday,' said Lydia. But she was obviously very satisfied with the result. [15]

On our return, we were greeted by unexpected cooking smells. Anatoly had been out shooting and had bagged three woodpigeons which Akulina was making into a casserole. I felt the time had come for some straight talking with my business partner. I found him putting his feet up on the divan and reading a book.

'How were your baths?' he asked.

'Splendid,' I said, rather curtly. I did not feel at all splendid at the prospect of cross-examining Anatoly about the true story of his property. I rambled on politely for a bit about our lunch, and Lydia's attempts to spread discontent among the worker's families.

'She won't succeed there. The wages and conditions at that mine are the best in Russia,' said Anatoly.

'Yes. It seemed a model enterprise in all respects. But they say that they turned down your offer to sell them your property.'

Anatoly swung his legs around and sat up, sliding his feet into his large slippers. 'And no doubt they failed to tell you the true story.' he

---

[15] The article by Lydia Hawthorne, 'A French Capitalist in the Wilds of Russia,' published the June 1914 edition of *Medea*, suggests that Miss Hawthorne successfully 'politicised' the women of the mine and left them determined to rouse their men to action, and to send 'Napoleon' beating a retreat back to Paris.

said. 'My father-in-law used to own the land on both sides of the river. Some years ago some French people came here and asked to buy all of it off him. They did not say what they wanted it for. He wanted to keep this house for a hunting lodge, and so he sold them only the other side of the river. Of course they swindled him. They gave him a fraction of its value. Now they want our side too, but we won't sell it to them. And so they make up these stories. That's the truth of the matter.'

Anatoly stroked his moustache, and I wondered if that might be a sign of dissembling, but otherwise he seemed entirely innocent. I noticed his gun propped up in the corner, and he had provided evidence today of the good shooting yielded up by the woods. I said:

'Cuny insists that this side of the river has been mined already and that there's nothing of any value left, if there was anything here worth finding in the first place.'

'Then Cuny is mistaken,' said Anatoly. 'His employers have instructed him to deceive us again about the true value of our land. But once bitten, twice shy.' (The English saying rolled of his tongue with a certain pride in his mastery of the language.)

'Perhaps I will have to come back here with an independent geologist in the spring to get a second opinion.'

'Of course, you will always be welcome at our humble country house. Come as often as you like, but it is rather far from London. The report I have commissioned and had translated for you is by a very respectable scientist. We can visit him in Yekaterinburg on the way back.'

My mind was put at rest. At least, while I was actually looking Anatoly in the eye, I somehow believed that he was being straight with me. It was only later, when I was lying awake that night, that I turned things over logically — hadn't Anatoly said that his father hated living out here? That he sold his house in Yekaterinburg and moved to Moscow? It was not entirely incompatible with keeping a hunting lodge in the woods, but it seemed rather remote and inconvenient for a Muscovite. It seemed more likely that the speculators did not want the remaining land because it did not have any worthwhile prospect for mining.

Thankfully, Lydia did not invade us that night. I expect she slept well after her bath and her second meal of woodpigeon in one day.

We managed to make it to Yekaterinburg in one day. We called on Anatoly's 'expert' who worked at the Imperial Lapidary in the Geology and mining department. Unfortunately we were told that he was on a business trip to St. Petersburg. Lydia's eyebrows told the whole story – it was suspiciously convenient for Anatoly but I did not see how he could have arranged it that way.

Chapter Eleven

Vera looked out of the train window. The province of Kazan was rolling by at about 40 miles per hour. The thaw was beginning, and flat fields of glistening mud were emerging. A vast pale blue sky arched over it all, peppered here and there by black crows. Vera's black shiner was almost healed, but there were baggy shadows under both her eyes. She looked vacant with boredom.

My conversations with Lydia had taken on a political tone since the day we had visited the French mine. I had asked her why she seemed to be so opposed to business on principle. She told me her theory – that while there is property there will always be inequality, and while there is inequality there will always be war because the have-nots will always desire the possessions of the haves.

'So you are a Marxist?'

Her little eyes opened quite wide. It was not a description she relished.

'I am an anarchist,' she said. She was the only person I knew who might have made that comment in earnest. Even so, I did my best to imitate her way of turning an eyebrow into a question mark. As far as I understood, anarchists were people who committed outrages with bombs. But no, she said that they were pacifistic utopians.

She explained that she was an admirer of Mikhael Bakunin, the founder of modern anarchism, and of Peter Kropotkin, the Russian anarchist dreamer. I am glad to tell you that up until then I had no knowledge of either of these gentlemen, but during the long journey back to Moscow I heard rather a lot about them and their differences with the Marxist line of revolutionary thought. I recall that one particular point of disagreement concerned the remuneration of the workers come The Revolution. Should they be paid wages? The Marxists said 'Each shall receive according to his contribution.'

Instead of money, a worker would receive a ticket denoting '8 hours of Labour in the fields' or '4 hours of labour at the artist's easel.' This could be exchanged at the shop for goods. I thought that the 'tickets' sounded rather like money. 'Exactly' said Lydia growing excited. 'That's why we anarchists believe in 'each according to his needs'. It is the only way to abolish money. If you need food, you shall be fed. If you need a house you shall be housed. If you need a nurse you shall be nursed.'

'And if you need a beautiful painting?' I asked.

'Art shall be held in common.'

She seemed to have the blue print for Utopia worked out in every detail.

The most surprising aspect of all our discussions was how Anatoly began to side with Lydia on a number of points. The nearer we approached to Moscow, the more the two of them were in accord with each other. They both dreamed that after the Revolution, humankind would evolve into a state of complete reasonableness. There would be no need of law-courts or police, no temples, and no money - free gifts taking the place of the exchange.

'This is the state of anarchy that we are struggling for,' said Lydia, 'When each receives according to his needs, exploitation and injustice will cease to exist. There will be nothing to argue about. It's that simple.'

'I recall only too well,' said Anatoly, 'that on the first evening of our acquaintance, you so eloquently expressed that the whole process of making money to get through life was distasteful to you. It is far better that each one of us be set free to pursue our own natural talents and to fulfil our dreams.'

Why then, I demanded to know, was he interested in making money?

'As I have previously mentioned to you, I have a responsibility for my family. In the present world – in which everybody believes in this illusion of money – we must try to acquire it for our needs. Any surplus we must dedicate to the good of mankind.'

'And Vera? How would she fit into your Utopia?'

Vera continued to look out of the window.

'She has her talents,' said Anatoly. Lydia did not contradict him. She merely said that in a society without money, women would be on an equal footing with everyone else. 'There will be no exchanges, except for love and kindness.'

'Both of you are just dreamers,' I said.

'It is the generality of mankind who believe in an illusion,' said Anatoly. 'People do not see that money is just a kind of trick. It is a game, that has no root in reality.'

He spread out a deck of cards on the table and picked up the King of Diamonds. He slid it into my breast pocket, before sitting back to look at me, and then sighing deeply.

'You are young. You have not had time to see through life's disguises and deceptions,' he said. He reached across the table and extended his hand inside my jacket. This felt like an intrusion. He took out my wallet and opened it. 'Here you have a note that bears the picture of our great leader, Nicholas II. I can take this paper and exchange it for a sack of sugar, a crate of vodka, or a rather high-class woman.' He nodded toward Lydia. She looked away frostily. 'Why? It is just a piece of paper. Is that not a fraud? Is it not an illusion? It's like a game of cards. It is exactly like playing fool. At the end, one player is left holding a hand full of useless cards. That player is the fool. Usually, as I recall, the fool turns out to be Ivan.'

'And the alexandrite mine. Is that an illusion too?'

'All investments are an illusion. Many mines turn out to be empty of gold. The fools are those who are left holding the shares and bonds when the truth becomes known. The winners are the ones who rid themselves of the property first and exchange it for something more important. It is a risk that investors take.'

'So what the Frenchman told us is true?'

Anatoly did not answer. I took his inscrutable expression to be an admission. I spoke into the silence left by his non-reply.

'I'm sorry Anatoly,' I said. 'I can't get mixed up in a caper like that. I'm the one who will be standing in the dock at the Old Bailey. I don't see a British policeman coming out to Moscow to feel your collar.'

Anatoly nodded. Now I was certain.

'Unfortunately,' said Lydia, 'The current powers in the world enforce the illusion of money through the law. We have to live with it until things change.'

I looked at Vera, who by now was dozing with her head propped against a pillow, and I really hoped that she would have approved of my stance, if only she could have understood what we were talking about. In her own way, she was in business, and her transactions could not be performed without a certain amount of good faith by both the parties. In any exchange, one side has to hand over the goods or the money first. The wisest traders know that repeat business depends on good service.

My greatest regret was that I would not have an excuse to return to Russia in the near future to see her again. It was a high price to pay for honesty.

I played over one or two future conversations in my mind.

'And by the way Papa. Russia proved to be rather an expensive place. I ran up a few bills.'

Had I returned with a deal worth signing, my over-draft would have diminished into insignificance. Papa would have almost cheerfully written out a cheque to pay it off. As things stood, through no fault of my own, the trip had been an expensive failure that might prove to be a millstone around my neck. My father would blame me, no matter how unreasonably. He might insist on me taking a job. I felt like a prisoner awaiting his sentence.

But Vera had been worth it all. Soon we would arrive in Moscow, and there would be little excuse for me to stay more than a day or so. I would be returning to London.

She knew that I was brooding. She took my hand.

'I won't be able to come back to Russia,' I said, 'Not now.'

She looked into my eyes and smiled tenderly.

The bed in my room at the Metropole, which did not rattle or move, was extremely welcome, but I felt that my Moscow days were at an end. The weather was dull and the pavements were banked with heaps of dirty slush that had been shovelled there by workers early in the morning. The walls of the Kremlin brooded.

My oriental dream was over and it was time for me to return to London. In an odd way, I wanted to get the parting with Vera over as soon as possible.

Unexpectedly, it was Anatoly who helped smooth things over. He suggested that Vera could live at Nina's flat, in place of her flatmate of old who had moved to St. Petersburg.

At the time, I thought that it was a sign of his trying to make up for things. Looking back now, I think that perhaps he was making a calculation: if I knew that Vera was waiting for me, I would have an extra incentive to return to Moscow. I drew another £25 from the bank – it was as much as I dared to draw – and I left it to cover her expenses. The banking system was, and always will be, thankfully, slow; and so my cheque would be following me to London.

We spent my last evening in Moscow, as we had done the first, at Nina's flat. Once again there were some funny stories, but they were tinged with a little melancholy for me. Vera did a good job of looking cheerful – perhaps too good a job for my liking.

We did not drink to excess, but Anatoly and I paused to smoke together one last time. This time we were able to fully open the window onto the balcony.

'You once told me,' I said to Anatoly, 'That a woman like Vera could never change. Do you still think that?'

'I cannot deny,' he said, 'that she has acquired a certain something. I must congratulate you. '

Before leaving Nina's flat, I placed the wad of 250 roubles on the table by the samovar. I trusted that Nina would use this great sum prudently for the upkeep of both women. 'Vera must find honest employment,' I said sternly. Then I added, 'Vera nada bit good girl, kharacho.' You might gather that I was becoming something of a Russian linguist.

Nina gave me a hug. I think she meant to reassure me that she would look after her.

Vera returned with me to the Metropole for the last time. I lay awake with my hand on her leg under the sheets almost until dawn.

On the platform of the station, it was difficult to say if it was Vera or Anatoly who gave me longest embrace: he showered me with bristly kisses and gave me a great bear hug that almost squeezed the life out of me. But as the train pulled away, I saw that it was Vera who was dabbing her eyes with a handkerchief. Even I, in all my innocence, had not dreamed on my first night that a lady in my nocturnal employment would shed tears for my parting.

I only woke out of my Russian dream when the train was approaching Berlin, safely inside a good Lutheran country. The German fields lay under a blanket of snow: so flat, so neat, so orderly. Even the cows looked as if they knew precisely how many hours and minutes were left until milking time. On the outskirts of the city, dark factories replaced the hedgerows.

After Berlin, I had to share my compartment with a shaven-headed, cigar smoking German. At a one stop in the middle of Germany, the blue eyes behind his horn-rimmed glasses were trained on the platform. I saw that he was looking at a tall woman wearing a mink coat. She seemed to be waiting for someone, glancing up and down the platform. She was smoking a cigarette, and I thought she looked cheap. The shaven German turned to me with a broad, wrinkly smile, 'Frauline gud, yuh?'

'Gud,' I said, just to be polite. He must have been two decades or more my senior, but I thought then, 'What a schoolboy!'

Chapter Twelve

"Give them a good dividend, and they will not come near the meetings. Give them bad news and they will crowd in. Show them any rubbish in print and they will be disposed to believe it."
                             Horatio Bottomley MP, Bottomley's Book, John Bull Press 1909

On my return from Russia, I slept practically the whole weekend in my lodgings. Most of the time it was raining outside on Sussex Gardens and a nasty wind rattled my sash windows. At least in Moscow they had proper heating – clever little stoves within the walls. The only thing to do in the English winter was to hide under a blanket or find a pub with a good log fire because my landlady, Mrs Greeson, was too stingy by half to provide any warmth.

I began to regard various women as 'possibilities.' I even asked Mary, the waitress in my favourite eatery, about what she was going to do on her night off. She thought about it for a moment and said she couldn't remember what she was going to be doing, but that she was sure it was important. I was relieved that she had rebuffed me, but at the same time quite pleased with myself for asking. Unfortunately, I was running so low on funds that I could not afford to eat out often and so I had little opportunity for trying out my new found confidence on any other waitresses.

I had received a snooty letter from Coutts Bank noting that my account was substantially overdrawn and asking me to remedy the situation forthwith. Of course I had been expecting the letter, but all the same, I was annoyed at the high-handed tone.

An invitation to lunch came along from an old school friend. I replied right away to say that I had a free slot in my diary the very next day owing to a last minute cancellation. My spirits soared when he replied: 'RIGHT-OH. SEE YOU AT JOSHERS HALF 12 TOMOR.'

I walked to my appointment along the rain-washed streets and across Berkeley Square, looking up at the bare arms of the trees and the great wedding cake buildings of Mayfair as if it was the first time I had seen them. I noticed all sorts of details; caryatids and flourishes in the stucco including Egyptian scrolls and faces with pointed beards and Persian helmets, none of which I had realised were there before.

I supposed that Drake and I had been thrown together at school because we were both tainted by the whiff of 'shop'. In my case, it was a great relief that the Sainsbury brothers had bought up my grandfather's grocery. It would not have done to have had vans driving around with my family name daubed on the side. On the whole I got off lightly at school, despite my family's 'new' money. Only once did I bear the taunt 'Munnings is a tea leaf'. I wasn't quite sure if that was meant to refer to a grocer or a thief in my family. Drake's father was some sort of antique dealer with a shop somewhere around St. James's Square, and I knew that the son had joined the family firm. I feared that the conversation with Drake would prove laborious. While he had been poking around with the smell of French polish in his nostrils, I had been sliding across snowy prairies and conducting an exotic love affair. I could not imagine how I could relate my experiences to my old friend without sounding like a man talking down to a boy.

Drake's club was relatively new, and most of its members were young men. It had taken over an Adam house, inconspicuous from the outside, but graceful on the inside. I found him sitting with a green coloured drink. He had sprouted a neat little moustache and his skin had gained a bronze patina that hinted of a winter holiday in Alexandria. He sprung up in a very lively fashion to shake my hand and to ask me what my poison would be.

'I've been meaning to get in touch for ages,' he said, 'But when your father dropped into our shop the other day, that spurred me on.'

'You saw my father?'

'Not alone. He's employed a lady to advise him on his collection.'

'That would be Mrs Crawford. She helps him with more than just his collection.'

'Is that so? She's a handsome woman.'

'Yes, I suppose she is.' I was truly surprised. We seemed to have communicated on a knowing level that would not have been possible in our former days. 'Did anything catch his or her interest?'

'Oh yes. She has good taste all right. She spotted the two most expensive objects in the whole collection straight off - two exquisite stone heads I brought back myself from Arabia.'

I had always imagined that his family dealt in old furniture – but of course the shops around St. James's stocked plundered antiquities. He spoke rather differently from how I had recalled at school. He had more poise and confidence; the veneer of adulthood.

'So that explains the fashionable suntan?'

'Oh yes, it's baking in the desert alright.'

'You were in the desert?'

'Four days by camel from Damascus.'

And so it turned out that, while I had had cold adventures, he had experienced hot ones. We enjoyed a long boozy lunch, exchanging tales – although I was more reticent than he was. Drake felt no embarrassment telling me how his Arabian hosts had provided everything a young man could need. I vaguely referred to an affair of the heart. When he pressed for more details, I told him that it was a discreet but passionate liaison with a Russian stage performer. We both agreed that the female sex was best encountered abroad. There was no pussyfooting around with English garden paths and iambic pentameters.

I tried not to devour my lunch like a starving man.

I was, of course, grateful to Drake for this hospitality, but I must admit that by the time we parted, he had started to irk me. He was so smug, and certain that he knew everything there was to know about business, women, and the world. I felt that my experiences had been more profound, but I felt at a disadvantage to him because of the state of my finances.

As I left the club, I thought, 'Well now. If a damn fool like Drake can succeed in business, so can I.'

Chapter Thirteen

I could not put off a visit to my father indefinitely. I feared that when he heard about my Russian failure, I would resume my job in the back office of his firm on the shitty wage of £250 a year. It was a prospect that filled me with despondency, but my empty stomach could hold out no longer. And so I took the train down to Guildford to pay my respects to the cunning old puppet master in his new villa.

He led me through some of the downstairs rooms pointing out objects of art and praising Mrs Crawford's good taste, for it was she who had chosen the Persian carpets, the Ottoman style couches and the huge onyx lamps shaped like urns. The drapes, cushions, and light shades would have done Leon Bakst and the Russian ballet proud.

The smell of fresh paint wafted through the rooms. Occasionally the lunatic sound of a hammer banging up-stairs. The house was full of young and helpful servants, still enthusiastic for their new jobs. Only the butler, Johnson, who had accompanied my father from London, had that cynical and superior air that servants acquire after twenty or thirty years of employment in one household – and he had only worked for my father for seven years. Someone had made up a bloody good fire in the drawing room. We warmed ourselves in front of it and sipped sherry. I spoke of the Russian houses I had seen – in particular Mr Shchukin's. He liked the idea of a businessman who was courted by artists and political types. He would ask Barbara to work on an event that could be held at Munnings Hall as a 'draw.' – 'Perhaps some of your Russian dancers?' he said.

'Perhaps.'

We took a stroll around the grounds. We were quite high up, overlooking a deep rift through the chalky North Downs. I would have said the view was spectacular, but after Russia's vastness, the English countryside was like a pale watercolour – attractive in its own way, but lacking imponderability. I could make out houses and farms wrapped in the mist on the other side of the valley. We could not actually see any other people, but a human presence was to be felt everywhere – not at all as in the Urals, where you sometimes feel like the only person in the world. Not here was there the possibility that your boot might tread on an emerald or an alexandrite that had been lying around for a millennium or two, devoid of any value or significance until it fell under the gaze of a human being – or possibly a magpie.

Only the lonely squawk of a crow reminded me of Russia. A pony looked over the fence of our neighbours' paddock hoping for a pat or a sugar lump. He had learned to expect human kindness. Sheer survival was not his pressing concern.

My father seemed invigorated by the crunch of his footsteps on his new gravel. He was, at last, a man of property and substance – no longer a mere high priest of occult financial rites.

He was in a chatty mood. I was pleased, as all I had to do was to listen and to respond to his meanderings. I could postpone the moment when I would bring up the subject of the mine.

'Something positive has happened to this country recently. Money is finally in fashion,' he declared.

'I never thought that money went out of fashion, Papa.'

'You might just as well say a good pair of female legs never was out of fashion, but until recently they were kept strictly from public view. Now you can see them in every review bar, not to mention on your Russian ballerinas. The same is true for money. Yesterday it was bad form to let on that you had any, unless it had been plundered around the time of the Crusades. In today's world, one can wear one's money openly, even if one has been so vulgar as to earn it oneself.'

When we reached the fountain of Diana the Huntress (which was badly in need of some green slime), we turned round to take in the turreted masonry that was Munnings Hall. At least it was not one of those "Tudor" piles, so beloved of Guildford stockbrokers. Munnings

Hall was solidly classical. The shadowy figures of builders could be seen walking along the balustrades. Unfortunately the new roof had sprung a leak after a recent gale. If you wanted to see Papa's blood boil, all you had to do was ask him about the builders. I avoided the subject, but he brought it up himself.

'Are Russian builders any good? We could ship some over here and give these boys the boot. That would do my soul some good.'

'I was told by a French manager that Russian workers are five times less productive than English or French ones.'

'By God! On that reckoning Munnings Hall wouldn't be finished before Christmas 1920!'

When father had started to build three years previously, the people across the valley had complained that his villa would be a boil on the chalky face of the North Downs. Not long ago, I turned up a cutting from the local newspaper documenting neighbourly hostility at the time. One Doctor Reave is quoted as calling the house a 'Plutonian Hall'. A Mrs Huntington ranted about 'This vulgar age that worships only money.' All work had ground to a halt for eighteen months while various legal actions had passed through the courts concerning various covenants associated with the title of his land. Papa pretended to laugh this sort of frustration off, but we all knew that he longed to own the sort of house that cultivated people are supposed to possess; that was what all those Corinthian pillars were about; it was why Mrs Crawford had been given a blank cheque to pick up bronzes and pieces of porcelain at the auction houses, and the older and more expensive the better; it was why Maples had been sending over a forest of furniture.

Now the house was almost complete. Papa took a lingering gaze at it. 'When this place is finally finished, we'll have the cream of the country down for the weekend. Mark my words we'll have Lloyd George hanging around hoping to pick up a few share tips.'

'What, the Welsh Windbag? I don't think any respectable people will visit if he's here.'

Father grunted his ascent to this political point of view.

'They say he's flogging off honours. He's asking £80,000 for a viscountcy, which is a bit steep if you ask me, but I might give £10,000 for a knighthood. It's a shame to give good money to a bunch of Liberals, but the Tories are yet to put conceit up for sale.'

Back in the house, my father's mistress ambushed me with a peck on the cheek. Just one, of course, but it took me quite unawares. I think she was laying claim to be family. Mrs Crawford was wearing broad trousers that almost looked like a skirt and had a silk scarf wrapped around her head. She was naturally elegant. I speculated that Vera would get on with her, in the far-fetched eventuality that they might ever meet up. We followed her into the half-finished dining room for a lunch of oysters and champagne. Papa had supplies of both sent down from Leadenhall Market, packed in ample ice. In my age of innocence, I had wondered why oysters were supposed to be a food of love, but that day they brought to mind quivering, salty coupling. While we ate I had a fairly graphic mental picture of my father alone with Mrs Crawford. At my father's prompting, the three of us chinked our champagne flutes.

'Well cheer-oh!' he said.

At school, my housemaster had said it was the height of vulgarity to clink glasses and, even more damnable, it was middle class. But I was gratified to have my glass clinked. It was Papa's concession that his son had graduated, finally, from the nursery. What Mrs Crawford made of my father's table manners in general, I never fathomed.

I did my best to describe my Russian experiences: the glittering crosses above the Moscow skyline; the gypsy singers; the reckless sleigh drivers. My account was, of course, the Bowdlerised version. When speaking to parents, one leaves out all the important bits. The last thing you want is for them to start up a cross examination about your love life. My father said:

'George found time for more than just sightseeing. He met up with a young lady.'

What gossip had the old man got hold of? Had his clairvoyant spied on Vera and me in her crystal ball? Mrs Crawford was all ears. I felt she was looking at me and seeing a youthful and more virile version of my oyster-sucking father. But I quickly regained my composure. He was obviously flying a kite, as they say. It is an old trick for bouncing the truth out of someone – to pretend that you know it already. My reply was to blush like a schoolgirl and to fiddle with my napkin. I think Mrs Crawford found my embarrassment rather sweet. She said:

'Russia always brings such romantic ideas into one's head. I'd wager that your eye caught a Countess Olga or a Princess Vera while you were out there.'

My heart missed a beat at the mention of the name. No, she could not possibly know anything about my Vera. It was a common English conception that all Russian women went by the name of 'Olga' or 'Vera'.

Papa wiped his mouth with his napkin.

'My son's not one to fall for a phoney foreign title. A little bird told me that she's English, by the name of Lydia.... Is your old father right, or is he right?'

'Wrong... and right. Lydia Hawthorne is just a friend.' I presumed that he was prefixing her name with 'Lady' because of his rum sense of humour. Perhaps he meant that she was well bred.

'More's the pity,' said father, 'I've heard she's a good looking young woman.'

'It would be ungallant to deny it. So, which little bird told you, mistakenly, about Lydia and me?'

'Quite a big bird actually; her father. He telephoned me to say that he was interested in taking part in our Russian project. I was a little surprised that our interest in frozen prairies had leaked out, and he told me all about how his daughter had met up with my one and only son in the Urals and had seen a placer mine with priceless gems lying around waiting to be picked up. I fancied that Lord Hawthorne considered our families to be as good as joined, or perhaps I was a bit too quick out of the starting gate?'

'A bit of a false start. But is she really the daughter of a Lord?'

'Certainly. I don't see why the old fox should pretend to be her father if he wasn't.'

'I hate to disappoint you father, but I'm afraid that your information is not quite accurate on a couple of accounts.'

But he would not quite believe me. Shortly afterwards he proposed another toast of bubbly to 'the younger generation.' Mrs Crawford gave me a sly look. I think she wanted to believe that I was practically engaged to Lydia too. I wondered if she was planning on coming to the wedding, and if so, in what capacity.

After lunch, we went into my father's library. The ancient head of the Syrian merchant that she had found in Drake's antique shop had settled on the side table. His was a proud face with a well-trimmed beard and shrewd eyes.

'Do you like him? Barbara says he looks a bit like me,' said Papa. 'While you are over there, would you mind fetching that box of cigars?'

We settled into two new shiny armchairs.

I did my best to explain to my father that my enquiries had revealed that the land was 'dead.' He dismissed the reports as 'rumours put about by a rival. We had a geological survey which we had received in good faith, and which was of greater credibility than any local gossip.

'But Anatoly Mizinsky as good as admitted to me that it was a hoax. Naturally he's very aggrieved that his family sold the valuable part of the land to foreign investors, and now he wants to get some money back.'

'But he did not actually say to you that the land was 'dead' as you put it?'

'Not in so many words.'

'And Lady Lydia knows everything that was said?'

'She was there throughout, and she's no fool, even if she is a bit eccentric.'

Father lit his and my cigars. It was the first time we had ever smoked together like this. He settled back and thought. Eventually he leant over and said to me in that mellifluous voice of his:

'If Lord Hawthorne comes to Angel Munnings and says, "What's this about your Russian project? I hear from a good source that it's worth a fortune?" Angel Munnings doesn't say, "I'm afraid that you are sadly mistaken," he says, "It's so promising that I'm planning to keep it all for myself, but since you've been so good as to take an interest, let's meet up and talk about it. Who knows? We might find some other project to work on together. Or perhaps there will be a big demand from the shareholders to take a bet on Siberia. Let's see how it turns out.'

My father knew so much more about these things than I did. I supposed that he must be right. I am afraid that I had more pressing concerns of the financial kind, namely another letter had arrived from the manager of the bank. I seized the opportunity to mention that my Russian trip had not been cheap, what with the expedition to Siberia, hiring sleighs, winter equipment, translators. Oh yes, and entertaining Lady Lydia, making sure that she had every comfort on the journey.

The important thing was that, before I left, he wrote out a cheque for £250 in my favour, 'to be getting on with.' I was out of trouble for the time being.

I sank into the calf leather of Papa's Rolls. Mrs Crawford sat with a straight back on the other side of the seat and waved to my father as we crawled up the drive. He blew us – presumably her in particular – a kiss.

'Such a dear man, your father,' she said.

Of course I had to agree, and it was true that he was treating me less negligently than he had ever done before. I had been expecting to rattle back to London on the train. He had been thoughtful enough to suggest that I wait a little while longer, and travel back in the Rolls with Mrs Crawford. It was quite unlike him, at least as far as his relations with me were concerned.

The road took us along the foot of Box Hill. It was good country for picnics and kite flying – two occupations which seemed to sum up my Papa's approach to life. I wondered about Mrs Crawford. She was undoubtedly his posh doxy – but did she really love him for his open-heartedness? Open-handedness more like. I knew almost nothing about her. Who was Mr Crawford? Was he dead, divorced, or merely cuckolded? These were questions too delicate for direct enquiry. And so I was none the wiser when she dropped me off at Sussex Gardens and continued her journey to Mayfair.

Chapter Fourteen

The 'gulls' – as private investors are sometimes referred to by those who work in the City - flocked into the ballroom of the Cannon Street Hotel – a room badly in want of the warmth of an orchestra and the dazzle of diamonds. Some flowers might have helped, but there were none. Instead, there were banners and posters bearing phrases such as: 'Gold From Guinea' and 'Nil Desperandum .'[16]

The truth that they all read in the newspapers was that their company was in a bad way. There was anger showing in some of the ruddy, bug-eyed faces, but no self-knowledge or self-blame that I could discern. They did not for a moment think that their own greed or folly or lack of good judgement had led them to lose their money down a faraway hole in the ground.

When I had seen father in his London office, I had expressed one or two 'moral qualms' about the Russian venture. He had told me that everything he did was always checked and double checked by lawyers. This did not entirely satisfy me.

'You are quite right to think about the interests of the shareholders,' he said, patting me on the back as I stood up to leave. 'I never forget them, which is why I have such loyal following among the investing public. I've looked after them over the years, and they've stuck by me. One of the companies I look after needs a new departure, and the timing of your Russian find is most fortunate – it will attract new money into the business and keep it alive for a few more years. Believe me, staying in the fight is half the battle.'

---

[16] "Never Despair." The share promoter Horatio Bottomley actually named one of his companies with this Latin tag.

He wanted me to come witness an 'extraordinary general meeting' of a company that had run into a 'spot of bother.' I would see how he always made sure that things turned 'alright in the end, come what may.'

The board of directors of New Guinea Gold Mining PLC took their places on the orchestral dais. The chairman – my father – looked relaxed and refreshed by his breakfast of champagne and kippers. He wore a colourful buttonhole. I sat in the front row of the audience. The man next to me said, 'I hope this bunch of scallywags get what-for today. I sunk ten thousand down this particular orifice.'

Of course many of the people in the room must have seen through his very thin veneer of social polish. They must have regarded him as an 'upstart.' But perhaps they calculated that a man who has made his own money probably knows a thing or two.

There was nothing that I could see in my father's looks that had contributed to his name 'Angel.' If anything, his broad frame and shambling walk reminded one of a cart horse. You had to hear him speak in public to understand why people were willing to believe that there was something divinely inspired about him. His own father – Munnings the Grocer – had been a lay preacher on Sundays. Both his sons had inherited his gift for oratory, Frederick going into politics and Gabriel into business. My father's voice was rich and naturally melodious, almost honeyed. He had an actor's knack of being able to speak without any discernible effort and yet be audible at the back of the hall. It was indeed like hearing an 'angel' singing in your cockleshell about wealth and dividends and fabulous fortunes. And at other times, when he pulled out the stops on his vocal organ, he had real power.

The stenographer's account of the speech my father made that day was among the papers which have come down to me. I use it here to reconstruct most of what he said:

'Gentlemen, after a brief and, one might say, brilliant, career, I think it is fair to say that the progress of your company has been somewhat rudely interrupted.

'During the year 1913, a year of some considerable depression in the mining market, your company made a loss of some £112,121, 17s 5d.'

'I trust that no one here today is unaware of the speculative nature of our enterprise. I think it is fair to say that we directors have risked drowning you in caveats and warnings from the outset.

A cry of 'Swindler' from the back of the hall is met by 'Sit down, you ass' from the front. A man stands up and says, 'Don't slander 'Angel' Munnings; he's one of England's finest.' 'Angel' Munnings thanks the gentleman for his kind words before continuing.

'I will not be party to a misrepresentation of the true state of affairs. Therefore I must inform you in no uncertain terms that, if we continue along the road we are now travelling, our journey will end sooner rather than later, at the door of the liquidator.'

An uneasy murmur spreads around the room. Someone shouts 'Shame!' and this time nobody contradicts him. 'Angel' Munnings's expression is grave, but determined. His voice grows in vigour.

'If you bear with me, you will soon understand that sombre danger is not the only prospect which lies in wait for your company. Far from it! If, at this juncture, we set ourselves in a new direction, on the path of opportunity, we may yet see happier days.'

But first some other business.

It is my sad duty to announce the resignation from the board of Major John Latherton. Major Latherton has provided us with three years of immaculate service, but some of you may have read in the newspapers of his present difficulties at another venture totally unconnected with this one. I hope that you will join me and my fellow directors in saying that we have always found him to be, and should be very surprised to find him anything else than, an officer and a gentleman!'

Polite applause.

'As it says in the Bible, out of the sadness of partings, comes forth strength. It is my honour to bring before you today, for your approval, a nominee for election to the position of director of our company.

He is a man of the highest profile and the most impeccable curriculum vitae; he is man whose association with our company will surely give the highest hopes to all those gathered here today – he is none other than the esteemed chairman of Ledermans' Bank, Lord Hawthorne of Malden.

"Hear, Hear!" Followed by thunderous applause and even some cheers from the back. My father indicates for calm with his hand, and his baritone voice soars above the dying embers of the audience's clamour.

'How is it? - Yes how can it be? - You may well be asking yourselves - that a man who has the pick of directorships; a man whose wealth, renown and integrity would open any door for him in the City of London, is joining the board of our company at this troubled hour in its career? Let me now lay the reason before you. We, the directors, have been assiduously applying ourselves these past weeks to a rescue plan. It is a plan which, if it meets with success, as I believe it is certain to do, will completely overcome the difficulties we face today.'

'Indeed, I for one would go a step further, and promise you an early and handsome dividend! One that would satisfy the most avaricious among you!'

Bravo! Hear-hear/!

'Only the natural caution and prudence of my fellow directors holds me back from making such a commitment at this juncture.

'Those of you with long memories will recall that in the year 1894, I was at the forefront of the Westralian mining boom. My friends, for I hope I may call you thus, I confidently predict that by this time next year we will find ourselves at the zenith of the Siberian mining Boom of 1915!

'We have an infallible channel of communication with that frozen part of the world – none other than my own son, George Munnings, who has spent these past six months prospecting in a region as rich in precious minerals as it is in snow and ice. He has identified a property at a bargain price that is ripe for development.'

My father beams and holds out his hand in my direction. As the youngest individual in the room, I cannot hide the fact that I am this man's progeny. I have been ambushed. The reference to myself and Russia has come as a complete surprise to me.

My neighbour, who earlier called the directors 'scallywags,' says to me, 'I only wish my son would go off and dig up a fortune somewhere.'

'The aforementioned property is rich in a mineral that is unique to Russia – a stone that is named after the late Tsar, his Majesty Alexander II. This priceless gem is so rare that some of you may not even be familiar with it. The fact which I put before you is this: one carat of Russian alexandrite sells on the market for two and half times the price of one carat of the finest South African diamond.

'My fellow investors, I humbly thank you for your kind and courteous attention. Let me leave you with this thought. Opportunities such as this come but once or twice in a lifetime.'

Loud applause

One of the many 'details' which my father omitted to mention to investors was that their company was to undergo what is known in the City as a 'restructuring': they would be asked to stump up money for an issue of new shares in their own company. He planned to raise £250,000 from the 'gulls.' After the company's debts had been paid off (mostly in the form of directors' bonuses and back pay), £150,000 or so would be left over for the purchase. All this came out only later.

There were one or two dissident speakers at the meeting, but the formal vote on the restructuring plan was destined to go my father's way. He had settled the matter with the largest shareholders – the ones that really counted - over oysters and champagne – two days earlier.

Chapter Fifteen

"It is maintained, for instance, that a lack of civilization in Russia, as compared with Western Europe, hampers trade relations with Great Britain, and renders it difficult, if not impossible, for foreign merchants and capitalists to conduct business operations within the limits of the empire of the Tsar."

Introduction by Baron Alphonse Heyking, Imperial Russian consul-General London in

The Russian Year Book for 1911 compiled and Edited by Howard P Kennard MD Eyre and Spottiswoode Ltd. 1911.

In those far off days, before we Europeans made a habit of machine-gunning one another, you could travel almost the entire breadth of the continent without once being troubled for your papers, but once you reached the Russian Empire, different conditions applied.[17] Anatoly had once quoted to me a phrase of Gogol - "a Russian without his papers does not exist" – or words to that effect. At the frontier station of Alexandrovo, rail-passengers had to descend from the train with their luggage, the contents of which was subject to a thorough examination. The customs officials were on the lookout for printed matter and even balls of newspaper used as padding were regarded with suspicion. On my first trip, I had found the whole process tedious, but I had not encountered any serious obstacle. On this occasion, I had a feeling that the officer had picked me out for trouble. He laboriously examined the articles of association for our newly founded limited company, turning the pages

---

[17] "No Single obstacle has had more influence in deterring tourist traffic to Russia than the passport bogie." – The Tourist's Russia. (a visa was also required). "If a passport is not in order, its unhappy owner has to re-cross the frontier, the train by which he came waiting for this purpose." – Baedeker.

to see if any seditious or pornographic material lay concealed within the covers. Disappointed in that quest, he pointed to Tatters (short for Tatiana), my Dalmatian pup. I had brought her, you see, as a present for Vera. A spotty dog had been her request during that very first dinner in the Metropole.

'Tshhh.' he said.

'I'm sorry. Is anything the matter with my dog?'

'Forbidden!'

I pointed to the customs form:

Articles not permitted for import
Munitions of war, explosive materials, daggers etc.
Firearms having the same bore as the military rifle
Playing cards of all kinds
Berries of the cocculus indicus variety
Margarine products
Artificial saffron
Bengal lights
Articles implying disrespect for sacred things
Wallpaper covered with arsenical colouring matter
Tickets for foreign lotteries

'No mention of dogs,' I emphasised.

His face was stony, unchangeable, and official.

My heart sunk. I did not relish the prospect of turning round and taking Tatters back to England – a journey of one and half days. My father, if he found out that my business trip had been delayed because of a lady friend and a dog, would be unlikely to be sympathetic. And so I demanded to see the officer's 'superior'. He did not seem to understand the word, and I flung a few others at him: 'Chief, Generalissimo, Imperator, Capitan...' He looked bemused and said, in a perfect English accent:

'I will ask if he will see you.'

While I was waiting for him to telephone the top-man, a French woman passenger told me with a sad face that I could 'kiss goodbye to my dog.' Madame Durran had lived in England with her diplomatist husband, and had picked up some idiomatic phrases. She explained that the only possible solution for me now would be to offer an immense bribe to the customs chief, for once he set eyes on a valuable animal, he would want to confiscate it.

'You should have asked the British delegation to send the dog in the diplomatic bag.'

'I don't think they would have obliged.'

'Then next time you must depend on France. My husband is M. Durran, the consul in Moscow. He will be honoured to assist you. There is so much corruption in Rosie. It is not like France, or England. They are very primitive.'

My wallet already felt lighter as I led Tatters down the corridor in search of the customs chief. I resolved that if the occasion called for it, I would not shrink from bribery and corruption, after all when in Rome… It would take courage, but it would also be another stop on the way to a mature accommodation with the ways of the world.

I was admitted into the chief's office. Canine claws scrambled on the wooden floor as Tatters strained on the leash, trying to rush over and greet, with nuzzle and tongue, the man who would send her back across the frontier. I hoped that he was a dog lover. First impressions were favourable. He was certainly more elegantly turned out than his surly underling, and spoke English with a polished accent:

'My officer is correct to say that livestock cannot enter the Russian Empire without official papers from the Ministry of Agriculture.'

'She's a dog, not a sheep.'

'Even so, she is still alive.'

'She has a passport.' I handed him an envelope containing her pedigree document – not because I naïvely hoped that he would be satisfied by any old official looking piece of paper – but because I thought he might be encouraged by a small gift that I had slipped alongside it. My attempt at corruption was in vein: he took out the pedigree while carefully ignoring the banknote.

'I am afraid that this paper is not legal in Russia. It has not been stamped by our Consul in London. But as you are an English gentleman, I will be honoured to assist in this matter. You may leave the animal in my personal care. You will collect her on your return to England.'

The dog, of course, was far more valuable than my 'gift', and I was convinced that I would not see her again once I had left her in the hands of a venal bureaucrat.

'It is a most kind offer,' I said, 'but she's a present for a lady who lives in Moscow.'

'I am sorry. I can do no more. The rules are the rules, as I believe you say in England.' He handed back the envelope.

I felt like Petrushka imprisoned in his box. On a return trip to Covent Garden, I had seen Nijinsky dance the tragic part of a wooden puppet, frustrated in his desire for a doll-ballerina (Karsavina). At the end of the dance, Petrushka flayed his arms in the air in gawky frustration and anguish, and now I wanted to do the same. I could see no option but to accept the official's offer and to leave Tatters behind. It was hard indeed to turn my back and walk out of the room without her. She trusted me so implicitly. When another being plants his or her faith in you, strong feelings of responsibility take root. I won't describe here her big mournful eyes and her little whines as I left her – for fear of overdoing the sentimental pathos of the situation, but please believe me I did feel truly terrible. I turned round at the door and asked:

'You couldn't make an exception? Just the once? I would be most grateful.'

I do not think I would have lowered myself to pleading, had it not been for Vera and Tatters. I must have had a very pained expression. The man thought for a moment:

'Mr Munnings. Another plan has come to my mind. Please be so kind as to sit down again. What you must do, sir, is this – you must sign a declaration that you intend to take the animal with you when you leave. By this you agree that you are not importing her. Then I can let her through. You will give the dog to the Russian lady friend. When you return, you will sign a declaration that the animal has, unfortunately, died, while you were in Russia. It would be as well if you could take a certificate from a surgeon to confirm this unfortunate event. I think your Russian friends will help find a kind animal doctor who will write what you require.'

Two trains were waiting on either side of the platform – the one on which we had arrived, which was heading back for Ottlotschin in Prussia, and the other continuing on for Warsaw, Minsk, Smolensk, and Moscow. [18] I boarded the Russian train with a feeling of triumph. When I met Madame Durran in the corridor she said:

'How much did you pay him?'

'Nothing,' I replied chirpily

'That is most extraordinary. You are very fortunate. Perhaps he was an Anglophile, like my husband. He will do anything for an English gentleman.'

As the train pulled out, Tatters sat on the opposite berth to mine, which I had booked for her at some expense to the firm, and I said: 'Well now, my dear dog. Your owner is not so lacking in powers of gentle persuasion after all. Perhaps I can put them to good use in the sphere of commerce. Here, have a biscuit.'

---

[18] The Russian rails were set on a wider gauge than in Europe, forcing a change of carriages at the frontier stations of Alexandrovo on the Moscow route and Wirballen on the way to St. Petersburg.

Chapter Sixteen

I had feared that the management of the Metropole Hotel might kick up a fuss about a Dalmatian dog with the potential to imprint muddy paw marks on the marble, jump up at the guests in the lift and leave black and white hairs on the bed spread – but nobody so much as noticed her as I registered at the front desk of the hotel, unless it was to pat her head or to admire her.

It was perhaps quarter of an hour after I had moved into my new room that the telephone rang. I was expecting to hear Anatoly who had failed to meet me at the station. But it was a female voice and the old rigmarole about whether Monsieur would be wanting a 'special service' that evening? 'I won't be needing that again,' I thought to myself as I put the receiver down.

I had a good idea that Anatoly would turn up sooner or later that evening. I imagined that he would bring Vera with him, and perhaps even Nina. I could see the look of delight on Vera's face – that pretty 'o' of her mouth as she took in the canine present with her green eyes. We could eat in the great dining hall of the Metropole, as on that first evening. Perhaps Vera would insist on bringing Tatters to our private 'kabinet' and spoiling her with titbits. These were the ideas turning through my mind as I lay on the bed and waited with a growing sense of anticipation.

I recognised Anatoly's knock on the door, and soon I was being subjected to bristly kisses which I could have done without. But Anatoly was alone. It was he who immediately made friends with an excited Tatters, play-fighting with her and ruffling her ears. Looking up, he remarked that I never travelled without 'a pretty companion.' I explained the dog was a present for Vera.

'Ah yes, my friend, Vera.' He said. Then he repeated, 'Vera, Vera, Vera.' He sat down on the chair, a big hand preventing the dog from jumping up, and he looked at me with an earnest face, as if he was trying to prepare me for some news of trouble. I said,

'I do hope that she's not caused you any inconvenience while I've been away.'

'No, no. Nothing like that. But we have been worried for her safety.' She had, he explained, simply disappeared. She had been living with Nina, staying out to Lord knows what time in the morning and finally, about two weeks ago, not returning home at all. She had vanished, 'just like that.' He snapped his figure and thumb as he said this. I shook my head in disbelief. 'I feel sorrow for you,' he said. 'But it has turned out that she is true to her breed. People do not change any more easily than animals. Take this black and white dog of yours. She is bred to be a domestic dog, chiefly a decorative dog. You can try to train your pretty companion, you can beg her, you can plead with her, you can bribe her with all sorts of delicacies, but she will never be a guard dog to scare away trespassers. You might as well ask her to change her spots to green or purple: she can no more change her nature. Women are the same.'

I no longer found my friend's insights into the 'sex question' quite as profound as I once did.

'And Nina? What does she think happened?'.

'I am afraid that she has gone too. Or more accurately, she has found a richer sponsor with a bigger and more luxurious apartment. So you see, we are both in the same boat.' For a few moments, Anatoly looked away and was lost in thought.

As we went out and walked along the corridor to the lift, he put his arm around me. I was glad that nobody was coming the other way. We dined in somewhat low spirits.

Before I retired to bed, I took Tatters for a little turn around the fountains of Theatre Square. I gazed over to the side on which the Bolshoi Theatre stood. Down a street I could see the spire of the department store where I had bought shoes and gloves for Vera. I wondered who was buying presents for her now.

'Well Vera, my girl,' I said out loud, 'You won't have your spotted dog after all. Tatters is mine now. At least she will always be faithful.'

I went to bed drunk and depressed.

This was the time of my disillusion with Moscow. The city was both familiar and strange at the same time, like one of those dreams that keep on returning in a slightly different form. Now, instead of the golden domes and the pink and yellow merchants' palaces, I noticed the unmade roads, the wooden sidewalks, and the man outside the Bolshoi Theatre selling pornographic postcards. I caught the last few flecks of snow of the winter, but after they had melted, a greyness washed over the streets. The population, once so exotic in their great variety of costumes, now seemed like actors in a play that had run for too many weeks.

Even the beautiful Metropole was tainted for me, especially in the evenings. I could not enter into its debauched spirit. The endless parade of women arriving in the great dining hall was still a one of the wonders of the Eastern world – but there was now a feeling a dread in my soul. I expected to catch sight of Vera on the arm of a man, as I had once done early on in my acquaintance with her. In the lift, I simply closed my eyes because I did not wish to see her. I thought of going upstairs to the women's boudoir to ask for news of her – but frankly I did not want to hear the answer, less still to find her there again, waiting for custom.

I would have been very lonely indeed had it not been for the young Dalmatian who, as I turned the key in the door to my room, would jump off the bed (I heard the thump of her paws), and who would do a little dance as I came in, licking my hand, and even my face if I was not careful. It is very hard not feel your spirits uplifted at such a joyous welcome. She was the best sort of companion in my condition, because I could not discuss my sorrows with her, and thereby indulge them. I would take her for walks two or three times a day in the Alexander Gardens beneath the walls of the Kremlin, but when I left her alone in the room, I always felt guilty as I pushed her nuzzle back into the room and closed the door. I do not know if she howled while I was away. I did not receive any complaints from my neighbours.

As far as work was concerned, one of my first priorities was to obtain for a licence for a British company to carry out business on the territory of the Russia Empire. Campbell-Fitzgerald, the vice-consul, was helping me to find a reliable lawyer to make all the necessary applications. On paper, should have been a straightforward procedure, but it practice, as is always the case, it was more time consuming and bothersome than you might have thought from reading the 'bible' of doing business in Russia.[19]

The company that I was representing was called Precious Gems of Russia Ltd, which had been formed by my father and Lord Hawthorne for the specific purpose of acquiring the Mizinsky land. I had come to Moscow armed with the following proposal: that the Mizinsky family relinquish the ownership of their 'mine' in return for twenty five per cent of the shares of Precious Gems. In the next manoeuvre, New Guinea Mining PLC (whose general meeting I had attended in London) would buy Precious Gems for a sum not far shy of £150,000. As its main sphere of operation would then move from New Guinea to Russia, it would then change its name to something more fitting to its new purpose.

My father and Lord Hawthorne had adorned the board of Precious Gems with a Knight of the Garter, a Rear Admiral and a smattering of names well known in the City of London, including my father's old friend, Horatio Bottomley MP, who was known as an expert in corporate 'reconstructions.' These persons had been chosen,

---

[19] "A request for foreign company to carry out business on Russian soil, and conditions on which such a request can be granted are determined by Government Authority, and are not directly provided for by the law. As a rule, if no special privileges are asked for, this permission is easily obtained. The Request must be presented in writing to the Department of the Minister for Trade and Industry, or to the Trade Section of that Department. It must be accompanied by a copy of Company's articles, a declaration of their validity from the Consulate, and by a Russian translation confirmed by sworn affidavit." - The Russian Year Book for 1911.

not for their financial acumen, but for their reassuring credentials. It was felt that the shareholders of New Guinea Mining PLC might baulk at buying a mine directly from some unknown Russians.

It had taken me a while to understand the reasoning behind the scheme, but now I saw it all from every angle with absolute clarity: the shareholders of New Guinea Gold Mining PLC would struggle to find any individual responsible for their next misfortune. They would not find a single piece of paper with my father's signature on it. Indeed, the personal interests of my father and Lord Hawthorne in Precious Gems of Russia Limited were hidden within an impenetrable maze of nominees, trusts and international holdings. The board of directors of both companies could say perfectly truthfully that they had no way of knowing with 100 per cent accuracy what lay beneath the ground in Siberia. No doubt, the Mizinskies would be blamed. It seemed unlikely that a British law suit would reach them in Moscow, but if it did, they could point to their elusive geologist who was far away behind the Ural Mountains, or even better, to Alexander Mizinsky, who was safely within the borne from which no man returns. If anyone recalled my involvement, I could blame the inexperience of youth and say that I had been badly let down and deceived; besides which, I was not personally a party to the transaction (thank God!). I was little more than the messenger boy, and I just hoped that everybody concerned remembered the adage, 'Don't shoot the messenger.'

I tried to imagine an enterprise where men work all day turning over the earth and never finding anything of value. Back then, it struck me as futile and dispiriting – but as I write now, from the perspective of hindsight and four years of trench warfare, an empty mine seems to be one of the world's lesser evils. After millions of men dug up or blew up a good chunk of Northern France and Flanders for no particular point, other than to create a giant cemetery, we learned that governments and generals have an almost infinite capacity to organise and compel futility. The harm that businesses do is on a far smaller scale, and there is no denying that, while the fantasy lasts, there is a community of people – managers, workers, suppliers and even some of the shareholders - which benefit from an enterprise with no economic point to it, and Russia has profited from many similar undertakings.[20] When it all collapses, of course, everyone has to think again, but men of resilient character just move onto the next project: in much the same way that a disappointed lover moves onto the next object of desire.

While we were waiting for the lawyers and the bureaucrats to complete the formalities, I had to remain in Moscow. During this period, Anatoly introduced me to the ritual of the Russian baths or 'banya', in which one strips and steams before plunging into an ice cold pool. While in the hot room, a helpful friend lightly flagellates your back with a small bundle of birch twigs. Strange though it might seem, the birch is quite pleasurable, for when you are so steamed up that you feel like your skin is a hot flannel, the dried leaves send little globules of sensation travelling across your back , confirming to you that you are still alive. Surviving a banya is a feat of endurance, but at the end of it you feel enormously relaxed and cleansed, both physically and mentally.

---

[20] See, for comparison, the Russian oil industry: "The effect of English capital has been to stimulate and inspire energy into the industry; and, far from financiers taking money from the country, they have invested more than £6,500,00 in Russian oil, a great deal of which will never be recovered, and it is doubtful whether more than a small proportion will ever pay a profitable return on account of the high prices paid for partially exhausted grounds." The Oil Fields of Russia by A Beeby Thomson, A.M.I. Mech. E, Late Chief Engineer and manager of the European Petroleum Company's Russian Oil Properties. London Crosby Lockwood And Son, 1904.

In between bouts of hot vapours, we wrapped ourselves in sheets and sat on oak pews drinking light Lithuanian beer. We talked, as men do, about the joys and sorrows of contact with the opposite sex. Anatoly informed me that he had been using a discreet and exclusive 'service' that procured respectable women: educated and married as a rule, but hard up for pin-money. It was entirely safe, he said, both from the point of view of hygiene and the maintenance of an uncomplicated life. Even I would be hard pushed to become entangled under such an arrangement. Every time that we met for 'banya', he urged me to try the service for myself and, I must confess that, on one occasion, I did.

The assignation was to take place in a room overlooking Malaya Nikitskaya Street. I had been given the key, and I let myself in. The only furniture was a bed, a chair, and a dressing table. There were utensils for washing, making tea, and taking a pee. A touch of pale colour was provided by dwarf daffodils, already wilting. I stood looking through the window, spying out women walking up the street, and wondering which of them was coming to me. I had been told that she would be fair, twenty-nine years old, and 'musical'. The knock on the door came forty-five minutes late. The expression on the lady's face was business-like as she removed her hat and gloves. I helped her to take her coat off.

'Chai?' I offered – pointing to the samovar and the tea .

'Nyet.'

She was rather more mousy than fair, but had she permitted a smile or some sort of expression to flicker across her face, she might have been pretty. She was long and slender, her cheekbones were high and broad, and her nose was rather sweetly turned. A bit of Mongol had definitely introduced himself into her family a few centuries back.

She turned away so that I could help her with her buttons on the back of her dress. Then I undid my shirt and shivered. We clambered onto the bed and she laid her head to one side on the pillow. I felt her breasts, more out of curiosity than passion, and since that was what we were both there to do, started to make sex to her. Afterwards she lay still for a few minutes, before getting up to make a pee in the chamber pot. I had never seen a woman do this before, and closed my eyes, but I could not block out the sound. Then she mixed hot water from the samovar with cold from the jug and washed herself in the brass basin. When she was dressed, I handed her the fee and thanked her, and she left.

It is an inevitable rule of life that the more you pay, the less you receive. I was twenty roubles poorer, had wasted an afternoon, and felt as weak as I did after the steam baths, without any of the benefits - the relaxed limbs, healthy glow and appetite for a good meal. The woman probably did not feel any better, but at least she had my roubles in her purse.

On my listless way home, I found myself behind the elegant back of another woman. A fox scarf was entwined around her shoulders. I wondered if her face was young and beautiful. She turned to visit a little white walled church with a blue copula. I followed her inside. On the way in, I bought three candles from a babushka who had positioned herself near the door. My kopek coins clattered into her tin. The price of a prayer was next to nothing, and servicing the soul was certainly less costly than attending to the flesh. Inside, I would have liked to have sat on a pew and held my head in my hands, but Russian churches have standing room only, even for old ladies with swollen legs, let alone the young and healthy. In a dark corner, a policeman was crossing himself before a blackened icon that depicted the one saint whom I easily recognised: St. George putting paid to a lizard-like dragon. I looked over to the other side of the church where the woman I had seen out on the street was now kneeling before an icon. I stationed myself by a pillar where I could gain a better sight of her. Her complexion was white and pink and her nose had a glossy shine. Blond hair fell in ringlets from beneath her hat. She looked innocent - almost like a Russian doll. She must have been about nineteen. She was praying before an ancient image of a Christ with dark eyes and long girlish lashes. I could not help wondering if she found the image before her sexually attractive. Was she a virgin? I checked myself. The afternoon's experience had poisoned my spirit. If the Almighty could police our thoughts anywhere, it was here with all his saints listening in. I went back to St. George. My patron saint had become available for supplication. First I asked him to slay the cold-blooded dragon in my heart. Whatever else happened, I did not want to grow into an old Anatoly, or still worse, my own father. Then I asked him to rescue Vera, wherever she was, and to bring her back to me.

I suppose that I was becoming a familiar sight to guests and staff as I walked out of the Metropole with my dog on the lead. People would often stoop to pat her head, and I had a struggle on my hands to prevent her leaping up with her paws. One morning there was a woman coming toward me whom I recognised. She was the striking redhead whom I had almost purchased on my previous trip: a 'colleague' of Vera's. The last time I had seen her had been up in the ladies' 'boudoir' on the sixth floor. This time she was rather better covered. Although her face did not look quite so unused by daylight, she certainly cut a figure with her magnificent proportions preceding before her. She had a haughty step as she came across the foyer, and you might have thought that she was at home in her own mansion. She seemed to recognise me too, and she stooped to give Tatters a pat. I tried to tell her – in my extremely limited Russian – that the animal was a present for Vera. She touched my arm and looked surprisingly concerned:

She said 'Vera', and then a word which I could not understand. She repeated the phrase and looked around to see if anybody nearby knew English. I pulled out an English/Russian pocket sized dictionary. She thumbed through the pages, but it became clear that the alphabet was not her strong suit. Fortunately a gentleman who happened to be passing by helped us out. He did not speak English, but he found the definition:

Propást: To perish

I was stunned: 'You mean she is dead?'

Oksana – for that was her name - shrugged her shoulders.

Taking the dictionary back I stared at the page. For a few seconds, my eyes did not see anything more than a blur. Everything in the hotel lobby fell silent. But gradually the letters took form. I realised that there was a second definition:

To disappear.

The difference was more than mere semantics. But all I could get out of Oksana was a 'Maybe.' I thanked her and continued on my way out. I walked with Tatters almost empty of thoughts. I had not yet got over my shock. But at least I had ceased to worry about bumping into Vera. On the contrary, I glanced at every passing woman's face, almost to the point of rudeness, hoping to catch sight of the definitive proof that she had not 'perished.'

Chapter Seventeen

One could surely be forgiven for assuming, as I did, that the Mizinsky family would have been counting themselves remarkably fortunate. I had returned to Moscow to make them a generous offer for their land which they knew to be practically worthless. But they were far from jumping with joy; indeed, they seemed remarkably cool. The land had been Julia's dowry. Her name appeared on the title deeds and her assent for the transaction was required. She was having second thoughts.

When we met over the dining room table of the their apartment, I did my best to explain the transaction to the lady – how the Mizinskies would exchange their land for shares in Precious Gems of Russia Limited and how these shares would soon be cashed when the company sold itself. Julia listened and nodded. She looked surprisingly business-like, almost frighteningly so.

'Without any disrespect to you or your father,' she said firmly, 'It might be imprudent to give this land to a foreign company in return for paper shares, but no money. We are far away in Moscow. It is difficult for us to judge whether the gentlemen who sit on the board will honour their obligation to us.'

I felt rising irritation. Here we were discussing the ins and outs of a polite fiction. Everyone concerned knew this, but did not say so. No doubt my father would have charmed the good lady and reassured her with his bonhomie, and perhaps he would have dropped a rye hint that we all perfectly understood the true state of affairs about the real prospects for the 'mine.' But I was not my father.

The young Madame Mizinsky frowned and looked almost annoyed as I tried to explain yet again about a limited company selling itself to a public company listed on the stock market. Anatoly started to speak to her in Russian. I could see that he was using his charm, but that his wife was impervious to it.

'I would not wish our family name to be traded on the stock market like Circassian horses,' she replied abruptly.

We both assured her that use of companies made her involvement more, not less, anonymous. She fiddled impatiently with the alexandrite ring which she had slipped off her hand. It was getting on in the day and the electric lights had been lit. The stone glowed crimson.

I was making no headway with the lady, and I was starting to feel angry. Quite frankly, I no longer cared if the Mizinsky tribe passed by this opportunity. In some ways it would suit me if they did, as I would be able to wash my hands of the whole business. I would return to London with no contract but with a clear conscience. On the other hand, I saw that if I had no stomach for helping my father in his business, I would have to find a job elsewhere. The only place to start my career would be at the bottom, and the climb to the top would be long and tedious. The family leg-up was a big attraction. One day, I would be in charge, and then I could look for worthy projects to finance. I might even leave my mark on the world. So in short, I was in two minds about whether or not I wanted this deal to go through. I would just see how things turned out, and let fate decide my next move. I think Anatoly understood my state of mind, even if his wife did not.

'Madam,' I said, defiantly pronouncing the word with an English intonation, 'You will forgive me for saying that you are behaving like the foolish virgin in the Bible. If you do not take this offer, there may never be another one.'

I managed to say this with a tone of grave finality that belied my youth. Her face did not show a flicker of concern, but Anatoly stroked his moustache. I arose to leave, and I had a feeling that there would be a blazing row and then she would come round to her senses.

I thought that I had grown wiser and more sceptical, but even so, I took Anatoly's statement that Vera had 'disappeared' at face value. The only doubt in my mind, after meeting Oksana, was that Vera might have 'perished' and my friend was holding back the worst from me. I had to know, and so I decided to find Nina. This was not entirely straightforward, given that Anatoly had told me that she had moved into a richer man's apartment. But I recalled that she worked at the Taganskaya Theatre.

I learned what it felt like to stand at the stage door of a theatre waiting to accost an actress. I thought I saw a fellow with a velvet collar bribe the commissionaire. At any rate, he managed to pass through into the theatre. I was left with two other characters smoking cigarettes. One of my rival 'Charlies' (as we had called them in my theatrical days), had brought a bunch of flowers. It occurred to me that Anatoly might have stood here once. I wondered how he had managed to attract Nina's attention and offer her his 'sponsorship.' I also thought that perhaps, after she had left him, he had stood here again with flowers trying to woo her back. I doubt that he would have told me if that had been so.

When Nina stepped out, she was already carrying so many flowers that she only accepted an admirer's offering with difficulty. When she saw me, she exclaimed with surprise and, deserting the giver of the bouquet, came to kiss me on the cheek. It was almost like kissing in a garden, she was so encumbered with blooms. I have never felt quite so superior to my fellow mortals in my life.

I gave Nina a lift back to her home in my hired cab. On the way she tried to explain to me what had happened about Vera. There was the same old problem with language, but I could tell from Nina's tone of voice that there was cause for concern. Despairing of any hope of making me understand, she indicated by gestures that she wanted to write something down. I gave her my pocket address book and she wrote on the back page:

III

БУТЫРКА

We drove to the address that Nina had given the cabbie. I recognised the street. It was where she had always lived – the 'Boulevard of Flowers' - and I realised that it was most probably untrue that she had moved to a richer man's apartment, as Anatoly had claimed. I declined her invitation to come up for 'chai' or tea. There seemed little point as we could not converse.

The word that Nina had written was not in my dictionary, not that I could find at any rate. The next day, I happened to be meeting Anatoly, and I showed the note to him. If he recognised the hand writing, he did not say so. He just shrugged his shoulders and claimed that the meaning of the word was as much a mystery to him as it was to me.

The weather had improved and we were enjoying bright, sunny days, although there was still quite a nip in the air. Sometimes I used to take Tatters for walks in Petrovksi Park around the Palace of the same name. [21]

It was on one of these walks, just as I was heading back home, that I saw a familiar person heading towards me: Lydia Hawthorne. I do not know what it is about Russia, but it is a place where you seem to bump into people you know quite accidentally on a regular basis. So much seems to happen there that it can easily be mistaken for destiny – and that is perhaps why the people are known to be such fatalists. The prancing dog, of course, proved to be our initial topic of

---

[21] "The Petrovski Palace, 1 ½ M from the Trumphal Gate was built by Kazakov in 1776 and was occupied by Napoleon in Sept 1812. On the latter's retreat it was plundered and set on fire by the French. The present handsome two storied building in the Lombard Gothic style dates from 1840. The palace is surmounted by a flat dome and surrounded by a colonnade. Its internal equipment is simple. Single visitors are generally admitted by the sentinel at the door, but a party must apply to the superintendent. The Tzars repair to the Petrovski Palace before their coronation and proceed thence in solemn procession to the Kremlin. The park, laid out by Tzar Nicholas in 1834 contains a summer theatre, numerous villas, and several restaurants. In the E half of it is a small lake with bath houses." - Baedeker

conversation, and I mentioned that I had brought her as a present for Vera.

'Oh, how lovely!' said Lydia, 'How is she?'

'That's just it, I don't know. She's vanished without trace.'

Lydia expressed surprise. She had seen Vera two or three times while I had been away in London. She had seemed happy to be living with Nina, and looking forward to my return, which was poignant to Lydia, given that she knew I might never return. This was partly why she had sent encouraging reports back to Lord Hawthorne about the mine. She thought his influence might revive the project and bring me back to Russia.

'It doesn't bother you that the mine is almost certainly worthless?' I asked.

'It's of no concern to me whether the men pick up pebbles or diamonds. They will have no share of it in either case. I just want them to be paid properly and live in good conditions. They will set a standard for the other mines in the area.'

On one occasion, Lydia and Vera had taken up Mr Shchukin's offer of a private viewing of his collection of paintings. Vera had been more taken with them than ever, and she had explained that some of her friends were painters and that she sometimes posed as a model. She could not for the life her understand why Vera might want to 'disappear' or return to her old life.

We were both heading back into the centre, and I was intending to hire a cab, but Lydia insisted that we take the electric tram: 'It's on one of the few occasions that one brushes up against the ordinary people,' she explained. And to say 'brush up against' was putting it mildly. On board the crowded tram we came into very physical contact with the people of Moscow with their inevitable bundles, bottles, and sausages rolled up in newspapers. I produced the scrap of paper on which Nina had written her mysterious note. I asked Lydia if she could make head or tale of it.

'Butyrka', she said, pronouncing the letters written on the paper. One of Lydia's neighbours on the tram, a man whose breath smelt not a little of drink and salted cucumbers, repeated the word - Butyrka - as if the puzzle had been addressed to him. Then he looked at his feet in an embarrassed sort of way. I had assumed it would mean as little to her as it had, apparently, to Anatoly, but she said immediately, 'I spent most of my last trip trying to get into there. It is Moscow's most famous prison. I wonder what she did to be sent there.'

'You sound almost envious.'

'Gracious me! How could you say such a thing? The poor, poor dear. It's just that I wanted to write an article about the prison system. I made many requests for a visit, but the officials of the Ministry of Interior never said "yes" and never said "no" exactly. They just treated me as if I was highly eccentric.'

We got off the tram in the square outside Brest Railway. As we stood on the edge of the busy square, she indicated the long avenue straight avenue leading North East to the Butyrsky region of Moscow. In fact, she said, it was just the other side of Petrovsky Park and I had been walking with Tatters practically beneath the walls of the prison.

'Of course I must see her,' I said.

Lydia shook her head. She doubted that I would stand any better chance of being admitted than Vera would have of escaping. The particular function of the gaol, said Lydia, was to hold prisoners who were either awaiting their trial or deportation to Siberia. The heroine of the story she had told me when we first met the young female revolutionist, Maria Spiridonova, had been kept in the Butyrka before her removal to the frozen north.

Nina also lived in this area, known as The Tverskaya Yamskaya Fields – although fields were not an apt description for the military barracks, beer dens and bordellos that gave the place its character. I found her street and her building without too much difficulty, and led Lydia up the unlit staircase.

Nina and the bubbling samovar gave us a warm welcome. She seemed greatly relieved to unburden herself of Vera's story which she had not been able to explain to me the night before.

Three weeks earlier half a dozen gendarmes had come to the flat at dawn under the supervision of a police superintendent of high rank. They had searched the flat, taking up floor boards and skirting, unscrewing the stove, and generally creating a mess. They had found nothing of any note, but they had not left empty handed – they had taken Vera. All she knew was that the charge against Vera was of theft – and not just any common pick pocketing or shop lifting, but of something that was of great value – otherwise the case would not have attracted the interest of so important an officer. It had taken all this time to track Vera down to her incarceration in the Butyrka. It was agreed that we would try and visit her the very next morning.

I walked Lydia to her apartment block. Before we parted, I said:

'Tell me, Lydia, do you think any Russian would know what Butyrka meant?'

'Well I should think so. You could hardly read a newspaper without coming across its name.'

I knew that Anatoly for one read the newspapers.

Chapter Eighteen

I had an attack of class-consciousness outside the prison gates at half past six in the morning. My new cashmere coat, bought on Bond Street before I left London, seemed to fit uneasily well around my shoulders when we joined the crowd of mostly women, padded and bundled up like mummies with ragged scarves wrapped around their heads and bandages on their hands in place of gloves. Nina, who had insisted on joining us, held her chin high above her sliver fox fur collar. Lydia rubbed together her hands, clad in calfskin. Even the Dalmatian's spotted coat was too chic for this place. I felt that everyone was looking at us and thinking how our wealth was no protection against our friends and relations falling foul of the law.

Prison visiting seemed to be a female occupation for the most part - but another representative of my sex, a gaunt student with a small tuft of a beard on his chin, made a fuss of my dog - a certain way to my heart - before cadging a cigarette. Nina had instructed me to keep my mouth shut, in case the guards felt some delicacy about allowing foreign visitors to tour their prisons. I tried to pretend that I was a man of few words, but the boy was talkative and fluent in several languages; I was forced to break my cover, and we started a conversation. His friend inside was a 'political'. I told him that I had no idea why Vera had been arrested. The boy was saying that the offence of a respectable young woman would have been against the autocracy, rather than against the people. He said that I should be proud of her. To be a 'political' was quite a different category from a 'thief' (or worse, a prostitute).

'You'll have to be a relative to gain admission,' said the student. 'Say that you are her English cousin.'

After we had smoked a few cigarettes and wandered up and down the pavement for quite a while, the heavy gates slowly opened just enough to let a single file of visitors through. The mummified women pushed forward and my instinct was to let them go first, but Nina and Lydia proved that elbows clad in expensive coats were just as effective as ones less finely attired. One of the guards was checking identity papers and slowly writing out passes. When our turn came, Nina spoke to him for quite a while. The foreign passports were the cause of frowns and looks in our direction. The dog met with little more approval. Nina placed her hand on the guard's forearm and she carried on chatting as if they were old friends, completely oblivious to the lines on his forehead which practically spelt out the word 'nyet.' She opened up her purse and I assumed that she was about to offer him money. Instead, she handed him two theatre tickets. He examined them slowly and carefully, and although he did not look to me like a member of the theatre going public, he thanked her. In return he wrote out not three but four passes. The fourth, as I discovered later, granted 'permission for one dog to enter and depart.'

We crossed the courtyard and entered an airless waiting room with long benches on either side. The only decoration was an icon on the wall. The smile on the Madonna's face promised mercy and tenderness. I doubted if there was much of that beyond the next door, the one that led to the inner part of the prison. Here I began to learn about the patience of the Russians. Collectively, they had suffered a thousand years of serfdom, so what account was another couple of hours in the prison waiting room? One or two people came to pat the dog – Vera's dog - and a young boy gave her a piece of sausage (I wondered if it had been meant for a poor inmate's mouth). The student asked what prisons were like in England. I had to admit that I had never seen inside one. He laughed and told me that this was a very prestigious prison in which to be incarcerated. One of the best. The male quarters housed at least three leading members of the Russian parliament - the Duma. In fact, these days all the best Russians were in gaol and the scoundrels were in the Winter Palace. He told me an anecdote about how, when the wife of a leading politician came to visit her husband, she had brought two suitcases full of warm clothes and provisions. She said to one of the guards:

'Well, aren't you going to help a lady carry her bags?'

'Madam. This is not The Metropole.' But he carried them for her all the same.

It was gone ten o'clock, when the guard called our names and we were escorted over a clanking iron floor down a long, poorly lit corridor. We were led out into another courtyard, and to my surprise, its centrepiece was a pretty chapel. Its gay copula seemed quite out of place under the gloom of the prison walls. Nina pointed out the notorious round tower named after its most famous resident of the past, Pugachev, who had rebelled against Catherine the Great.

Eventually, having passed through at least two iron barred doors, we reached the visiting room. About twenty prisoners were waiting inside individual metal coops fronted by double layers of wire mesh. They had a ghostly appearance on the other side of the gauze – almost like shadows of human beings without the power to touch or feel. For a moment it was eerily silent, but soon the sound of human voices began to hum as inmates and visitors recognised one another. I picked out Vera's frail outline inside a baggy pair of overalls. I caught just a hint of her green eyes and the red of her lips. She was standing with her hands and nose pressed against the mesh, but she had not yet recognised us. Then, I think, she saw the dog, because she started to gape down at her. I gave Tatters a sharp tug on the lead – for she was not keen on this room – and stepped forward towards Vera's cage. At some point she recognised me because a loud squeal of 'Giorgi!' soared above the general babble of conversation.

It is said that the most beautiful sound in the world is that of your own name (even in its Russified form), and hearing my name called by Vera certainly backed this view up.

I intended to press my lips against the wire but Vera came down to greet the Dalmatian, whose tail and rear quarters were in a frenzy of wagging. Vera was babbling away with affectionate baby sort of noises. I was growing a little impatient before she finished with the dog and stood up greet me. Then she pointed to Tatters and said one of the dozen or so words of Russian that I understood. I think it is fair to say that, had I been the worst linguist in the world (which I might have been), it would have been hard for me not to have learnt this word after so much time in the company of Vera: it was 'padarok' – a present or gift.

'Yes, a 'padarok' – for you – her name is Tatters.'

'Tatters' she said, opening her eyes wide and laughing with girlish pleasure.

'Short for Tatiana', I added – but I could not tell if she had fully understood. It did not matter. We stood in silence looking at each other through the double mesh. Language was superfluous. I could tell that she was studying my face – trying to hold my image in her mind to recall in detail later on. I knew because I was doing the same thing. I was beginning to realise that this person who was a few feet away from me, but whom I could not reach out and touch, was bonded to me, and that I could not desert her.

Perhaps this is what is meant by destiny – when life has given you a roll and you must act it out. At last I had discovered the purpose of George Munnings: it was to rescue Vera. Perhaps I would never succeed in doing anything else – but this would be worth while.

It was becoming quite noisy in the visiting room. Other people seemed relaxed, as if the situation was quite normal. Lydia and Nina had been standing back to give us our moments together, but now they came and joined me in front of the cage. Nina and Vera started to exchange news, speaking at breakneck speed, perhaps trying to utter as many words as possible before our time was up, but Lydia butted in, saying that she must translate for me.

And so I learned via the medium of Lydia's no-nonsense Englishwoman's voice that Vera had seen me in a dream the previous night. We had been walking arm in arm through a strange city. She realised it was London because the air was foggy. We had stopped at a shop and I bought her a hat. Lydia recounted this last part with a note of dry irony in her voice.

A door opened at the back of the cage for a few moments and a guard shoved in the provisions that we had brought. Vera picked up and cradled the string bag as if it was a baby.

Suddenly, Vera said in English:

'I - love - you.'

She had said it before in jest, but this time I think that quite possibly she meant it. I blew a kiss back at her.

I looked at my watch. Our twenty minutes would soon be up. I told Lydia that she must find out what she was charged with. Vera launched into her account. She was telling the story in a lively fashion, and Lydia and Nina were exclaiming with astonishment, but before she could finish, the guard started to usher us out.

'Tsiluyu, Tsiluyu', Vera was saying. 'I kiss you, I kiss you, ' translated Lydia faithfully. It was one of those occasions on which a silent look would have spoken more elegantly than words. As we walked through the iron frame of the door to the visiting room, I longed to blow one last kiss - but I did not dare turn around because I had an eerie feeling that by looking back I would lose her.

After we left the prison, we walked around the Butyrski ponds and Lydia told me what Vera had said. Nina's intuition had been correct. She was indeed charged with no petty theft. It seemed extraordinary, but her alleged crime was to have stolen the very same alexandrite stone that we had seen on our trip to the Ural Mountains. The charge had been made by Monsieur Cuny, the French owner of the mine himself. I was baffled by how he could have got such preposterous idea, and still less how he managed to pinpoint Vera's whereabouts; she was hard to pin down at the best of times. Nina had the answer: the only possible route by which they could have found her was via the Frenchman's neighbour in the Urals, Anatoly Mizinsky. And while we were on the subject of Anatoly, Nina denied that she had left him for a another man – not that she had any shortage of offers. He had begun to treat her as if he owned her – issuing edicts when she should be at home and whom she could and could not see. After they had quarrelled, he had bought her an expensive birthday present for which she had not asked. He had not succeeded in placating her. She was too proud to be 'bought' by any man. She had thought of returning the sapphire pendant and matching earrings. Then a better idea had occurred to her. She had sent them to Anatoly's wife. She very much hoped that Julia Mizinsky was pleased with the unexpected gift from her husband.

Anatoly Alexandrovich Mizinsky had some explaining to do - not for the first or the last time in the course of our acquaintance. First he filled out some of the details he had received from the police and Mr Cuny about the alleged 'theft.'

It had gone unnoticed at first because it was not everyday that he took his prize exhibits out of the strong room, but a month after our visit, he had received some of the leading shareholders of the enterprise. Naturally he showed them the 'museum' and was shocked and embarrassed to discover that alexandrite had been substituted for a worthless piece of crystal. One could imagine that suspicion fell upon himself and on his chief engineer, and perhaps rightly so. He recalled that we had been the last people to whom he had shown the alexandrite. The police had come directly to Anatoly's door. They had been received by Julia who was wearing her own alexandrite ring. It had taken all of Anatoly's powers of persuasion to prevent them from taking his wife to the police station. He had no choice but to point to a more obvious culprit, and Monsieur Cuny had confirmed that he too suspected the young lady who had been sporting a black eye.

Of course Anatoly had understood perfectly well the note bearing one dreadful word – 'Butyrka' - but he had feigned incomprehension – not for his sake, but for mine.

He sat in the leather chair of his study. His face behind his thick moustache looked as innocent as ever. He did not even blush. He told me that he held me in great esteem; he had an enormous respect and affection for me. He felt a responsibility to look after me.

'So why did you lie to me?' I flung back at him. To call your friend a liar is almost like pointing a gun at his heart and pulling the trigger. It might be just, but it can only be done in anger. But Anatoly did not flinch.

'I did not want to trouble your soft heart with this sordid affair,' he claimed.

'But surely you know that I would want to see her?'

'That was precisely the suffering from which I wanted to save you. Vera and this dog have exactly the same approach to life. They look at you with their sad eyes and you cannot hold anything from them.'

I was so furious and I did not even know myself what names I was calling him. I might have kicked the waste paper basket. Tatters shrank back to hid under Anatoly's desk. At the time I could not have said why I was so angry, but I suppose that when a person lies to you, he treats you like a child. Anatoly had deprived me of the facts. Any choice I might have had in the matter, any decision about what to do or not to do about Vera, had been taken away from me. He had decided for me that I should not see her again – and there lay the profound insult.

It was not a particularly dignified outburst, especially given that I was in his home and God knows who could have heard me. Perhaps his family thought that we were arguing about the land. Anatoly kept on trying to interrupt, raising his voice slightly louder each time - 'If you will please calm down, take a moment to listen to me…' he said. And I supposed I gained some satisfaction that he was becoming flustered. I felt an impulse to strut out slamming the door behind me, but I flung one final insult at him and gave way to his demand that I sit down and listen to him for a moment. I was still quivering with anger when he said,

'I have an idea for getting your Vera out of prison…Are you interested to listen to me?'

'Go on then.'

'My father had a school friend who will help us. He is a powerful man. If he cannot get her out, nobody can.'

Anatoly's 'friend of the family' turned out to be the one and the same gentleman whom Lydia had spent so much time trying to see when I first knew her. He was a Privy Councillor and Moscow's highest ranking official in the Ministry of Interior. All Lydia's long and patient efforts at gaining an audience with had had been rebuffed. Anatoly explained that he was a man marked by anarchists for a bomb or a bullet, and that his officials were obliged to protect him with contact from 'strange looking females'; but when we dropped in at the residence of His Excellency M. Basile De Sanarazov that very evening, he received us without delay in his spacious study where he was working at his papers. Such is the power of a family 'connection.' His Excellency's features were somewhat severe behind his silver beard and rim spectacles, but he expressed deep regret that 'my fiancé', as Anatoly had politely termed Vera, had befallen such a misfortune as to be imprisoned by an administrative 'error.' He surmised that there had been a most unfortunate case of mistaken identity. He would ask an official, a Titular Councillor, to look at the papers first thing in the morning, and he would see what could be done. After we left his Excellency, I felt reasonably reassured. I was ready to head back to the hotel, Anatoly wanted to try and recapture some of the spirit of our earlier friendship. He invited me to a popular nightclub called The Bat (or La Chauve Souris).[22] It was situated in a basement, and we dined while watching light hearted men and lightly clad women perform a series of songs and sketches. We ordered Champagne to wash away any bad taste from our argument.

'Do you still respect me?' Anatoly asked.

'Well, more than I did earlier on today,' I said.

And we drank to mutual respect.

---

[22] The impresario Nikita Baleiff escaped to the west with his performers after the Revolution and the 'La Chauve Souris' appeared in Paris, London and New York.

The Titular Consul took about a week to complete his enquiries. The result was not quite as I had hoped for. He had arranged for me to marry my 'fiancé' inside the prison chapel.

'Marry?' I said to Anatoly in disbelief when he told me. 'Why does he think that I might want to marry her?'

He told me that it was not quite as strange as it seemed. It was not so unusual for people to marry inside a Russian prison, and it was a logical step – from Vera's point of view. She would acquire a new family name. She would receive new papers – and might be issued with new social class, which in her case would be particularly expedient as she was currently classified as a prostitute on her official document. It might even be possible for her to become a British subject. It was quite likely that her old documents and identity would become lost. A few hundred roubles in the right hands would increase the likelihood of such a mishap. It would then be more 'comfortable' for Anatoly's high ranking friend to order her release on the grounds that the papers for Mrs Vera Munning's arrest could not be found and her detention was not in accordance with the law. Anatoly assured me that it would not be the first time that a female prisoner had been released by such a ruse. It all made perfect sense to someone familiar with the Russian 'system', in which justice appeared to be about as hit and miss as an anarchist's bomb. Confusion and lost papers were the norm. It was not unknown for the wrong prisoner to be hanged due to a muddle. The whole plan would cost around 400 roubles which Anatoly himself would provide. Obviously, I said that I could not possibly allow him to pay such a sum on Vera's behalf, but in the end I allowed him to. After all, the plan would no doubt cost me a great deal more.

I spent most of the next day taking a very long walk around the garden ring boulevards, tracing up and down Moscow's seven hills. Spring was already in the April air. Tatters was in full fettle cantering backwards and forwards and running up to greet children in prams and French poodles on red leads. I walked and worried.

Lydia had said that I was doing 'a fine thing' and 'not shirking my responsibility'. She told me about Russian prisons: about how beatings and molestation were common, and there was a constant fear of tuberculosis. If Vera was found guilty of this 'trumped up charge' of theft, she would be sent to a labour camp. She did not think that Russian courts were in the habit of delivering innocent verdicts. It seemed like the moral pressure for me to 'do the right thing' was insurmountable.

I wondered at what stage I had 'become responsible' for Vera. We could so easily have maintained a clean arrangement along the lines suggested by Anatoly. I paid. She provided a service. Right from the first night, I had never been comfortable with this simple setup. It was, perhaps, too brazen for my oversensitive feelings. I had allowed a business relationship to turn into a romance. Anatoly had warned me of the dangers of letting her cross the line from concubine to 'attachment', but I had become jealous of rivals. I claimed a proprietor's rights over her – and with ownership came responsibility. Vera now 'belonged' to me. By dint of the fact that I had been kind and open handed, I had allowed myself to become her patron and her protector. This thinking it through was not quite enough to explain it all to me. I felt that some external force, not my good judgement, was driving me towards this reckless but 'noble' act.

Tatters and I went up and down hills and past little chapels. I stopped off at a street market and looked aimlessly at a pair of leather boots. I had not the slightest intention of buying, but the old man who was selling them (nothing else), thought that God had sent me to him. I gave him two roubles. Only when I got home, did I notice that the boots were different sizes.

The next time I saw Vera in prison, all my doubts melted away. This time I visited her on my own. She placed her palm against the mesh and I covered it with my hand on the other side. I felt that I had reached out to touch an apparition and had found a real, substantial person. I thought about how may thousands of miles we had been born apart, and in what different circumstances. The long odds against such a coming-together as ours seemed to make our intimacy all the more priceless. Chance and destiny are sometimes indistinguishable. And now we were separated, not by distance, but by this thin wire, and such an abstract force as due process of the Russian criminal code. We spent a long time just looking at each other's outlines, refracted through the mesh. I had a strong impression of the paleness of her cheeks, the red blush of her lips and the darkness of her fringe and eyebrows. It even seemed to me – though perhaps I imagined it – that I could see clearly into the greenness of her eyes. I did not feel that there was any intensity or pleading in them, only tranquillity.

The voice of doubt no longer spoke inside my head; I loved her.

After about quarter an hour of this silent communion, Vera called to the guard. He took me to see another woman prisoner - Vera's friend. The lady was called Sasha, short for Alexandra, and she was the singer who had been arrested for performing at the funeral of a revolutionary and was detained without charge. She said:

'Vera told me all about you. What a kind and good-hearted gentleman you are.'

'Perhaps you can ask her something for me when you are in the cell together.'

'Certainly. What is your question?'

'Will she marry me?'

'So you're going to get hitched?'

'Well there's something I wanted to ask you about. Does a marriage in Russia, count? Back home, I mean.'

I was in the office of our vice-consul. My resolve was still subject to violent swings. When I was in Vera's company, I had no doubt that love and destiny compelled me to marry her. As soon as I was on my own and had time to think over some of the practical implications of such a course, the doubts began to return.

'Oh yes, it certainly does count,' said Campbell-Fitzgerald. 'There's a Foreign Marriage Act that recognises unions made under Russian law.' I thought for a moment about the ramifications of what he had just said. Anything the matter?' he asked

'I was just thinking that it could prove rather expensive for me.'

'I have a card here which sets our consular fees.'

Marriage Fees: The Foreign Marriage Act 1892

1) For receiving notice of intended marriage - 10 s

2) For receiving notice of a caveat - 1 s

3) For every marriage solemnised by or in the presence of a marriage officer and registered by him - 10 s

4) For the certificate of a notice having been given and posted up - 1 s

5) For registration by a consular officer of a marriage solemnised in accordance with local law - 2s

He tapped point '5' with his pencil. Foreign marriages did, indeed, count.

'This isn't going to be the most usual of weddings. My fiancée is currently residing in the Butyrka Prison. It's all the result of a big misunderstanding, of course. I think the Russians would take more notice of her case if a foreign power was involved. When we are married, will you be able to make representations on her behalf to the Russian authorities?'

'Hmm.' I got the impression Campbell Fitzgerald did not come across cases like this too often, but he seemed very knowledgeable. 'In this matter, as in so many others, various Russian laws contradict one another. The Russian legal code does not permit a natural born subject of the Empire to transfer allegiance to any other State or Crown. However, according to another law, a married woman is a subject to the same state as her husband. Part of the appeal of this country is that you can always choose which law you wish to follow. I think that in this case we can go along with the second choice. In that case, I will do the best I can on her behalf.'

'The Russian officials want you to be there, at the wedding. Will that be possible?'

'Inside the prison? That will be a first. Yes of course. I'm afraid it will cost you 10 shillings though.'

'I think it might cost me a good deal more than that.'

Anatoly and Robert Campbell Fitzgerald were my fellow stags at my pre-nuptial lunch. We had a little table in the corner of the Slavyansky Bazaar, a high vaulted, gaily painted hotel on Nikolskaya Street – no more than 200 yards from the Chapel of the Iberian Virgin, where I had asked the blessed Icon to arrange for me to marry Vera. How carelessly I had made that prayer.

I suppose that on a normal wedding day, I could have enjoyed the traditional banter about 'signing up the for the full catastrophe' and 'starting a life sentence of my own.' I smiled rather feebly. Anatoly, roaring with laughter, pointed out that my fork was vibrating its way across the table.

'Perhaps it's a sign,' he said quite hilarious. I wondered for a moment, before I traced the cause of the vibrations back to my knees which were trembling uncontrollably.

Campbell Fitzgerald softened the tone of the conversation.

'I say old chap, how did you meet young Vera?'

The simple question completely stumped me. My jaw dropped. I tried to think up some plausible story but my mind was totally blank. Eventually I croaked, 'Anatoly was there right at the beginning.'

'Yes, indeed. I translated their first words to each other. As the saying goes, 'Their eyes expressed the language of love.'

Campbell Fitzgerald smiled sympathetically. 'Sometimes I wish that my own dear wife and I could communicate rather less.'

I did not eat my sturgeon with much relish, and I was slurping at my Crimean wine rather fast. Anatoly and Campbell Fitzgerald were not far behind with the drink. Anatoly was poised to pour again, but the vice consul put his hand over his glass: 'It's a good thing I don't have to preside over the ceremony. I sometimes have to marry people in my cramped little office. I've got a crib for the vows, but in my current state I might find it hard to command the words on the card to stand still.'

When we were on the brandy and cigars he gave me a little pep talk to stiffen my resolve:

'May I congratulate you on your fine taste in taking a Russian lady to be your wife? I'm sure Anatoly will back me up in this when I say that a Russian woman makes the most splendid spouse a man could desire - excepting my own Jane, who happens to be English through no fault of her own, you understand. From my observation of my friends and acquaintances here, every Russian wife I know is loyal, loving, as well educated as any man, and has a plucky independence of spirit. There isn't any of that moping about the house and muttering pointed ironies that you find in some English households I can think of. I'd rather have a go-ahead woman any day. The most delicately brought up young Russian girl speaks straight from the heart. And as for natural beauty, well they have buckets of it. I swear to you, Russian women don't walk, they float like swans. Good deportment isn't the word for it. There's none of that stiff corseted look they teach English girls in Swiss finishing schools. No, Russian women are all natural. I've seen common streetwalkers defy all of Isaac Newton's laws with weightless grace. It's only to be expected that you're a bit nervous George. Perhaps you'll look back on this day as one of the less orthodox chapters in your life. A wedding behind bars is a first for me too. But I'm sure you'll always remember it as the best thing you ever did. Now let's get going and tie the knot before you have a chance to think twice and jilt the girl at the prison gate.'

I did not feel in control of my own steps as we walked across the prison courtyard. Anatoly and Campbell Fitzgerald escorted me on either side. I could not say if my feet were being lifted up and moved along by the sublime strings of love, destiny, kindness, drink, weakness of character, past mistakes, or general confusion. I was aware that the prisoners who had walked this way before me must have felt bewilderment for other reasons. I, however, was a free man - at least in theory.

There was a tune playing in my head – the lone violin from the Russian ballet. Why oh why, it asked, must we submit to fate?

The iron door in front of us clanked and heaved open. I recalled that this was the way into the visitor's waiting room. The interior, however, had been transformed. Candles shed their gentle light on all sides and the soothing aroma of incense hung in the air. The same cheap icon of the Madonna and Child shimmered with a mysterious life. We were honoured by the presence of His Excellency M. Basile De Sanarazov. I had not expected to see his elegant figure on the very same bench that was used by ordinary prison visitors. He was in conversation with Lydia who was seated next to him. Anatoly gave a little bow to Nina, and she acknowledged him with the briefest of nods. Oksana, the redhead from the hotel, dabbed her heavily outlined eyes with a handkerchief.

We were led by no lesser a figure than the prison governor himself out of the waiting room, across the yard, and into the prison chapel. Here about fifteen or so female prisoners and about as many guards were standing under the vaults and among the incense burners and icons, almost as casually as the crowd in the Church of the Iberian Virgin. Only their uniforms reminded one that the prisoners were not free worshipers.

The bride was waiting near the altar with a prison guard by her side, in loco parentis. She stood with her back to us, her white headdress falling over her baggy blue prison uniform. A red carpet had been spread out on the ground just in front of her.

'Be sure to be the first to step on the red carpet,' said Anatoly. 'If you let Vera put her foot there before you, she will always rule you.'

From a dark corner, a little priest stood up and took his place behind the lectern, bearing a heavy bible. A gold embroidered mitre perched on his head like an exotic bird, and his flowing robes were embroidered with silver. A small choir of women prisoners began to chant an anthem. Anatoly and I walked side by side up to the edge of the carpet. When I reached Vera, he lit candles and handed them to us. We both stepped forward and knelt. It was only then that I realised that Vera's foot had touched the carpet first. The hot candle wax ran onto my hand. I bowed my head, as if waiting for an axe to fall.

For such a small man, the priest had a magnificent baritone voice. He read his verses, half in speech, half in song, and the mostly unintelligible words echoed around the chapel. I picked out a few names from the cast of the Old Testament including Isaac, Rebecca, Moses, and Zebedee. Then we stood up and the priest took the candles. He handed us both the rings and began to ask us questions. I had been tutored how to respond by Anatoly. The first question would be if I knew of any impediment to our wedlock and I should answer 'Nyet'. The questions that followed would ask if I took Vera as my lawful wedded wife, to cherish and to hold etc., and I should answer 'da' to all of them, except to the ones which were directed at Vera when I should just shut up. To my great surprise, I got through this without any slip-ups and even managed to catch my cue to put the simple gold ring on her finger.

At this point, Vera's prison friends began to sing a psalm. The women's voices were, I swear, the sweetest I had ever heard.

In the final part of the ceremony, we kneeled side by side while Anatoly and Oksana held crowns joined by a ribbon over our heads. The priest intoned some more verses which seemed to go on for an awfully long time. Finally we sipped sacramental wine from a golden goblet. The ceremony just fizzled out and people started to mill around, shed tears and congratulate us. One of the women singers came up to us and said out loud 'Gorka!' Others joined in with a chant, 'Gorka! Gorka!' Vera turned her mouth up towards mine, and I got the general idea. I kissed her. (In fact, Gorka means 'bitter' and you have to make it sweet).

A select group of us – all free persons apart from Vera - passed through the gaol, over metal floors, past stinking cells, groaning prisoners, guards playing cards and drinking black tea, through heavy gates with keys as big as your arm, and finally through an oak door into the Governor's office. Here the Governor poured out Armenian cognac. The big man was all smiles and warm congratulations and we drank the inevitable toast to our happiness. Then it was time for formalities. Campbell Fitzgerald was in charge of my papers and he stood up to place them on the Governor's desk where Vera's passport was already laid out and waiting. I saw a look of astonishment pass over Campbell Fitzgerald's face when he saw Vera's yellow document denoting the fact that she was a prostitute officially registered with the police.

The Governor donned a pair of silver spectacles and considered the array of papers before him. He sighed deeply. 'Tac' (well now) he said. He took a gold fountain pen out of its ink well and sat with it poised. After a minute or so he apologised, and said he wasn't used to officiating over wedding ceremonies. M. De Sanarazov and the priest came over to help him sort things out. I do not know how many papers the gentlemen passed around to sign and counter sign and witness and stamp. I was slightly taken aback to see my British passport being submitted to the rubber imprint, but Campbell Fitzgerald did not object. He produced a consular stamp from his briefcase and merrily banged the ensign of the Lion and the Unicorn over any documents put in front of him. All the time, Vera sat in an armchair with the white veil again over her nose.

At the end of it all, Vera had two new non-yellow passports. One was her documentation for the interior of Russia, and the second was her passport for foreign travel. Naturally, they had assumed that it was our consummate desire to join up back in England. Her husband's authorisation was required before she could go abroad. I did not want Vera turning up on my doorstep unannounced in London - but I could hardly decline in front of all those people and look like a cad. I duly signed.

I do not know if the Governor was ever harsh to his prisoners. Lydia has sent me cuttings of dreadful stories in the English press about the floggings that went on in the Tsar's gaols. All I can say is that on our wedding day he showed nothing but warmth and consideration to Vera and myself. Well I suppose he had been well paid. When all the official signings were done, he proposed one more toast before announcing that he would leave us alone in his office for half an hour so that we could be together before Vera went back to her cell. He locked his desk, and the group shuffled out and left us.

Vera sat on my knee. I slipped the veil from her nose. That was the time that I discovered that a kiss really can take away life's bitter taste. I felt that we were more joined, more physically and spiritually united, than I had known was possible. Certainly our clothes came between us - or at least proved a partial obstacle - but I was not aware even of them. My hopes and fears became hers. Hers became mine. We shared the same breaths, the same heart beats. It seemed like only a minute before a rattling of the lock to give us warning before the Governor and the warder entered. We disentangled ourselves. The guard led Vera back to her cell. She pulled the veil over her face so that I could see the outline of her nose and mouth, pressed against the material, where a few moments before my kisses had been.

Campbell Fitzgerald and I left the prison in silence, as if from a funeral. The gates shut behind us, and we were locked out on the street where Anatoly and the women were waiting for us.

We celebrated at 'Yar', a large restaurant glittering with gilt and chandeliers. I sat next to an empty place laid for Vera. Campbell Fitzgerald proposed a toast in two languages to 'the absent bride and to the groom.' I was forced to make a speech and I thanked everybody who had helped such unusual a wedding to come about. At the end I said, 'To Vera', which needed no translating. We all raised our glasses to the empty place. Everybody was telling me how beautiful she had been in the simple blue overall and the white veil, and the women were saying how they had wept buckets. Even Lydia admitted to having resorted to a handkerchief. I began to feel enormously proud of my bride and my decision to marry her.

Lydia and Basile De Sanarazov were getting along famously, and later on they went off into the ballroom together, presumably to dance. Even Anatoly and Nina managed to exchange some words, and I wondered if his part in the wedding had helped to restore his status in her eyes.

By the end of the evening, I was extremely drunk and trying not to show it.

'But you're certain that they'll let her go?' I said to Anatoly.

He assured me that we had paid good money for the system to fail, and it would surely not let us down.

I tried to imagine what it would be like meeting her at the prison gates on the day of her release. I had an idea that it was going to be the highpoint of my life.

I did not, however, have the opportunity to remain in Moscow. The next day, alongside my coffee brought to me in my room at the Metropole, I received a telegram on a silver plate. I could see that it was from London as I opened it, and I wondered with a guilty shudder if news of my secret wedding had reached my father. On opening it, however, the only thing that was clear was that I was summoned back to London as a matter of urgency.

Chapter Nineteen

"I would write a long and very interesting book on the joys and sorrows of a company promoter. If the child of your brain should turn out a success then you are the finest fellow in the world and nothing is too good for you. But should it happen that the company is a rank failure, and that the shares you have sold to your friends should steadily drop down to nothing, then you are an errant rogue, a common swindler, and a subject for criminal proceedings."

Hooley's Confessions by Ernest Terah Hooley Squire of Risley Simpkin, Marshall, Hamilton, Kent & co Ltd London 1924

'That shitty, shitty, little man.'

The solicitor's chubby index finger trembled as he stubbed it down on the table. For a moment I thought that Mr William Verity of Greville, Black and Verity had been referring to my own dear Papa, but of course that was quite the wrong end of the stick. The next thought to flash through my mind was that there had been some sort of accident, and that the 'shitty little' man, whoever he might be, was responsible. I was still dazed from my long journey from Russia and was lacking information. All that I had to go on was the telegram that I had received from Mr Verity while I was still in Moscow:

URGENT. YOUR FATHER NEEDS YOU. RETURN TO LONDON IMMEDIATELY. CALL AT MY OFFICE AS SOON AS YOU ARRIVE.

On the evening of my return, I had telephoned to both of my father's houses, and had been told that he was 'not at home.' This had not caused me any special alarm at the time, but now I could see that something had happened which was very much troubling Mr Verity. Whatever it was, it had better justify the urgent summons back to London. If Verity had called me back on some false alarm, I was going to give him what-for.

'Which man do you mean?' I asked.

'Crawford,' he said dejectedly. 'Naturally we are suing for defamation, but his work of wanton destruction is done. Financial reputations are such fragile things. It will take more than an award of damages to repair your father's standing now.'

'Forgive me,' I said. 'Who is Crawford and what is this all about?' I did know a certain Crawford of course, a 'Mrs' Barbara Crawford, my father's 'artistic adviser', but I was yet to make the connection.

'Crawford is the scoundrel who made the baseless imputation in the first place. Haven't you read the papers? No, of course, you've been abroad.' He gave me a look which caused me some concern – a look of pity - before gathering his strength to summarise recent events.

It had begun with 'a disgraceful disturbance' at an Extraordinary General Meeting of The Southern Slope Gold Mining PLC. The company chairman, my father, had just proposed a capital restructuring to the shareholders. The dire state of the company's finances left them with few alternatives. The shareholders, for the most part, had faced the situation with equanimity until Major Clarence Crawford rose to his feet brandishing his certificate for five ordinary shares of one shilling each which he had bought for the specific purpose of gaining entrance to the meeting.

The crux of Major Crawford's address was a matter at once both delicate and devastating. He claimed to have in his possession the most irrefutable evidence that the company Chairman had drawn deep into the firm's accounts to fund the 'most extravagant wooing of a certain lady'. A flat in Mayfair had been acquired out of company funds for the sole purpose of 'sordid rendezvousing'. Further monies had been made available to the 'certain' lady for the furnishing and decoration of the Chairman's country home and for the throwing of an orgiastic party. It was only at the end of his speech that he revealed that the surname of the 'certain lady' was the same as his own, for it was his own wife whom he was denouncing publicly along with 'Angel' Munnings. The newspapers, perhaps for fear of libel proceedings, had so far reported the story using the 'certain lady' formulation.

For some reason, perhaps complacency, my father had failed to pack the meeting with his supporters. Worse still, a faction of his fellow directors and 'guinea pigs' had grown disaffected, owing to a disagreement over their emoluments. Major Crawford was no mean orator. His military bearing commanded respect, and he refused to give way to Chairman's repeated attempts to intervene. Such was the uproar among the shareholders that, in order to avoid the necessity of calling the police to quell the disturbance, the board of directors conceded a full and independent inquiry into the allegations. A firm of auditors of impeccable credentials, unconnected to my father's 'pet' accountants, was appointed by the close of business the following Tuesday.

When Mr Verity had finished telling me this, I tried to put it all into perspective: 'Surely it will all blow over,' I said.

'I'm afraid,' said Mr Verity, 'that your assessment reveals that you have not yet comprehended the gravity of the situation.'

'But these allegations are groundless. I don't deny that my father has seen rather a lot of Mrs Crawford these past years, but it's quite clear that Major Crawford is seeing things through the eyes of a jealous husband. These expenses he mentions will all turn out to be legitimate.'

I still believed that Mr Verity was overreacting and in a funk. He had practically acted as my father's private secretary for as long as I could remember, and handled most of his business correspondence. My father had an aversion to signing his name on any document. It was said later that his signature was about as rare as Rembrandt's, and a letter from Mr Verity was about as near as many people, including these days my mother, came to receiving a personal communication from my father. No doubt if there was something amiss on the legal front, he was in danger of being dragged into it himself. I suspected that regard for his own hide was at the bottom of all this. He had probably invited me to his office hoping to persuade me to take some unilateral action without the knowledge of my father. My annoyance with him was growing. If I was to miss Vera's release from prison because of this.....

'One might like to think,' he said, 'that a lifetime's work would receive better protection from the law, but try telling that to the official receiver and the director of public prosecutions.'

'You mean they refuse to take any action against this Crawford fellow?'

'Crawford? They're not concerned about him. Didn't you know? Your father had little option but to surrender himself to the City Police, or else they were threatening to come to his door and lead him away in handcuffs. The newspapers reported it on Thursday morning.'

On Thursday morning, my train had been passing through Warsaw. I had been completely cut off from the world's news. I had bought a newspaper on the way to Mr Verity but I had not had time to read it. Had I turned as far as page four of the Daily Mail, I would have discovered that questions about the Munnings Affair were being asked in Parliament. Rumours of insolvency and accounting fraud had spread like influenza across my father's business empire. Loans were being called in, debts were being defaulted on, and share prices were tumbling down. My father was a director of no less than thirteen companies, and of nine of those he was chairman. It had become apparent that many of those companies held each other's shares on their books and lent each other money. It was, as the papers liked to say, 'a financial house of cards,' and a card of particular structural importance had been pulled away – that of my father's good name. His arrest came as a surprise to nobody but myself, but his failure to stump up the bail caused wide spread comment. The matter was sub judice. For the time being at least, the avenging pen-pushers saved their ink.

Verity explained all this in some detail. At several points he was obliged to clear his throat with a gurgle. He seemed to be in a bad way that morning.

'The problem is raising the money,' he explained. 'The bail is set so astonishingly high. £25,000. I've never heard anything like it. The judge must be one of those old family types who hate the plutocratic classes.'

I shook my head: 'Well I suppose the judge took into account that my father is a wealthy man.'

'Not so as to have £25,000 lying around. None of the banks want to know him all of a sudden. If anything, they are calling in loans.'

'Do you mean to say that my father is languishing in gaol for want of £25,000! It's hard to credit. Couldn't you lend it to him?' I could see from the expression on Mr Verity's face that this novel suggestion did not find favour with the lawyer. 'Well couldn't he mortgage the house?'

'Has done already. Up to the hilt. The Guildford villa has been making a considerable strain on his expenditure. The costs overran frightfully. Our best hope is to sell his race horses, but that can't be done overnight.'

I was beginning to feel rather irritated by Mr Verity. He seemed to be holding up the white flag of surrender. Now he came to the point of the meeting. My father had given me his power of attorney. I now had signing rights for all his bank accounts and could buy and sell assets, take out loans and so forth on his behalf. I could, in fact, instruct Mr Verity. The solicitor advised me to go through everything and see what I could find to sell, especially if it could be done without attracting too much attention.

'When can I see him?' I asked.

'Any day, while he is on remand. Visiting hours are between three and five thirty.'

When I left Verity's office I understood that I was not longer the heir to a certain fortune or the offspring of an 'Angel' of the City. As far as the public was concerned, I might as well be the child of Lucifer. There was nothing to fall back on. My destiny was, for the first time in my life, in my own hands, and more than that, I was now responsible for my father, his employees, his investors and – it should not be forgotten – my new wife.

'Mrs Crawford?'
'Gabby, is that you? Can it be? Oh God it is you.'
'No, it's George, his son.'
'Oh Lord. You sound just like your father.'
'I'm sorry to give you a shock, Mrs Crawford.'
'I am supposed to be in hiding. How did you find my number?'
'Mr Verity.'
'I see. You heard, of course.'
'Some of it' - sound of sobs – 'I'm going to see Papa. Is there any message you want me to give him.'
'Tell him I love him.'
'Yes, I'll say that.'

There were no wire cages in the visiting room of Wandsworth Prison. My father sat across the table from me, real and substantial. The only barrier between us was the regulation that we must keep two feet apart.

Of course, every British prisoner on remand is innocent until proven guilty, but even so, there is something about a pair of prison overalls that makes a dirty rascal out of the average man, even before his own family. Some of the inmates in the visiting room at Wandsworth might have looked more dignified stark naked than in their uniforms. In Papa's particular case, the overalls rather suited him. He looked quite relaxed in them. His silver hair was a little longer than usual, but neatly combed. His moustache had a carefully tended look. His powerful presence had not deserted him. I can only describe it as a sort of spirit which seemed to spread out from his head and fill the visiting hall. An aura is a requirement of the job for a great actor, politician, captain of industry, or indeed, for any professional dissembler. Such an aura provokes a reaction in those who are around it. You have to respect it, fear it, love it, or hate it. My father had such an invisible force about him. He was one of those men whose face seemed to be made of something not quite flesh and blood - perhaps of tough rubber. His hair seemed to grow with more vigour than was natural. His lines and contours spoke of experience and strength of character – but I would go further; there was something more than human about him. I read an account of Rasputin recently, and people said similar things about the Tsarina's favourite holy man. That was how my father was: people regarded him as a prophet. I could hope that a jury might find it hard to believe that such a man – with all his dignity and confidence in tact - could be guilty of a base crime.

'How was Moscow?' he asked.

'Well, you know, a bit slow, but I came as soon as I received word.'

My father spoke in a low voice, but it was so clear that I think the warder at the back of the hall could hear it. He said:

'The present situation is a bit of a bugger, but I'll clear my name soon enough. I'm sorry, but it's too bad for your Russian deal.'

I told father that all was not lost. I had visited Lord Hawthorne, who received me for about the time it takes to boil and egg, but as I left his office he had said, 'Why don't you try to sell the Russian property to The Lena Goldfields Limited? I'll ask my secretary to make an introduction for you. I'm doing this on account of the good report I have received of you from my daughter, you understand. No other reason. The Munnings Affair has caused me no end of trouble.'

And so our future financial solvency still depended on Anatoly's land. Before I left Moscow, Julia Mizinsky had given me her 'final' offer – she would accept nothing less than 51 per cent of the company in return for her land. At the time, it had seemed to me like a preposterous cheek on her part, but now her terms did not seem so unattractive, especially if I had the Lena Goldfields Company lined up as a buyer.

When I had finished explaining this to my father, I could see that there was deep paternal pride in his expression. He was relying on me. We discussed what I might sell to raise some money – and I am afraid to say that the antiques and oil paintings purchased by 'a certain artistic adviser' were at the top of the list. On a more personal note, I had to pass on the message from the lady herself. I was squeamish indeed to tell my father that his mistress wanted to him to know that she loved him. Therefore I said, 'Mrs Crawford asked me to assure you that the affection and regard in which she holds you has not lessened.'

'That is most kind of her,' said my father. 'I believe that she must be suffering rather more than me.'

I could not bring myself to tell him that I was now a married man. It was more than enough to have one gaol bird in the family. I wondered if I would ever be able to let him know about my marriage. Indeed, I was not sure who would be more shocked – my father by my wife, or my wife by my father.

I was grateful that we had a good deal of business to discuss. It kept us off personal matters and gave me a sense of purpose. I left feeling almost uplifted. I was going to sort out the mess.

Chapter Twenty

Nothing in the days that followed proved straightforward. The Lena Goldfields Company was, it seemed, in no hurry to meet a businessman by the name of Munnings, even if he did come armed with a reference from Lord Hawthorne. The official receiver had laid claim to both my father's antiques and his race horses, saying that they were company assets as they had, in one way or another, been paid for out of company funds. I consulted my friend Drake about whether, if I smuggled some of the antiquities out of the house, he could manage to sell them sell them discreetly to private collectors (he agreed to do his best). Mr Verity was trying to track down and sell some overseas properties that belonged to my father personally, but he was having difficulties receiving replies from Australia and Southern Africa. Even Anatoly was delaying sending a reply to my telegram about our willingness to accept his wife's offer. There were, however, plenty of people who wanted us to settle various accounts (I told them to wait until my father was out of gaol). Of Vera, there was no news at all.

One rainy Saturday morning, I took out my old Crombie overcoat that I had worn on my first trip to Russia. I was about to take it to the second-hand shop as I now possessed a newer and much nicer coat bought before my second visit to Moscow, in the belief that a successful businessman's shoulders should be covered in a cashmere and wool mix from Bond Street. There was a hole in the pocket of the old coat, and a collection of English and Russian coins was jangling in the hem. The hole was just big enough to let coins through into the lining, but not large enough to let me fish them out with any ease. I tried, unsuccessfully, to retrieve them by finesse, and, losing patience, I decided to push my fist through the hole. Round the back of the garment, in among bits of fluff and old theatre tickets, I found something like a small pebble. It had smooth surfaces and sharp edges. I pulled out my hand and unfolded my fingers.

A green eye stared at me from the middle of my palm. It was almost as if the stone was looking at me, and taking in my image. I sat for about half an hour, staring back at the gem, occasionally closing my fingers around it, feeling its cool hardness, and thinking of my Russian days and nights: the ballet, the Metropole, Shchukin's paintings, the mine in the Ural Mountains, the wedding in the Butyrka, and above all, the bride with green eyes.

Outside there was a flash of lightning, which probably landed in Hyde Park, followed by a thunderclap. For a moment the stone glowed red like a fiery coal and a tiny beam of light sprang out from within it. An electric thrill ran through my body. The sky had grown as dark as late evening. I got up off the sofa and looked at my discovery under the electric lamp. It was consumed by a crimson hue.

I knew exactly where the alexandrite had come from and which thieving little minx had slipped it into my overcoat pocket. She must have done it sometime toward the end of my first trip to Russia. What baffled me was why she had given it to me. Was it as a talisman to bring me back to her? Or was she hopping to see it set in a ring? Or both?

I left the house in the rain and hopped onto an omnibus heading for the centre. Sometimes I like the gay, underworld atmosphere of Edgware Road, but on a snivelling day it is brooding and menacing, even from the top deck. Fortunately, it only took about five minutes to escape the pawnshops, the music hall, the ironmongers, and the men standing in doorways with shapeless hats pulled down over their eyes. The bus turned up Oxford Street and past the clock on the front of Selfridges. Soon I was hoofing it down Bond Street and looking through jewellers' windows. The rain had slowed to drizzle and I hardly noticed it. I was too involved in my quest. As I went down the slight hill towards Piccadilly, I realised that the big, cavernous establishments like Cartier and Tiffany were on the right-hand side, while the smaller jewellers had colonised the left of the street. Even though I had walked down here many times before, I had never paid much attention to the jewellers. My interest in gemmology was only recent.

I thought a smaller place might be more helpful - but they all looked like enemy territory to a young man: quite forbidding. Black was the colour of choice for the shop fronts. On the whole, they exhibited clumsy objects like diamond encrusted stars and dark brooches. Even the diamonds did not really sparkle. I stepped inside one or two shops along the way. It was almost like standing in the drawing room of a country house. The British display of wealth lacked exuberance, like the slow, heavy step of an impeccable but unwelcoming butler. When I thought of Moscow's shopping streets, Petrovka and Tverskaya, I recalled how the brightly illuminated shop fronts brought cheer into the dark winter. Children of all classes stopped and gazed at the sparkling gems.

I wiped the sweat of my brow and found myself outside a shop called Sweetnam & Co. It looked more inviting than the other places. Through the window I could see a moulded fireplace and fancy chairs. It made me think of a ridiculously up-market pub.

Inside I found young and not so young men choosing engagement rings, balancing prices against their chances of acceptance when they presented the little box, no doubt on one knee; and there were also a few doe-eyed couples who had moved onto the next stage of fitting wedding rings. It was a while before I got the attention of one of the assistants. I explained that I was hoping for an expert valuation.

'You'll be needing to speak to Mr Sweetnam, sir. His office is through there.'

Mr Sweetnam, it turned out, was an elderly gentleman in semi-retirement. His movements were slow and precise and his eyes squinted like a mole's. I wondered how well he could see, but I supposed that his long experience would make up for any waning of his senses. I placed the alexandrite on his desk.

'I'm sorry to trouble you with this trinket,' I said. 'I bought it in Russia for a few bob, but a friend thinks it might be worth a lot more.'

'It is more usual,' said Mr Sweetnam with a long face, 'that a customer brings a stone to me believing it to be many thousands. It is my sad duty to inform them that the family heirloom is made of paste. The customer remonstrates with me as if it were I who had robbed them. Many years ago, a lady accused me of slipping her emerald up my sleeve.'

'So I have nothing to lose,' I said cheerily. 'I believe this stone to be worth next to nothing, but I would be most grateful for your expert opinion. '

He placed an optical instrument in his eye and held the crimson stone between some tweezers and informed me in a neutral voice that the style in which it was cut, 'en cabochon', was rather unusual in the London market. Then he rose rather slowly from his desk and took the stone over to the window. The rain had cleared and the sun was reflecting in the bright puddles. The alexandrite turned verdant green.

'I congratulate you. You have not one, but two stones: an emerald by day and a ruby by night.' He turned it again, and it did its trick of shooting out a ray of light. 'In more years than I care to remember, I have seen only two or three such stones. You have an alexandrite cat's eye.'

Mr Sweetnam's old face smiled at me with a good deal of satisfaction. I had made his day.

'And how much is such a stone worth?'

'A few bob - in Russia - as you have told me. Here, a few thousand pounds.'

I persuaded Mr Sweetnam to prepare his expert valuation of the stone for me: £15,000. I watched him very carefully as he placed it in a little bag, and I clutched it tightly all the way back on the bus.

It took me another couple of weeks to persuade Coutts to accept Vera's stone as collateral for a loan. After that, my account was again replete with funds. Mr Verity had persuaded the courts to reduce my father's bail to a more realistic sum. I was now able to remove Papa out of remand in Wandsworth. I greeted him at the prison gate with a bottle of Pommery, his favourite champagne, in one hand, and the Dalmatian tugging at the lead in the other. My heart secretly harboured many regrets. I had dreamed so often of meeting Vera as she was released from the Butyrka Gaol. My father was my father, and filial love and respect was due to him and all that, but I have to say that his pat on the back, warmly meant though it was, was a poor substitute for what Vera would have given me.

A few days later I received a telegram from Moscow with some long expected news:

FREE. SEND FUNDS MOSCOW COMMERCIAL BANK, KUZNETSKY MOST. I KISS YOU.

I wired £100 to my wife. I thought for a while of asking her to come and join me in London. Then I hesitated. Naturally, there was the worry that what seemed beautiful and mysterious in an exotic foreign setting, might seem out of place back home in drab conservative old London. That was a risk that I was prepared to take when the time was right. But just then I had so much on my plate. I did not think that it was the moment to start introducing a wife who spoke no English into the British way of life. What would people make of her? How would I explain her to my father? How would she take to discovering that she had married into a family whose fortune mainly rested on a stone which she had purloined?

No, I thought. The time to begin the adventure of married life with Vera would be after my father's trial was over. If he was cleared of all charges, then the revelation of my marriage would surely blend into the general jubilation. If the worst came to the worst and he went down for a prison sentence, we would at least have a clear idea then of what 'for better or worse' would really entail.

I cabled Vera my love telling her to stay put and wait for me until the end of the Summer.

Chapter Twenty One

I suppose we all have vivid memories of that last summer in 1914. For the Munnings father and son, it was not just the events rumbling away in the Balkans that unbalanced our equanimity. In London, the lawyers, the investors, and the police were conspiring to bring us down. You might have thought that the fate of nations would have given them better things to do – 'There are bigger devils to slay than Old Munnings,' said Papa. 'I think they'll probably put my case in a drawer now.' But they did not. Lawyers, unfortunately, belong to a reserved profession; they are a species protected from the ravages of war, like members of parliament and other parasites. The newspapers might tell of mobilisations and declarations, and the roll of honour for the dead is printed on page after page, but there is always a space reserved in the paper for the law reports. Lord So and So was called as a co-respondent by Mrs Such and Such... A scoutmaster in Peckham was sentenced to seven years with hard labour for interfering with a boy... The news from the legal front was hardly promising. A date had been set for committal proceedings at which it would be decided whether or not the Crown had a built a case strong enough to justify a full trial. Only the prosecution would call witnesses, and the press would be restricted from reporting what was said at the hearing other than the final result.

I went to stay with my father in Surrey and Mr Verity was our most frequent visitor. The news we received from various quarters was hardly reassuring: the City police were working closely with Section 10 at Scotland Yard which had been set up recently to investigate frauds. They were said to be digging deep into a mountain of papers. They had been sniffing around former employees and builders at Munnings Hall. They had called on many of the shops that my father and Mrs Crawford used to frequent. And most disgustingly of all, they were threatening Mrs Crawford that she would be standing in the dock alongside my father unless she agreed to give evidence for the prosecution.

Each morning, throughout the committal proceedings, we breakfasted on kippers and Champagne at the Connaught. When our party arrived at Bow Street Magistrate's court, just opposite the Opera House, my father's face did not betray the slightest hint of concern or, heaven forbid, bad conscience. It was, you might have said, quite angelic.

Mr Spicer, the council for the prosecution, was a tall wiry man, with no chin and long arms. His nickname, said Mr Verity, was 'Spicer the Spider,' both on account of his dangling looks and his reputation for patiently ensnaring defendants in his web. He specialised in financial cases. My father was represented at the hearing by himself. He did not believe that there was a barrister in the country who could match him 'word for word' for oratory.

On the third morning, Major Crawford gave evidence. He explained how he had suspected his wife of an intrigue with Mr Munnings. He coloured red when The Spider had asked him for clarification: 'What nature of intrigue?'

Crawford paused to place his monocle in his eye before standing almost to attention and saying:

'I suspected her of an affair de coeur.'

'On what grounds?'

'On the grounds that she was frequently out late, discussing artistic matters with Mr Munnings. I knew Munnings' reputation for coarseness, and it seemed peculiar that he had developed so lively an enthusiasm for the arts.'

The ushers had to call for silence in court. The press, even though they were under reporting restrictions, had turned up in force. They were a noisy bunch.

Major Crawford went on to explain how he had opened his wife's desk. He had found no billets doux, but he had taken the opportunity to examine her cheque books – now exhibits A, B, C and D. He was surprised to discover that she had the signing rights for various mining enterprises and commercial concerns. He looked through the stubs: furniture from Maples, food from Fortnum's, antiques from Sotheby's, the Strand Theatre, a theatrical agency, a race horse trainer - and not small sums – all paid for on the company cheques. He knew that she had been helping Munnings to organise a party at his new home in Surrey on the First of May. The Major had turned up at the last moment, without giving his wife warning. He was amazed at the decadence of the affair. The Emperor Nero would have had a few tricks to learn from 'Angel' Munnings. Two jazz bands, one black, the other white, screeched cacophonies into the night sky. Men prominent in public-life chased nymphs around the swimming pool. A dog was served Champagne from a bucket, which it lapped up with relish before staggering off and falling into the pool. A white substance came round on silver platters, served by girls clad in white veils. A bare-chested black man led a cheetah or some such wild beast on a chain. The arm of the attendant appeared to be dripping with blood, though in probability it was paint. He was disgusted to think that all this had been paid for out of shareholders' money, but the part that hurt him most personally was the sight of his wife in her fancy dress costume: baggy trousers and a blouse that was almost transparent. She would not have looked out of place in a harem. When he accosted Mrs Crawford and demanded that she change into something more suitable, she looked right through him as if he were a ghost. As he recounted this episode, tears welled up in his eyes and he was obliged to remove his monocle The Spider turned to my father and said, 'Your witness.'

My father decently waited for Crawford to regain his composure. His military backbone seemed to have deserted him completely. 'Major Crawford,' said my father at length, 'Be so kind as to take a good look at me in the eye, man to man.'

The eyelids of the witness flickered in the palpable silence. The two men were square onto each other, like boxers in the ring.

He continued: 'Do you imagine me to be your rival for the affections of your wife?' Crawford croaked a couple of words, before clearing his throat and saying,

'I have already given testimony to that effect.'

'Thank you, Major. Let us set aside for the time being for the question of whether or not you have misapprehended the situation. Please consider my question carefully: is it not natural for a husband in your position to feel jealousy?'

'"Righteous anger," would be my preferred phrase.'

'Come, come, Major Crawford. Remember that you have taken the oath. Do you deny that you feel any jealousy toward me at all?'

'You say "jealousy", I say "anger".

'A seething jealousy that keeps you awake at night.'

'That would be going too far.'

'You have not lost any sleep over this matter?'

'Of course I've lain awake, wondering. Any husband in my position would have done so.'

'You have never considered taking your revenge on me?'

The judge said that Major Crawford would be excused for answering the question.

It had been a sordid and exhausting session. Papa looked white and sapped. Never mind the punishment, due legal process is enough to take away a man's vitality.

In the afternoon, the Spider produced a witness who had worked at the party. She was a Guildford girl whom father had employed as a mermaid. She had sat in the middle of an indoor fountain wearing nothing but a silver stocking pulled over both her legs. Only her long blond hair had provided some strands of modesty. Black caviar and selections of salmon and trout had been stored on ice around the base of the fountain. She had complained of the cold and goose bumps and father had promised a supplement to her wages – but she did not receive the extra payment. When Papa cross-examined her, he tried to imply that she bore a financial grudge against him – but she pouted and won the sympathy of the magistrate.

'You told the court,' said father, 'that your modesty was covered only by your hair.' There was a snigger from press gallery. The girl had a look of brazen cheek in her eyes.

'You could say that both my upper modesties were getting goose pimples.'

I wondered how long the magistrate would allow such a cross examination to continue, but when I looked up the bench, I rather think its occupant was rather enjoying it.

My father pressed on bravely but, in retrospect, foolishly.

'But were you not provided with an ample covering? I refer to a garment given to you by Mrs Crawford, with rhinestones and silver tassels.' (more laughter)

'I couldn't wear that thing! It was too small for my build, and besides it scratched something awful.' Oh how the press must have been sorely tempted to break into print and risk contempt of court. What hints and euphemisms they would have resorted to – making their reports sound even worse than the reality. The court was in raucous laughter, but the girl would not shut up: 'It was that sort of party, if you understand my meaning. You should have seen what was going on in the bushes outside.'

Things were going badly for Papa. He protested that this was all irrelevant to a fraud case; the magistrate in charge of the hearing had an appetite to hear more.

The day that damn nearly killed my father was the one when a very meek and reluctant Mrs Crawford took the stand. The Spider got his pound of flesh by cross examining her all morning and continuing after lunch. He made her account for every stub in every cheque book. She tried to keep her eyes downcast, but she could not help the odd sideways glance at my father. She had not understood the significance of the cheque books. She thought that the companies belonged to Mr Munnings and he could spend their funds how he wished. All that legalese about shareholders and their funds was, quite frankly, beyond her understanding.

The Spider saved up the crux question until after lunch.

'Have your personal relations with the accused ever entered the realms of physical immorality.'

Mrs Crawford composed herself before answering:

'If you are asking have I, do I, will I always, love Mr Munnings, the answer is an emphatic "Yes."'

'So you admit to immorality with him?'

'If it is immoral to love he who is twice the man one's husband is – then the answer is again "Yes"'.

Spider looked pleased with himself. He knew that father was done for now. How could a magistrate deny a jury and the British public a trial as entertaining as Rex V. Munnings?

'Your witness, Mr Munnings.'

'I have no questions.'

Father's final summing up for his own defence was one of the best speeches of his life, but I think that even he knew in his heart of hearts that the decision would go against him.

He admitted, frankly, to the mutual love and respect which he and Mrs Crawford felt for one another. He knew that society would frown upon their relationship, but this was not a divorce proceeding. A man's liberty was at stake. The prosecution's chief witness, Major Crawford, was blinded by sexual jealousy. His protestations that he acted for the good of the shareholders were not to be taken seriously, for his actions had done irreparable harm to the companies, and if any value was to be salvaged for he shareholders, the misguided legal proceedings must be brought to a halt. Yes, the expenditure on entertainment might have been on the high side, but entertaining the rich and famous was part and parcel of the work of a company promoter. It was the way that a modern business operated. If he had not courted the great and good, his companies and their shareholders would have been at a competitive disadvantage.

In deference to the wishes of the magistrate and the court, he would not name the members of the cabinet, the clergy and the House of Lords who had enjoyed his hospitality. But he warned that if the case went to trial, he would be forced to call certain influential people as witnesses for the defence: men who would be diverted from work vital for the survival of the nation; men whose reputations might be tainted by such a trial. This eventuality could only bring comfort to the Kaiser and the enemy. At a time of War, the erring ways of mankind had to be seen in the context of much greater evil - and here we were salaciously pouring over the details of a trivial private scandal from a bygone time of peace. He therefore moved that Mr Hetherington, the magistrate, should see fit to dismiss this false and malicious prosecution and spare the nation from a trial that would only sully it.

Hetherington kept us waiting almost a day for his decision. When he recalled the court, he was curt: the prosecution had brought forward evidence that suggested, prima face, that the funds of publicly listed companies had been expended on private revelries. The defence had claimed that this was part of the legitimate expenditure of a shareholding company. This was a matter for a jury to decide. Therefore he committed my father to trial at the Old Bailey.

'I plead innocent and shall contest my case vigorously,' said father. The court began to rise. It was almost an anti-climax.

The Times Law Report September 20th, 1914

At Bow Street's magistrate's court, yesterday, Theodore Gabriel Munnings was committed to trial at the Old Bailey. The charges under the Larceny Act related to alleged irregularities in the accounts of a number companies under the control of Mr Munnings.

As is well known, father did not fight his case. His body was fished out from The Thames near Hammersmith Bridge three days later. I am sure that he would have gone on to the bitter end, had not it been for Mrs Crawford. He felt a terrible responsibility for putting her through the ignominy of a public trial. He must have loved her. Besides which, it was increasingly apparent that any hope of salvaging his financial reputation was a vain one. Never again would he be able to captivate an audience with one of his tales of a pot of gold beyond the rainbow. He had lost all credibility.

The hostilities with Germany had made the journey from Russia to England a hazardous one. It involved running the gauntlet of the Baltic Sea where there were frequent sinkings. I wrote to Vera telling her that it would be safest and most practical for her to stay in Moscow. I had little doubt that I would soon be in France, and I privately expected that my bones might remain there for all eternity. I had no particular desire to defend king and country after what they had done to my father, but the pressure on all young men to enlist was enormous. I pre-empted conscription by one month.

It was a great comfort for me to receive letters from Vera during those dark days, both in France, and during the periods I spent in hospital in England recovering from wounds. The letters would arrive infrequently and written in a variety of hands and with varying standards of English grammar. She at least seemed acquainted with two or three people who could write English for her. I learned that she had found work in the props department of Nina's theatre. The performances were very patriotic in those days, and after the curtain fell the orchestra played the national anthem of each of Russia's allies in the War in turn. There had been anti-German riots in Moscow, and Vera regretted that shops belonging to subjects of the Tsar who possessed Germanic names had been looted by the mob. She had visited Mr Shchukin who had wrongly believed, at first, that the war would soon be over. Now he seemed very grave. The war had damaged his fortune.

She did not hold back in more delicate matters – saying how the day of our wedding had been the happiest in her life, and how sad she was that this terrible war had separated us, and how she longed for me to take her in my arms again. There was the odd hint that she hoped for a ring with a 'special stone' when we were once again reunited.

I must admit, I found most of the sentiments expressed in her letters surprisingly graceful (although usually she ended up with a request for funds.) I wondered how much help she had received with the composition as well as with translation.

The letters became more infrequent as the situation became darker. Perhaps some did not find their way to me. After the Russian Revolution of February 1917, (a period during which I was in hospital in London) I received a letter describing shooting and barricades in Moscow, but now that the Tsar had stepped down, it seemed that the streets were full of smiling people milling around and waving banners and flags. They hoped for peace.

In October, the Bolsheviks staged their putsch against the Provisional Government. Lenin and Trotsky were now in charge of Russia. Vera's letters ceased.

Chapter Twenty Two

"We are thus faced in Europe with the spectacle of an extra-ordinary weakness on the part of the great Capitalist class ... Now they tremble before every insult — call them pro-Germans, international financiers, or profiteers, and they will give you any ransom you choose to ask not to speak of them so harshly."

John Maynard Keynes The Economic Consequences of the Peace, 1919

My late, disgraced father would have hated England just after The Great War: income taxes at 30%, excess profits duty on companies at 60%. Churchill growling from the Liberal benches for a levy on 'War Wealth' and receiving a chorus of 'Hear! Hear!' in the House. Perhaps it was for the best that he did not live to see it. Money was right out of fashion once again. It was supposed to have been bad form to have kept your business intact throughout the slaughter, and the Government did its level best to see that any that survived the War would be done in the by the Peace. Not that people had any sympathy for the wealthy classes. Oh no, they were suspected of having started the whole damn conflagration just to make some 'excess profits.' Had father survived and continued to prosper, envious little toads would have pointed him out in his favourite watering hole, the Connaught Hotel, with a bottle of bubbly and perhaps a chorus girl or two set before him, and they would have whispered: 'Old 'Angel' Munnings looks like he did rather well out of the War.'

I was of the age and sex that was supposed to have been machine-gunned or shelled or gassed. I must here pass on my heartfelt thanks to one particular Hun whom I never saw through the fog of battle, but who shot me in the groin. He missed the important bits by the width of a hair, and although I walk to this day with a slight limp, it was enough to end my war but not my life. Good Shot Fritz! Dankerschöne.

After I was discharged from hospital, somebody important recommended me for a post at the Board of Trade on the Russia desk. I have always suspected, but never confirmed, that it was Lydia's father who was my guardian angel in this particular instance. The Board paid for me to take up Russian lessons and finally, under the strict discipline of a Crimean count in exile, I came to grips with the syntax. I managed to gain some sort of linguistic proficiency. It was of little use to me. After Lenin and Trotsky pulled Russia out of the War in January 1918, we cut off trade relations. My duties were therefore rather light. I commanded a certain respect among my bureaucratic colleagues: few of them had been closer to the fray than the tea rooms in War Office building. I had been wounded in action. Nobody really expected me to get too much office work done.

I hoped that Vera thought of me sometimes, and perhaps cherished my memory. I now regretted deeply that I had not seized the chance to bring her to England before War and Revolution had fallen down between us like invisible curtains. It had been the biggest mistake of my life, proving that misfortune begets more misfortune.

There remained a chance that, when Britain and the Bolshevik Government normalised relations, I might yet be able to discover her whereabouts in Russia. And contrary to what most people thought at the time, I believed that British diplomacy would cosy up to the Bolshevik bosom sooner rather than later. I had no doubt that Lloyd George was a Communist at heart and would soon be embracing Vladimir Lenin on the steps of Number 10. The Bolshevist trade emissary, Comrade Krassin, a member of the Soviet Central Committee no less, was calling on the PM for tea on practically a daily basis. His aim was to persuade the prime minister to re-establish trade relations. The Manchester Guardian photographed Krassin in his vulgar white trilby hat buying a rose from a flower lady on Oxford Street. I remember thinking that back in Russia, the flower-seller would have been arrested for the new crime of speculation.

In May 1920, I received a letter which absolutely scotched any lingering hope of a reunion with my wife. It came from my long lost friend, Anatoly Mizinsky, and had been posted in Paris and forwarded by way of Verity.

My Dear Old Friend,

I pray that you receive this letter with body and soul still together on this Earth. Too, too many friends have departed for a better world. In my heart I know that you are still alive. You may call this Russian mysticism, but it is something I truly feel.

How are my affairs? Nothing to grumble about, as you English might say. I have employment here in Paris, and a sufficient wage. It is an entirely new experience for me, and I might say not such a bad one. I spend my time not so differently from when you first made my acquaintance, in the best company, with the best food and wine, at one of the best restaurants in the city. As before I keep late hours, and creep into my bed practically as the sun is rising. The only difference from old times is that now I am waiting at the tables of Le Cossack Qui Ris. You can congratulate me. This last week, I have been promoted to the respected post of sommelier. No one could be found with a better knowledge than I of both Crimean and French vintages. At first it was a little inconvenient when I found myself waiting at the table of old acquaintances, but I soon came to realise that more often than not they were eating and drinking their last francs, just as I had done, before applying to the owner for a job. He is a kindly man, a Crimean Tartar whose family have been in France for 25 years, but he cannot support Paris's 'White Russian' community in its entirety. I say without irony that I am not unhappy. I have learned Christian humility. I am tired, but it is an honest and useful tiredness. I am chaste too, if only because I have no time for women.

You might have thought I could have learned the benefits of an honest day's endeavour in the new Workers' Republic of Russia. There are many of my class who would have gladly taken up laborious jobs in the name of equality and justice. I myself volunteered to work as a hotel barman. When the commissars came to our flat and said that three workers' families must move into our spare rooms, we did not complain. As for our money - it was made worthless by the war in any case, but we understood that the respect formally shown to our class must go, and we did not shed any tears for it. We felt purified by our new equality. But sadly our relief at shedding our former class distinction did not last long. Our new rulers did not differentiate between those who were ready to give up their privileges and those who wished to cling to their former positions. No. They hated us, the middle classes, bourgeoisie, 'former-people', exploiters, Capitalist scum; they despised us and wanted first to humiliate us and then to rob us of our will to exist, and finally, if we did not crawl away and die like cockroaches, or join the White Army, they wanted to arrest and shoot us. It was for us that they instigated their 'Red Terror,' of which they boast, and from which, I am glad to report, we escaped 'just in the nick of time.'

My mother and wife send you their warmest regards and beg that, should you find the time to visit Paris, you pay us the honour of a visit; in the meantime I drink to your health

Salut!

Your faithful and affectionate friend

Anatoly

PS You would not believe what has become of your little Vera. She mingles in the ranks of the new ruling class and has become extremely rich. Before we departed from Moscow, I saw her stepping out of a Rolls Royce such as only party members and their wives, mistresses, whores, children, etc. are privileged to use. She went into the Kamerny Revolutionary Theatre where Nina now performs. She was dressed in sable and looked just like a lady.

It was not long after I received the letter from Anatoly, that I decided to sell the alexandrite stone that Vera had so judiciously stolen off the Frenchman. After the long period of probate of my father's estate (during which my father's remaining creditors were either killed off by the war or exhausted by Verity's delaying tactics), I was good for a few thousand which I used to pay off my debt to Coutts Bank. I redeemed the little gem from their vaults. I again held the potent memory of Vera in my palm. But what use was it to me?

I felt the time had come to exclude Vera from my dreams. She was doing rather well for herself in Russia and had no need of me. At least I knew now that she had found a good patron, somebody close to the top of the Communist tree. I understood, of course, that this was the best thing for her, but I could not help feeling regret at the news. The postscript to Anatoly's letter had been the final confirmation that she was no longer mine. I had to find a new man within myself, and I needed a new woman to go with him.

I took the alexandrite round to Sweetnam's of Bond Street. I found that the old man had passed away, and I met the son in the upstairs room. I expressed my condolences, hoping to imply that I was a long standing customer of the family business. Young Mr Sweetnam had a pious face, one you might trust. He said:

'My father was that rare beast: a true expert. There wasn't an ounce of balderdash in his body.'

He held the alexandrite up to the window. Its green eye gazed back into the room with intensity.

'It belonged to my wife,' I said.

'I am sorry,' said young Mr Sweetnam. 'It seems my condolences are in order too.'

'You weren't to know,' I said. 'It pains me to part with such a wonderful stone – but circumstances are not easy.'

'You are not alone in that particular boat. We see a steady flow of people selling treasures which they would never have dreamed of letting go before the War. Death duties play their part. I am afraid that some of our customers find our valuations disappointing. I must tell you frankly, Mr Munnings, it is not a seller's market today.'

He observed the alexandrite's colour change under the electric lamp. I thought that even in these difficult times, such a marvellous stone must be worth a bob or too.

'I can give you £8,000,' he said.

He had been correct. I was disappointed.

'Your father thought it was worth a great deal,' I protested.

'Ah, but that was before the War. As I indicated, times have changed.'

I said that I would have to think over his offer. Once I was out on Bond Street, I walked into a bigger place across the road. After a little wrangling, their expert agreed £9,500. I took the cheque from the cashier and left, not feeling any jubilation. Vera was erased from my life with the same finality as the world's set-up pre 1914 – or so I thought.

I handed in my notice at the Board of Trade. I could get by now without their £260 per annum. I bought a flat near Hyde Park for £1,200 and filled it with the few possessions which I had managed to whisk away before the creditors got their hands on them. Thanks to the good taste of Mrs Crawford, Papa had owned one or two rather good objects. I spent my days reading several newspapers, and walking Tatters in the park. The Dalmatian was my last souvenir of Vera.

My plans to find a new female element in my life did not progress well. For a while I used the services of an Italian in Shepherd's market. I confess to her without making any excuses or asking you to overlook my depravity. She bore a passing resemblance to Vera, but she demanded cash in advance. I gave up my Moaning Lisa, partly as an economy measure, and partly because I thought I really ought to attempt a relationship with a woman on non-monetary terms. Next I formed a brief attachment with a student at London University. Our relations were frustratingly pure. I was not at liberty to progress things further, because I could not hold out the hope of marriage.

It was about that time, that I came across a short article in the legal columns of The Times about an interesting but sordid case. I have kept the cutting pasted onto a page in my diary. The proceedings were entitled Higgs v Higgs. A Russian born lady, Mrs Natalie Dimitrievna Higgs, had married her English husband in the chapel at the British Factory in St. Petersburg before the War. Now the swine had deserted her and was trying to deny that marriage was lawful in this country.

Mrs Higgs was suing for restoration of her conjugal rights. I am glad to say that the judge was a gentleman and ruled in the lady's favour. So Campbell Fitzgerald had been right: a Russian marriage did count over here, and I was still married to Vera.

It was dear old Lydia who fixed my visit to Red Russia.

Only Lydia could have simultaneously had one foot in each of the following camps: The Communist International (recently founded in Moscow), and Bearfields Bank, (recently founded in the City of London). Naturally all her shares in the merchant bank (which her father had set up during the War to finance foreign trade) were tied up in various secretive trust arrangements. She only accepted the dividends because they helped fund her work in the realm of international socialism.

In those days, the main hazard of visiting Lydia's flat in Bloomsbury Square was that one felt obliged to buy a copy of The Worker's Dreadnought. The latest editions were spread over the coffee table. Its banner proclaimed itself to be a pacifist Socialist journal – but its difficulty was that Europe's socialists were anything but pacifist. The Dreadnought's illustrator found ways to feminise rioting workers in Berlin and the Bolsheviks attacking Warsaw. To depict these violent events, she conjured up Pre-Raphaelite drawings of women in peasant scarves and floral shawls, peacefully marching through the streets of Budapest. Lydia saw me smile. She frowned:

'It's a good cause. You would hardly know from the pages of the Capitalist press that Communism is spreading across Europe like wildfire...' And then she added, with a persecuted look, 'It's too, too humiliating, trying to raise advertising for a publication putting forth the leftist point of view. You can't imagine the language that some company directors use when we ask them for sponsorship.'

I rummaged in my trouser pocket for a shilling..

'Why don't you take a second copy for your maid?' she said.

'What? And incite Beth to join the revolution against the idle exploiters? That would hardly be in my best interest.'

I felt the razor edge of Lydia's disapproving gaze, and so I rummaged in my pocket for another coin. Lydia did not know that Beth read my Daily Mail every day and told me that her Archie believed that the country was going to the dogs what with all those unpatriotic shop stewards calling for everyone to go out on strike.

Over tea and ginger nut biscuits, Lydia said:

'I've got something exciting to tell you.'

I looked at her long, slightly freckled, English face. She did not appear to be blooming with an unborn child (that would have flattened her progressive ideas) or even a male admirer – but I guessed that I was going to be briefed on a love experience. And so what she said after a long pause for effect surprised me: 'I'm going to Moscow.'

'What? To join the Bolsheviks as a Commissar?'

'Not yet. I am to be a delegate at the Second Congress of the Third International.'

This somewhat baffling statement required further explanation. The Third International was an organisation formed in Moscow under the leadership of Comrade Zinoviev, and was dedicated to the immediate overthrow of international Capitalism. It was the biggest jamboree on the socialist calendar and Lydia had wangled an invitation through the editor of The Worker's Dreadnought, Sylvia Pankhurst, the Communist daughter of Mrs Emmeline, the woman suffragist. Many of the other delegates from Britain would be trades unionists and leading members of The Labour Party.

Lydia spoke of her excitement about the social change that was taking place in Moscow. It was, she said, mankind's bravest experiment. There was a firmament of creative energy bringing forth new art forms, new buildings, new communal ways of life. Soon, money would be abolished and each would receive according to his or her needs. The movement was truly international in its spirit. She could believe that not too far away in the future, a new civilisation would spread across the world without borders, countries, or conflicts.

'Well have a nice trip,' I said, not without a pang of envy. If only I had belonged to the socialist side of my family – my Uncle Fredrick's – Russia would have still been my playfield. I did not agree with any of that 'progressive' rot, of course, but I missed the crazy side of Moscow – the feeling that even the maddest of dreams can take wing any moment. It might be magnificent, it will probably be a flop, but it is bound to be exciting.

Lydia said, 'I thought you might have plans to visit Moscow again.'
'Me? How?'
She raised that eyebrow of hers:
'You are aware of the talks that are going on with Russian trade representation here in London?'
'I am.'
'The new Republic is looking for outside help to develop its industry. It recognises the need, during the transition to a Communist society, to enlist the help of foreign capitalists. My father is privy to some of the negotiations. A small group of industrialists are travelling in secret to Moscow.'

'Business will never get anything but grief out of the Bolsheviks,' I said. 'Besides, I don't think I would care to get in too deep with your chums. They're a bloodthirsty lot, so I hear.'

Lydia did not pick up the bait:
'I am not suggesting that you go so far as to set up a business in Russia – I merely thought that you may have a desire to see Moscow again … and perhaps your wife. The business would be more of a pretext for your trip… I think, perhaps, not for the first time.'

Oh, that eyebrow of hers! It was as sharp as a sickle.

I spoke to one of my connections at the Board of Trade, and he arranged for me to visit the Russian trade delegation in Mayfair where I was received with great charm and courtesy. Comrade Krassin himself shook my hand. The young man who worked as his secretary gave me tea in Russian style, with hot water from the samovar, and chatted to me about myself and my essay into the Russian mining industry, which I explained had been cut short by the war. I had no sense that he disapproved of my commercial connection with his country in Tsarist times; indeed he seemed quite nostalgic about the 'days that were gone forever.' I returned a week later and was told that my participation in the secret conference of 'Industrialist Friends of the Revolution' had been approved at the highest level. I was warned that, owing to the trade blockade by the Allied Powers, the situation in Russia was rather difficult. I was not to expect great comfort or convenience. Above all, there was a strict 'gentleman's understanding' that my trip was to remain confidential. I was to make my own way to Helsinki where I was to visit a certain address where I would be given documents to continue my journey through Russia to Moscow. My only instructions for once I arrived in the Bolshevik capital were to report to Comrade Karakhan, the deputy commissar for foreign affairs, whose office so happened to be inside a building that I knew well: The Metropole Hotel.

Rather disappointingly, it was not possible for me to travel with Lydia. The Russians did not wish the foreign representatives of the toiling classes to mix en route with the 'Industrialist Friends of the Revolution.' Who could say what embarrassment or misunderstanding might ensue?

Chapter Twenty Three

'Several members of your delegation questioned me with surprise about the Red terror, about the absence of freedom of the press in Russia, of freedom of assembly, about our persecution of Mensheviks and pro-Menshevik workers, etc. My reply was that the real cause of the terror is the British imperialists and their allies.'
V. I. Lenin LETTER TO THE BRITISH WORKERS June 17, 1920

Now I know what it feels like to enter the Butyrka as a prisoner. I have been driven through the eighteenth century gates of the fortress-prison inside a truck marked 'Bread.' I have been marched along the clanking metal floors by a guard armed with a pistol and a sword. I have been handed a questionnaire to fill in – name, nationality, date of birth and 'crime with which you are charged.' I have been asked to remove my clothes. I have stood naked while my things were examined minutely before being returned to me, minus my belt, shoe laces, money and travel documents.

It feels cold, for one thing. It is like entering one's own tomb.

I did not notice any fear at first. There was nothing left to fear. How quickly I had become a former person! It was almost as if the outside world, the streets of Moscow, England, my rooms on Sussex Gardens, George Munnings, no longer existed. The walls of the Butyrka marked the outer limits of the universe.

I had been expecting solitary confinement. I was almost indignant to discover that I was to have company during my stay. I was lucky, I was told, to be sharing the cell with only three other men. I would have found it much more crowded had I arrived a day earlier, before the latest round of executions. This far from comforting information was imparted to me by one of my cell-mates, a British officer: a prisoner of war, who had been incarcerated in the Butyrka Prison for six months. He had landed in Vladivostok with the British Expeditionary Force, a half-cocked attempt to intervene in the Revolution.

'No need look so down in the mouth old chap,' he said, 'They haven't shot any of the British contingent so far.' But after he had looked up and down my civilian clothes, he added, 'But, then again, if they suspect you of espionage, perhaps you might be a different case.'

'I assure you that I am not a spy or anything of that sort.' I spoke firmly. I hoped that he was a stoolpigeon and that my comment would reach the proper authorities.

'Ah,' said the Captain. 'I should warn you, they take a good deal of convincing, these Bolshevist fellows, in my experience.'

After that, he seemed to treat me as 'not quite the right sort,' or perhaps I was imagining it. In any case, I was in no mood for conversation. I spent most of my time squatting on the iron 'bed' hugging my knees. I drifted in and out of consciousness, some of the time not sure if I was in the Butyrka dreaming of the trenches, or in the trenches dreaming of the Butyrka. Either way, there was a strong feeling of déjà vu about the coldness and the soldiers' gallows' humour. Actually, the things people normally go on about when they describe prison life – the diet of thin gruel, the bed without a mattress, and the bucket for a convenience - were relatively easy to endure. It was the not-knowing why I was there or what would become of me that was my worst enemy.

Only after I had been there a day did I endeavour to decipher some of the Cyrillic graffiti inscribed on the walls:

Tell family at 31 Klyebny Street that they shot Dr. Malyevich.

I did not bother to read any more inscriptions after that.

And my trip had been going so well, so it had seemed. Up until the moment of my detention, I had thought that Moscow had almost belonged to me.

My train had pulled into Moscow around daybreak – a mere fourteen hours late. I had a feeling that Moscow had been asleep for seven years while I had been away, and now that I was back, it was gently stirring itself like a beautiful woman waking from her slumbers. The sky was a hue of Revolutionary red. 'Bliss it was that dawn to be alive,' not because I had any soggy sympathies with the Bolsheviks, but because I felt that I had arrived back at the centre the of my lost youth.

The air that morning was sooty, and not as fresh as it ought to have been at that early hour. I learned later that the peaty earth around the city had caught fire, and that tens of thousands of Red Army soldiers were deployed to beat it with blankets.

The first omen was promising: plenty of cabs were waiting for hire in the great square before the station; at least that aspect of Moscow's commercial life could never be abolished. Gone though, were the drivers' uniforms and smart caps. The cabbies looked as though they had come directly from ploughing the fields. Gone too was the cheerful banter of the former days. I made a sullen bargain with a man, and bid the price of his hire down to a wedge of Bolshevik roubles as thick as a book. I needed not a wallet, but a briefcase for my money. My bumpy ride along the potholed streets filled me with fresh wonder. Away from the station, only a few citizens of the Workers' Republic were on the streets so early. A young man walked down the incline of Tverskaya Street. I fancied that he had spent the night with his girl, but perhaps he had some more prosaic night-time occupation. A solitary black motor vehicle came up the other way from the Kremlin, swerving to avoid a crater in the road, and puffing blue kerosene smoke into our nostrils as it passed us. The car had been as crowded as a bus. A man clad in a long leather coat had been hanging standing on the running board, and I caught a glimpse of a holster for an enormous pistol on his hip. When the automobile was out of earshot, the only sound left was the squawking of a crow, such as you would normally hear on a farm. Many of the shops were boarded up, rather as in London on May Day when the trade unionists march down Oxford Street. At the bottom of the hill, nearer the Kremlin, I saw evidence of the street fighting during the

Revolution. The Hotel National on the corner looked like it had been transported to France and back for the War. Despite the general dilapidation, the golden crosses on the churches glinted as they had always done, and no doubt will for all eternity, long after the Bolsheviks have gone to blazes.

The doors of the Metropole were open, though nobody helped me haul my kitbag into the marble entrance. The genial desk manager of old had been replaced by a woman whose hair had been dyed with henna. When I presented my papers, I was met with a scrutinizing look of intense suspicion. I thought that perhaps she had misunderstood my inadequate Russian. It was no use regretting the passing of the former desk manager and his excellent English; those days were gone for ever. At least it was a chance for me to use the Russian I had learned while I was at the Board of Trade.

'I have a letter,' I said, 'from Comrade Krassin in London.'

She took my letter without a word and placed a pair of half-moon spectacles on her broad nose. She looked at me and said, 'You need the Commissariat of Foreign Affairs.'

'Where?'

'Sixth floor; it opens after ten o'clock.'

A single chair remained in the lobby – I remembered that there had been cluster of comfortable places to sit in the old days. I claimed it and I closed my eyes. I opened them a couple of hours later and found a more friendly looking face behind the reception counter. I went over and was informed that I could take breakfast in the cafeteria.

'I know where it is,' I said. It came back to me now: the tinkle of spoons and the aroma of coffee, the little cakes and honey-soaked crepes, all of which had delighted Vera and even Lydia, not to mention me. However, breakfast was the absolute confirmation that things had gone seriously downhill under Communism. It consisted of a couple of pieces of dry bread and a glass of weak tea without sugar. I paid with a ration coupon which had been given to me by the Russian representative in Helsinki. It proved a popular meal. Most of the other breakfasters wore worn-out suits, and looked as if they belonged to the clerical classes or were, perhaps, eccentric academic types.

Around nine thirty, I went in search of the Commissar of Foreign Affairs. The lift was out of action, and so I went up by way of the staircase. There was no carpet, and the steps were covered in dust. All the same, old memories came back of climbing up here with Vera. The stained glass windows were in want of nothing more than some soapy water to revive the swans and stalks depicted on them. The upper reaches of the hotel had not changed much. The sixth floor had always been a bit dusty, even in the hotel's prime. The alabaster faces of young women still looked out from the columns of the stairwell, but the gold that had once adorned their hair was gone. There was no trace of the rouge heart that had once been painted on the door of room 606. I knocked in some trepidation, half expecting a corseted ginger beauty to open up. Speculation and trade were banned, but one could not help wondering whether the oldest exchange of all kept going somehow. The door did open, and I was confronted by a woman – an enormous bosomed woman of about fifty years of age. I wondered, for a moment, if she was one of the girls of old, now ravaged by time and revolution. As it turned out, she was not one for providing service of any type.

'I am listening to you,' she said. As time went by, I became more familiar with notions of politeness currently held in Communist Russia. The foulest insult you can use against a man is to call him 'Mr or 'Sir' or worse still 'Your Excellency.' They have a saying, 'All the misters are in Paris.' People hail each other as 'citizen' and 'comrade' or simply 'young man' or 'girl' or just nothing at all. 'I'm listening to you,' is a way of saying: 'I am probably going to ignore you completely, but in the meantime don't get any ideas that you are better than me.'

I handed the letter from Krassin to the lady and said, 'He is a member of the Central Committee of the Communist Party and the most senior representative of your government in London. He asks that you help me get a room.' She looked at the letter and responded:

'I know who Comrade Krassin is - but you are wrong to say he asked me to do anything.'

Nonetheless, after only a brief wait, I was admitted in to see the Deputy Commissar for Foreign Affairs, a devilish fellow, with a dark moustache and a little beard. He puffed a cigar and his manner reminded me faintly of Anatoly.

'I am very sorry you have had such trouble,' said the gentleman who went by the name of Karakhan and who spoke good English.

'Not at all,' I replied, 'I've been making myself comfortable.'

'We have so many problems; the lack of transport, the shortage of rooms, the Allied blockade…'

'Quite. I'm here to see if I can help to do my little bit as regards trade.'

'You are a friend of our Government and a guest in our Republic. I will do all I can to help you,' he said. And he did.

He picked up the telephone and shouted into it. Some weak tea was brought for me while Karakhan got on with signing some papers. About half an hour later the telephone buzzed and a little light flashed on it. They had found me a place to stay. When you take into account that I was not a Glaswegian shop steward, nor was I an American millionaire, nor a world famous writer with socialist inclinations – in other words I was just about the least important foreigner in Moscow that hot summer of 1920, he had done well for me.

I found myself billeted in a mansion, heavy with oak-carved gothic gloom, but magnificent all the same. Before the Revolution it had belonged to a wealthy merchant, Moscow's 'Sugar King', or so they said. I slept in a room with rich tapestries hanging on the walls. My window looked across the river to the Kremlin. To my mind it was the best view in Moscow, if not the entire world. In addition to those fairy tale domes and towers, it had an added advantage of not being interrupted by any scenes of proletarian squalor. You could almost imagine that the world had not changed, so long as you did not wonder too hard while you slept in the Sugar King's bed, about what fate might have befallen its owner.[23]

The other guests at the house were, like me, 'Industrialist Friends of the Revolution,' none of whom seemed particularly troubled by the fact that they were living in the confiscated property of a comrade in commerce. Money is the most pragmatic force in the universe – it adapts to new conditions without any sentiment for the old. Money will deal with anybody, even those who promise to abolish it. This was one of the many lessons that I learned first-hand on my third and last trip to Russia, for I was a very different George Munnings from the young man who had arrived there in 1914. I had shed all the romantic delusions of youth. In this respect, I was the very opposite of the great majority of foreigners in Moscow that summer. Lady Lydia and her comrades, gathering for the Second Congress of the Third International, were determined to see the New Republic as Paradise Regained. Even the 'hard-nosed' capitalists who had come for the parallel congress of 'Industrialist Friends of the Revolution', had convinced themselves that Lenin was just another politician whose speeches and slogans should be taken with a pinch of salt, because in the end he would have to deal with economic reality. Whatever they saw with their own eyes, they longed to return home and make far sighted and visionary recommendations to their boards, if only to justify the time they had spent in Russia at the shareholders' expense.

I shied away from conversing with my fellow English representatives, fearing that my name might be recognised. I overheard grumbles about delays and cancelled meetings, not to mention the food and accommodation.

In the morning, a line of black Rolls Royces waited to take us to the conference. I slipped past them, preferring to walk over the

---

[23] It would seem that George stayed in the Kharitonenko Mansion which later became the British Embassy.

bridge. I had no trouble finding my own way to the venue; it was back at the Metropole Hotel.

Our conference was held in the grandiloquent dining hall where I had eaten with Anatoly and Vera that first night in Moscow. Over the dais, where the musicians used to hammer out frenetic waltzes, a red banner was strung up bearing the, by now, hackneyed slogan, 'Proletariat of the World Unite!' One of the porters, who had been there in the former days, recognised me and greeted me like an old friend. 'Oh comrade,' he said, 'how you used to climb up the candelabra and dance in the pond!' (The pond was now empty of water and the golden cherub spouted no more). I nearly replied, 'Actually that wasn't me, I never went quite that far,' but why disappoint a nice old fellow?

'Yes, we did have a good time,' I said. 'By the way, do you remember my lady friend, Vera Borisovna?'

'Vera? There were so many beautiful young women here in those days. Nowadays the female comrades are, you know – more the clever sort.'

'Yes, I know what you mean – not like the old days.'

The Russian woman of 1920 wore a mannish haircut and a severe expression, but she could arrange a handkerchief around the head with certain style. By contrast, some of the Russian male delegates had given way to shabbiness. One or two wore ties wrapped around their necks without collars.

I had been provided with a translator, Nadia, who whispered English versions of the conference speeches in my ear. Nadia, who I would say was a lady of about forty odd years of age, had been born into a good family. She told me, in between translating speeches, that women from the 'former classes' were much in demand for positions as stenographers and translators, but that their wages were lower than factory workers'.

I was grateful for Nadia's help. The Russian language skills I had acquired while working at the Board of Trade were certainly not up to following the convoluted conference proceedings. The Chairman gave a special welcome to the foreign 'sympathisers' who had broken the Allied Blockade and travelled through difficult and dangerous conditions. He made an unashamed appeal to our charity; the fledgling workers' state was in urgent need of locomotives, cutting tools, dredges, winches, boots, winter clothes, grain, potatoes, tobacco, alcoholic sprit… his list went on for a long time.

The second speaker was rather more animated, but no more concise. He explained that 'under Communism', gold would have no value. I noticed that the comrades always spoke of Communism as a future state of bliss that would one day encompass the entire universe. He ran through the history of mankind, explaining how ancient priests and oracles had valued gold because they believed it to be the colour of the Gods, and later the Bourgeoisie had made a living from buying and selling the metal, and had promoted the notion that it was somehow important to mankind. Now the entire capitalist system was constructed upon this fiction.

He concluded with a rousing crescendo:

'Comrades!' No one can name the day when gold will lose all its value on the Capitalist exchanges, and will be seen for what it is: nothing more than a soft and shiny metal.

'Comrades! Mining is the most urgent of all economic tasks facing the new Republic. As urgent, even, as the harvest.

'It is necessary for the Revolution to be cunning as well as bold. Let us dig the gold out of Russia's soil and sell it abroad – let us exchange it for tractors and machinery, ball-bearings, boots, overcoats, etc. But let us work quickly, Comrades, before even the Capitalist fools comprehend the worthless value of our shining gold!'

This nonsense was too much for me. I made some excuse to Nadia and slipped away from the conference and the Metropole. On the way out, I nodded to a fellow foreign Capitalist 'fool' who was also rising from his seat. I hurried past him.

The icon-kissers still crowded into the Church of the Iberian Virgin. I had a feeling that if I closed my eyes and opened them again, I would see Vera, in the same way that she had appeared there seven years beforehand, but I tried and she did not manifest herself among the incense and the candles. All the same, I had a strong sense that she came there sometimes and remembered me. I stood before the famous icon of the Virgin and asked her if she could perform a very small favour for a businessman who had fallen on hard times. She had brought Vera to me here before, and would she mind repeating the miracle once again? I wasn't really a bad man, as men go. Surely it was better to be a Capitalist than a Communist in God's eyes, if only just? At least we Capitalists did not go in for iconoclasm, which was an important consideration if one happened to be an icon. I looked into the Virgin's dark face and I felt comforted. She had retained her looks through good centuries and bad, and there had probably been more of the latter than the former. Love, she seemed to say, can overcome the politics, philosophy and economics of the day. On the steps I asked a long haired priest if people were able to worship freely – he replied that people could do what they liked, so long as they did not mind being watched. He gave a nod in the direction of two men in black leather coats who stood with fixed glares in their eyes. They, or their friends, were no doubt responsible for the notice set inside an icon frame and affixed to the church. It bore the slogan: 'Religion is the opiate of the people!' I watched an old man stop before the frame and cross himself. He must have been illiterate. One of the watchers called out:

'That's right Uncle!'

I found myself walking up the hill toward Lubyanka Square. Of all the qualities which I recalled from the Moscow of my wasted youth, the one which was now most remarkably absent was the feeling of leisure. Russians, as I remembered them, had sauntered along the pavements with a nonchalance that you might have expected to find in sunnier climes. Now everybody hurried along with a look of intense introspection on their faces. Eye contact was avoided at all costs. People carried small bags and darted in and out of shops, often, it seemed, failing to make a purchase. I soon learned why: most of the shelves were empty of goods.

The Extraordinary Commission for Combating Counter-Revolution and Sabotage, or the Cheka as it was known in its abbreviated form, had taken over the building at Lubyanka Square No.11. The name of the building's former owners, The Russian Insurance Company, was inscribed over the door. The new occupants also advertised their business: a red banner bearing the words, 'Death to Counter-Revolutionaries and their Imperialist Allies' was draped over the facade. It took me a minute or two to decipher, and when I had succeeded, a chill ran down my spine. It would not do for a foreigner to be standing and staring at such a building. I set off at a brisk pace. Now I understood some of the fear that drove the Russians' feet over the broken pavements in such a hurry. Minding your own business was the essence of survival.

It was odd how Moscow had so easily taken on a seedy disposition. Some of the old one storey houses seemed to be crouching and skulking like conspirators. I passed a place advertising itself as a 'Flower Salon' but there was nothing fresh or sweet smelling about it. Say what you will against the old bourgeoisie,[24] but at least he used to keep his premises spruce and cheerful. Now, the faded pink and turquoise paint of the buildings had the air of old dresses. Moscow's favourite motif, the stone face of a pretty girl above a door or window, had grimy cheeks. Whereas formally the girl-motifs had been virgins, now they were slatterns.

Children were always around my feet begging for food or roubles. I had to learn how to be tough and brush them away. I pressed on and found myself under the Sukharev Tower. The old 'Thieves

---

24 24 Marx and Engels in their Communist Manifesto do not hold back: 'Our bourgeois, not content with having the wives and daughters of their proletarians at their disposal, not to speak of common prostitutes, take the greatest pleasure in seducing each other's wives,' etc.

Market' was still operating, almost as before. Here, if anywhere in the city, human beings were animated by contact with each other for the ancient purpose of exchange.

On the whole, it was perfectly possible to distinguish between the members of the 'former' classes. The round shoulders of the peasant, versus the wan frame of the aristocrat, provided a rough and ready indication. Style also gave a few clues: the man who had made good under the new regime, exhibited a penchant for leather riding boots up to the knees and a large buckled belt, and, often, a side arm. The upper echelons of old did their best to conceal their origins, but you could catch them out by their refined steps, their straight backs, their abbreviated chins, their kempt finger nails, and their frayed clothes that had been of such quality that they never quite lost the whiff of tailor or couture.

I spoke to a lady with her goods spread out on the ground at her feet. She was offering a set of six cups and saucers, along with a silver samovar. Her pedigree was all too visible beneath her tarnished skin: her chiselled nose and cheek bones were no less fine than her porcelain. I thought it would be jolly to keep a Russian samovar on the table by the window in my dining room back in London. I pointed to it and asked, 'How much?' She replied with admirable cheerfulness, demonstrating to me what a good samovar it was, and how all the pieces fitted together nicely.

'But how much?' I said

'What have you got?'

'Roubles and English pounds.'

'Sir,' she said, (she was the only person to address me by that term), 'what use is money these days? Only a fool takes cash. It is worth less and less every day. Soon it won't be worth anything at all. If you had flour or sugar or potatoes, I would be glad to sell you my samovar. You can go to the kitchen in your hotel and buy whatever food you like. They will have everything they need there – white bread, porridge, butter, tea, good sausages, perhaps even chocolate. Bring something here tomorrow and I will be standing on this spot.'

I wondered how the exchange rate of sausage for samovar stood, but made no further enquiries. I asked her, instead, if free trade had not been banned at the market.

'Everything is illegal, therefore everything is allowed,' said the lady. Then she leaned over and spoke to me in good English: 'Sometimes the police come here. They ask for money but if we do not have it they take what they please, or smash something for fun. Then they leave.'

'I see', I said, and I took a few ration cards out of my wallet and placed them in her hand. They were the only currency of any value in town, as they could be exchanged in special shops and eating places for food that was considered fit for party members and foreign visitors. She asked the Lord to grant me my dearest wish, and I thought of Vera.

Before it gets dark in Moscow, grit speckles the light. It was especially so that sootiest of summers. I felt particularly grimy as I walked back to my lodgings. Vagabonds were lighting fires in the squares and grilling some sort of meat. I dreaded to think what it might be; dog... cat... rat? Small, shoeless boys bothered me for money, looking like sweet little rogues behind their dirty faces. I gave what I could, but they soon became nuisances like flies. 'Go on, briss!' (shoo!). One tried to get his hands into my pocket, and I resorted to threatening him with my fist. He spat back at me, but fortunately the yellow globule fell short and landed by my boot.

A girl stood in an archway. I could not say how old she was – perhaps twelve, but perhaps an undernourished fourteen or fifteen. She looked at me with intense eyes that reminded me of Vera's hungry look of old. She called out:

'Give me a piece of bread.'

I had no bread. I made a resolution. I was not going to give her money. There were so many people – young and old – whom I could help, and I was not going to be swayed by her young femininity. I would give fifty useless roubles to the next toothless old hag or legless soldier, the uglier the better. The girl beckoned. It was an unmistakably sexual gesture. I stopped and looked at her. The low sun was setting behind her giving her dirty hair a kind of halo. She pouted and lifted up her ragged skirt to show me some leg. I could not help smiling.

'Get away,' I said in English. 'You're far too young for that game!'

Now she was walking toward me. I was rooted to the spot. I knew that I could not hurry away – she would think I was scared – I would have to turn and walk down the street, but I was momentarily mesmerised by this young hussy. And then she did something which quite shocked me. Odd thing that. You would think after all my experience in love and war that I would have lost the capacity for shock. She stopped and lifted up her skirt – right up above her waist so that the hem was almost at her chin. I could see her grubby stick of a body, the matted triangle of her pubic hair, and even the bones of her pelvis. Her breasts were like two small sausages. She said:

'Your Excellency, I am hungry.'

'Please… your skirt', I said – then I felt flushed with panic. The Russian words for 'skirt' and for 'fuck' are easily mixed up by a foreign tongue: yubka and yobka (I blush to mention how I had previously encountered this hazard). I hoped that I had used the correct word. I took a wedge of notes out of the canvas satchel that I wore at my side – probably enough to buy a loaf or two of bread – and held it out at arm's length to the girl. She took it. 'Go home!' I commanded. And she ran back through the archway, skipping as she went, before stopping to bend over and lift up her skirt once again to show me her bony posterior, and then disappearing round the corner.

I returned to my mansion that night feeling completely drained and exhausted. I had to force myself to go to the oak panelled dining room and eat. They had laid out black and white bread with salted fish and caviar and hams and cheeses and three or four salads. On the side they had a selection of vodkas. It was only after a quick shot that I felt myself come to.

The next day I tried to attend the other conference – The Second Congress of the Third International which was gathering just down the road from the Metropole. Lydia was there, and I had promised to drop in on her. But my attempt was unsuccessful. Guards were posted on the door of the Delovoy Dvor Hotel where it was taking place. I did not have the correct papers to enter.

I had a plan for locating Vera, but I delayed implementing it for several days. She might not at all welcome her poor capitalist foreign husband. Contact with me might endanger her position. But as the time went by and the industrialists' conference droned on, I found myself hoping that she would walk into the Metropole and find me there in the great dining hall. It was no use waiting for destiny. I decided to take my own action.

Anatoly had written that he had seen her stepping into the Kamerny Revolutionary Theatre where Nina now played. I knew therefore, that she was still in touch with our mutual actress friend. I made enquiries with Nadia, my translator. She told me that the Kamerny was indeed a prestigious dramatic group, at the vanguard of Revolutionary experimentation. Its name literally meant 'a cell' and it had taken over the building of the 'Small Theatre' around the back of the Bolshoi, not more than a few hundred yards from the Metropole.

Chapter Twenty Four

Butyrka Prison

It was the small hour in the morning when the guards come to the cells and call out names. On this occasion, he called out mine.

I walked with my customary war limp alongside the guard to whom I was manacled by the wrist. At this brisk pace, my bad leg forced me to bob up and down like a madman. I was led me through an old door with metal studs, beyond which was a moonlit courtyard. Through the dark I made out the prison chapel. I had been wondering when I might catch a glimpse of it. An image flicked through my mind of a bride waiting by the altar. But this was not a good sign. I had heard that they shot people against the wall of the chapel.

'Oh Please, Holy Mother of Iberia, please don't let them shoot me.' A Ford motorcar waited by the gate. I thought for a moment that they might turn the engine on to mask the sound of the shots with the inevitable backfiring. An old Ford farting, those would be the last sounds I would hear on earth. We got inside the car. Perhaps they did away with foreign guests further out of town. We drove through the huge prison gates and down the dark avenue toward Brest Station. That squashed-up trip with two henchmen in leather coats sitting on either side of me is hard to forget. The moon was bright that night. I took in the shadowy sights of Moscow as we drove. They seemed as vivid to me as when I had first seen them in 1914. Perhaps the last impressions are as strong as the first.

Our Ford had the streets to itself. We passed the arch celebrating the triumph of old regime over Napoleon in 1812, and a little further on I saw the silhouette of Pushkin's statue standing with his head bowed in poetic contemplation, and we continued down Tverskaya with its once grand, still imposing shops, and toward the Kremlin. At the bottom, we turned left up to Theatre Square and my old haunt, the Metropole. My spirits soared. They were taking me home!

It was too dark to make out the mosaic mural on the side of the Metropole – the one depicting the dream woman taking flight alongside a boat – but I could see her in my mind's eye. 'So I'm saved.' I thought, 'by a woman.'

Unfortunately we passed the familiar building and continued up the hill. Now I knew for certain where we were heading.

'Sit down please. I hope you have had some food - all I can offer you is tea without sugar.'

My courteous interrogator was a laconic Latvian called Jacob Peters – the number two at the Lubyanka. He had spent time in England before the Revolution where he was known by Scotland Yard as 'Peter the Painter.' He had been arrested on a charge of murder, but the trial collapsed for lack of clear evidence. His English wife and baby were still in London. He told me all this with a note of depression in his voice. His face was round, puffy, and white. I thought that, perhaps, signing too many death warrants could get a man down.

'You must have been missing your wife too,' he said slowly.

I was not quite sure whether this question came from knowledge or ignorance of my exact marital state. He presumed, perhaps, that I had left a wife at home. I just nodded.

'When did you last see Vera Borisovna?' he asked. My mouth opened, probably like a fish, but no words came out. 'She is a beautiful woman. One could miss a woman like that,' he went on, as if he understood and sympathised.

Peters stood up and I saw that he was wearing a leather holster around his waist. He removed the huge Mauser pistol from within it and placed it on the desk. He covered it with a podgy hand. His finger nails looked as though they had been bitten down to the quick, but he told me later that they had been extracted in a Tsarist gaol. The British had treated him rather better, he said, when he had been in their custody. Thankfully the weapon was pointing to the side, not at me.

'Have you used one of these, comrade Munnings?'

I looked up at him: although he was not a tall man, the effect of his standing while I remained seated was to diminish me to about the size of a schoolboy.

'An Enfield rifle, during the War.'

'Not close up. Not at point blank range.'

'No.'

I had not got very far 'over the top' before Fritz had halted my progress with that lucky bullet that had been my ticket home. Now I was beginning to wonder if it might have been better if he had done for me.

'Then, you have been more fortunate than me.'

The lines of his grey brow expressed deep regret. He picked up his pistol and took a little walk around his stark office in silence. I felt him pass around behind me and circle back to his desk. I got his drift. Shooting me was going to pain him as much as it was going to hurt me — or something along those lines. In fact, I had a feeling that he believed that one day he would pay for his crimes, either in this world or the next, and that the premonition gave him his lachrymose air. I almost felt sorry for the Bolshevist bugger — but not for long. No. I just prayed that I could hold on to my urine before I embarrassed both of us. I thought of begging to be excused for a minute or two.

'Now let's start at the beginning,' he said. 'How did you find your wife's address in Moscow?'

I told him the only lie which came into my head. It was a pretty stupid one, given the chaotic state of affairs in the city, but he seemed to accept it. He could have walked across the room to pick up the book which would have completely disproved my statement — but he did not. I must have uttered the falsehood without blinking. I said:

'I looked her up in the telephone directory.'

'I see you are a man of many resources. And you take an interest in the Worker's Revolutionary Theatre?

'I've long been a fan of the Russian theatre,' I said. There seemed no point in denying what he knew already, that I had visited the Kamerny.

'And it just so happened that Vera Borisovna was in the audience too that night.'

'Really?'

'Please Mr Munnings. All I ask from you is the truth.'

'I am speaking the truth.' But of course I was trying to impart as little of it as possible.

At the theatre, I had found that it was the opening night of the season, and it struck me that Nina might have invited Vera. No tickets were available at the box office, but I purchased one off a tout who was openly speculating outside. I paid a lot of roubles but not much money.

The programme was somewhat surprising. I had bought a ticket to see Salome, the last play of Oscar Wilde.

Inside the theatre, the general atmosphere was none too fresh. That sultry summer in Moscow, odour was the great equaliser. Soap was almost as hard to get hold of as proper food.

I peered over the balcony and looked around at my fellow spectators: quite a few wore the loose Russian blouses of the sort that one used to see on waiters and railway officials. I saw through their disguises. It was my guess from the preponderance of trimmed beards and little round spectacles, that the majority of those gathered there belonged to the 'intelligentsia'. The women had done the best to dress smartly, without too much ostentation, in the fashion of school mistresses, although some of those in the front stalls were a little more showy. I even noticed one or two fetching hats, rare sights indeed in the Moscow of 1920. I wondered if Vera's head was underneath one – perhaps the purple cap with a jaunty feather in it. And then I partly caught sight of the cap-wearer's face as she turned to chat to her neighbour: it was not the face I was looking for – not unless it had grown a double chin. I was not decided, in any case, what I would do if I saw her. I thought, on balance, that it would be enough for me to catch sight of her from afar – to have an image of what she looked like under her new circumstances. To approach her, I felt, might be a mistake. I wanted to remember her as the love of my youth, not as a woman who cut me because of an understandable fear of endangering her position and perhaps her life.

Strange sounds emitted from the orchestral pit – throbbing drum beats and cacophonous wind blowing. Before us hung a black curtain, embossed with the golden images of a goat and a leopard standing on their hind legs. As the lights in the auditorium went down, I noticed two shadows of late-comers taking their places in the front row of the stalls: a man and a woman.

The curtain rose to reveal a spiky geometric sun and a pale green sickle of a moon suspended over a shadowy flight of steps. A terrace at the top of the steps was bathed in red light. Two soldiers stood guard with spears and pointed shields. If this was Herod's palace it was a disturbing, cubist fantasy.

The soldiers admired the trim figure of a girl as she slinked onto the terrace wearing a black cloak. It took me a moment to realise that I was looking at Nina – she must have lost weight, and she really did seem like a young girl. Her dark hair – the longest and thickest I had seen in Moscow - was amply suited to the part of Salome, the Eastern temptress, but for the time being it was hidden under a pointed hat. Her white arms extended from the cloak.

The guards were unsettled when Nina / Salome came up to them and pleaded for the release of a prisoner, John the Baptist. Her appeal to the soldiers was straightforwardly sexual as she strutted around them and ran her hand clad in a long black glove up and down their spears. John, as it turned out, was living at the bottom of cistern, and occasionally we heard his voice as it echoed up from the well in a deep, rich baritone. The only masculine sound that I had ever heard so beautiful had been that of the priest at our wedding. Salome begged and flirted, and the guards reluctantly hoisted the prophet up from his well. Then, horror of horrors, the princess took it into her head that she wanted to kiss The Baptist. The ragged, bearded giant was having nothing of it; he retreated back into his well.

I think the story is well known from the gospels. Herod enjoyed talking politics and religion with his prisoner down in the well, but his queen was filled with envy and distaste at his strange friendship. The king had an eye for Salome, the Queen's daughter by her first marriage, which happened, rather unnaturally, to have been to his brother. When it came to his birthday, Herod fancied the idea of Salome dancing for him. He offered her any reward she might choose, up to half his Kingdom.

The drama built up to its climax: Salome's Dance of the Seven Veils. The musicians blew their horns and beat their drums with primitive frenzy. Nina swooped across the hall, like some exotic bird of prey, gliding towards Herod and pulling herself away at the last moment. Now the drum beat grew faster, the horns more insane, and her dance more wild and free. I would not say that she was a graceful dancer – she stomped this way and that on her bare feet, running and jumping across the stage – but there was a veracious energy about it. Veils started to fly away from her body. Once or twice she paused to remove one slowly and Herod's face would looked pained with desire. At the moment when she tore the sixth veil away, the lights went down apart from a torch or two. Thus we saw her fulsome body in silhouette as she unwound her seventh and final covering. Herod rose to his feet to applaud with delight.

Salome and her mother demanded their horrific tribute for the dance – the head of John the Baptist on a golden plate. The trophy with its curly hair and full beard was brought to Salome by a black soldier almost naked and drenched in blood. At first she revolted from it, but then she grasped the Baptist's hair at full arm's length, and raised the head aloft. The blood of the prophet dripped onto her face. She pulled it toward her and at last kissed John the Baptist on the lips.

Herod could stand it no more. He bellowed a terrible command and the soldiers rushed forward and crushed Salome to death beneath their shields.

Personally, I had found the spectacle quite revolting, but I suppose that Oscar Wilde and the Bible have to take their fair share of the blame. Still, there was a lesson there for the revolutionists if they cared to see it: you can take something beautiful that does not belong to you, but you can also pervert and destroy it in the process.

I stood up to leave while the applause and cheering filled the auditorium, but I was in the middle of the row and could not make my way out without rudeness. The brass instruments started to drone the melody of The International and everyone respectfully rose to their feet. I noticed an empty seat in the front row of the stalls. One of the pair of latecomers had left during the performance. I looked at the woman who still sat next to the place he had vacated. There was something about the languid way she held herself. I recalled the phrase that I used to say to her, half affectionately, half critically, – though she could not, of course, understand it – you slinker-slouch. Yes, I was certain it was her. I began to slide my way past the comrades who were still rooted to the spot, some of them singing along to The International, others silently mouthing the words. There were tut-tuts and one woman even slapped me on the back, but I was pulled along by some impulse that I could not resist.

I found that the exit from the circle was locked. God help the Russian theatre going public if ever there is a fire! By banging on the door, I elicited an opening. I pushed my way past an annoyed-looking usher, and headed for the stairs with the Russian words for 'Young Man! Where are you rushing?' following after me.

It required a small emolument of 100 roubles to work my way past the woman who stood guard to the stalls. As I re-entered the auditorium, the audience was again seated and motionless, and a man in a collarless suit was on stage making a speech. He stood before the golden curtain depicting the dancing goat and leopard. He was saying, Tavarishi! – Comrades! - with great frequency. I did not pay him much attention, and I doubt that I could have followed his drift very much if I had, but I suppose that he was instructing the audience in a proletarian interpretation of Salome. I have sometimes wondered what he made of it all. I can only suppose that John was the oppressed proletarian, Salome and the Queen were the vulgar bourgeoisie, and Herod was the evil Tsar.

Fortunately, Vera was sitting not far from the end of the row. Her hands were neatly placed on her lap, and she was looking straight ahead, and not in particular at the man up on the stage. She seemed extremely bored.

I worked my way over, and sat down next to her. She turned to look at me. Her green eyes opened wide like those of a startled feline. Oh no! I thought, she's afraid! But I think now that she was just astonished. A few moments later, her fingers were quietly entwined in mine. After a while, she stood up and we left our seats. We slipped through the door and walked down the corridor away from the usherette. We could not escape the door-woman's view without stepping out into the public foyer, but we did not care. We locked each other in a tight embrace and she began to kiss me passionately. When separated – so as to stand looking at each other, hand in hand, she said to me with wonder,

'What are you doing here?'

'I came to find you.'

'Oh,' she said with that pretty 'O' mouth of hers. Her face had a few lines, but she was more of a woman now. If anything, the years suited her. Her embrace had been somewhat fuller and softer than I had recalled from earlier times. Her face seemed wiser, and less naïve. I remember thinking, 'this woman could prove even more fatale than when she was a mere girl.' I told her a little about the conference at The Metropole:

'The Metropole!' and then she added. 'You speak Russian now. I must watch what I say.'

'I speak very badly, I'm afraid.'

My modesty belied the truth that I was rather proud of those skills in her language such as I had acquired. And then Vera began to speak quickly and excitedly, and I had to ask her to slow down and repeat herself. I understood that it was dangerous for us to be seen together. She took a silver pencil from her purse and wrote down an address on my theatre ticket. I must go to a building which faced the river and was not far from Mr Shchukin's old house, later that evening. I must enter the building at precisely 11.pm, not a minute sooner and not a minute later. She took my watch out of my pocket and compared it to her own, a tiny little gold and emerald timepiece on her waiflike wrist. She told me to move the hand of my watch two minutes forward.

'So precise?'

'You must be exact. There is a doorman on duty. He is a spy who examines the papers of everyone who comes in and out of the building. If he knows that an Englishman is coming to see me, that would lead to all sorts of trouble, big trouble. I will distract him at 11.pm. He has a general key to all the flats, and I will tell him that I have lost my own. He will not refuse my request. You must go in and up the stairs to the sixth floor where you will wait until 11.15, not a minute sooner. At 11.15, descend one floor and come to my apartment, number 507. If the door is open, you may enter. If it is shut, it is not safe and you must leave straight away. You must not speak to anyone on the way out, especially the duty doorman. Walk straight past him with your hat pulled down. Do not go back to your hotel directly. Jump on an electric tram just as it is about to leave. It is harder to follow you that way. Am I clear? Do you understand?'

'I understand. 11 o' clock, not a minute sooner.'

'And at 11.15 come through my door, number 507. If it is locked, go straight out.'

'I understand.'

We did not have time to kiss again. The first members of the audience had been liberated from the auditorium, and within a few moments, Vera was lost in the crowd.

I walked along the river bank to Vera's address. I thought I had left time enough, but I had not allowed for the difficulty of locating a house in a city where few of the buildings displayed street numbers. Eventually I worked up the courage to stop a woman who was hurrying through the night. She almost walked straight past me before halting. I showed her the address written in faint pencil. She squinted by the light of a rare street lamp. The chief source of illumination that evening came from the almost full moon. She looked around and pointed to a solid shadow of a building. I checked my watch. It was two minutes to 11.00 p.m.

At a few seconds past 11.pm, I pushed open the heavy door to the building and walked in. I saw the booth where the duty doorman would normally be stationed. It was empty. I started to climb the wide, uncarpeted staircase of grey stone. The building was as solidly built as the Butyrka. I turned the corner of the staircase; it was not lit.

I must admit, I was not sure how many floors I had climbed, but by good fortune I emerged on the sixth floor, as Vera had instructed. The landing was illuminated by moonlight from the window, and I could make out the number of a door – 601. I had enough initiative to seek out flat 607. The layout of the fifth floor was likely to be the same as the one above. After I had found it, I returned to the window and looked at my watch; it was 12 minutes past 11pm. I lit a cigarette. There were footsteps on the stairs. My heart pounded for a few seconds and a woman emerged. She looked at me with a start and I just nodded. She nodded back without a word and looked for her keys in her bag. She opened a door and went in. I heaved a sigh of a relief and must have spent a few minutes thanking St. George for my salvation. Then suddenly I remembered the time. It was 11.17pm. I hurried down stairs and rushed to door 507. For a moment I thought it was locked, but I leaned on it and it gave way. I almost fell into the apartment and Vera's arms. She led me into the spacious main room. It was lit by a couple of lamps. I could make out some shadowy paintings on the wall. A large window and a spectacular balcony overlooked the nightscape of the river, and the view to the Kremlin about a mile or so away.

'What will you drink? I have some beer. There's not much else. The Allied blockade, you know.'

She went to the kitchen and returned with two bottles of Riga beer on a tray with some cut tomatoes, cucumbers and sausage. I do not think I had seen her carry a tray before.

'We are alone,' she said, apart from Grisha.'

'Grisha?'

'My little boy – don't look so alarmed - he's not yours – he's five years old.'

'And the father?'

'He's away. He works nights at the Ministry of Culture.'

'That's peculiar.'

She laughed.

'Don't worry. He won't be back for hours yet, perhaps not for a day or two. He's out with some whore. He's taking a bath in her perfume between her enormous bosoms and he'll come back stinking of it. I know its smell. It's called Triple Cologne.'

Whoever he was, he must have been important. The apartment was spacious and well appointed. The lamp consisted of a small statue of a naked woman. And the paintings were becoming clearer as my eyes adjusted to the light. I went over to take a closer look at one: it was of an extremely pretty lady in large black hat and a green dress. Her lively face was not so unlike Vera's own. The whole effect was achieved with great simplicity and charm.

'Do you like it?' she asked.

'Matisse?'

'No. It is by a Dutch painter, by the style is not so different from Matisse's.'

'Shchukin's?'

'Yes. He used to say that the woman in the picture was just like me.'

I thought of the alexandrite. If Vera wanted something, she just took it. It was as simple as that. The laws of property did not apply to her. She was a natural born Communist. I was still a little hot and fraught following the drama of my arrival at the flat. I felt a rising anger.

'How?' I asked. I was speaking in monosyllables due to my less than perfect mastery of the Russian language. My diction must have sounded staccato and not so very enamoured. Vera looked at me expressionlessly, but there was something defensive about the way she spoke.

'My husband – my Russian husband - arranged for the pictures to be brought here.'

'Did you say pictures?'

'Yes, the picture over there is a Matisse, and there is a Gauguin in the bedroom.'

I shook my head in dismay. I found it very hard to come to terms with the idea of a harlot hanging the old merchant's collection in her bedroom.

'You think I have stolen these pictures?'

I looked straight at her: 'Well they're not yours,' I said. And a more disturbing thought ran through my mind. It was the kind of suspicion that would never have occurred to the youthful George of the pre-war days. I wondered whether the 'former owner' of the paintings had been sent to the wall before he could protest against the redistribution of his property among the 'workers'. Was I looking at my very own Salome?

'And Shchukin?' I asked dryly.

I think she could almost read my mind. She had so much practice in the old days when we had almost no words to express our thoughts, but before she could answer we were interrupted. A small sleepy boy came into the room:

'Grisha darling. Can't you sleep?' Vera looked tired. He wanted a glass of warm milk.

'This is mama's secret friend. Don't tell Papa. Promise?'

'Yes.'

Then she said to him in heavily accented English:

'The friend of mama speaks English. You can speak to him.'

I was amazed. To hear Vera speak reasonably proficient English was something that I had not been expecting. Again she knew what I was thinking: she looked round at me and said: 'I have an excellent English teacher, a university professor no less. I want Grisha to speak English too. So you see; I have never given up hope of joining you.'

Grisha looked at the floor shyly. I asked him how old he was in English. After some hesitation he answered 'five' and went to sit on an arm chair with his legs folded up beneath him. At least I had confirmed that he really could not have been mine.

Vera went into the kitchen to warm her son's milk. I must add that even at the privileged guest house where I was staying, they did not have milk. I decided that the less of an impression I made on Grisha, the better he would keep the secret of my visit. I thought how typical it had been of Vera to have omitted any mention of him in her letters during the War. She liked to keep all her options open. I believe that she might have arrived in England after the peace, had it been possible, bringing Grisha to me as a surprise. No doubt in that case, the date of his birth would have slipped back a year or two.

I took another look at the picture of the lady in the hat. It really did remind me of Vera – as she used to be – playful, girlish, perhaps believing that the world was hers by right of being attractive and pretty - but now there was something different about her. She seemed to have cares, responsibilities, worries. All these had come with material success because, by the standards of Moscow, I was sure that she was very successful indeed. If a woman must be kept, this flat was the cage to be kept in.

Vera returned and while Grisha was drinking milk she said: 'I want to tell you something important. But first I must take my little boy back to bed.'

I still found it miraculous to hear her speak English. I also found it a little scary. I was not sure why at the time, but I suppose, looking back, because I had carried her with me as my fantasy for so many years. Fantasies do not have the power of expression.

When she returned from putting Grisha back to bed, she spoke to me at length, partly in Russian, partly in English. It did not matter which. I understood her perfectly. She paced up and down a little, as Russians are wont to do, and she gestured with her delicate arms. But there was no attempt to use her looks to touch the soft points in my character. This was more or less a 'straight-talk' as might have come from a man.

'Even if we had shared a mutual language in the past, I would have been ashamed to tell you all about myself. Now we have words and time and I have nothing to lose. It might be interesting for you to know what sort of girl you married in a prison chapel.'

'I think I can guess,' I said, but she took no notice of me. She was far too concentrated on weaving her story.

'My mother used to give me "The Three Female Commandments" (Vera now enumerated these on her fingers)

'(i) a girl might as well love a rich man as a poor one;

'(ii) a woman must have courage to make use of her beauty; and

'(iii) to be afraid of committing a sin when everybody else is busy sinning, is both stupid and unprofitable.

'Not that my mother was ever very successful in the world, but those words of wisdom were her 'dowry' to her daughter. You may not believe this, but I was a great disappointment to her. I thought differently. For me, art or books or music are an honourable kind of poverty. I did not have any real knowledge about these lofty subjects, but I believed this in my soul.'

(I must have been in a cynical mood, for I hardly suppressed a smile at hearing of her honour for the arts.)

'When I was fifteen, I ran away with an artist to Moscow. But Denis, my painter / lover, soon found a second muse and model for his paintings. You may recall her. She was Oksana, the redhead who used to work at the Metropole in the old days. I would sit and watch as he painted her in the nude, and one time he painted us together.'

'Why didn't you invite me?' I said, but she ignored my 'witticism.'

'Oksana was already starting to support herself by 'working.' He used to praise her, saying she was a clever girl who knew how to make money. He said a lot of things not so different from my mother. I started to think that he loved Oksana more than me. I needed his respect. And so I asked her to introduce me to 'Madame' at the Metropole, and she brought there me for a job interview. Oksana told me to say that I was a student at the University: Madame approved of education because she said it gave a girl a filthy mind.

'In a way, I was starting my career at the top, in the most prestigious position for that line of work in Moscow. I had to pay half my wages to 'Madame' but it was worth it to live and work in a hotel de lux and to command high prices. But I could never compete with Oksana for popularity - most men prefer the fuller figure – but there were plenty of customers to go round. My first man was sociable and wanted to entertain me and buy me flowers. He was unusual. Some of the men were disgusting to me. Sometimes I felt that I had to kill any beauty or goodness in my soul. It was not long before I had to see a doctor to take measures. After that I was ill and lost weight. Still, I told myself that I was doing this for 'art'. That is how Denis explained it to me when I brought him money. I also helped my mother in Smolensk.

'I was not very happy to be chosen by you. Young men are the worst payers – they think they are doing the girl a favour. But you fed me and took me to Nina's flat. We had a merry time. It was just like an evening with the artists and students, when everybody talks and drinks and makes love, but I did not think it was the beginning of anything, other than perhaps a friendship with Nina. After all, you would soon go back to London and forget all about me.

'When you found me in the Church, I was about to pray to the Virgin to bring me a rich lover, or, even better, a husband. I had in mind a Russian merchant or noble. I was very surprised indeed when I looked round and saw you. But I knew that the Virgin does not play jokes. She had given her answer: you were my future. All I had to do was to understand the sign and act accordingly.

'And so I gave up my work at the hotel and dedicated myself completely to you. My painter told me that I was out of my mind, and that hard cash was the only way to run a business. As you recall, you and I did not have any firm financial arrangement. I still needed money and clothes. I had to look my best or else you would lose interest in me. Madame and the hotel footmen still kept on demanding that I pay my dues. And so occasionally I had to drop a few hints to you, and you usually understood and were always generous. I liked that. I can't stand a man who is stingy. But I must say that I often wondered if the Virgin had not been playing a joke on me after all. On that long journey to Siberia and back, you and Anatoly and Lydia would talk and talk and talk, always in English, and how could I join in? Your friend Anatoly Mizinsky always treated me with as much respect as a cockroach, and after you left for England he tried to sleep with me. I gave him a black eye and after that, Nina got rid of him, and not a day too soon either!

'Sometimes I would go back to see my painter and his friends, and we would all talk about interesting subjects until late in the night: about whether there is any such thing as love, or only animal instinct; about the relationships between men, women, parents, children, artists, patrons.. All sorts of funny stories and anecdotes about the court in St. Petersburg, the Tsar and Rasputin. They would always tease me and tell me that my rich Englishman would never marry me, and I would say that, if they did not have faith in me, I would not invite them to come and stay in my palace in London.

'When we weren't in company, I was happy just being quiet with you, and because of that, I began to wonder if I loved you. You would take me to the theatre and the Tryetekov and Shchukin's Party, and show me so many things I had never seen before. How I loved Mr Shchukin's paintings!

'I could not wait to get home to tell Denis and to invite him to come and see those works by Matisse and Picasso. I thought that there was so much that he could learn. But all he could say was that it was impossible for a richbourgeoisie to appreciate art. It was all for show and I was foolish to be impressed. That was the first time that I realised that Denis was not so wise after all. And of course, when I was in prison, it was you not he who came to see me. As soon as I saw you, I knew that the blessed Virgin of Iberia had sent you, and that you would set me free. I just knew. But I was amazed when you offered to marry me. That was when I realised that you were the only good man I had ever met. All the others wanted was my body, and they could easily buy another.'

At this point I felt compelled to interrupt her torrent of words. 'Please tell me,' I said, 'Why did you take the alexandrite stone.'

She laughed but it was a guilty laugh; 'I couldn't help myself! It just spoke to me. The way it changed colour from red to green and back, reminded me of Matisse's paintings of the red dancers and musicians on the green hill. It was as if it was saying, 'Take me, I'm a Russian stone. I belong to you, not this pompous Frenchman.' But when we got to Moscow I realised that I could never wear it or sell it without causing suspicion. And so I gave it to you, just before you went to London. It's probably the first time that a girl like me has slipped something valuable into a man's pocket while he was sleeping. I thought that you would find it when you got home, and you would find it impossible not to be thinking of me. Perhaps you would exchange it for a French painting. I know it was wrong, but I was young and foolish, Have you still got that stone, by the way?'

'I had to give it back to its owners,' I said, not wanting to set a bad example.

'Oh,' she said, 'How strange. If the stone had stayed inside Russia, it would not belong to them now. Nobody owns anything after the Revolution. If a person wants to keep something valuable, he had better hide it away, and what good is that? But please don't think that I took these paintings from Mr Shchukin. This is quite a different story.

'When the Bolsheviks took over, Denis found a job in the Commissariat of Culture and Education, directly under Lunacharsky, the Commissar for art. It was almost as if we had stepped into a lift that was taking us straight to the top of the country. There was hunger and fighting all around. The rich were being thrown out of their houses, or forced to live in their bathrooms, and to sell their jewels on the streets for bags of flour – and that's just those that were not killed, or fleeing abroad. And I was moving into an apartment and meeting all the top people in the new Government. I was the respected wife, so to speak, of a commissar. I think Denis keeps me because I am popular with all the big leaders and they invite us to their parties. It was not quite as good as being an aristocrat in the old days, but it is the best that Moscow has to offer now. My mother is so proud of me. I did not forget my old friends. I have always tried to bring food and clothes to Oksana and Nina. And I visited Shchukin. I wanted to see if I could help him, perhaps save him. I wanted to make good use of my new position. I wanted to do what you would do.

'I found that he was living in the gatehouse of his former mansion, but he was full of dignity and did not show any regret for what he had lost. He only feared for his collection. The proletariat were breaking so many things - icons from the churches, porcelain from the houses - just to get revenge on the former masters.'

(She spoke the word 'proletariat' with a note of disgust that you might have expected to hear from the mouth of a deposed duchess).

'There were many pretenders for every mansion that had belonged to the old merchants and aristocrats. Every day a new Bolshevik committee was being formed. I spoke to Lunacharsky. He arranged that the Shchukin mansion and paintings should be given to a special Museum of Western Art under State protection. Not long after that, Shchukin disappeared, and it's rumoured that he escaped to France. And as for what became of the collection – well tomorrow I will take you there and then you will understand everything, I promise. You will see that it is absolutely no crime at all for me to have these pictures on my wall. In fact, you will say that I did the right thing and should have taken more under my protection.'

As she came to the end of this soliloquy she gave me a tour of the flat. A Gauguin, full of somnolent brown skin and a pink sky, hung over the bed. It was a sensual, beautiful painting.

'I know you don't think I should have these pictures,' said Vera.

'Well, I'm starting to understand.'

'But look at this too.'

And she went down on her hands and knees and pulled a suitcase from under her bed. She opened it: 'You see it's packed with a spare set of clothes, sugar, tobacco. You know everybody in this house has the same. Yes, we live better than everyone out there. Much better. But a woman like me can fall in a moment. All it takes is one word from an enemy. Maybe the woman upstairs will denounce me, in case I denounce her. They come in the middle of the night, and you don't have time to pack. If the Chekist is kind, perhaps he will send my son to Nina. If not, Grisha goes to an orphanage.'

She was almost in tears, and I wanted to join her on the floor and take her in my arms, but we were interrupted by a hammering on the door. Vera looked up at me, her face full of strain and said in a low voice:

'It's only the doorman.' And then she added, 'Mudak![25]. He's got the skeleton key. He might come in.'

And so she went to open up the door. While he was in the front room, his voice booming compliments to the lovely Vera Borisovna, I slipped down the corridor and out of the apartment.

---

25   A profanity indicating a practitioner of onanism

Lubyanka

Peters offered me a cigarette. He apologised for its poor quality, but said that when he was working so late he would be ready to smoke donkey shit. I did not think the remark was particularly funny, but I laughed just to be polite.

'Soon, however, I will be getting some healthy sun on my pale face. You can congratulate me on my new position. I am to be our chief commissar in Tashkent.'

'Is that a promotion?'

'A change is as good as a rest. In any case, I am tired of this work. It is not good for the health. I am up late at night. So many of the people one meets are saying goodbye to this world. To speak to ghosts, quite frankly, can depress the spirits... Oh, I see from your face that my remark might have been tactless? Do not worry Comrade Munnings. You will be going home soon to London. Maybe. The price of your ticket home is not extortionate – all I ask is the truth. I hope that you will give it to me. In return I will gladly give you your freedom. Had I not been expelled from your country, I would like to go with you. I have fond memories of perfidious Albion. But before I can let you go, you must tell me the whole truth and nothing but the truth – ah! What memories those words bring back to me! British justice! Do not lie to me Comrade Munnings. This may be my last official conversation before I depart for Tashkent. I hope that my memory of it will be a happy one. Now tell me. What did she do with the paintings?'

'Mr... I mean Comrade... Would I lie to you? I really have no knowledge of any paintings. Paintings are not my thing at all. I am a total philistine when it comes to art.'

'So tell me – when did you next see Vera Borisovna?'

'After we bumped into each other at the theatre, we agreed to meet the following evening. She wanted to hear Alexandra Kollontai speak at the Kremlin, so we both went there together. That was the last occasion on which I saw her. '

I admitted this much because I suspected that Peters would have received information about our being present at so official an event.

It had been the final day of the conference at the Hotel Metropole and I thought I had better turn up for form's sake. My translator met me in the lobby with a furrowed brow:

'Where were you yesterday?'

'I went for a walk.'

'Mr Munnings. You are in Moscow. You can't just go for a walk. Yesterday, I told that you were confined in bed after drinking too much bad spirit,' (my translator did not say whom she had 'told' but I could well imagine).

'Thank you.'

I sat at the back of the hall, and she whispered translations of the speeches in my ear, but I was not listening. I was full of regrets at my cowardice for having bolted out of Vera's flat the previous evening. I also saw how foolish I had been to feel angry at her for taking the paintings. You cannot read a moral lecture to a woman of her sort. It had been better, quite frankly, when we had not had the opportunity to converse at all. In the old days, I had to keep all my qualms to myself. They had always passed, soon enough. Now, I supposed, I would never see her again.

An hour or so later, a woman wearing an attractive scent, decidedly not a Russian eau-de-cologne, sat down on the wooden backed chair next to mine. She put her hand on my lap. My translator stopped translating and started to read a book. After about five minutes the woman and I got up. I told the translator that I would be back in half an hour, adding, 'I promise.'

Vera led me up the first flight of the marble staircase of the Metropole Hotel. We passed various comrades in their tunics and breaches. On the first landing, we took a more business like attitude, striding past a man working at a desk. She took me down a dark corridor and she tried some door handles. Finally she found a door which pushed open. I should have known where we had been heading. We were in one of the private Kabinets which overlooked the dining hall of the Metropole. For a few moments we stood on the balcony, just as we had done that first night in 1914, and looked down into the great hall where the conference was taking place. About two thirds of the wooden chairs were empty. I saw Nadia, reading her book. An American delegate, whom I recognised from our boarding house, was fast asleep.

Vera pulled me down onto the floor, out of sight and into her arms. The sound of a delegate giving a speech droned on. They really did make some terrible orations. It did not take long before his voice faded from my consciousness.

When we had finished, we helped each other to dust down our clothes. It had not been the cleanest of floors. We sat on chairs in a dark corner facing each other and held hands. Occasionally we kissed. Vera leaned over, rubbed her nose against mine in the manner of Eskimos (or Chuk-Chuks as the Russians call them), and whispered:

'George, don't ever leave me.'

'Darling. How can I stay in Moscow?'

'Take me and Grisha with you to England.'

'Of course I have been dreaming of that,' I said. 'But how?'

I had read of dramatic escapes from Soviet Russia. None other than my heroine of old, the beautiful ballerina, Tamara Karsavina, had fled by sleigh to Archangelsk with all sorts of hair raising adventures on the way, but then she was married to the British Ambassador and must have had plenty of help.

Vera said:

'There is a big delegation of foreign Communists in Moscow right now.'

'I know,' Lydia is among them. I tried to get in the other day, but they would not let me through without a pass.' It occurred to me that Vera was still the sort of woman who knew the ins and outs of hotels.

'We will need official permissions,' she said. 'And I know where we can get them. It is a place upstairs. Somewhere you have been before.'

When we reached the sixth floor of the Metropole, we paused to catch our breath. Vera said, 'You remember this place?'

'How could I forget?'

'You will never guess who is located in room 606.'

'I know, because I have been there already. The deputy commissar of foreign affairs has an office there with a tiger skin rug.'

'You know everything.'

She knocked softly on the door and entered. What memories that room must have held for her. 'See how it's changed,' she said.

She pushed the door open to Comrade Kharakan's room. The deputy commissar appeared to be out. It was strange that he should have left the door unlocked. Perhaps he was not far away. Vera went round to the other side of his desk and slowly opened his top draw. She pulled out an elegant little hand gun and smiled at me. It was a pretty thing, with an ivory handle. I could see that she fancied it.

'Put that away, Vera, are you mad?' I hissed.

'Don't worry,' she said, and slipped it into the pocket of her skirt. 'I think I might take this as well,' and she picked up a paper embossed with an official emblem and went over to a typewriter. She started to wind the paper into the roll.

'You know,' she said, 'My Russian spelling and grammar is not so good. Fortunately the policemen who will read this letter are as badly educated as I am.'

'I didn't know you could read at all.'

'Me? I went to school until I was twelve. My father was a member of the intelligentsia.' She spoke with obvious pride, and she was lost in thought for a few seconds. Then she added, 'but he left, and my mother, well she was not the clever sort.'

Her fingers were poised above the typewriter. My heart was beating rather fast and the fear of being discovered in the act of forging an official document. I wondered whether I should make my excuses and go to relieve myself. But I realised that I could not be so cowardly, not openly, in front of a woman: one to whom I might still be lawfully married and whom I might – I could not really be sure of this – still love. A woman might be reckless, immoral, and mad; but a man could not be a coward.

She finished thinking and started slowly to work the machine: clunk, clunk, clunk. Vera was no typist. She was obviously not familiar with the layout of the instrument. The letter was going to take a long time. She paused to think again.

'I don't suppose you know how to spell 'народныхь'? Does it have a soft sign on the end?'

'I'm sorry Vera, I'm not an authority on your language.' I wished that she would hurry up.

Clunk, clunk

My conscience told me that forging a document was wrong. But was it a sin to forge a Bolshevik document? After all, the regime was born illegitimately and conceived outside the constitution; it was a bastard Government with no right to issue edicts and orders and sentences of court. And yet it did. And its orders were followed. And people were shot against the wall.

'Vera, I'm sure I can hear footsteps out in the corridor.'

'One minute.'

'We don't have a minute.'

I could hear somebody coming in through the outer door.

'There,' said Vera, and pulled the paper out of the typewriter. The sound of the mechanism revolving back as it released the paper out was all too loud. Surely the person, who was now in the hall, could hear us? He or she would be coming through the office door any second now: 'Oi! I nearly forgot,' she said, and grabbed a rubber stamp from the desk and banged it on the bottom of the document. Then, just for good measure, she took another stamp and bashed that on it too. As the door opened, she was stuffing the paper down the front of her cleavage. I wondered if the fresh ink might leave marks on her chest. Would I have a chance to find out later on?

Lev Karakhan, the deputy commissar for foreign affairs, looked surprised to see his uninvited guests. I do not think that I have ever worn such a guilty expression in my life. Vera looked as innocent as a new born baby.

'Darling!' she said and tip toed up to the comrade and kissed him.

'Vera Borisovna! He said. And gave her a hug, as Russians do.

'I just came to see your handsome face,' said Vera. She was holding a photograph which she had picked up from his desk. He had apparently been signing his way through a pile and posting them to Bolshevik camp followers. He laughed. She turned to me and said, 'I believe you have met Comrade Munnings.'

'Of course. The English engineer.'

I nodded.

When we had got through all the pleasantries, and fortunately Karakhan was a most polite man, Vera admitted that we had come to beg a favour. Comrade Munnings wanted to see some Soviet factories and design bureaus and, as everyone knew, transport in the city was sadly lacking. Might it be possible to arrange a car for just one morning?

'I would be pleased to oblige,' he said, 'My car will be round in the morning. You are still at the mansion house across the river? I hope you are finding it convenient?'

'Very. I don't know how to thank you, Comrade.' I said.

'Don't worry. Now that I know that you are a friend of Vera Borisovna, the most charming member of our Party, no favour is too great.' He was a tall man, and of course he had to dip his eyes to look at Vera, but still I thought his eyes dipped a little lower than was necessary. Did he notice anything odd about her cleavage? I hoped that the old adage was true, that the eyes only perceive what they are looking for, and I knew that what his eyes were looking for was not a piece of paper. I wondered then, and I often still do, what it must be like to have a pretty face, a nice figure, and no scruples. As we left, he offered his car for half an hour to take us to our next appointment.

Downstairs, as I held Vera's coat (the cloak room attendants in Russia do not know how to behave anymore), I said, 'My translator is going to be furious. I think she might report me.'

'You must give her a little present,' said Vera, and reaching into her handbag she pulled out a bottle of French scent. I took it back into the hall, sat down next to my translator, and put the bottle into her hand.

'I am not feeling well,' I said.

'You are going for another stroll? Be careful. I do not want you to catch your death of cold, especially as it is summer.'

Vera settled into the back seat of Comrade Karakhan's Rolls Royce. I wondered who the vehicle's 'former' owner had been. She spoke briefly to the driver, and we were conveyed alongside the walls of the Kremlin, along the river bank toward the great Cathedral of the Saviour. Before we reached Vera's apartment block, we turned up the hill, and into a small side street, before halting before the way into The First Museum of Western Art. A hoot of the horn elicited a sleepy looking sentry to come out of his box and open up the gates.

As we climbed the great oak staircase, I looked up to the wall above us where Matisse's primeval figures used to dance. It was now draped in a red banner. At the top, Vera was greeted by a demure young woman with kisses on either cheek. She held out her hand for me to shake. Her name was Yekaterina Sergeievna Shchukina.

The merchant's daughter led us to the start of the exhibition. She turned to me and said in toneless English.

'The first task of the museum's committee was to remove the absolutism of the personal taste of the former owner and to rearrange the pictures according to rational and historical principles.'

I laughed and she turned red. Of course, the party line was completely abhorrent to her. After that she spoke more or less freely to us, but in whispers. Matisse's dance had found its 'rational' place in a space above a doorway. We had to crane our necks to look at it. It was still a magnificent picture, but it had not sense of belonging in this position, and it was no longer the heart of the collection. It was just another 'example' of modern French art. I recalled how, before, the rooms, the arrangement, and pictures combined to create and exotic, almost perfumed effect that Vera had said reminded her of her holiday in the South. Almost as if by magic, the eighteenth Century furniture and décor had been in perfect harmony with the 20th Century paintings. No longer. The pink wallpaper had been replaced with grey canvas; the gilded furniture with stools.

In the former dining hall, we found that the tropical collection of Gauguin's Tahiti paintings had been kept together in a sort of 'iconostasis', but they had somehow lost a little of their force. I could not quite put my finger on it. Ekaterina Sergeievna explained that, whereas formally they had been arranged so that the frames touched each other, now they were with 'rational' spaces in between. The almost religious power of the former arrangement had been lost. Of course, the eccentric brilliance of the previous arrangement had been down to the vision of one remarkable individual – the former owner. A committee, by its very nature, hated individualism. A Communist committee hated it still more. Inspiration is not rational.

Irena told us that her main task was to show round groups of workers who arrived in trucks from local shops and factories. At best they would look bored and baffled. At worst they would jeer and say that their children could do better. When her father had been in Moscow, he had born all this with great courage, saying that in the 'old days' they had said just as bad things about his paintings, if not worse.

Just after February Revolution, before the Bolsheviks took over, there had been a plan to create a giant museum of art in the Kremlin. Her father had been more than willing to give up his collection for such a project, so long as the collection was kept together safely. He had, in any case, made a will in 1907 in which he had left his pictures to the people of Moscow with the one stipulation that the integrity of the collection be maintained. But the Bolsheviks had moved into the Kremlin and killed the plan to build a 'Moscow Acropolis of the

Arts.' Now the committee that 'owned' the paintings saw its main task as to purge the collection of its tainted past.

It was true, she admitted, that Shchukin was now in France and, she hinted, she and her Latvian husband might try and join him there before too long.

When we left, I was convinced by Vera's argument. The three small pictures were indeed better on her wall. A painting needs a good home – otherwise it ceases to be a work of art, and is merely paint on a canvass.

We could not return to Vera's flat where her husband lay sleeping, and so we spent the afternoon walking round the boulevards and drinking weak tea in one or two little cafes that still operated, hidden away in basements, that only a few people knew about. She would only reveal a little of her plan to me. That evening she wanted to join the Congress of the International. There would be an interesting talk inside the Kremlin by a female comrade. She was certain that Lydia would want to be there and we could all meet up.

I did not believe that even Vera's eyes could sparkle our way through the Spassky Gate on Red Square and into Kremlin – but they did not need to. The letter that she had typed on Comrade Karakhan's machine, and long patience were all that were required to take us through the manifold checks and glances of the guards.

Vera said: 'I would like to look around.'

We slipped into the dusk and found ourselves walking over grass and among trees alongside the Kremlin wall. It was already beginning to smell of autumn: woody and fruity, and of course there was still that infernal smoke in the air from the peat fires. She spotted a ripe apple on a branch just within my reach and asked me to stretch up and get it, and so Vera tempted me to steal a little of the Kremlin's fruit. It was still a mystery to me what this was all about:

'What are you plotting, my dear, in that pretty little head of yours?'

'Not to know is safety,' she replied in English. She pronounced the last word as 'safe-et-y.' It was charming the way she said it, but the effect was to make me feel quite unsafe.

As we walked hand in hand through the trees, a shrill voice called out:

'Who's there?'

'Who asks?'

'Sergei Trotsky.'

He came running up: a proper little blighter he was, not much older than Grisha, but far more cocky. Soon he stood before us. He wore a worker's blouse with a very fancy band around his middle. On his head, a cap sat at a jaunty angle. His chest puffed out like an old trooper.

'Are you Anarchists?'

'No we are Bolsheviks,' said Vera firmly. He put his head on one side and examined us suspiciously. Vera said: 'A brave boy like you is not afraid of a woman like me, is he?'

'Papa says it was a woman who shot Lenin.' [26]

'So it was. But we are not going to shoot anyone. We are going to the Congress. Can you show us the way?'

Young Trotsky led us to the Kremlin's Cathedral Square, which I had visited with Lydia in 1914. I was not sorry to see the little bugger skip off after he had shown us to the Kremlin Palace and the correct staircase for the conference.

Red banners and placards draped the walls of the granite stairwell.. One wall had been painted with a mural of a naked, god-like worker,

---

[26] Fanny Yefimovna Kaplan.
On August 30,1918, Lenin spoke at a Moscow factory called "Hammer and Sickle". As Lenin left the building and before he entered his car, Kaplan called out to him. When Lenin turned towards her, she fired three shots with a Browning pistol. She made the following statement to the Cheka : 'My name is Fanya Kaplan. Today I shot at Lenin. I did it on my own. I will not say from whom I obtained my revolver. I will give no details. I had resolved to kill Lenin long ago. I consider him a traitor to the Revolution. I was exiled to Akatui for participating in an assassination attempt against a Tsarist official in Kyiv. I spent 11 years at hard labour. After the Revolution, I was freed. I favoured the Constituent Assembly and am still for it.'

whose torso was expanding to bust his capitalist chains. At the top, we turned the corner into the Hall of St. George. I remembered the impression this vast white room had made on me when I had toured the Kremlin with Lydia in 1914. You could almost see the power of the Romanovs reflected in the dazzling white marble and the shining parquet floor. When Vera and I entered this Elysium, it was echoing with the tinkling of tea glasses and the low babble of conversation in a variety of languages. The majority of foreign delegates were clad in Russian blouses, issued as souvenirs of the Second Congress of the Third International. The Russian peasant blouse sits well on the shoulders of a skinny revolutionary fed on dry black bread and weak tea, but it tends to hang over the pub-gut of a British shop-steward rather less elegantly. I noticed a group of my compatriots eyeing up some of the young women in white caps who poured tea from pots and topped them up from samovars. Dishes with salads and sandwiches were spread over the side tables in some of the side halls. The inner walls of some of the other alcoves were draped in banners and placards, covering up the gilt inscriptions bearing the names of the soldiers who had won the Medal of St. George in the service of the old regime.

We stopped to glance at a great map of Europe covered in red sweeping lines ending in arrow heads. These showed the impressive advance of the Red Army on Warsaw, sweeping up the Western territories of the Tsar's empire which had been given up to the Germans by Lenin in Trotsky in return for peace in 1918. And from Poland, who could say where the World Revolution would stop? It might well sweep on, like Attila the Hun, across the central Europe and to the gates of Rome.

It was only when I returned to England that I read that the Red Army was actually in retreat.

At the far end of the hall, a woman who looked like a gypsy stood on a podium as she orated and waved her arms. Her hair was, quite frankly, a mess. Vera said that she very much wanted to hear the lady speak, and we moved up the hall to where those who were interested in her words were gathered. We found ourselves chiefly among the women delegates.

I tapped Lydia on the elbow. She looked round and greeted me with a look of pleasant surprise, her little eyes opening quite wide. Lydia was at her most English when she smiled – sincere but somewhat nervously strained. She had only a few seconds to take in the fact that Vera was with me before she found herself wrapped in Vera's hugs and kisses. Lydia always did her best to adapt herself to the Russians' warm nature. She patted Vera affectionately on the back. Once she was free, we spoke our greetings in low whispers, and Lydia put her finger over her lips. At least those gathered in this part of the hall wanted to hear the words of the woman up on the podium. I understood that the general topic was something to do with the family under Communism, but my Russian was not up to following her properly. One had to wait until the end of the speech for a dry translation to be read out. Here I quote from an English text of that very same speech of Alexandra Kollontai published in a pamphlet by the Worker's Dreadnought Press (I bought it recently from Lydia for 3d). The other titles in the series promise doctrinaire boredom. This speech, however, was a corker. Vera was all ears.

"Comrades!

"We have to explain unequivocally that the old form of the family has been outstripped. Communist, society has no need of it.

"In Soviet Russia, the life of the working woman should be surrounded with the same ease, the same brightness, with the same hygiene, with the same beauty, which has thus far surrounded only the women of the richer classes.

"Down with the unproductive labour of housework and child-minding! "

(Her exclamations were greeted with intermittent applause from the few women who could follow the original. Vera and Lydia joined in.)

"The working woman will no longer have to spend her, alas, too few hours of leisure in cooking. In the communist society there will be public restaurants and central kitchens to which everybody may come and take meals.

The working woman will no longer be obliged to sink in an ocean of soap suds and filth. She will simply carry the linen and clothes to the central laundry each week. Under Communist society the Commissariats of Public Education and Social Welfare are already beginning to relieve families of the burden of the minding and the instruction of children.

"The woman under Communism no longer depends on her husband, but her work. Already, thanks to a decree of the People's Commissars, divorce has ceased to be a luxury available only to the rich. Marriage will be purified of all material elements. Free union will take the place of conjugal slavery.

"After marriage has given place to the free and honest union of men and woman who are lovers and comrades, another shameful scourge will also disappear: prostitution.

"Prostitution arose as the inevitable shadow of bourgeois marriage, which was designed to preserve the rights of private property and to guarantee property inheritance through a line of lawful heirs. The prostitute guaranteed that the daughters of the respectable citizens remained chaste and their wives faithful, since a single man could (for a consideration) turn to prostitutes for comfort.

"Bourgeois society rose its hat respectfully to the 'lawful wife" of an industrial magnate who had obviously sold herself to a husband she did not love, and turned away in disgust from a girl forced into the streets by poverty.

"With the rise of capitalism, the sale of women's labour, which is inseparably connected with the sale of the female body, steadily increased, leading to a situation where the respected wife of a worker, and not just the abandoned and "dishonoured" girl, joined the ranks of the prostitutes: a mother for the sake of her children; a young girl for the sake of her family.

"Comrades! When the Communist collective has eliminated property and the material dependence of woman upon man, the trade in women will cease to exist. Sexual relationships have nothing in common with prostitution.

"Under communism all the elements of material calculation found in modem marriage will be absent. Sexual relationships will be based on a healthy instinct for reproduction prompted by the abandon of young love, or by fervent passion, or by a blaze of physical attraction or by a soft light of intellectual and emotional harmony. Healthy, joyful and free relationships between the sexes will develop.

"The Red flag of the social revolution already proclaims the heaven on earth to which humanity has been aspiring for centuries."

"Let us get to work, comrades. The new family is already in the process of creation, and the great family of the triumphant world proletariat is growing stronger by the day."

Vera vigorously applauded at the ends of both the Russian and the English versions of the speech. Lydia bellowed 'Bravo!' repeatedly. Her English voice did not seem suited to the task – the cheering came more naturally to the Italians and Russians.

A comrade began to read out a German translation. This was too much even for Lydia to bear, and we began to retreat back along the hall. On the way back down the crowded staircase, we fell in with a party from our homeland. Lydia asked them if they had heard Kollontai's speech.

'Just the sort of thing that gets Communism a bad name back home,' said one man. Lydia was astonished. What did he mean?' 'Nationalising women,' he replied, adding that you could hear that sort of nonsense from a man in the public house any Friday evening, but it was quite something to hear it coming from a lass.

'Come, come,' said Lydia, 'Don't let's do the work of the Daily Mail in spreading myths about the revolution.' But he and his fellows would not be budged from their belief that the speech had been 'pure unadulterated filth.'

Lydia, Vera and I walked back across the shadowy Red Square and down beyond St. Basil's Cathedral onto the bridge overlooking the Kremlin. The night sky that stretched behind the golden domes and the red turrets was a shade of darkest, deepest blue, and it easily might have come off the pallet of Leon Bakst, the designer of the Russian ballets. The scene was Russia at its most Russian. Vera took my arm and we stood close together.

Lydia began to speak excitedly:

'Wasn't it wonderful what Kollontai said tonight? Russia's despotic past has given birth to freedom. The Russians have stood up and challenged all the assumptions that have supported chauvinism and force through the ages. The rational side of human nature has triumphed here in Russia. Doesn't it thrill you to be here right now?'

I recounted some of the disturbing sights I had seen, including the young girl who had lifted up her dress.

'All that squalor existed under the Tsar,' said Lydia, 'but you were blinded by your romantic adventures and did not see it for what it was.'

I admitted that she might have a point, but that that Kollontai was still making a good deal of use of the future tense to describe what Communism would do for the people. Lydia was ready with her reply:

'Well of course, the realisation of the Communist Society has been delayed by the Allied Blockade and the civil war with the White Russians. While the necessities of life are in short supply, the force of law is a temporary requirement to ensure equal distribution and to prevent exploiters and capitalists bringing back private ownership. But as soon as soon as Russia is left in peace, and food and commodities are plentiful once again, then government authority can recede. There will be no need for laws and policemen. The great communal family that Kollontai was describing will come into being. Money will be abolished and each person will live to his or her full potential without acknowledging the superior rights or authority of any other being. I do believe that a Buddha or a Jesus Christ would be proud to call himself a citizen of the Soviet Union today.'

I said,

'Let's ask Vera. She lives here.'

Vera continued gazing at the Kremlin with childish wonder. Lydia butted into her reverie by switching into Russian and demanding to know her opinion of Kollontai's speech. Without turning her head, Vera said:

'Kollontai has a beautiful dream. She has no need for the theatre or paintings. She has a wonderful vision in her head.'

'You see,' said Lydia, 'She agrees with me.'

I could not blame Vera for supporting a feminist point of view. I decided to change the subject. I asked:

'What happened to that woman comrade from the past? The one you used to admire, Maria…'

'Spiridonova'.

'Yes that's the one. I recall so well how you were always trying to visit her for an interview. Is she still alive? Are you going to meet her now?'

Vera had obviously understood of whom we were speaking, for it was she who answered, still looking out at the Kremlin:

'Spiridonova tells the people that the Red Commissars have taken seeds and grain away from the peasants and now the people are dying of hunger in the countryside. Of course we all know that the Allied Blockade and the greedy kulaks[27] are to blame for the shortage of food, but poor Spiridonova became insane during her long exile in Siberia under the Tsar. Comrade Trotsky says she must be kept away from sight until her condition improves.'

I turned to Lydia. I am not sure that she had even noticed Vera's s deadpan inflection: it had certainly been a revelation to me that she was capable of expressing a political truth with such irony. Lydia was unperturbed. She was aware of the circumstances of Maria Spridonova, confined in the familiar Butyrka once again. She said,

'Miss Pankhurst has asked Comrade Lenin to grant me an interview with Spiridonova.'

'And what did Comrade Lenin say?'

---

[27] Kulaks = 'rich' peasants who were frequently accused by the Bolsheviks of hoarding grain.

'He will ask Comrade Trotsky's view and let us know what they decide.'

Before we parted that evening, Vera told me not to attempt to see her again in Moscow. She would call me when she reached London. 'How will you get there?' I asked, but she would not say. I gave her a few English pounds and a tight embrace.

I myself was due to leave three days later. At four in the morning, on the eve of my departure, there was a knock on my door at the guest house. I was given a few minutes to throw a toothbrush and a change of clothes into a grip bag and led down stairs and onto the street where a truck marked 'bread' was waiting.

***

Lybyanka

Peters was silent for a good two minutes. I think he was hoping that I would speak into the void. I did not. I kept all that I have written here to myself. Eventually he leaned back in his chair and asked me casually,

'Do you recall if you or Vera Borisovna met an English comrade called Miss Annabelle Welcome?'

'I should think I would recall a name like that. But no, I don't. Why?'

'She lost her purse during the address in the Kremlin Hall by Comrade Kollontai. It contained her official papers and her passport. We have an idea that Vera Borisovna took it and planned to use it to travel to England.'

'I have no idea about that.'

He leaned forward across the desk and looked me in the eyes for a good long time, hoping to divine the truth there. I met his gaze steadily. I thought of my late father and I could almost feel his presence. He gave me a kind of electric charge from beyond the grave. I could feel the current in the air around my body. Eventually

Peters said slowly and deliberately, so that the words would sink in almost syllable by syllable:

'We arrested Vera Borisovna four days ago and she has confessed to everything. She put special emphasis on your guilty actions and the part you played in stealing the French works of art which are the property of the state and the toilers of the Russian Federation.'

'I don't believe you.'

'Vera Borisovna will be set free. She has convinced me that you are the guilty party, and that she is an innocent victim of your deception. She panicked and went into hiding. You, however, came to Russia to steal those valuable works of art and to take them back to the West and to sell them.'

I did not say anything. He drew a deep breath: 'But if you sign this confession, the Revolutionary Tribunal might look at your case more leniently. In this, the true version of events, you describe how Vera Borisovna confessed to you her criminal plans to steal state property and to sell the works of art in a Capitalist country. You tried to dissuade her, but she would not listen. If you sign, I will use my personal authority to ask the Tribunal to commute your sentence to expulsion. Here is the pen. Sign.'

I made no move to pick it up. I just sat back in my chair, and smiled at him.

'No,' I said very softy.

'You go to your death for Vera Borisovna?'

For a second, I felt cold fear, and then I heard my father's voice whispering in my ear. I swear that I did actually hear his silky voice. Papa said one word to me, quite distinctly:

'Cobblers.'

'I won't sign,' I said firmly.

Then all of a sudden, a look of exhaustion came over Peters. He had aged twenty years in one minute. He sighed deeply and picked up his huge revolver as if it were a dead weight. He put it back into the drawer and began to write out an order on a form. He moved the pen with great weariness, before standing up to open the door and call the guard. A car was waiting for me in the courtyard of the Lubyanka. I was driven past Brest Station and up the long straight road back to the Butyrka Prison.

Once again I found myself in the small cubical of an office where I had surrendered my possessions on the night of my incarceration. After a long wait, and a good deal of form filling, my things were found and returned to me. I did not count all the rouble notes in brief case, but I had the impression that each and every note was present and correct. I waited another two or three hours in that little room. Prisoners were escorted in and out, and I witnessed the strip searches and the goose pimples and the trembling. At length, I was told, 'Prisoner Munnings. Stand up. You are expelled by official order from the territory of the Russian Federation. The penalty if you are found inside Russia after the next 48 hours is death. Do you understand?'

'Yes.'

As I squeezed into my place on board the train, on a hard bench between two Chekist escorts, I pulled down my hat and tried to doze. Poor Vera, I thought; the Russian authorities will be waiting to arrest Miss Annabelle Welcome and son on the border.

But Vera did not leave by the official crossing into Finland. She walked across an unguarded stretch of country with Grisha riding piggy back. Shortly after crossing, they were stopped by a Finnish patrol and detained in a guard post. In those days the Finns were sending any Russian refugees they intercepted back to the Workers' State and certain death. British subjects, however, were a different matter. She produced Miss Welcome's papers and, after a call to the British Consul in Helsinki, she was sent on her way and wished 'bon voyage'.

Afterword by Misha Munnings

I have only a few memories of my great-grandmother, Vera Munnings. I was six years old when she died in 1987. I recall an elegant old lady in a mink coat walking her dalmatian on Hampstead Heath. When we visited 'Babushka', as we called Vera, she would prepare 'Russian tea.' She was fond of a dish made with sour milk, sugar and nutmeg. Much better for us children were her pies filled with plums and cherries.

Most of what other information I have about Vera has filtered down through my parents, grandparents, and family 'legend.' She was famous for beginning dinner parties at her house with shots of neat vodka straight from the freezer and served in silver tumblers. Her husband George always declined to join in. He said he had drunk enough vodka while in Russia to last him a lifetime. She also often kept a good supply of caviar, smoked-sturgeon, and other delicacies passed onto her contacts at the Soviet Embassy. There were sometimes Russian diplomats present at her parties, despite the fact that she held strong views against Communism. Western apologists for the Soviet Union often found themselves on the sharp end of her tongue. There have long been whispers in the family that she had a number of love affairs after she joined George in London. What is certain is that she retained her piquant sense of humour. My uncle has passed on the following anecdote which he says caused both raucous laughs and horrified looks when she told it at a dinner party where both the Duke and Duchess of Kent were both present. A Soviet diplomat pulls on his trousers, adjusts his tie, and is about to leave the woman whom he met half an hour ago. She cries out: 'Hey what about the money?' He replies, 'Soviet diplomats don't charge.'

The fate of the three Shchukin paintings which she brought from Moscow has been a matter of some controversy within the family. She herself often used to relate how she tracked down the old merchant in exile in the south of France and restored the pictures to him. The story ran that George was initially furious when she found out that she had given away their most valuable asset at a time when they were running short of funds, but later he realised that she had done something truly noble. She maintained that in her own way she had 'Put right a small part of the Revolution.' She was a firm believer in 'the sacred right of private property' and would lecture that when property rules are overturned, civilisation falls apart.

My uncle used to do an imitation of the old lady saying, in her Russian accent,

'I could not bear to keep those pictures hanging on my wall, when I knew how my old friend Sergei Shchukin wept each day for what he had lost.'

The rival story runs that Vera secretly sold the Shchukin paintings. Certainly, Vera and George seemed, after a number of years of scraping by, to have become suddenly much more prosperous by 1927 when they bought their house in Hampstead. For a long while the cause of their sudden enrichment has remained a mystery.

I have finally discovered the source of their good fortune. My researches at Companies House led me in turn to the City Library and the transcripts of an Extraordinary General Meeting of the Lena Goldfields Company for 1926. In that year, the British company — notorious for its pre-revolutionary suppression of its Russian workers — was granted a 'concession' to mine its former goldfields, in return for royalties of 8 per cent paid to the Russian Government. In the same year it purchased 'Precious Gems of Russia Ltd' for a sum of £75,000. In doing so, it bought out the only shareholders: George and Vera Munnings. It would appear that shortly prior to the sale, 'Precious Gems' had won a Soviet Government concession to mine emerald, topaz and alexandrite on a site near the town of Galino not far from the city of Sverdlovsk (formally Yekaterinburg).

Another rumour in my family —which may or may not be connected with the Russian mining concession — was that sometime in the mid-1920s my great grandmother had an affair with a Russian trade official working at the Embassy in London. Whatever the truth of this scandal, it does seem certain that she had friends at the Soviet embassy and sometimes attended receptions there.

George eventually found his metier running a small theatrical agency which, though it probably never showed much of a profit, made him, for a time, a well-known figure in London's theatrical and cinematic world. I am told that their house in Hampstead was always full of artists, actors and writers. By one of those Russian coincidences their neighbours and friends in Hampstead included the Russian ballerina Tamara Karsavina and her diplomat husband, Henry James Bruce.

Readers may be interested to know the ultimate fate of some of the people and places and works of art mentioned in "Vera."

After Sergei Shchukin left Russia in 1918, and like many white Russian émigrés, he settled in the South of France. Later he bought a flat in Paris. Fortunately he had kept a reasonably well funded bank account in Stockholm, but even so he was forced to economise. He even sold a casual sketch given to him by Picasso as a memento of old times. But Shchukin must have been more confident of his financial position later on when he bought four works by Ronald Duffy. He died in 1936 and is buried in Montmartre.

Shchukin himself always claimed to be untroubled by the loss of his extraordinary collection (which included 50 pictures by Picasso, 43 by Matisse, 15 by Gauguin, 13 by Monet, 8 by Cezanne, 4 by Van Gogh, and 3 by Renoir). He had in any case bequeathed them to Moscow in his will of 1907. His one stipulation had been the collection should be kept together, but after the Second World War it was divided between Moscow's Pushkin Museum and Leningrad's Hermitage. The ideal venue for a reunified Shchukin collection would, of course, be the merchant's former mansion on Znamensky Periolok which is currently occupied by the Russian Ministry of Defence.

Maria Spiridonova, the 'white rabbit' whom Lydia was forever chasing for an interview, escaped from prison in the Kremlin in 1920. She had been arrested for plotting to overthrow the Bolsheviks.

While in hiding she was met by the anarchist sympathiser, Emma Goldman. In her book, "My Disillusionment with Russia", Goldman writes,

"Before the desk, piled high with letters and papers, sat a frail little woman; Maria Spiridonova. This, then, was one of Russia's great martyrs, this woman who had so unflinchingly suffered the tortures inflicted upon her by the Tsar's henchmen. I had been told by Zorin and Jack Reed that Spiridonova had suffered a breakdown, and was kept in a sanatorium. Her malady, they said, was acute neurasthenia and hysteria. When I came face to face with Maria, I immediately realized that both men had deceived me…

"She dwelt on the razverstka, the system of forcible requisition [of grain and produce from the peasants], which was devastating Russia and discrediting everything the Revolution had been fought for; she referred to the terrorism practiced by the Bolsheviki against every revolutionary criticism, to the new Communist bureaucracy and inefficiency, and the hopelessness of the whole situation. It was a crushing indictment against the Bolsheviki, their theories and methods."

Spiridonova was later re-arrested and spent twenty years in the camps before her execution in 1941.

Sergei Trotsky, the young son of Leon Trotsky who met Vera and George in the grounds of the Kremlin in 1920, grew up to be a mathematician and scientist with no interest in politics. His father rivalled Stalin of the Party leadership and was expelled from the Soviet Union 1929 and eventually moved to Mexico where he was murdered with an ice-pick by a Soviet agent in 1940. After Leon Trotsky's exile, all members of his family were suspect, and those within Stalin's reach, both at home and abroad, were eliminated. In

1935 Sergei Trotsky was accused of attempting to poison a worker's canteen and sent to the Vorkuta Labour Camps. He was shot in 1937. His father never learned his exact fate.

Jacob Peters, the deputy head of the Cheka Secret Police (and said to be their chief executioner), was removed to Tashkent shortly after he interviewed George and was executed in the purge of 1938.

Alexandra Kollontai, the Bolshevik feminist and 'prophet of free love', faired rather better, despite criticising the Bolshevik leadership and setting up a faction with the party called 'The Worker's Opposition'. In 1921 she advocated free speech for members of the party and for trade unionists. She also called on the party to cull its burgeoning bureaucracy. Lenin hit back by banning all party factions (including hers), and by publicising his condemnation of free love while calling for a 'Soviet morality'. Kollontai was sent abroad as an unlikely diplomat. Between 1923 and 1945 she was posted to Norway, Mexico and Sweden. She also turned her hand to writing racy novels including 'Red Love' (1927) and "Great Love" (1928). She died of natural causes in Moscow in 1952.

The fate of Chapel of the Iberian Virgin, where George met Vera for the second time, is best described by the Intourist Publication, "Moscow Past Present Future" published in Moscow in 1934.

"The narrow gates with the Chapel of the Iberian Virgin which once throttled the entrance to the Red Square, have now disappeared; the narrow, stony slits which formerly jammed the traffic have been replaced by one wide approach through which, on the great Revolutionary holidays, the massed columns advance unimpeded under their fluttering banners, standards and streamers."

The Resurrection gate into Red Square, with the tiny Iberian chapel that stands between its twin arches, was rebuilt in the early 1990s.

The Foreign Ministry house on the bank of the River Moscow where George stayed in 1920, played host to many of the Bolshevik's guests of the era including the 'Young Turk' Enver Pasher, HG Wells and Winston Churchill's niece, Claire Sheridan. Before the

Revolution, the magnificent mansion designed by Moscow's greatest Art Nouveau architect, Fyodor Shekhtel, had belonged to the merchant family, the Kharitonenkos. In 1930 it was given to Britain for use as her embassy as a reward for being the first Western power to recognise the Soviet Government. Churchill hosted a dinner for Stalin there in 1941. It is now the British Ambassador's residence.

Bruce Lockhart records that the Kharitonenkos' eldest daughter escaped to Munich where she lived in a 'two-roomed servant-less flat.' In 1930 she came to London to protest to Lord Thomson, a Labour Government Minister whom she had entertained in the mansion, about its occupation by the British Embassy. She did not receive compensation.

The 'Trading Rows' on Red Square (where George bought a one rouble necklace for Vera) became an office building for Bolshevik five-year-planners in the 1920s. In 1932, the body of Stalin's wife who had committed herself, was laid out in there by Stalin, who noted those who came (or failed to come) to pay their respects. In 1952 it reopened as the Soviet emporium, 'Gum', which was privatised in 1993.

The Scottish owned store, 'Muir and Merilee's', (on Petrovka Street near the Bolshoi Theatre), became Soviet Moscow's second most famous department store, Tsum, and is now home to some very expensive boutiques. Unfortunately, the façade has been disguised with concrete. When it too was privatised in the 1990s, the heirs of Andrew Muir and Archibald Merilee were invited to Moscow to receive compensation for their property of £400.

A building which remains remarkably constant on the map of Moscow is the eighteenth century fortress, the Butyrka, which still functions as a prison and retains its 'Pugachev' tower. During the Stalin era, 140 prisoners were crammed into a cell which under the Tsar had housed 25; and 2000 prisoners were kept inside the prison chapel (which has since been destroyed).

The Lubyanka is home to Russia's secret police in their latest incarnation, the FSB, and it is impossible to walk past it without feeling a chill.

The Metropole still stands and functions today as a first class hotel. George Bernard Shaw stayed there and met Stalin (whom he greatly admired) for two hours in 1931. It closed for several years during the late 1980s while undergoing renovation works, partly due to an underground river that threatened its foundations. At its grand re-opening in 1991, guests discovered that they had no hot water. Things have improved since. Many of the building's features, including the great dining hall with its golden fountain, the stained glass windows, and the motifs of girls' faces on the upper floor, can still be seen. Some of the atmosphere, however, has been 'internationalised' in the rooms and corridors. Bruce Lockhart stayed in the Metropole in 1912 and confirmed my step-great-grandfather's depiction of some of the Metropole's pre-revolutionary residents in his book, 'Memoirs of a British Agent':

'Most of my neighbours were women, gaudily painted and gaudily dressed, who, after discovering by exhaustive telephone enquiries both my innocence and my modest purse, lost all interest in this new arrival.'

I myself have received such nocturnal telephone calls while staying in some modern Russian hotels (I replied after the fashion of Bruce Lockhart, rather than my great step-grandfather).

As for Vera's original profession and how it fared under 'Communism', I think it is best to quote the words of Nikita Khrushchev; 'There are no professional prostitutes in the Soviet Union, only talented amateurs.' My guess is that if Alexandra Kollontai could visit Moscow's bars and nightclubs today, she would be depressed to see how things have turned out.

From Hugh Fraser

I wrote Red Fortunes some years ago, and it did not see the light of day until recently. Much of its flavour is drawn from my own years spent living in Russia (1990-1993). I invested almost as much time researching and writing the book. Vera exists in my mind as a real person and perhaps George is part of me too. I would like to just clarify what I hope is obvious - that the mildly prejudiced and sexist attitudes in the book are meant to be seen as anachronisms - not my own.

In the years since I finished this book, I have been writing children's stories for the audio site, Storynory.com - Storynory has an underground cult status among discerning families. If you have a children, drop by and listen to some of my words read by some talented actors. Many of my thoughts and preoccupations, as well as my experiences of travel, are expressed through the medium of Storynory these days.

I do hope that you have enjoyed Red Fortunes - if so, please leave a nice review on Amazon to encourage me to write another historical novel. I have a vague idea to write one about a female star of the silent movies.

Please feel free to contact me at hugh@storynory.com.

Select Bibliography

Precious Stones and Gems, Their History, Sources and Characteristics by Edwin W. Streeter FRGS, MAI, 1898 edition.
http://www.palagems.com/alexandrite_russia.htm
The Times
The Annual General Meeting of the West Australian Loan and General Finance Corporation, 1898.
The Gold Mines of the World, Third Edition, 1905. JH Curle
Bottomley's Book by Horatio Bottomley 1909
Hooley's Confessions by Ernest Terah Hooley Squire of Risley Simpkin, Marshall, Hamilton, Kent & co Ltd London 1924
The Tourist's Russia by Ruth Kedzie Wood, Andrew Melrose 1912
The Russian Year Book for 1911 compiled and Edited by Howard P Kennard MD with an introduction by Baron Alphonse Heyking Imperial Russian Consul-General London Eyre and Spottiswoode Ltd. 1911.
My Russian Year by Rothay Reynolds Mills & Boon Limited 1913
The Mainsprings of Russia by Maurice Baring Thomas Nelson and Sons 1914
Russia with Tehran, Port Arthur and Peking – a handbook for travellers: Karl Baedeker, Baedeker, Leipzig, 1914
Changing Russia by Stephen Graham, John Lane, The Bodley Head 1915
The Russians and their Language by Madame N. Jarintzov, B.H. Blackwell, 1916
Six Weeks in Russia in 1919 by Arthur Ransome George Allen and Unwin 1919
Russia in the Shadows by HG Wells Hodder and Stoughton 1920

Speeches of Alexandra Kollontai based on Marriage and the Family, a speech delivered in 1918, translation appeared in the worker, paper of the Scottish Workers Committee, in 1920. Published in 1984 by the Socialist workers party and the International Socialist Organisation (USA) - and Selected Writings of Alexandra Kollontai, Allison & Busby, 1977; Translated by Alix Holt.

Soviet Russia as I saw it by Sylvia Pankhurst Dreadnought 1921

Morgan Philips Price Reminiscences of the Russian Revolution 1921

Memoirs of a British Agent by R.H Bruce Lockhart, Putnam 1932

Pocket Guide to the Soviet Union issued by Intourist (State Tourist Company USSR) Moscow, 1932 Vneshtorgisdat Moscow and Leningrad.

Spiridonova Revolutionary Terrorist, I Steinberg, commissar for Justice in the first

Soviet Cabinet, translated and edited by Gwenda David and Eric Mosbacher Methuen & Co 1935

A life of Alexander II Tsar of Russia: Stephen Graham, Ivor Nicholson and Watson 1935

Москва и Москвичи - В. А Гиляровский - Московский Рабочий 1968

The Rise and Fall of Horatio Bottomley by Alan Hyman – Cassell 1972

Памятники Архитектури Московы – Москва Искусство

The Russian Revolution 1899 – 1919: Richard Pipes, Collings Harvill 1990.

Collecting Matisse: Alber Kostenevich and Natalia Semyonova Flammarion Paris 1993

French Painters, Russian Collectors: by Beverly Whitney Kean Hodder & Stoughton General 1994

The Ninth Circle: The Lena Goldfield Workers and the Massacre of April 1912," Slavic Review, Fall 1994

The City of London Volume II Golden Years 1890 – 1914: David Kynaston Pimlico 1995

Leon Bakst and the Ballets Russes: Charles Spencer, Academy Editions 1995

The Incomparable Anastasia Vial'tseva: Louise McReynolds in Russia Women Culture Indiana University Press, 1996

A People's Tragedy The Russian Revolution 1891 – 1924: Orlando Figes Jonathan Cape 1996

Interpreting the Russian Revolution: The Language and Symbols of 1917: Orlando Figes and Boris Kolonitskii, Yale University Press 1999.

Merchant Moscow, Images of Russia's Vanished Bourgeoisie, Edited by James. L. West and Iurii A. Petrov, Princetown University Press, 1998

Printed in Great Britain
by Amazon.co.uk, Ltd.,
Marston Gate.